MW00881590

Mary, Mary, How Extraordinary

The Adventures of Miss Mary Bennet, Volume III

S.M. KLASSEN

Jane Austen's *Pride and Prejudice* Continues...

ISBN 13: 978-1512227451

⟿ Also by this author ⟿

Writing as S.M. Klassen

What Really Happened Before Mr. Darcy's Wedding
A Prequel to Mary, Mary, Not So Ordinary

Mary, Mary, Not So Ordinary
The Adventures of Miss Mary Bennet, Volume I
(Jane Austen's *Pride and Prejudice* Continues...)

Mary, Mary, Oh So Contrary
The Adventures of Miss Mary Bennet, Volume II
(Jane Austen's *Pride and Prejudice* Continues...)

Mary, Mary, How Extraordinary
The Adventures of Miss Mary Bennet, Volume III
(Jane Austen's *Pride and Prejudice* Continues...)

Mayhem at the Minster
A Regency Era Above-Stairs/Below-Stairs Mystery, Volume I
(the characters of Jane Austen's *Pride and Prejudice* live on in this
series, continuing the tale of *Mary, Mary, How Extraordinary*)

Writing as Shelly McDunn

City of Dread
A 1919 New Orleans Mystery

Spies, Lies, & Shoo-Fly Pie
A Jamey Knight Mystery

CAST OF PRIMARY CHARACTERS

{n.b.: Characters taken from *Pride and Prejudice,* with grateful acknowledgment to the imagination of Miss Jane Austen, except those marked with an Asterix (*), which have been added to the story by S.M. Klassen.}

Annesley, Mrs.: companion to Georgiana Darcy
*Ashton, Major: would-be suitor to Mary Bennet
*Babcock, Mrs.: cook, Darcy House in London
Bennet, Mr. & Mrs.: of Longbourn in Hertfordshire; daughters: Jane-Elizabeth-Mary-Catherine (Kitty)-Lydia
Bingley, Mr. (Charles): of Netherfield Hall; wife: Jane, née Bennet
Bingley, Caroline: unmarried sister of Mr. Bingley
*Braxton, Dr.: physician to Darcys in Derbyshire
*Burnabys: (daughter, Deidre): neighbors of Darcys
*Burney, Fanny: (aka Mrs. D'Arblay - taken from history)
*Castlereagh, Lord/Lady: government official (from history)
*Chandler, Mr.: childhood friend of Georgiana Darcy
*Clay, Mr.: friend of Freddie Arbuthnot & Caroline Bingley
Collins, Mr.: Hunsford/Kent; wife: Charlotte, née Lucas
Darcy, Mr. (Fitzwilliam): of Pemberley/wife: Elizabeth, née Bennet; sister: Georgiana
*Darnell, Edward: friend of Mr. Bingley
de Bourgh, Lady Catherine: aunt to the Darcys & Colonel Fitzwilliam; daughter: Anne
Dawkins: maid to Lady Catherine de Bourgh
*Egerton, Mr.: Mary Bennet's publisher (taken from history)
*Exeter, Lord: society gossip
Fitzwilliam, Colonel (Richard): first cousin of the Darcys & Anne de Bourgh
Gardiner, Mr. & Mrs.: brother/sister-in-law of Mrs. Bennet
*Grantly, Miss: friend of Miss Bingley's in London
*Halifax, Mrs.: midwife (sister of Mrs. Annesley)
Hill, Mr. and Mrs.: Bennet family servants, Longbourn
Hurst, Mr. & Mrs. (Louisa): sister/brother-in-law of Bingleys
*Jameson, Captain/Lord, wife: Morna, née Drummond
Jenkinson, Mrs.: companion to Miss Anne de Bourgh
*Leigh, Diana & Catherine: formerly of Beechwood Manor

*Linley, Mrs.: the Bingleys' nursemaid (to Little Eliza)
Long, Mrs.: friend of Mrs. Bennet
Lucas, Sir William & Lady: of Lucas Lodge/neighbors of the
Bennet family; daughters: Charlotte & Maria
Lucy: maid to Georgiana Darcy
*Matlock, Lord and Lady: (the Earl & Countess of Devonham)
Colonel Fitzwilliam's parents/aunt & uncle to the Darcys
*Molly: maid to Mary Bennet
Nicholls, Mrs.: the Bingleys' housekeeper, Netherfield Hall
*Paige, Miss: assistant to Mr. Egerton, publisher
*Petersham, Mr.: American; alleged spy
Philips, Mrs.: sister to Mrs. Bennet, of Meryton
Reynolds, Mrs.: housekeeper at Pemberley
*Samson: Mr. Darcy's spaniel puppy#
*Steinman: butler, Darcy House in London
*Thomson, Mrs.: midwife to Jane Bingley
*Walker: the Bingleys' butler, Netherfield Hall
*Webb, Vicar (& son, Mr. Webb): Longbourn chapel
Wickham, George: nefarious, childhood companion of Mr.
Darcy, wife: Lydia, née Bennet
*Wickford, Lord: suitor to Miss Anne de Bourgh

Locations
*Beechwood Manor: new Bingley family home in
Derbyshire
*Darcy House: Darcys' house in London
*Devonham: Colonel Fitzwilliam's family home in Derbyshire
Longbourn: Bennet family home in Hertfordshire
Lucas Lodge: near Longbourn in Hertfordshire
Netherfield Park: Bingley's (rented) estate in Hertfordshire
Meryton: town near Longbourn in Hertfordshire
Pemberley: Darcy family home in Derbyshire
Rosings: de Bourgh family estate in Kent

Mary, Mary,
How Extraordinary

CHAPTER ONE

Netherfield, 20 December 1813

As the longcase clock in the Netherfield vestibule struck one, a bleary-eyed Charles Bingley led a tight-jawed Fitzwilliam Darcy down the hall, each holding a candle aloft.

Mr. Darcy knocked lightly on the door of his cousin's chamber before entering, then moved silently to the bed.

As a member of His Majesty's Regiment, Colonel Richard Fitzwilliam was a light sleeper. Without warning he gripped Mr. Darcy's wrist. "What is it?"

Mr. Darcy's terse response caused the colonel to jump from his warm bed. He struggled into his buckskin breeches in the dim light given off by the two candles and a dwindling fire. "What kind of addle-brained—pardon me, Bingley—" he shrugged into his dressing gown "—who would...why would anyone with half an ounce of common sense do such a thing? And in this weather?"

Mr. Bingley was uncharacteristically silent, eyes cast down.

"We can discuss it in Charles' study, Richard, but first we must wake Major Ashton." Mr. Darcy saw his cousin reach for the bell-pull and held out a hand to prevent him. "It might be best not to rouse your batman just yet."

The three gentlemen then went to Major Ashton's chamber, where they found him sitting near the fire with a book in his hands—one he attempted to hide from the colonel's curious gaze.

"I see you are reading Miss Mary Bennet's novel again." Colonel Fitzwilliam did not bother to hide his amusement.

"I am." The major eyed each of their states of dishabille. "To what do I owe the pleasure, gentlemen?"

Colonel Fitzwilliam gave a brief explanation and within minutes the four men were in Mr. Bingley's study, where his valet had stoked the fire and set out two trays—one with a pitcher and glasses, another with bread, cold meat, and cheese.

"Now, tell us exactly what you know about Miss Bingley's elopement." The colonel impatiently pulled his long dressing gown out of reach of stray sparks from the fire.

Mr. Bingley handed him a letter with a broken seal. "This came by express just before we woke you—it is from my sister, Mrs. Hurst. If you would consult the third paragraph particularly."

The colonel read quickly, his frown deepening as he handed the letter to the major. "She may already have met up with Petersham."

Mr. Darcy filled four glasses before handing them round. "Charles made the excellent point that Caroline never travels without copious baggage and at least three maids—as well as the equivalent of footmen." He took a sip of the mulled wine. "It would slow her down considerably."

They soon began the business of deciding upon the best course of action. When Mr. Bingley suggested riding out immediately in search of his wayward sister, Colonel Fitzwilliam objected in the strongest terms. "I think not, Bingley, especially considering your wife's condition. Also, someone must remain behind to organize additional search parties and to maintain contact with Lord Castlereagh." He finished his drink. "No—you and Darcy stay here; Major Ashton and I are obviously the ones to go in search of Miss Bingley." He turned to the major. "We should try to get what little sleep we can, and be off at dawn."

Major Ashton set his own empty glass on the tray, addressing Mr. Darcy and Mr. Bingley. "I am happy to do whatever is required to prevent Miss Bingley from taking what can only be considered a calamitous step. If you will please convey my apologies to the Bennets and to your charming wives—it would seem that the colonel and I will be unable to attend the wedding, and will no doubt miss the holiday festivities as well."

"Yes, Darcy—please convey our apologies to each member of the Bennet family." Colonel Fitzwilliam smirked; the major pointedly ignored him.

"We will—" Mr. Bingley turned to Mr. Darcy "—but what can we tell Mr. and Mrs. Bennet? Certainly not the truth!"

Mr. Darcy shook his head firmly. "No, we must do everything possible to prevent this unfortunate event from becoming fodder for gossip."

"Simply tell them the major and I were called away on official business for the crown." Colonel Fitzwilliam opened the door. "It will no doubt be true once Lord Castlereagh learns of this."

"I cannot thank the two of you enough." Mr. Bingley wiped his brow with a handkerchief. "If it were not for Jane's present condition, I would be off myself in search of my wayward sister."

"You need not concern yourself," the colonel interrupted. "We would have been ordered to intercept Miss Bingley regardless." He turned to his cousin. "Darcy, will you write to Lord Castlereagh? I must warn my batman about our early departure, which could take some time. He can be devilishly difficult to wake."

After the other two men went off in search of their beds, Mr. Bingley and Mr. Darcy returned to their chairs.

Mr. Bingley held his head in his hands. "What could Caroline be thinking? And how far could she have traveled by now?"

The two gentlemen remained in the study, discussing the many possible escape routes Mr. Petersham might choose for himself and his prospective bride, and the various ways in which the plan could be thwarted.

At dawn, Mr. Darcy penned a letter to Lord Castlereagh and sent it off express, he and his good friend not returning to their beds until after venturing out in the cold to see Colonel Fitzwilliam and Major Ashton off from the Netherfield stable.

Elizabeth was fully aware of the hour when Mr. Darcy finally came to bed. She snuggled close to him, holding tightly to him until she felt the chill leave his body and heard his deep, even breathing. When she rose a couple of hours later, Mrs. Darcy sought her sister in order to recommend a later breakfast than was normal at Netherfield.

Therefore, it was nearly noon before the ladies met their husbands for the first meal of the day, Mr. Bingley dismissing the servants before he and Mr. Darcy explained the situation.

Jane Bingley's normally placid countenance was marred by a frown, the piece of toast in her hand forgotten. "What if the colonel and the major do not find Caroline in time, and she and Mr. Petersham are married? What will happen to her?"

"Neither of them will ever be able to return to England, for one thing, and should they try to escape to America they will find the British waters unaccommodating—especially given Petersham's accent, which he never could fully disguise." Mr. Darcy's jaw was clenched as he looked across the table at his sister, Georgiana, who had given up all pretense of eating the piece of seedcake on her plate. "Unfortunately, it is possible our families will suffer from the association." His eyes caught Mr. Bingley's. "We must be prepared for it."

Elizabeth Darcy sipped her heavily sweetened tea, the drink agreeing with her far better than her usual coffee since becoming an expectant mother. "Surely Caroline cannot remain forever ignorant of Mr. Petersham's traitorous activities?"

Mr. Darcy folded his napkin into a perfect square before setting it alongside his empty plate. "If Petersham believes Caroline has fully succumbed to his charms, he may well disclose some of his iniquities to her. But sadly, as we know from our experiences with Wickham—" his expression softened as he gazed upon his wife and sister, whose cheeks had gone slightly pink "—Mr. Petersham will no doubt manage to convince Miss Bingley of his being both unjustly accused and shabbily treated." He stood, suddenly impatient. "I wish Lord Castlereagh had seized Petersham's estate, or at the very least his bank accounts, immediately upon his arrest. No doubt the scoundrel has managed to divert funds enough to keep himself in the manner to which he has long been accustomed."

"Caroline's fortune will also be available to him, and under his complete control," remarked Elizabeth a trifle drily.

Mr. Darcy strode to the bank of windows to look out, unseeing, at the falling snow. "Richard and Major Ashton will not have an easy ride today."

Jane set her teacup down thoughtfully. "If we are not to allow word of this to go any further, how are we to explain the absence of the colonel and the major to our guest, Mr. Darnell? He will soon be Kitty's husband after all, and part of our family." She gazed at Mr. Bingley, her eyes wide. "And what are we to say to my mother and father, and to our neighbors?"

Mr. Bingley had not slept, and his normally cheerful countenance was morose. "We decided it might be best to imply that the colonel and major were called away on business for the crown. It will be the truth—they have simply anticipated the order."

Mr. Darcy turned away from the white landscape and came to stand behind his wife's chair. "I think the best we can do is guard this secret and wait."

Elizabeth tipped her head up. "I agree with you." She then addressed the others. "We cannot allow Caroline's recklessness to adversely affect the wedding—or the Christmas activities, which will include all of our neighbors at one time or another. If we all agree to remain silent about the matter, everyone else will be happily ignorant."

Jane looked up. "Charles, how long had Caroline been gone before Louisa sent word of the proposed elopement?"

Mr. Bingley pulled the well-worn missive from his waistcoat pocket to examine it. "She wrote on the eighteenth of December; her letter arrived just before one o'clock this morning." He looked up at the ornate ceiling, calculating. "Caroline probably has a lead of more than thirty hours, but as Darcy pointed out, the prodigious amount of baggage she insists upon bringing with her on even the shortest of journeys may well lead to her downfall. Not only will her travel time be slower than two experienced men on horseback, but such a spectacle as she generally creates will not go unnoticed, especially in the smaller villages." He smiled for the first time, his eyes on Georgiana. "And as we know from at least one experience you shared with Mary, the colonel is extremely good at finding people."

Mr. Darcy tried to sound optimistic as he added, "It is not only the colonel and the major who will be searching for Caroline—someone is bound to intercept her before she reaches Petersham."

Unfortunately, it was unclear to the others whether or not he believed his own words.

CHAPTER TWO

Longbourn, 21 December 1813

Due to the unceasing snowfall and unseasonably cold temperatures, it was not until the day before Kitty Bennet's wedding that Jane Bingley, Elizabeth Darcy, and Miss Georgiana Darcy could safely travel the two miles between Netherfield and Longbourn.

Kitty Bennet flew down the stairs to meet them in the front hall before they were able to remove their winter wraps. "Whatever shall we do? Mr. Webb is ill and cannot perform the service tomorrow!"

Elizabeth, waiting for a pause in Kitty's sniffles, calmly handed the housemaid her fur-lined pelisse, hat, and muff. "I am not surprised to hear the vicar is ailing—Lady Lucas told me only last week that he visited a family in Whitchurch, where six of their seven children were extremely ill."

"You should be nearer the fire, Kitty," Jane put her arms around her distraught younger sister and led the way to the sitting room, always the warmest at Longbourn in the wintertime. "Where are the others?"

Kitty sniffed, tucking her handkerchief away. "Mamma has gone to speak with Cook about the white soup, Aunt and Uncle Gardiner have taken our little cousins out in the snow, and Mary has been writing all morning." Tears began to well up in her eyes, and Jane pulled out a fresh handkerchief.

Elizabeth took the handkerchief and dried Kitty's eyes before handing it to her. "It may well be fortuitous that the infected vicar cannot perform the ceremony tomorrow, for he might otherwise have spread sickness to others." She rested a hand on her midsection before leaning closer to the fire to warm her hands, smiling when she saw her sister Mary enter. "Kitty tells us you have been working all morning—how are you getting on with your novel?"

"I do not believe Lady Catherine will be pleased." Mary grimaced while she hugged her two elder sisters. She had been taking advantage of the morning light to rewrite a chapter dictated by Lady Catherine de Bourgh, the Darcys' officious, demanding aunt, when she had seen the Bingleys' sleigh arrive from the window of her chamber. After straightening the loose pages of her novel and attempting to hide yet another ink spot on her cuff, she had hastened downstairs.

Mary then noticed Kitty's red eyes and damp face. "Whatever has happened to cause this?"

"The vicar is ill and cannot perform the marriage ceremony tomorrow," Georgiana explained with a sympathetic glance at Kitty.

Mary sat down, visibly relieved, having assumed something untoward had happened to Mr. Darnell. "Surely someone else can read the service? The young Mr. Webb, perhaps?" She saw Elizabeth's lips twitch in amusement at the mention of the young man Mrs. Bennet had once hoped Mary would wed.

"Apparently the young Mr. Webb has gone to Dorset, as the vicar there suffers from gout." Jane placed a finger under Kitty's chin, who sniffed one last time before raising her head. "Perhaps now you might consider Mr. Collins' oft-repeated request to officiate?"

Mary looked at her eldest sister with horror. "Is there no one else? The last time he took the pulpit here, he made it a point of honor to extend the length of Mr. Webb's sermons by at least two times!"

Kitty's eyes were wide as she looked to Elizabeth for support, who purposely glanced at the ticking clock on the mantle. "He appears to be your only choice, my dear—and if we are to enlist his aid, we must act quickly."

Fewer than thirty minutes later, Mr. Collins, the Bennets' second cousin and heir to Longbourn (due to the entailment which had long been the bane of Mrs. Bennet's existence), divested himself of his capacious outer garment, tall hat, woolen scarf, and mittens, handing each item one-by-one with great ceremony to the slight maid. He stomped his feet to remove traces of snow and entered the drawing room where Mrs. Bennet, four of her five daughters, and Miss Darcy awaited him. He stood in front of the fire, effectually blocking the heat from the ladies, and eyed them from beneath his up-pointed nose.

"Miss Kitty Bennet—" he addressed the bride-to-be, although his small dark eyes scanned all the unfortunates in the room "—tomorrow morning, at Longbourn Chapel, you will become the wife of Mr. Edward Darnell." His eyes narrowed suddenly. "Why is the groom not here?"

Mrs. Bennet, speechless and wide-eyed, turned to her daughters, one hand at her throat as if she were one of Mary's heroines.

Elizabeth spoke quietly, but with discernible firmness. "Mr. Darnell is at Netherfield with the other gentlemen, including my father, and my uncle, Mr. Gardiner."

"How unfortunate." Mr. Collins looked down at Kitty, his unruly brows well-nigh meeting in the space between his eyes. "It is imperative I speak with your fiancé before I can consent to officiate at your wedding." His displeasure was evidenced in a great sigh. "But as you are already assembled, I will take this opportunity to remind you of your duties as a wife." He took a deep breath, unaware of any stifled giggles, and proceeded to lecture Kitty on her role of a dutiful and modest help-mate, warning against putting on airs above her station in life, and demanding she acknowledge the superiority of her husband in all things, subject to the laws of the Church of England. "Woman was put on this earth to serve man—" he began yet another harangue, and Mary, who could bear no more and was closest to the door, left the room before Mrs. Bennet or any of the others could object or do the same.

"My dear, what has happened?" Mary's Aunt Gardiner was just coming down the stairs as Mary started up, and they met in the middle. "You look as though you might have a fever, you are so flushed!"

Mary pointed back towards the drawing room door. "Mr. Collins has come to instruct Kitty on her wifely duties."

Mrs. Gardiner looked somewhat shocked. "I see. Shall I inform Cook that tea will be delayed?"

"I suppose so," Mary said with regret, for she was quite hungry. "And no matter if he has already taken his own at Lucas Lodge, Mr. Collins will no doubt be joining us." She pointed again to the closed door. "In the meantime, I suggest you do not go in there."

"Sound advice, my dear. I will go below-stairs and have a nice chat with Mrs. Hill, for Mr. Gardiner has gone off to Netherfield and the children are finally resting in the nursery." Mrs. Gardiner descended the last few steps and disappeared through the green baize door, no doubt in search of something to curb her appetite.

Surprisingly, Mr. Collins did not accept Mrs. Bennet's invitation to remain at Longbourn for tea, as he wished to speak to Mr. Darnell without further delay. "For otherwise I cannot possibly write an appropriate sermon," he complained to his hostess as she waited in the chilly hall for him to don his winter things, the fireplace in that part of the house having never been terribly efficient.

Mrs. Bennet nodded her head absently as he spoke, all the while worrying over details about the wedding breakfast and the dance to follow. "We shall see you tomorrow morning in church, Mr. Collins," she said, waving good-bye before hurrying to the same door Mrs. Gardiner had passed through more than an hour earlier.

Shortly after Mr. Collins' departure, the ladies reconvened in the sitting room for tea. Kitty's eyes filled with tears as she cried, "Aunt Gardiner! Mr. Collins will not allow us to tie ribbons at the end of the pews! He said—" she lowered her voice in a fair imitation of their second cousin "—Miss Bennet, the church is no place for such frippery and nonsense. My esteemed patroness, Lady Catherine de Bourgh, would never allow it." She coughed a little. "He is going to ruin everything! Mr. Webb thought my plans for decorating the chapel were charming!"

Mrs. Gardiner, next to Kitty, patted her niece's arm, clicking her tongue sympathetically.

"Given the alternative, Kitty, do you not think it better to do as Mr. Collins wishes?" Jane calmly handed the teacups round.

"Otherwise you may have to wait for the return of one of the Mr. Webbs, and we do not know when that will be."

Kitty frowned, paced up and down, and shook her head fretfully until she finally took a seat next to Georgiana. "You are right of course, but the chapel was so beautiful for your double wedding last December...." She looked first at Jane, then Elizabeth.

"It will be perfect despite the lack of ribbons," promised Elizabeth, her merry eyes catching Jane's.

"Will Miss Bingley arrive in time for the wedding tomorrow?" inquired Mrs. Bennet before biting into a warm scone, too concerned about hundreds of other details to think any longer about ribbons.

Jane did not even blink. "I am afraid the weather has caused Caroline to postpone her return to Hertfordshire. She will be sorry to miss the wedding, of course, but before departing from Netherfield, she left a gift for Kitty in my care." She paused to sip her tea. "I believe she made it herself."

"What a shame to lose three of our number, especially two gentlemen," mused Mrs. Bennet. "I was depending upon Colonel Fitzwilliam and Major Ashton to dance!"

"Well, Mamma, one can neither forecast the weather nor foretell when those in the service of His Majesty will be called away." Elizabeth looked down at her dress, which hid her increasing waistline. "Jane and I will not require partners, at any rate."

Mrs. Bennet's attention was successfully diverted by the topic of her forthcoming grandchildren, and she beamed at her two eldest daughters. "Oh, Jane—Lizzy, sometimes I do not know how I can bear such happiness! To be a grandmother not only to Mr. Bingley's child, but now to Mr. Darcy's as well!" She reached across to take hold of their free hands. "It is just as I told Mrs. Long on your wedding day—we will soon hear little feet pattering about at Longbourn!"

About the same time Mr. Collins was addressing the ladies at Longbourn, Mr. Bennet and his brother-in-law, Mr. Gardiner, arrived at Netherfield in response to Mr. Bingley's invitation.

"Good afternoon, Walker. Where might we find my sons-in-law?" Mr. Bennet removed his greatcoat and handed it to Mr.

Bingley's frail, elderly butler, who in turn gave it to the footman who assisted him.

"The gentlemen are in Mr. Bingley's study, sir." Walker's voice was growing so weak, the two men had to lean forward to hear.

"Thank you, Walker—we can find our own way. It is far colder today than yesterday, is it not?"

The butler responded by lowering his head for a moment before shuffling off, the laden footman following closely behind.

When the two men entered the study, they saw five wingback chairs arranged in a semi-circle facing the fire. Mr. Bingley, Mr. Darcy, and Mr. Darnell were already seated, cigars in hand.

Mr. Gardiner smiled. "Is this in some way the last rite of a gentleman soon to be married?"

Mr. Bingley jumped up. "Mr. Bennet! Mr. Gardiner! So good of you to come. Please have a seat—" he motioned to two empty chairs "—would you care for a cigar? Madeira? I have only just procured some very fine bottles."

The two newcomers gratefully accepted his hospitality, taking their respective seats.

Mr. Darcy spoke while Mr. Bingley poured the drinks. "I am sorry to say we asked you here not to celebrate as we should, but to impart news of a distressing nature regarding a serious matter, which could affect us all."

Mr. Bingley's face looked almost haggard as he sat down, handing over the well-worn letter from Louisa Hurst. "Darcy, will you read the pertinent section of Louisa's letter aloud? I do not believe I can bear to see it even once more."

Mr. Darcy took the letter, explaining to the other three men, "Mr. Bingley received news before dawn yesterday morning from his sister, Mrs. Hurst." He read aloud:

I write with shocking news—Caroline has left London this very day to elope! Before taking leave of me (Mr. Hurst was indisposed), she confessed to having received a letter from an undisclosed emissary directing her to travel to Cornwall, where Mr. Petersham awaits her. They are to be married immediately upon her arrival. From Cornwall, she claims they are to travel 'to distant shores.' (I would like to note that against my better judgment and advice, our sister instructed her maid to pack all of her jewels, and has taken them with her!)

Mr. Darcy set the letter on a side table. "Colonel Fitzwilliam and Major Ashton left at first light, but they may not be able to overtake Miss Bingley in time to prevent this elopement. We must therefore prepare ourselves for bad news, for Miss Bingley unwittingly plans to ally herself to a man who is an admitted traitor to England." Mr. Darcy's expression was grim as he looked upon the surprised, disconcerted faces of Mr. Bennet, Mr. Gardiner, and Mr. Darnell.

"There are some facts with which you should be familiar," Mr. Darcy admitted, and for the next few minutes all attention was riveted on the tale of Mr. Petersham's suspected association with France, the final proof of his activities as a spy against England, his arrest, subsequent promise to spy for England instead, and finally, his escape. He neglected to speak of Georgiana and Mary's experience, not wishing to alarm Mr. Bennet unduly. "It is possible Petersham's activities will become general knowledge if Caroline Bingley does in fact go through with this marriage, and we might all—through the association—be adversely affected. It could even go so far as to affect your business interests in the north," he warned Mr. Darnell.

Mr. Bennet, who had listened with great patience, removed his pince-nez as he addressed his prospective son-in-law. "No doubt this news is even more of a shock to you." Mr. Bennet's piercing gaze then went to Mr. Darcy, who shifted slightly under the scrutiny. "I do not believe you have told us all that occurred at Devonham, my son—" he held up his hand when he saw Mr. Darcy was about to respond "—and I do not expect you to tell any state secrets, though I have been wondering if Mary might have gotten some inspiration for her tales while she was in Derbyshire." He turned again to Mr. Darnell. "I assume Mr. Darcy and Mr. Bingley thought it best to warn you before you take your vows alongside my daughter tomorrow morning." His eyes again sought Darcy, who lowered his head in accord.

"It is still possible for the elopement to be prevented, is it not?" Mr. Darnell asked.

"Yes, it is possible," replied Mr. Darcy. "However, Miss Bingley departed London many hours before Mrs. Hurst posted the letter." His disgusted glance fell upon the worn page. "Caroline clearly did not wish to give us time enough to stop her. Sadly, we cannot be sure of her actual destination, though Petersham no doubt has many friends in Cornwall, it being a notorious hiding place for criminals and pirates. But there are many other places from which he could launch his escape, and a small boat might easily slip past our fleet."

"There are others out searching for them, surely?" asked Mr. Bennet, the pince-nez back in place.

Mr. Darcy nodded. "And sent in all directions, I assure you. Our hope is that Caroline will travel in her accustomed manner, no matter what warnings Petersham might have thought to give her."

Mr. Bennet leaned back in his chair, hands steepled, eyes once more focused on Mr. Darnell. "Well, my boy, do you still wish to marry my daughter, risking the association?"

The eyes of the other three gentlemen were on Mr. Darnell, who took a deep breath. "Mr. Bennet, even with the threat of tainting my own family, I would still wish to marry her—as long as you have no objection?"

"I have no objection at all." Mr. Bennet smiled kindly. "We have weathered many storms, my son. Rest assured, all will be well."

Mr. Bingley let go a great sigh of relief. "You are a good man, Edward—a good friend, and a most welcome addition to our family! I am certain Caroline will be found long before she can take this, er...misstep."

Mr. Bennet thoughtfully tapped cigar ash into the tray. "I agree with you, Charles. Assuming Miss Bingley is traveling to Cornwall, it will be especially slow as the roads are prone to flooding and ice this time of year. Any carriage passing in this weather will be especially noticed—hopefully by someone willing to share a bit of information in exchange for a few coins."

"I believe you are correct, sir," said Mr. Darcy. "It stands to reason that my cousin and Major Ashton will overtake her, for they are accustomed to hard riding and are unencumbered." His expression grew darker. "I cannot imagine Caroline would knowingly wed herself to such a man—by comparison, Wickham seems almost high-principled."

Mr. Bennet looked at Mr. Gardiner and raised his glass. "Now we are finished with serious matters, it is time to celebrate, for there is to be a wedding tomorrow—or so Mrs. Bennet has informed me once or twice. Please allow me to offer the first toast—to my three sons-in-law!"

After the toast was justly recognized, Mr. Darnell frowned. "If you do not mind my asking, why does no one speak of the other one—Mr. Wickham?"

Mr. Bingley held his glass out with a smile. "Darcy, my good friend, I think we are going to need a bit more of this."

Just then there was a knock at the door and a harried-looking Walker appeared, barely able to make his announcement before their unexpected visitor entered the room, his face bright red from the exertion of riding a horse against the cold wind.

"The Reverend Mr. Collins!" Walker announced, closing the door and leaving the gentlemen to fend for themselves, per Mr. Bingley's previous orders.

Later that afternoon, Elizabeth and Jane were together in the drawing room at Longbourn, Elizabeth standing at the window looking for signs of the gentlemen's arrival.

"Lizzy—" Jane was thoughtful "—do you truly think Caroline has no knowledge of Mr. Petersham's iniquitous behavior?"

"I sincerely hope not," Elizabeth replied sharply, turning away from the view of the drive and snowy landscape. "But if she cannot be stopped, it will be an unpleasant discovery that she is wed to a man of more questionable merit than even Mr. Wickham." Her eyes grew wide. "You do not think Mr. Darnell would no longer wish to marry Kitty because of it, do you?"

Jane set her knitting down with a sigh. "I do not think so. It is obvious to anyone with eyes how much he cares for her. I would think Mr. Collins' presiding over the ceremony would be more of an incentive to cancel the wedding."

"Jane!" Elizabeth tried to look shocked.

Jane smiled, holding up the tiny little stocking she had made. "What do you think, Lizzy?"

Elizabeth tipped her head to the side. "What is it, exactly?"

Before Jane could reply, Mary and Georgiana entered the

room, having gone outdoors to cut some sprigs of holly at the request of Mrs. Bennet. Georgiana shivered as she approached the fire. "It is still uncomfortably cold outdoors," she observed, holding her hands near the heat.

"Whyever did Mamma send you out on such a day as this?" inquired Elizabeth.

"She is apparently trying to make up for lack of decoration in the chapel," Mary said dryly as she too moved closer to the fire.

"But why did Mr. Hill not go? He claims the cold weather does not affect him," Jane remarked, still admiring her handiwork.

"He is busy with a thousand other tasks, and it took but little time to do it," Georgiana said before sitting next to Jane with a quizzical look. "What are you holding?"

Elizabeth laughed heartily as Jane threw the stocking at her.

CHAPTER THREE

(An Entry in Mary Bennet's Diary)

Longbourn, 21 December 1813
Major Ashton has gone away without so much as a by-your-leave, which I find odd given our last conversation. Of course I cannot take his proposal seriously, and consider his absence fortuitous as it will allow time to organize my thoughts. With him gone there will be less distraction, and I can finish the book and move on to another. I do hope he stays warm and safe, however. Travel can be dangerous at any time of year, but the snow and cold must make it doubly so. Enough about the major.

For Mamma's sake, I hope he and the colonel find Caroline Bingley soon, so they might return to Hertfordshire in time for the Christmas dance. I do not understand Miss Bingley's decision to elope after planning such an elaborate wedding. Happily for her, the invitations had not yet been sent, for she meant to have nearly every member of the ton witness her triumph.

Georgiana seems to have forgotten she ever thought herself in love with Mr. Petersham, for she is her normal cheerful self once again, and never mentions his name. I have not yet said so to her, but I do not believe she was ever truly in love with either him or Mr. Wickham—only perhaps enamoured with the idea of being so. I feel certain she is destined to marry, however. The only question is who the gentleman is to be. For my part, I have begun to think I was never in love with Captain Jameson, for if I had been, should I not still be suffering from a broken heart? He was simply the first man who treated me as if I were a person of some intelligence, and whose company I enjoyed (one must also consider his heroic actions in the Thames, leading to my rescue, for which I will forever be grateful). Of course, my feelings are unclear regarding Major Ashton, whose penchant for teasing is a great source of exasperation to me. He hides it well, but he is a well-read man of many interests. Only last evening he and Papa had an interesting discussion about the novel by William Chetwood (one of Papa's favorites) about one Captain Robert Boyle, and I am determined to read it.

CHAPTER FOUR

Longbourn, 22 December 1813

On the morning of the wedding, the powdery blanket of snow which had fallen overnight upon Longbourn and its environs sparkled like diamonds in the sunshine.

It was unseasonably cold, however, and Mrs. Bennet, who had been up and bustling since dawn, could not approve Kitty's plan to walk the short distance to Longbourn Chapel as had long been the Bennet family tradition. "Remember how you suffered last spring, my dear—you must take special care not to catch a chill as you would by traipsing about in this horrid weather." She pulled her shawl tighter about her shoulders, sniffing into her inadequate lace handkerchief. "Who will remind you of such things when you are so far away?"

Kitty left her seat at the dressing table to embrace her mother. "You must write to me each day, Mamma, to give me advice, for I will certainly need it." Her eyes grew wide with trepidation. "How will I ever manage a home of my own?"

"If you do not allow Molly to finish your hair, we may be subjected to Mr. Collins' lengthy admonitions regarding those who come late to church," Mary said drily, looking at her own little time-piece.

Kitty giggled nervously and sat down.

Molly, with a hidden smile, swept up her curls and completed the coiffure with a smart cap edged with Brussels lace.

"You look like a princess, my dear!" Mrs. Bennet adjusted the gauze overlay of Kitty's gown before pulling a more serviceable handkerchief from inside her sleeve, dabbing at real tears.

One of the housemaids, who had come to Longbourn shortly after the fortuitous marriages of Jane and Elizabeth, entered Kitty's chamber to announce the arrival of the Darcys, Bingleys, and Mr. Darnell. "They are waiting in the drawing room, ma'am," she said, her eyes on Kitty. "And may I offer my best wishes for your happiness, miss?" Kitty's answering smile was radiant.

Mrs. Bennet looked into the mirror, pinching her cheeks and tucking away a stray curl. "It is time, my dears!" She moved to the door and waited as Molly helped Kitty into a satin pelisse made especially to complement her wedding gown.

"I do hope Mr. Collins will not go on and on about my wifely duties," whispered Kitty as she and Mary proceeded slowly down the stairs.

"Even an irksome sermon given by our cousin could not make this day any less happy for you." Mary spoke with confidence, though she had little hope Mr. Collins would refrain from lecturing the bride and groom at great length. Her greater concern was for the unfortunate family and friends in the cold, unadorned chapel, as well as for the townspeople who would wait outside to offer their congratulations.

The chapel being small—and custom being what it was—only the family members witnessed Mr. Bennet embrace his daughter before he presented her to Mr. Darnell, who stood nervously before Mr. Collins.

The service would have been relatively short had Mr. Collins not chosen to offer his wisdom via an extended sermon on the desirability for certain persons about to be married to overcome their questionable upbringing, to avoid the contamination of unsuitable connections, and never to admit into their homes those infidels who had taken a false step. He concluded with a lecture on the necessity for brides (and females in general) to learn proper humility and to refrain from headstrong and foolish behavior (at which point his narrowed eyes focused directly on Mary).

When it came time to read the solemnization ceremony, Mr. Collins enunciated each word. He gave greatest emphasis to those which caused the most discomfort, Kitty visibly trembling when he intoned:

> *I require and charge you both, as ye will answer at the dreadful day of judgment when the secrets of all hearts shall be disclosed, that if either of you know any impediment, why ye may not be lawfully joined together in matrimony, ye do now confess it.*

But, however hard he tried, Mr. Collins could not forestall the vows forever. The bride and groom pronounced "I will" at the proper time and with satisfactory humility, and Mr. Darnell slid the ring on Kitty's finger. When, with a severe glance at the young bride, Mr. Collins intoned, his arms opened wide, "wives, submit yourselves unto your own husbands," Elizabeth rolled her eyes, while Mary began to meditate on the true nature of marriage. Vicar Webb had accommodated his audience at Jane and Elizabeth's wedding by reading speedily through the text after the vows were exchanged, and the mumbled words had not resonated so in Mary's mind.

After Mr. Collins read the final blessing, the bride and groom, followed by all their guests, fairly fled out the door to be greeted with cheers from the thoroughly-chilled townspeople and Longbourn servants.

The Bingleys were hosting the wedding breakfast at Netherfield, followed by a dance, and those guests who did not attend the ceremony—the most prominent citizens of Meryton and the four-and-twenty families with whom the Bennets commonly associated—had been invited to assemble there, where Mrs. Nicholls, the housekeeper, was to maintain order until the arrival of the wedding party.

The long table in the largest of Netherfield's dining rooms was laden with tempting delicacies of every sort: rolls both sweet and savory, eggs, ham, bacon, tongue, fish, savory pies, sweet pies, hothouse fruits, nuts, negus, chocolate, the white soup Mrs. Bennet had deemed absolutely necessary, and as a measure of the occasion, a large cake decorated with marzipan flowers set upon a high silver stand in the middle.

"I believe I would rather not be married at all than to have Mr. Collins officiate at my wedding, if you will pardon me speaking in such a manner about your cousin," Georgiana said in a quiet voice to Mary as they stood apart from the crowd, sipping cups of chocolate.

"Nor I—" Mary watched the object of their discourse as he tried to ingratiate himself to a somewhat unreceptive Mr. Darcy, Charlotte Collins looking on with pink cheeks "—and you need not apologize." She turned away from the spectacle. "But despite his best efforts, he could not mar the day for either the bride or the groom." She indicated Kitty and Mr. Darnell, looking a bit bewildered as they accepted the congratulations of their guests.

"I think Kitty was fortunate Mr. Darnell came to Hertfordshire when you were not here. Do you ever wonder what might have happened had you been, for was not his original intent to visit you?"

Mary smiled, shrugging. "I hardly think so. At any rate, you and I had other things on our minds at the time, and as you know, it has always been my intention to remain unmarried—"

Georgiana laughed outright. "Yes, my good friend—I know, and I believe your resolution to remain so has become infectious—you may well start a new trend in society. What would Mr. Collins have to say about people remaining unmarried, I wonder?" She set her empty cup on a passing footman's tray. "I see Mr. Collins eyeing the Darnells. Perhaps we should go speak with them."

They soon accomplished their goal, Mrs. Darnell responding happily to Georgiana's request to tell them about her other children. While listening politely, Mary caught sight of Walker shuffling in Mr. Bingley's direction. A note was passed discretely, Mr. Bingley frowning as he glanced at the contents. He soon sought out Mr. Darcy, both of them leaving the room after a brief, discreet word with their wives.

Mary stopped wondering about Mr. Bingley's note, as her attention was caught. She listened with increasing horror to Mr. Darnell's tale of a treacherous stretch of ice on the western edge of Hertfordshire that nearly caused their horses and the carriage to topple over the side of a hill. "We feel fortunate indeed to have escaped serious injury," he said, taking his wife's arm. "One hears of such accidents, but I never thought to experience one myself."

"I cannot imagine how frightening it was," said Georgiana,

her eyes wide. "How horrible for you."

Before anyone could respond, Mr. Collins approached with his signature obsequious pomposity, rubbing his hands together as he pleaded, "Miss Darcy, will you please introduce me to your friends?"

Once the introduction was made, Mr. Collins launched into a detailed description of Rosings, the grand home of his patroness, Lady Catherine de Bourgh, followed by his whispered news of the soon-to-be-announced betrothal of her only daughter (and heir to her entire fortune), Miss Anne de Bourgh.

Just as he took a breath to extoll on the endless virtues of his patroness, Mrs. Bennet wafted across the floor towards them, crying out when she came near, "Oh, my dear, dear Mrs. Darnell!—" she took hold of that lady's arm "—you and I have so much to talk about!" Mrs. Bennet's glance slid to Mr. Collins, her expression not particularly friendly, his recent sermon no doubt the cause. "You must excuse us, Mr. Collins. It is the first opportunity we mothers will have to speak with one another privately." She did not wait for a reply, but tucked her arm beneath Mrs. Darnell's, leading her away as she exclaimed, "Did you not think my dear Kitty and your dear Edward the handsomest couple? Their looks were enough to decorate the chapel, which unfortunately..." her voice faded away and Mr. Darnell took advantage of the moment to excuse himself. Happily, when Mr. Collins realized he had only Mary and Georgiana for an audience, he went off in search of other prey.

Mary set her cup on a tray, pulling Georgiana into an unoccupied corner behind a large potted plant brought in specially for the occasion from the hot-house. "I think Mr. Bingley may have just received news regarding you-know-who!"

"He will have gone to his study to send a reply." Georgiana spoke through a false smile, slowly leading the way towards the southernmost doorway. However, their progress was halted when Elizabeth came to join them, her lips formed into a thin line, whispering sharply, "Did you hear Mr. Collins hinting at *further* troubles visiting upon us? The man is intolerable!" She lowered her voice even more. "If he has learned something about Miss Bingley, Lady Catherine will soon get wind of it, and who knows where things could lead!" She eyed their cousin coldly as he leaned over the buffet table, struggling with a piece of turbot.

Georgiana turned away from the sight, her expression unreadable. "Even though Caroline might actually deserve her fate, I hope my cousin and Major Ashton are successful in preventing her from making such a blunder—" her eyes lit up "— Mary believes Mr. Bingley may have just received news from Cousin Richard and Major Ashton."

Elizabeth nodded thoughtfully. "I wondered what could take them away." Her eyes swept the room, her expression softening when she saw Mr. Darnell hand a piece of cake to his bride.

Later that evening, after the final dance, the bride and groom proceeded with much pomp and circumstance to the sleigh that was to take them the short distance to the recently-redecorated hunting lodge at the farthest edge of Netherfield. Mary observed Kitty's expression as it changed from excitement to near-terror, believing herself lucky never to have to experience such fear.

Shortly thereafter, the guests (who had been celebrating for some hours) either departed in their own sleighs or retired to their rooms. Mr. Bingley and Mr. Darcy waited until the last of them disappeared from the landing above before asking their wives, Mary, and Georgiana to accompany them to the study.

"Colonel Fitzwilliam and Major Ashton were able to overtake Caroline," Mr. Bingley said without preamble, "although it took a great deal of time to convince her to change her plans. She has not admitted much, but was definitely following Petersham's instructions given her by an emissary, whose identity she has not yet disclosed." He passed around a tray of glasses filled with negus. "Colonel Fitzwilliam said she is unharmed. Her greatest concern is for the fortune she signed over to Petersham without my knowledge."

"She has lost her fortune to him?" Elizabeth leaned forward. "But they were not yet married!"

Mr. Darcy looked about to respond to his wife's question, but stopped. "Why are you smiling, Bingley?"

"Months ago, when she told me she was engaged to Mr. Arbuthnot—can you imagine!—I arranged with my banker to disallow Caroline from signing over her fortune to anyone without my written consent. She has always been so headstrong." He took hold of Jane's hand, still smiling. "I am her guardian, after all." His smile became even wider. "But the best part of all is she is unaware of my actions, and does not yet know her fortune is safe."

"When do you plan to inform her?" Elizabeth's looks were teasing.

Mr. Bingley smiled deviously. "She will not learn of it until she comes to me on her knees, begging forgiveness for this confounded escapade!"

"So the situation is resolved?" Georgiana asked, just managing to hide a yawn. "Miss Bingley will return to Hertfordshire in the company of the colonel and the major?"

"And several maids," Mary reminded her.

Mr. Bingley shook his head. "No—I am afraid she will not be joining us. She insisted on being escorted back to London, where she will once again reign supreme over our poor servants." He sighed and turned to Jane. "Remind me to have a few extra guineas added to each of their boxes."

"And word of the escapade has not spread? We are safe?" Elizabeth was jubilant. "Mr. Collins implied there was trouble ahead—thoroughly enjoying his prognostication, I might add."

Mr. Darcy moved away from the wall he had been leaning against, holding his hand out to his wife. "Caroline's absence from London will not necessarily have been remarked upon, as she travels with great frequency. She will return to London just as she was before she left—an engaged woman whose fiancé is apparently away, seeing to his business interests." He put his hand on the door handle, turning back to say to Mr. Bingley, "When the time is right, we will need to formally terminate the engagement, but that should not be difficult." He looked at the others. "Now, if any of you are as tired as I, you have been longing for your warm beds this last hour."

CHAPTER FIVE

By the time Georgiana and Mary entered the Netherfield ballroom the day following the wedding, they saw with some regret that the servants had already put the room to rights and had removed all traces of the ornate chalk design drawn on the floor by a local artist.

"It was so lovely," said Georgiana. "I had hoped to see it again, but without so many feet upon it." She went to the pianoforte and ran her fingers up the entire keyboard in a glissando, something Mary had attempted without great success when she thought no one could hear.

"There would have been little left to see this morning." Mary looked thoughtfully at the shining floor.

"When Fitzwilliam and Elizabeth give a ball at Pemberley, I will ask them to hire the same artist—do you think the chalk really prevents people from slipping? Mr. Collins certainly did not seem to benefit from it."

"A spectacle not easily forgotten." Mary rolled her eyes. "He would not let go of poor Miss King's hand, and nearly took her and half the guests down with him when he fell."

Georgiana was clearly remembering the incident with amusement. "At least young Mr. Webb was there to prevent Miss King from falling."

Mary recovered her composure. "Even though the chalk might have kept the rest of us safe, it seems a terrible waste of an artist's work."

Georgiana nodded, looking through the stacks of music before choosing a Clementi piece familiar to each of them.

She then broached another subject altogether. "We have not

had a moment to ourselves since we were out walking on Monday. Can you now finally tell me all of what transpired between yourself and Major Ashton?"

Mary sauntered through the instruments, idly strumming the strings of a harp. "Major Ashton is a fine conversationalist; he does not center his talk on the weather and hunting." She half-smiled at the memory. "We talked of many things, including your aunt's determination to see me in service as a governess."

"My aunt will never succeed in making you do anything against your will—but surely such an intense exchange was not entirely centered on her?"

"There is not much more to tell. He threw the stick for Samson several times, told me about the friendly relationship between his mother and father, and—" Mary paused for dramatic effect "—asked if I would consider the possibility of a similar relationship with him, based on mutual esteem." She opened one of the violin cases and peered inside, not touching the instrument.

Georgiana's eyebrows rose, her looks incredulous. "He asked you to marry him?"

Mary closed the case, frowning. "It was certainly not what one would consider a conventional proposal."

Georgiana waited for Mary to continue, unrewarded, and finally asked a trifle impatiently, "How did you answer him?"

Mary flipped through a piece of music resting on an upright stand. "I did not wish to be rude, and agreed to consider his proposal. He claims to be a patient man and as I have no intention of marrying at present—and told him so—I will take him at his word. At the moment, I wish only to write novels and spend time with my dear friend Georgiana until *she* decides to marry."

Georgiana sat down at the pianoforte. "Well, my friend, while you are *not* considering his proposal, perhaps we can work through the pieces for this evening." Mary obliged and sat down before the instrument.

Later, while Georgiana searched for another piece, Mary asked, "What would you do in my place?"

Georgiana set the music on the rack, opening it to the first page. "As you know, I have thought myself to be desperately in love with *two* men, each with despicable characters hidden beneath flawless manners and handsome looks, thereby proving my judgment poor and untrustworthy." She looked up at the nymphs on the painted ceiling. "I have come to think it would be best for me to follow your example and remain unfettered—at least for the time being. You, on the other hand, have had two marriage proposals from two fine, respectable men—one with whom you *might* have been in love, but we will never know for certain as his mother prevented the match, and the other a brave, noble gentleman who apparently loves you, but is willing to settle for a marriage based on friendship."

Georgiana sighed. "I wish to marry for love, just as Elizabeth and Fitzwilliam, and Jane and Charles have done. Nothing less will satisfy me, while it is possible you may be perfectly content in the type of marriage Major Ashton proposes." She looked kindly upon Mary before placing her hands on the keyboard, ready to play once more. "You have to know that you would be allowed more freedom as a married woman than as a spinster, in many ways." She took a deep breath. "Sadly, I will need a husband if I am to get my wish for a hoard of children."

Mary laughed. "It is traditional. But what of Mr. Chandler? You seemed to enjoy his company at Devonham."

"He is quite nice, and I have known him since I was a child, but—" Georgiana frowned "—I begin to wonder if I am actually *attracted* to bad men."

Mary did not admit to having that exact thought. "In which case you might consider marrying someone you like, and hold in high esteem—perhaps you would be happier in the end with a marriage based on friendship."

Georgiana shook her head vehemently. "The idea is not at all appealing to me. But there is time for both of us, you know, despite Aunt Catherine's hints about my advancing age and your imminent slide into servitude. No—I am perfectly happy to go on as we have been, until one or both of us decides to marry." Georgiana motioned for Mary to ready her hands, and soon the strains of a Purcell melody filled the room.

In the meantime, Mr. Darcy and Elizabeth were at opposite ends of the settee in their shared sitting room at Netherfield, Darcy's legs stretched out in front of him, Elizabeth's feet upon his lap. She said sleepily, "So, Caroline Bingley is now safely back in London, her reputation intact?"

Darcy nodded, his lips forming a thin line. "Thankfully, yes. But it was a narrow escape from a well-deserved fate."

"Mr. Darcy!" Elizabeth feigned shock.

He lifted a single brow in imitation of his wife. "You saw through her veneer early on. It was only when you were in this house nursing Jane that I first began to see Caroline in a new light."

"Oh, do not remind me." Elizabeth shook her head to clear the image. "I did not behave so well at the time either; it would be unfair to judge her too harshly. She hoped to become Mrs. Darcy, you know, and for some reason saw me as a competitor even then."

Darcy grinned. "I told her I admired your fine eyes, which in part probably led to her vindictive behavior towards you and your family."

Elizabeth's brows rose. "Then I believe I am in her debt, for had she not pointed out my faults so assiduously, you may never have noticed me!" She rested her hand atop his. "Do you still admire my fine eyes?"

"Let me think." Darcy leaned his head back against the settee, his eyes closed. Elizabeth shifted away from him.

"I did marry you, you know," he said, eyes still closed.

Elizabeth settled back against the cushions with a contented sigh. "Yes, you did. And it is a kindness for which I will be forever grateful."

For a long time they stayed exactly where they were, Darcy occasionally opening his eyes to view the dancing flames in the hearth, Elizabeth not fighting the languidness she had begun to experience each afternoon. The crackling of the fire was the only sound for some time, until Mr. Darcy said reflectively, "I wonder what we should do about Georgiana."

Elizabeth half opened one eye. "Georgiana? Is something the matter?"

"She has never had a season, you know. She begged me not

to force one upon her, and I allowed her to have her way, as society is filled with puppies and popinjays—all seeking young ladies of fortune. But now I begin to wonder how she will ever find a suitable mate."

Elizabeth opened both eyes, sat up, and took a moment to tuck the folds of her dress around her bent knees. "Mate? You want her to be married so soon?"

"I do, certainly, and to someone of strong character, for I fear I have completely lost control of her—just think of what has happened within the last year alone! It was only by the greatest luck I was able to prevent her from eloping with Wickham when she was but sixteen years old. And now...." He sighed. "Richard says I have always been far too lenient with her—and since becoming Mary's friend—" he looked apologetically at his wife "—you must forgive me, my dear, but the two of them have an uncanny tendency to get into scrapes of the most outlandish nature. The only remedy is for one or both of them to marry, though Georgiana is clearly the more likely candidate since Mary seems determined to remain a spinster."

Elizabeth thought for a moment. "They will not be separated, Fitzwilliam. Georgiana and Mary are as close as any two friends could ever be—it would not be fair to them. Not yet at any rate." She placed a hand upon her husband's arm. "Richard shares in Georgiana's guardianship—does he feel as you do about her having a season?"

Mr. Darcy shook his head. "It is only a recently-formed plan of my own." He relaxed against the cushions once more, holding his arms open and she snuggled against him as he mused, "Perhaps Mary would like to go to London with Georgiana. I believe I can convince my Aunt Matlock to chaperone them, as well as sponsor Georgiana's presentation at court, as she is forever lamenting no daughter of her own to take to routs, balls, and the theatre. Surely they could not get into trouble in so short a time?" He rested his chin upon Elizabeth's head, a dubious look on both their faces.

CHAPTER SIX

"Mrs. Long told me of the strangest tradition in foreign parts—people actually bring a fir tree into the house to bedeck it with birds' nests, apples, nuts, and even candles!" Mrs. Bennet was at the moment arranging an evergreen bough on the high mantle in Netherfield's main drawing room, per Jane's suggestion. "She has so far been unsuccessful in trying to convince Mr. Long of its desirability in her own home. Can you imagine?" She laughed, shaking her head in disbelief, while taking up another aromatic branch from those gathered earlier by the servants.

"It sounds like a delightful custom, Mrs. Bennet," said Mr. Bingley from his comfortable chair, watching as the ladies decorated the room with evergreen boughs, holly branches, ivy, hawthorn, rosemary, and Christmas rose. "Perhaps Jane and I should have that enormous pine felled at the third turn in the drive. Our coachman nearly drove right into it after the most recent assembly we attended in Meryton." He thought for a moment. "It was uncommonly foggy, as I recall."

Mr. Bennet looked up from the book he had borrowed from Mr. Bingley's library. "A tree inside the house might greatly increase the danger of fire, especially at this time of year, when our wives—" he gestured with the book "—are intent upon placing wood branches dangerously close to the flames."

At the table, Mr. Darcy held a branch of holly out to Elizabeth, who placed it in a vase holding other treasures from the winter woods. "One would have to rearrange the furniture to accommodate an entire tree. However, if it is a tradition you wish to adopt at Pemberley, my dear...."

Elizabeth took another branch from him. "I would not wish to do anything to endanger Pemberley, Mr. Darcy. We shall keep to our English traditions, if you please."

Just then Walker appeared, clearing his throat, followed shortly by the young Darnells.

"Happy Christmas, my dears!" Mrs. Bennet rushed over to the newly-wed couple, embracing each of them in turn before addressing Mr. Darnell. "I am sorry your parents had to leave us so soon—we found them charming, absolutely charming!"

Mr. Darnell bowed his head. "They were sorry to go, Mrs. Bennet, but my father is not one to change plans already made, no matter the circumstances."

"Where are the others?" Kitty asked, her eyes scanning the room.

"Jane has enlisted Aunt Gardiner, Georgiana, and Mary to help prepare the gifts for Boxing Day," Elizabeth said, holding her hand out for another bough.

"We were waiting for you, Darnell." Mr. Bingley rose from his chair. "Darcy and I hoped you would join us for a ride while the ladies finish their...decorating." He turned to Mr. Bennet and Mr. Gardiner to include them in the invitation.

"Riding out in such weather is a game for the young, my boy. Brother Gardiner and I will retire to your library if you please, and pass the time in a much more reasonable manner," Mr. Bennet said cheerfully.

Mr. Gardiner nearly jumped from his chair. "A fine idea—most fine!"

Elizabeth turned to Mr. Darcy. "It is unusually cold today, as you know from our thwarted attempt at walking outdoors earlier. You must all wear your warmest outer garments."

The younger gentlemen nodded obediently, but their immediate departure was forestalled by Mrs. Bennet. "My dear Mr. Darnell, before you go galloping through the countryside you must sit with Kitty on the yule log. It is sure to be added to the fire by the time you return."

Kitty looked shyly at her new husband, who smiled and gently pulled her towards the large log set close to the fire. "It is a tradition in my family as well." He took out his handkerchief and valiantly dusted the bark before they sat down, Kitty's cheeks a becoming pink.

"There, now we have all done!" Mrs. Bennet clapped her hands as Mr. Darnell helped Kitty to her feet. "You are sure to have good luck the year long!" Before anything else could detain them, the younger gentlemen left to change into their riding clothes.

Jane entered the drawing room a short time later, followed by Darcy's spaniel puppy, Samson, who found a comfortable spot near the fire. "Mamma—" she hurried towards Mrs. Bennet "—did you and Papa remember to bring a piece of charcoal from last year's yule log?"

Mrs. Bennet's hands halted above a hawthorn branch. "Oh, dear! I must see your father immediately!" She rushed from the room.

"I take it that means no," said Elizabeth dryly, turning to Kitty. "Did you find the hunting lodge comfortable?"

Kitty's eyes lit up. "It is a cozy, wonderful place, Lizzy!" She twirled around to face Jane. "It was so thoughtful of you and Mr. Bingley."

Jane smiled. "Charles will be happy to hear you are happy there. It was his pet project these past weeks."

Mrs. Gardiner brought a basket of evergreen boughs over to the table. "You look the picture of a contented young bride, my dear."

Kitty twirled around, her arms out wide. "More than I ever hoped to be!"

By the time one of the servants had gone to Longbourn and back, bringing with him the lump of coal preserved from the previous year's yule log, the gentlemen had returned from their ride. The Gardiner children, back from a sledding expedition with their tutor, were the last to join the party assembled in the drawing room to watch the ceremonial lighting and to welcome the season with elderberry wine.

On Christmas morning, the inhabitants of Netherfield traveled in two shining sleighs to Longbourn Chapel for services, while the Bennets and Gardiners walked the short distance. The building was cold despite the fire, the ladies keeping their hands in their swan's-down muffs, the gentlemen not removing their greatcoats during the entire service. (Mr. Collins once again took the pulpit, as the vicar had not yet recovered.) However, neither the cold nor the grim, over-long sermon could dispel the general feeling of goodwill amongst the flock.

After a traditional meal of roast goose and plum pudding, the Bingleys and their extended family assembled in the music room, where all those who could play the pianoforte—including the Bingleys' new nursemaid, Mrs. Linley—took a turn, while the others danced. Mary was not the only one watching Georgiana as she laughingly joined the Gardiner children (whom she had asked to call her 'Aunt Georgy') in a country dance.

By mid-afternoon, the largest of Netherfield's tables was once more filled with good things from the kitchen, the guests serving each other (with a great deal of mirth), while the Bingley servants celebrated below-stairs.

Boxing Day brought even more snow, the thick blanket on the ground increasing each hour, the wind making it difficult to see, ruling out travel of any sort. Therefore, the Bennets and the Gardiners stayed near the warm fires at Longbourn, the young Darnells remained snug in the hunting lodge, and the Darcys and Bingleys, after distributing gifts to the servants, were left to their own devices at Netherfield.

Elizabeth and Jane were together in the morning room after breakfast, watching the snow fall while keeping their feet warm on the fender near the fire. "I do wish you would try to convince Mr. Darcy to remain at Netherfield until the baby is born, Elizabeth. I spoke to our physician, who claims you should be safe traveling as late as March since your own baby is not due until the latter part of June."

Elizabeth turned to her sister with a smile. "Mr. Darcy spoke to your physician about this very topic recently, and has agreed to stay. I am happy to say we will be here to celebrate the safe delivery of your child, and will not leave until we are fully acquainted with him—or her." Elizabeth leaned back with a sigh. "I asked Mamma about traveling while I am gravid—" she grimaced at the term "—and she said it would be far safer to travel when the weather turns warmer and the snow and ice have melted. She believes we could return to Pemberley as late as April, though I do not think I could convince Mr. Darcy to stay quite so long."

Jane squeezed her sister's hand, a contented smile on her lips.

Mr. Bingley unlocked the ornately carved box holding his precious ivory billiard balls and placed them carefully on the baize-covered table. "Shall we play to twelve?" he asked, handing Darcy a cue. "It is your turn to begin."

"As you wish."

Mr. Darcy was about to line up his first shot when Walker entered, followed by a footman carrying a laden tray.

"Excuse me, sirs, but Mrs. Bingley thought you might enjoy some refreshment during your game." Walker directed the footman with a discreet gesture.

"How thoughtful!" Mr. Bingley glanced at the brimming pitcher. "The wassail is excellent this year—have you sampled it?" he asked his butler, who was pouring the frothing mixture into two glasses.

"We all took a portion with Christmas dinner, as was kindly suggested by Mrs. Bingley, thank you, sir." Walker bowed, motioning with one gloved hand for the footman to precede him from the room.

"Despite any infirmity, your butler does seem to enjoy his duties," Mr. Darcy commented quietly after setting down the glass and realigning his shot.

Bingley nodded, picking up his cue. "He is a good man, and will no doubt insist upon working until he can no longer stand.

Before you came in, I found him iron
indicated the fabric-covered surface, grin
"—well done!"

Darcy stood aside. "You have not y
letter I received earlier—it was from Ric...
wait to tell us in person exactly what transpired ...
caught up with Caroline. It will not be for some time, however,
for he is to remain in London in hopes of discovering any others
involved in the scheme for Petersham's escaping England. Lord
Castlereagh suspects at least one accomplice was a guest at
Devonham."

"I wonder who?" Mr. Bingley could not hide a smile as his
cue ball knocked Darcy's into the left corner pocket. He picked
up his unlit cigar. "Mark me for two points, will you, Darcy?"

Darcy obliged with good humor, sliding the markers across.

"And Major Ashton? Will he return to Hertfordshire?"

Darcy missed another shot and frowned. "The major is also
remaining in London, ostensibly as part of his regimental
duties, but in actuality to keep company with your sister." He
waited for Mr. Bingley's turn before asking, "Charles, are you
aware of any particular friendship, for lack of better word,
between Mary and the major?"

Bingley thought for a moment, then shook his head. "I have
noticed nothing unusual between them." He shot again, Darcy's
ball sliding into a pocket.

Darcy used his cue to add two more markers to Bingley's
score. "Lizzy suspects he has grown partial to her. Who would
have guessed she would have two beaus vying for her attention
simply because she removed her spectacles and stopped reciting
passages from Fordyce and the other pedantics? And who can
tell what she will choose to do next? One minute she is
convincing my sister to take pugilism lessons, the next she is
selling novels, all the while proclaiming her wish to remain a
spinster—crazy notions." Darcy shook his head with frustration,
squinting as he made his shot.

Mr. Bingley watched as the ball stopped far wide of the mark.
"Something is bothering you, my good friend—" he set his cue
aside and motioned for Darcy to take one of the chairs nearest
the fire. "What is it? It is nothing to do with Elizabeth or the

, surely?"

Darcy laid his cue on the table before refilling each of their glasses, handing one to Bingley. "It is kind of you to ask, Charles. I thank you, but Lizzy and the baby are fine. It is Georgiana's future that concerns me."

CHAPTER SEVEN

A thick fog covering all of London and its environs to the southeast gave the Gardiners good reason to postpone their return to Gracechurch Street until after the Twelfth Night celebrations. On the morning of their departure, Mrs. Bennet stood outside with only her husband and Mary (all of her other daughters now married), alternately waving her handkerchief and dabbing her eyes as the carriage proceeded down the drive, for she was in fact quite fond of her brother and his family.

Mary waved good-bye absently, for her mind was already on the journey she and Georgiana would soon undertake to Rosings, Lady Catherine having insisted they return so she could oversee (dictate) the completion of the sequel to Mary's first published novel, *The Turret Room*. Despite the constant, almost overwhelming interference of that lady, Mary felt a little thrill at the thought of traveling again as she followed her parents indoors, excusing herself to work on the book.

The following day the Bennets came to Netherfield to wish farewell to young Mr. and Mrs. Darnell, Kitty waving out the carriage window long after they had passed through the Netherfield gates, though no one could see her. While she was hiding her tears against her husband's shoulder, her mother was making good use of the sturdiest of all her handkerchiefs.

"Oh, my dear, dear, Kitty!" Mrs. Bennet cried upon entering the sitting room. "What shall I do without her?"

"She is going to York, not the West Indies." Mary tried to sound comforting, but her words only brought more tears and cries of "poor, poor Lydia!" (Despite her desire to see them all married, Mrs. Bennet did not like to part with any one of them, even Mary.)

"Mamma," ventured Jane, "would you care to help me choose the paper for your rooms at Beechwood Manor? We could try several in the model house." Mr. Bingley had commissioned a miniature model of their new home in Derbyshire so his wife might expend her energy on something other than having the Netherfield nursery repainted each week. His scheme had worked, for Jane happily worked each day on the extremely elaborate miniature model of Beechwood Manor, endlessly painting and papering the walls, making curtains from scraps of fabric, and rearranging the tiny pieces of furniture which a craftsman in Meryton had made to her specifications.

Mrs. Bennet sniffed and tucked her handkerchief away, her eyes regaining some of their brightness. "I would be happy to, Jane. I described your little house to Lady Lucas; she has already commissioned her own model of Lucas Lodge."

Elizabeth, who secretly wished for just such a model of Pemberley, took her mother by the arm. "I have been longing to have a go at the ballroom—gluing miniscule pieces of plaster onto the ceiling will be a pleasure."

Mr. Bingley insisted upon helping Jane up the stairs and to the nursery, where the model was kept, for the baby had grown so large his wife could not always see her feet. "It is time we exercise our horses, Darcy," he called down to his friend when they reached the upper landing.

Mr. Darcy had been watching their progress with a bemused expression, no doubt picturing Elizabeth in the same condition as Jane in the near future. "I will meet you at the stables!" He took the stairs two at a time.

❧

"Shall we begin with the Mozart piece for two pianos?" Georgiana's voice was muffled as she dug in the music cabinet. "I feel like something in a major key."

Mary found the comment interesting, given her friend's recent propensity to play the most ferocious of works, all in minor. "A piece with a slow tempo might be nice," she suggested.

"Certainly, but even so, we should warm up properly for the house has not yet recovered from the long string of frightfully cold days—Maestro Clementi is forever warning against injury."

Mary went to the second piano and rubbed her hands together before beginning to work slowly through an exercise Georgiana had taught her, designed to warm the hands and relax the muscles.

"Mary—" Georgiana was thoughtful as she played a simple pattern "—my brother wants me to have a season this year."

Mary stopped playing, and though she could not see Georgiana's face over the music rack, could guess at her expression. "In London?" She hesitated. "Have you agreed to his plan?"

The arpeggios Georgiana was banging out indicated some amount of temper, but once she completed the exercise she spoke calmly. "I have, but with one proviso—I asked if you could come with me to have a season yourself. And he agreed."

Mary opened her mouth to object, but Georgiana did not let her interrupt, adding quickly, "He is writing to my Aunt Matlock to inquire if she, in company with Mrs. Annesley, will act as our chaperone. My aunt loves to go to the opera—*The Magic Flute* is to be performed at Covent Garden in the spring, and there will be numerous plays, musical events, and lectures we can attend, all of which will be pleasantly diverting. Remember the demonstration on static electricity we saw at the Royal Institute? We will *not* limit ourselves solely to societal drawing rooms and Almack's!"

Mary laughed. "I would love to accompany you, Georgiana; you need not try to convince me. There is clear merit to the plan for me, as the experience should lead to ideas for future novels." She began to play the exercise again, but after a few moments stopped. "There may be a problem, however. You may have no difficulty in attaining a voucher of admission to Almack's Rooms, but it may not be the case for me. Caroline Bingley revels in tales about people even of the highest rank being turned away by the lady managers."

Georgiana's expression was complacent. "You need not worry. Lady Castlereagh is one of the Lady Patronesses—we will each get vouchers, never fear." Georgiana brought the music to

Mary's piano and set it on the rack. "Are you ready to play?"

"As ready as I will ever be," Mary responded.

⌒～⌒

Mr. Darcy and Mr. Bingley stopped to rest their horses at the crest of a hill, from where they could view much of the land belonging to Netherfield and Longbourn, as well as the rooftops of Meryton in the distance.

Mr. Darcy patted his horse's neck. "Have you heard yet from Caroline?"

Mr. Bingley dismounted and pulled a package wrapped in burlap from his saddle bag. "No, I have not." He grinned. "But she will write soon, I am certain of it, for Louisa will not be able to give her much money—my brother-in-law walks a fine line, as you know."

Mr. Darcy, well-acquainted with Mr. Hurst, nodded.

"So, once she realizes I am the only person to whom she can turn for funds, she will write. In the meantime, I take great pleasure in knowing what she does not: her fortune is safe. She does not deserve it, nearly giving it away to that...that—"

"Rogue?"

"Rogue, traitor, what have you—Petersham fits the description. He has proved to be a far worse villain than Wickham ever could be."

Mr. Darcy considered for a moment. "As Elizabeth noted only the other evening, there are not enough fine qualities between the two of them to make *one* good man, but I will allow that Petersham's villainy might slightly outweigh that of my brother-in-law."

Mr. Bingley opened the package and pulled out two sandwiches, passing one to Darcy, who looked at him quizzically. "I know we ate only a couple of hours ago, but I seem always to be hungry of late. The physician calls it 'sympathetic hunger pains.'"

Mr. Darcy opened his. "Your cook does make a fine sandwich."

They ate while standing, looking out upon the snowy fields, but before either they or their mounts caught a chill, started back to the house, allowing their prized horses to trot side-by-side.

Mr. Darcy dropped the reins momentarily to rub his gloved hands together. "Georgiana has agreed to have a season," he said casually.

Mr. Bingley stopped in the midst of rewinding the overlong woolen scarf Jane had knitted for him. "Indeed? How did you manage it?"

Mr. Darcy shrugged. "She simply agreed it was time she entered society properly. Had she voiced any objections, I might have yielded—I am not in the habit of denying her anything, as you know."

Mr. Bingley nodded, choosing not to respond.

"But she and Mary will not go to London until after your baby is born, and they have been to Rosings."

Mr. Bingley's eyes lit up at the mention of his forthcoming child. "Jane claims the baby will not wait until the middle of February, and thinks the physician has calculated it wrongly."

Mr. Darcy smiled, and for a time the only sound was the horses' hooves against the frozen ground and crystallized snow.

Mr. Bingley was not one to remain silent for long, however. "So Mary will go to London once again." He looked for his friend's reaction, but received none. "I thought you wanted Georgiana to be away from her influence, though I cannot say I agree with you on this point, for ladies need lady friends, you know, especially if they do not have sisters. And as Mary's sisters are now all married—well, I do not understand why you cannot view their friendship as the ideal situation it is."

Mr. Darcy looked at his good friend as if he had never seen him before. "I think my misgivings began shortly after they were kidnapped, Charles. But you surprise me—I had no idea you had given the subject a moment's thought."

"You have never asked me," Mr. Bingley grumbled. "Caroline might have gained much in the way of common sense had she a friend such as Mary Bennet—you look at me as if I were crazy, but I believe I speak the truth. Caroline has for too long been allowed to do and say anything and everything she desires. I, as her brother, have never been able to control her, and her actions have for too long been dictated by society. She would have benefited greatly from a friendship with someone like Mary, who cares not what people think of her. Louisa is much too malleable and has always done exactly what Caroline wishes." He took one hand off the reins to point at Darcy. "You have no idea how lucky Georgiana is to have such a sensible friend."

Mr. Darcy grunted. "Pugilism! You call that sensible?"

Mr. Bingley laughed. "Well, from what you tell me, it came in handy at Devonham."

Mr. Darcy's face suffused with color as his mind went to the scene. "She did not exactly strike him—"

"Punched, perhaps?"

Mr. Darcy's lips compressed more tightly. "Petersham!" he growled. "Petersham and Wickham!" He rolled his eyes. "Richard will be the strictest of guardians. Neither Georgiana nor Mary will be allowed to get themselves entangled in *any* type of predicament."

Mr. Bingley smiled, but chose to remain silent on the matter. "Care to race back?" He did not wait long for Darcy's nod. Their horses needed little encouragement, and the two galloped off in the direction of Netherfield Hall.

CHAPTER EIGHT

(A Letter from Caroline Bingley to Charles Bingley)

Belgrave, 9 January 1814

Dearest Charles,

I write this letter to you on a Sunday, directly after services, for the early sermon on brotherly love moved me greatly.

At the time of my engagement I was of course completely unaware of Mr. P's penchant for perfidious conduct, and acted only as a young woman blind with love could, doing what was asked of me without question, the real affection I felt (no longer, I assure you!) dictating my actions. When Colonel F and Major A appeared at that absolutely vile coaching inn where I was forced take refuge from the atrocious weather, it was the first I had heard of my fiancé's treachery. Upon learning of his deceit, I was overcome and lay insensible for hours. Even my special smelling salts could not revive me, and upon waking I was hardly able to take nourishment.

Dear brother, the saddest part of my tale is yet to come. I was persuaded—as if by dark magic—to allow Mr. P access to my fortune before the marriage ceremony took place (I made the arrangements just prior to leaving London). I write now to ask that you reverse this unfortunate situation by whatever means you have at your disposal, returning control of my inheritance to me. I do not believe it will be completely intact, but even he could not have spent it all in so short a time. We must of course all keep this episode to ourselves. I am doing my part, for the more often I am seen in the company of Major A, the sooner Society will assume I have simply changed my mind about Mr. P. You will of course understand this vexing situation has made me too ill to travel to Netherfield.

Your loving sister,
Caroline Bingley

CHAPTER NINE

Mr. Bingley opened the door of his Netherfield's library and leaned inside to call out, "Darcy!"

"Yes, Charles?" Mr. Darcy's amused voice came from across the room, nearest the windows.

Mr. Bingley entered, marching over to his friend, holding out the letter from his sister Caroline. "I think you will be interested to read this."

Mr. Darcy read the letter once, frowning, then a second time. "She does not say how 'Mr. P' contacted her about the elopement, nor how she knew where to meet him." He carefully refolded the trimmed foolscap before returning it.

Mr. Bingley had read the letter so many times it was burned in his memory, but he looked at it once more. "She believes her fortune may be lost," he said triumphantly.

Mr. Darcy was thoughtful for a moment. "We might use her misapprehension to advantage." He tapped his fingers on the chair arm. "With careful handling, someone—say Major Ashton—could earn her confidence enough to learn who acted as Petersham's emissary. The restoration of her fortune could be the carrot leading the horse, if you understand my meaning— he might even intimate that Lord Castlereagh is willing to intervene on her behalf in exchange for useful information."

Mr. Bingley looked up, his expression stern. "Her actions could well have led to a disastrous state of affairs." He handed the letter back to Mr. Darcy. "Send this to your cousin, and let them do their worst. I will tell Caroline nothing."

Mr. Darcy took up a pen to compose a brief, urgent message. Just as he was about to seal it, a messenger arrived, cheeks bright red from either the cold or extreme exertion. He brought with him the latest news from Colonel Fitzwilliam.

London, 10 January 1814

Darcy,

I apologize for the tardiness of this report, but after many days of playing at an annoying game of cat-and-mouse, we have finally learned where Miss B was to meet Mr. P—it really was Cornwall. But of course, by the time our men arrived there was no sign of him, and none of the natives saw a thing. Mr. P's final destination is yet unknown, and we still do not know who contacted Miss B as to where and when to meet him. She was told to burn all of his letters, and followed his instructions strangely enough. Needless to say, it is a devilishly frustrating business. She now insists the major take her to endless soirées, operas, and dances, claiming she is frightened of the repercussions of her actions regarding Mr. P. It is possible she knows nothing more, but Lord C wishes him to continue escorting her. Give my best to all those we left behind, and for my sanity send pleasant news from the shire.

Yours,

R.A. Fitzwilliam

"Your sister's letter came at the right time, Bingley." Mr. Darcy rang for the messenger. "The return of her fortune will give them the power they need over her."

Four days later, a letter arrived from Rosings, addressed to Miss Mary Bennet.

"I believe it is your summons from Lady Catherine," Elizabeth said as she, Jane, Georgiana, and Mrs. Bennet waited for Mary to open the neatly-folded packet with the deeply-embossed red wax seal.

Mary, who believed it to be exactly what her sister proclaimed, opened the letter with little trepidation. She read quickly before handing it to her mother. "It is as Lizzy suggested, Mamma—a summons from Lady Catherine. She wants us to return to Rosings immediately."

Georgiana was the last to read her aunt's letter. "She makes no mention of Jane's upcoming event," she mused. "Perhaps she does not remember what you told her before we left Rosings, Mary—that you would remain in Hertfordshire until after the baby is born."

"Oh, you must not leave before then, my dear!" Mrs. Bennet cried, looking at her eldest daughter. "Jane will want all her family about her—or as many as can be here, with Lydia so far away, and Kitty...." Up came the handkerchief, never far from reach since learning Kitty was to move north with Mr. Darnell, and that Mr. Bingley had bought an estate in Derbyshire. "You must tell her you cannot come!"

Mr. Darcy, entering the room with Mr. Bennet, heard the last part of the conversation. "If you would feel more comfortable, Mary, I will write to Lady Catherine to inform her neither you nor Georgiana will be going anywhere until after the baby is born, and you have had plenty of time to become well-acquainted with him."

"Jane is convinced it will be a *her*," Elizabeth whispered to her husband as she looked over at Mrs. Bennet. "And so is Mamma."

Mr. Darcy considered his mother-in-law for a few moments before saying softly, "Since she bore five girls herself, she may well be correct. But I will not say a word of this to Charles, who is convinced it will be a boy."

"Lady Catherine will not be pleased," Mary said, grimacing. She looked over at Georgiana. "I wonder if her wish to see Miss de Bourgh engaged to Lord Wickford has been granted?"

The day after Mr. Darcy responded to Lady Catherine's letter on behalf of Mary and Georgiana, Mr. Collins arrived unannounced at Longbourn, breathless and red-cheeked. He insisted upon being shown into Mr. Bennet's library, although the servants had strict orders against it. When the poor maid suggested he wait in the drawing room, he drew himself up and confused her with Latin words she did not understand until she had no other choice but to lead him to his host's inner sanctum.

"Mr. Bennet!" Mr. Collins lowered his head in the briefest of bows. "I have come to discuss a most serious matter with you!"

Mr. Bennet removed his pince-nez and motioned vaguely towards a chair. "Please sit, Mr. Collins—I beg you not to tower over me." He pulled out a handkerchief to wipe the glass lenses.

Mr. Collins sat, looking a little deflated, but he recovered his energy. "Mr. Bennet, you must control your daughter!"

Mr. Bennet leaned back in his chair as he eyed the heir to Longbourn. "To which daughter do you refer, Mr. Collins?"

"To your daughter Mary, of course!" Mr. Collins removed his waterproof hat, having not taken the time to remove his outer garments upon entering the house despite the poor maid's entreaties. "She has most ungraciously refused the request of my patroness, Lady Catherine de Bourgh, to come to Rosings! Such an invitation is a great honor. You must force your daughter to apologize before it is too late to make amends. She must retract her refusal, and go obediently, humbly—and immediately—to Rosings, as Lady Catherine has requested."

Mr. Bennet placed the pince-nez upon his nose and leaned forward, picking up his pen and dipping it into the ink before jotting something in his ledger. "It is my understanding—" he looked above the lenses "—that it was Mr. Darcy who wrote on behalf of my daughter Mary, and Miss Darcy, informing Lady Catherine they would remain in Hertfordshire until after Jane's baby is born, as is their right and privilege." He saw Mr. Collins' mouth open to protest and quickly added, "And no one will force them to do anything against their will as long as I am around to prevent it!"

It was the strongest statement Mr. Bennet had ever made to Mr. Collins, despite repeated provocation. Mr. Collins, his face aflame, stood, sniffed, bowed formally to Mr. Bennet, and left without another word, his nose at such an angle he was forced to hold one hand atop his hat to prevent it from falling off.

Mr. Bennet waited a few minutes before ringing for a servant. "Ah, Mr. Hill—would you be so kind as to bring a fresh bottle of port?"

CHAPTER TEN

The next weeks passed without major incident, and as Jane Bingley's time grew nearer, Mrs. Bennet visited Netherfield nearly every day. She frequently suggested Mr. Darcy take Mr. Bingley out riding, declaring his nervousness affected not only his wife, but the baby as well.

Mr. Bennet did his best to allay the fears of both his sons-in-law regarding childbirth. "It surprises me no more than it will you when I say, with complete honesty, that Mrs. Bennet's judgment can be trusted in this matter—both Jane and Lizzy will be safe while in the care of the midwife, *and* their mother."

By strange coincidence, a letter to Mary regarding her second novel was delivered to Longbourn on the very day Jane went into labor. The letter from the publisher was hand-delivered to Netherfield by Mr. Hill, a great fan of Mary's, having read *The Turret Room* three times with his wife as they sat together in the evenings by the fire below-stairs, referring to 'our own Miss Mary' with great frequency. Mary's thoughts, however, were not on books, and she absently placed the unopened letter in the pocket of the apron she had donned.

Hours went by, the carpets in the drawing room, study, and billiard room nearly worn through by Mr. Bingley's pacing, until Jane eventually brought a tiny, fair-haired baby girl into the world.

After the new mother was given time to rest, and Mr. Bingley was allowed to greet his child properly, the Bennets and Darcys were invited into Jane's chamber to meet their new family member.

While the others looked on as Mrs. Bennet gathered her first grandchild into her arms, Georgiana said quietly to Mary, "Are you not going to open your letter?"

Too excited about the baby to care much about the contents of a letter from her publisher, Mary broke the seal and quickly read the note before handing it to Georgiana.

"He wants to publish *The Count of Camalore*!" Georgiana cried, causing everyone else in the room to look away from the baby briefly, and the midwife shushed them.

"Congratulations, Mary." The soft words were spoken by Jane, who had been proudly looking on as each family member took a much-awaited turn to hold the baby. Her guests' attention once again focused on the new mother, for though they would not voice it, they were far more relieved than they cared to admit that both the mother and the baby had survived.

"Well, Jane, what will you call her?" Mr. Bennet asked as he watched his daughter take back the precious, swaddled bundle.

Jane looked up at her husband with a gentle smile. "We are calling her Eliza."

Mrs. Thomson then took advantage of the momentary silence, and with the assurance of experience began to usher them all from the room. "Mrs. Bingley needs her rest. You have had a chance to see the child and may now go to your own beds, where I am sure you will sleep soundly—as will our young mother." She managed to remove all but Mr. Bingley, who could not take his eyes off of his wife and baby, blissfully unaware of anything else. The experienced, no-nonsense woman seemed about to take hold of his arm, but her face softened as she looked upon the three of them. Instead, she whispered, "I will be back soon, Mrs. Bingley, after I have summoned the physician." Mrs. Thomson had safely delivered so many babies in Meryton and the surrounding villages that Jane had convinced Mr. Bingley not to call for the officious doctor until after the baby was born, unless there were signs of trouble.

Jane could no longer hold back her tears as she caught Mrs. Thomson's eye, mouthing "thank you."

Despite Mrs. Thomson's assurance, no one could even think of sleeping, and the Bennets and Darcys retired instead to the drawing room. Once there, Mr. Bennet asked Mary if he might read the letter from her publisher.

He read it three times at least, all the while shaking his head in wonder. "What a remarkable achievement, my dear. I could not be more proud of you." With a twinkle in his eye he added, "Apparently additional congratulations must be offered for the excellent reception of your first novel—" he looked around at the others "—Darcy tells me they have exceeded £175!"

Just then Mr. Bingley entered. "Darcy—I believe you owe me a cigar!"

"Why not play a game of billiards as well?" Mr. Darcy suggested. "If it were not the middle of the night, I would suggest getting a bit of fresh air, my nerves are so taut."

"A fine idea! But first, I must go below-stairs to share our good news with the servants and offer them a glass of ale." Mr. Bingley turned to Mr. Bennet. "Would you care to join us in the game, Grandpapa?"

"Late hours are for the young, my boy—it is time Mrs. Bennet and I were tucked into our warm bed." Mr. Bennet glanced at his wife, who was shaking her head in a bewildered manner, whispering to herself, "One hundred seventy-five pounds!"

"Very well then—we shall see you in the morning," said Mr. Bingley before rushing out to share his good news with the servants.

Mr. Darcy looked at Elizabeth, whose tired smile answered the question in his eyes. After a brief bow to the Bennets and Georgiana, he whistled for Samson and left the room.

Elizabeth positioned herself more comfortably on the couch and rubbed her face with both hands. "How exhausting! I had no idea a birth could take so long."

Mrs. Bennet opened the gold watch she wore on a filigreed chain, a recent gift from Mr. Bennet. "Seven hours, forty-two minutes." She closed the watch with a sharp click. "You took one hour longer than that to arrive, my dear," she said to Elizabeth. "The last three of my girls came much faster—which is the way of things, according to my own mamma." She eyed Elizabeth's mid-section. "I did not like to say anything before Jane's baby was born, Lizzy, but I do believe you are carrying a boy."

Elizabeth laughed. "You may be right, but it matters not. A baby girl will please us just as well."

There was a discreet knock at the door before the Bingleys' housekeeper entered, the physician close behind her. After curtly inquiring as to Mr. Bingley's whereabouts, Dr. Grey appeared ready to excuse himself. However, Elizabeth prevented his immediate departure by asking, "How did you find Jane, doctor?"

He did not reply immediately, but took a deep breath, drawing himself up, his posture and expression revealing his displeasure. "Mrs. Bingley and the child were fortunate to have survived the birth without my care."

He declined refreshment and left after only the briefest of bows, the housekeeper hurrying to keep up with his stride as he went to speak with Mr. Bingley.

Mary, her eyes on the closed door, asked, "You had only the assistance of a midwife when we were born, did you not, Mamma?"

"Indeed I did—physicians are all well and good when one has quinsy, dropsy or the chin-cough, but when it comes to babies, my own mother and her mother before her would only allow a midwife in the room." Mrs. Bennet glanced towards her husband, whose eyes were closed. "And Mr. Bennet was very understanding about the matter."

Elizabeth was thoughtful. "I must convince Mr. Darcy to allow the same for me. The Pemberley physician, Dr. Braxton, is—"

"Pompous and arrogant?" Georgiana interjected, surprising them all. "I for one would feel far more comfortable with Mrs. Thomson overseeing the birth of my own children."

"Will there soon be a wedding at Pemberley?" Mrs. Bennet's eyes betrayed a particular glimmer, familiar to each of her daughters.

Georgiana responded graciously. "Not as yet, Mrs. Bennet, but I have begun to consider each gentleman with whom I come in contact as a prospective husband and father, as any young lady of sense should do."

Her words caused Elizabeth and Mary to laugh outright, but Mrs. Bennet was serious. "My dear Miss Darcy"—Mrs. Bennet had yet to call Georgiana by her given name, even after many entreaties to do so "—I wish you had told me sooner, for we are acquainted with many eligible gentlemen in Hertfordshire, and would be so pleased to have you settled near us!"

At this, Mr. Bennet's left eye opened.

"Georgiana is to have a season this year, Mamma." Elizabeth looked apologetically at her young sister-in-law. "It may be that she will meet a suitable young gentleman or two in London in the coming months."

Georgiana hastened to reassure her. "It is time I had a season, Elizabeth. I am not so fearful of society as I once was, and am determined to bear it with grace and fortitude."

"A season will require a vast wardrobe and constant fittings," mused Mrs. Bennet with a glance at her husband.

Elizabeth sat straighter and said abruptly, "I do not care what Mrs. Thomson says. I cannot bear to wait any longer to see Jane again." She looked at the others, a challenge in her eyes.

"Jane no doubt wonders why you have not come to her sooner, Lizzy," said Mrs. Bennet with surprising insight. "Send Mrs. Thomas to us—" she winked at Georgiana and Mary "—we will ask for as many tempting dishes from the kitchen as can be brought so late in the evening."

Elizabeth would have skipped from the room if she could have, and Mrs. Bennet went off in search of the Bingley's housekeeper, rarely content to simply ring for any servant.

Watching Georgiana's expression as she stared into the flames, Mary felt sure her friend was thinking ahead to the day when she too would become a mother. Mary was not willing to admit to her own fiercely protective feelings towards her new niece—so strong, in fact, they caused her to wonder (briefly) if her plans for an independent future might be a bit short-sighted.

Two weeks passed and little Eliza Bingley thrived. Jane recovered quickly, leaving her bed after only two days, and was soon in the habit of walking the long, wide halls of Netherfield's first floor with her child in her arms. Mr. Bingley was often beside her, making cooing and other strange sounds, eliciting quiet giggles from the Netherfield maids as they went about their work.

Lady Catherine had not yet replied to Mr. Darcy's letter, written weeks earlier, and though Mr. Collins' assurance of her displeasure was no doubt warranted, neither Georgiana nor Mary were unduly concerned. If they were no longer welcome at Rosings, they were happy to remain in Hertfordshire until Colonel Fitzwilliam could escort them to London. Georgiana had already begun to meet with the seamstress in Meryton, and Elizabeth had been working assiduously to convince Mary to do so as well, insisting that if she were to accompany Georgiana to any society gatherings in London, she would have to be appropriately dressed or otherwise risk embarrassing Miss Darcy.

It was Mary's desire to purchase her own gowns, and not to burden the Darcys further, but even Mr. Darcy had begun to impress upon her the need to dress appropriately. Indeed, he and Elizabeth were finally forced to imply that if she refused their assistance, she would not be allowed to go at all. It was this particular argument which won her over, and after a fortnight of resistance, she too began to visit the seamstress in Meryton.

"You will of course have a modiste in London prepare the formal gowns," Elizabeth told them matter-of-factly while holding her young namesake, Jane taking a rare break from carrying her child.

"I will repay you somehow, Lizzy," Mary promised.

"You have repaid us many times over, Mary—you have been a loyal friend to Georgiana, and we have watched her confidence increase with each of the...let me just say *unusual* experiences you have shared."

The compliment was unexpected and for a moment Mary knew not where to look.

CHAPTER ELEVEN

(A Letter from Lady Catherine to Miss Mary Bennet)

Rosings, 28 February 1814

Miss Bennet,

    I feel it is my duty to remind you of the commitment you made to finish your novel under my guidance. To assure your timely arrival at Rosings, therefore, I am sending one of my finest carriages for you and my niece. You will no doubt wish to break the journey in London, where I believe you have an aunt and uncle with whom you can stay so as not to necessitate the opening of Darcy House. I understand they are not of the ton, *but respectable enough. You will commence your journey the following day to arrive here early in the afternoon, at which point we will resume work on the novel, for we have much to do and time is of the essence. I have only recently heard from my excellent friend, Lady Gordon, who was shocked by the ending of your first book, as you neglected to conclude with a wedding (I do not approve of elopements, even in written form). My carriage will arrive at your home in Hertfordshire in a sennight—on seven March. You must each instruct your maids to pack your heaviest gowns, for thin muslins will be of no use to you here.*

    I understand your sister is safely delivered of a girl. Tell her for me she should settle a considerable sum upon the child as soon as may be, so she does not have to suffer the near-misfortune of her mother, save Mr. Bingley's patronage.

Yours,
Lady Catherine de Bourgh

CHAPTER TWELVE

"Fitzwilliam, may I speak with you?" Georgiana had entered the Netherfield library so quietly that she surprised her brother, who was immersed in a book. Even Samson, lying at his master's feet, did not immediately sense her presence.

Mr. Darcy set his recently-acquired copy of *A New View of Society* on a side table. "Of course."

Georgiana, kneeling down to pet Samson, reached inside her pocket for Lady Catherine's letter. "Our aunt has written to Mary, saying she will send a carriage for us in seven days! Must we go back to Rosings so soon?"

Mr. Darcy read the letter, frowning. Then he turned towards the window, his expression undergoing several changes while Georgiana continued to pet Samson, finally turning back to his only sister with a look of determination. "I think you must oblige our aunt in this." He held up a hand to prevent argument. "It is reasonable to assume you and Mary will remain at Rosings for three, perhaps even four, weeks before proceeding to London to enjoy the offerings of the season." He was unusually stern, and Georgiana looked hurt and confused. "I will write to Lady Catherine to accept the offer of her carriage." He opened the writing desk, ignoring his sister's look of shock, and sharpened the tip of his pen with great deliberation.

In her room at Longbourn, Mary was writing as fast as she could to get on paper a new scene in *The Wine Cellar*. The two heroines had just been kidnapped and forced to inhale opium fumes.

Both Miss Benjamin and Miss White were nearly overcome, about to fall into a deep stupor, when suddenly the door was smashed open, and Captain Trumbull appeared in the dark, dank cellar. It took but a moment for his eyes to adjust, but he soon spied the two young ladies and rushed to their sides, gently cutting the painfully-tight rope from their delicate wrists and ankles with a folding knife before covering the spiraling, noxious smoke with his voluminous cape. Miss White fell into Captain Trumbull's arms, her large, innocent eyes full of wonder. "You saved us, Captain, you saved us!"

Unfortunately, before the captain could stop it, Miss Benjamin lifted the cape, which was protecting them from inhaling additional fumes. The smoke wafted all around her and she swooned, nearly falling to the stone floor, but was caught in the arms of Major Jenkins, who had run to her side. "Miss Benjamin!" he called to her, but to no avail, for the drug had taken its evil hold upon her once more.

"Mary? Are you here?"

Mary looked up from her work, eyes unfocused, mentally in the dungeon where her heroines had been left by their evil captor, Monsieur Villainneau.

"Are you not cold, sitting so far from the fire?" Georgiana was looking at the window panes, nearly covered with wind-driven snow.

Mary pulled her wool wrap tighter, exhibiting her fingerless mittens. "I wished to take advantage of what little sunlight there is today."

"How does the story progress?" Georgiana peered over Mary's shoulder, reading the recently-written paragraphs. "I do not believe my aunt will condone the use of an exotic drug."

"No, I venture she will not. But—" Mary put the loose pages together, tapping them against the surface of the table before placing them in the desk drawer "—I hope she will grant me some amount of freedom. Surely having a second book published gives me some right to choose what happens to my characters?" She raised her arms and stretched, causing her wrap to fall to the floor.

Georgiana bent to pick it up. "I am afraid I come with bad

news, Mary. My brother has written his response to my aunt's demand for our return; we are to leave for Rosings in seven days' time." She looked out the window with a definite pout.

Mary put her pen and ink inside a cavity on the desk. "I guess I had better work faster, then." She sighed and moved to the fireplace. "If the weather does not change, perhaps our journey will be delayed—but if not, we can console ourselves with the thought of being at Rosings in time to see Miss de Bourgh thoroughly engaged to Lord Wickford and his three children—or was it four?"

The next day Mary brought Molly into the sitting room at Longbourn, where the fire was warmest. Mr. and Mrs. Bennet were at Netherfield visiting their baby granddaughter, and although Mary invited Molly to sit, she refused. Instead, she stood in front of her young mistress like a schoolgirl, reading aloud from Mary's own volume of *Lyrical Ballads*.

"*Twas sad as sad could be—*'" Molly enunciated each word with care "—*and we did speak only to break the silence of the sea.*"

"You have improved ten-fold, Molly—though I wonder why you chose to read such a long, depressing tale."

"My uncle was lost at sea, miss. This poem makes me think of him."

"I am sorry to hear it." Mary paused briefly, reflecting on how little she knew about the younger girl. "Have you read all the way to the end?"

"No miss, I haven't made it that far. I've been reading the lines over and over, just like you said to." She grinned. "Mrs. Hill sometimes lets me read to her when she has a cup of tea, but she likes stories with a bit of romance better. With some fun in them, you know."

Mary, not surprised, chose a book from the short stack on the table. "I think you have improved enough for this; Mrs. Hill should find it more to her taste." She handed her own copy of *The Mysteries of Udolpho* to Molly, who hesitated at first, but Mary insisted.

"Thank you, miss. I'll take good care of it."

Mary smiled. "I know you will."

"I told Mrs. Hill I'd help with the pies this morning, miss, if you don't mind me leaving now."

Since asking Molly to be in her employ, Mary had wondered if she were doing the right thing for an intelligent girl who showed such promise. Before her maid could leave the room, Mary asked, "Molly, are you satisfied with your position? Do you feel the decision to remain with me was a good one?"

"Oh yes miss, I do." Molly's eyes grew wide. "I never dreamed I'd have so many adventures. I've already been to Pemberley and Devonham and Netherfield and Longbourn—" she counted off on her fingers "—and now we're to go back to Rosings! Lucy and I are ever so excited, even though the servants there are so uppity." She took a breath. "And as if that wasn't enough, we're going to London too. Believe me—I am happy to go wherever you and Miss Darcy go!"

Molly, her face pink, curtseyed and hurried out before Mary could respond, holding the precious books tightly against her chest.

⁓⌣⌣⌐

Georgiana entered Elizabeth's private sitting room at Netherfield, determined to broach a subject upon which she had been ruminating for several days.

"Georgiana!" Elizabeth viewed Mr. Darcy's sister through the mirror while her maid completed a lovely coiffure with little pearls strung through, highlighting her dark curls. "Would you care for tea? The water is still hot."

"I would, thank you." Georgiana drew closer to her sister-in-law's dressing table just as the maid arranged one final string of pearls.

Elizabeth excused her maid, waiting until the door had shut behind her to say, "Her skills in dressing hair have greatly improved, thanks to Molly's tutelage."

"Molly is teaching Lucy as well." Georgiana turned her head back and forth to show her maid's latest efforts before motioning to the tea tray. "Shall I pour?"

Elizabeth moved to the couch and watched as Georgiana prepared the tea. "I have been taking it sweeter than usual of late." She looked down with a soft smile. "The baby seems to appreciate it."

Georgiana stirred three full spoons of the grated sugar into Elizabeth's tea and handed her the cup, taking a sip of her own before broaching the reason for her visit. "I wish to ask your opinion about something personal." She hesitated, aligning the handle of the tea pot with the edge of the tray, a habit similar to one of Mr. Darcy's, while her sister-in-law looked on, amused. "It is a somewhat delicate matter; you must forgive me if I cannot express my thoughts completely or clearly."

Elizabeth inclined her head. "I am honored that you would confide in me; you may always speak freely, my dear."

Georgiana took a deep breath. "Then I will not prevaricate— I would like to know why it is that I seem to fall in love with gentlemen with less than desirable character traits."

Elizabeth gently replaced the tea-cup in the saucer and took a moment to consider Mr. Darcy's sweet sister. "You expressed yourself quite clearly." She smiled wryly. "Do you know that I too was—for a time—attracted to Mr. Wickham? I once found his conversation easy and his company entertaining—far more so than any other gentleman of my acquaintance at the time. I am ashamed to admit to ignoring his frequent breaches of proper behavior, as I was completely blinded by his charming manner." She put the cup and saucer on a side table. "But you and I were not his only victims—at the time of Lydia's debacle, we learned that Wickham had broken several hearts in Meryton while he was stationed there, and I can but imagine what damage he had done before then." She sighed and shook her head, lips in a thin line. "And now he is married to poor, silly Lydia."

"But I was one of his *first* victims, I believe, and grossly— unforgivably—blind to his faults." Georgiana set her cup on the table between them. "If my experience with him had been generally known, especially by your parents, Lydia would not have fallen into his clutches!"

Elizabeth leaned forward. "Georgiana, please do not take any blame upon yourself for my youngest sister's irresponsible actions. She was determined to have him." She sat back with a sigh. "At any rate, if Lydia's accounts of their life in the West

Indies can be trusted, it would seem she and Mr. Wickham are extremely well-suited."

"One can only hope. But my judgment was again proved poor in the case of Mr. Petersham. My brother's suspicions prevented anything serious from developing between us, but if he had not, I might have accepted an offer of marriage from a man who is a despicable, treasonous traitor." She looked horrified.

"Mr. Petersham fooled all of us, Georgiana. He is a most attractive man with fine manners and a great fortune. Just think of Miss Burnaby when we were last in London. She did her best to catch him, even when he was obviously visiting at Darcy House to see *you*." Elizabeth shook her head. "He might easily have chosen her for his next victim, rather than Caroline Bingley, who despite her extensive experience did not divine his true character either." She tilted her head and looked openly at Mr. Darcy's sister. "You may have been unable to correctly assess a gentleman's character in the past, but I think by now you have gained experience enough to prove otherwise in the future. I know you agreed to a season only to please your brother, but I do hope you can enjoy yourself thoroughly. You need not feel pressure to make an attachment with any gentleman, you know. But, since Colonel Fitzwilliam will thoroughly investigate each one you meet, you can compare notes with him to see if you can correctly identify the scoundrels!"

Georgiana laughed. "You may be joking, Elizabeth, but I believe you have hit upon an excellent plan!"

CHAPTER THIRTEEN

(A Letter from Colonel Fitzwilliam to Mr. Darcy)

London, 2 March 1814

Darcy,

How contrary is woman! One would assume the replacement of her lost fortune would induce Miss B to tell us all she knows. But we do not stand upon solid ground when dealing with this species, cousin—excepting your wife and Bingley's, of course. We have learned nothing more than the proposed location and date of their meeting, for she maintains her only contact with P was through messages delivered by an unknown confederate. Lord Castlereagh is increasingly certain that one of the guests at Devonham was in league with Mr. P and his valet and has initiated further inquiries, enlisting the aid of Lord Harold, who has proven to be a worthy choice despite my doubts.

Major A has agreed to take charge of the investigation, which will allow me to accompany Georgiana and Mary to Kent sooner than expected. I will remain with them at Rosings for a period of up to four weeks, but no longer, as my duties require my return to London. I come to Hertfordshire soon, and wish to spend some time in pleasant company prior to going to our aunt's home.

Please instruct Bingley not to yield to his sister's pleas regarding funds as yet—Major A continues to act as her escort, per Castlereagh's plan, who is yet hopeful of gleaning something useful from her.

Yours,
RAF

CHAPTER FOURTEEN

Mr. Darcy, sitting across from Elizabeth at a table in their rooms at Netherfield, liberally buttered a piece of toast. "I have written to Aunt Catherine regarding Richard's plan to personally escort Georgiana and Mary to Kent. Though I imagine he will not be in a hurry to leave Hertfordshire once he arrives."

"Four weeks at Rosings is a very long time." Elizabeth smiled, tapping her egg.

"I remember—nearly two years ago—when you were a guest of Mr. and Mrs. Collins at Hunsford, and Richard and I were at Rosings. Four weeks did not seem long enough." Mr. Darcy looked across the table.

Elizabeth looked into her husband's eyes, her cheeks a becoming pink. "Each moment I spent in your company while in Kent is as clear as if it happened only days ago, Mr. Darcy."

"My dear—." he hesitated, suddenly busy with the jam jar "—we have not yet come to a decision about our departure." He spread the marmalade on his toast with great deliberation. "I think it is time we return to Pemberley."

"Do you realize, Mr. Darcy, that when you wish to tell me something you do not think I will like, you frequently begin your statement with the words 'my dear'?" Elizabeth's eyes danced merrily. "You are right, of course—it is time we were at home. At least Mamma has little Eliza to distract her, for she reminds us with growing frequency how she is soon to be deserted by all of her daughters." She dipped her toast point. "Papa would like to travel to Beechwood Manor soon after Jane and Charles are settled there; with any luck, preparations for the visit to Derbyshire will keep my mother so busy she will not notice we have gone."

Mr. Darcy looked decidedly relieved.

Later the same day, Mary was in her chamber at Longbourn, re-working the final chapter of *The Wine Cellar*. Frowning, she crossed out several "indispensable" lines dictated by Lady Catherine. Just as she took up a clean sheet of paper, there was a light knock on the door.

"Have you finished the book?" Georgiana, who had recently arrived with the party from Netherfield, came over to the little writing table placed near the window to peer over Mary's shoulder. "This looks to be the final chapter."

Mary nodded. "It *is* the final chapter. I am reconsidering your aunt's ending—she wants a double wedding. I, however, am inclined to leave Miss Benjamin single and leave the marrying to Miss White."

Georgiana grinned. "My aunt might accept an ending in which one of your heroines marries a handsome, eligible gentleman of great wealth, but only if the other becomes a governess."

Mary groaned and turned back to cross out more lines.

"Your pen is wearing down." Georgiana picked up a fresh quill and began to sharpen it with implements from the ornamental tortoise-shell box she herself had given Mary. "You can finish the book at Rosings, you know—you need not work so hard before we leave." She finished the pen and picked up another quill. "Elizabeth and Fitzwilliam plan to walk to Meryton. It is such a fine day—would you not prefer to join them?"

Mary laid her now-useless pen alongside the page. "It is muddy and cold despite the sun—I would *much* prefer it."

Before Mary and Georgiana reached the stairs however, a breathless Mrs. Bennet stopped them. "If you are going to join Lizzy and Mr. Darcy in this questionable scheme of theirs—imagine walking out in the middle of winter when she is going to have a baby in fewer than three months—then I would have each of you promise you will not allow her to grow too tired, or to catch a chill. Lizzy absolutely forbade me to ask Mr. Hill to follow them with the carriage!" Mrs. Bennet drew a sturdy handkerchief from her pocket to dab at her eyes. "And do not tarry, my dears. Mrs. Hill and I have planned a very special tea today." She sniffled. "Goodness, how am I to bear it when you are all gone?"

Mary rested her hand gently upon her mother's arm. "Jane and Mr. Bingley will be at Netherfield for several more weeks, and when you and Papa finally see Beechwood Manor and Pemberley, you may decide to remain in Derbyshire indefinitely." She placed her bonnet on her head and turned to Georgiana. "I cannot *imagine* the preparation necessary to assure the smooth running of Longbourn while Mamma is away."

Mrs. Bennet's chin lifted and she tucked away the handkerchief. "There will indeed be far too much to do, and no time at all to waste. I must begin immediately!" She reached over to retie the ribbons of Mary's bonnet more tightly under her chin. "Now, do not forget about Lizzy—she does not always use reason when she wanders about the countryside. I am relying on each of you."

"We will be vigilant, Mrs. Bennet," promised Georgiana.

"You are too good, Miss Darcy," Mrs. Bennet replied, waving them down the stairs before hurrying to her morning room, where she kept her note paper and pens.

Mrs. Bennet need not have worried, however, for the path between Longbourn and Meryton grew too muddy for even someone as intrepid as Elizabeth, and the small party returned to Longbourn after only twenty minutes.

When the Bingleys, Darcys, and Colonel Fitzwilliam returned to Netherfield a few hours later, Mr. Bingley asked the gentlemen to accompany him to his study, where he showed them a letter. "It is another from Caroline—I thought you might be interested in the fourth paragraph especially."

Mr. Darcy set the letter on a table so he and the colonel could read it simultaneously. The first three paragraphs were made up of Miss Bingley's entreaties for money (the modiste was demanding payment for the wedding clothes she could never bear to wear); critical reports of Mr. Bingley's London servants (she threatened to dismiss several); and complaints of being abandoned, at a time she feared for her very life, by Colonel Fitzwilliam (she 'could not have survived without Major Ashton' who continued to see her safely to all the routs and balls she must necessarily attend).

It was indeed in the fourth paragraph their attention was caught:

Last night at Almack's, I was introduced to a Scottish woman recently wed to Captain Jameson—pardon me, not captain any longer, as his older brother has 'moved on' (I have heard, on good authority, that he was something of a wastrel, and brought the illness upon himself; luckily, the wedding took place before this event). Lord Jameson was not with his wife at the time, so I cannot attest to his current state of health and happiness, but his bride is quite pretty. I thought Miss Bennet would like to know.

Mr. Darcy looked up. "Mary may find Lord Jameson's presence in London difficult to bear."

Mr. Bingley took the letter back, carefully folded it, and tucked it inside his desk. "Jameson and his wife may not be in residence for long." He moved to a sideboard to pour three glasses of his favorite digestive.

Colonel Fitzwilliam accepted the proffered glass thoughtfully. "Ashton is no doubt pulling his hair out by the roots in frustration, and might welcome any kind of assistance." He sipped the bitter liquid before setting his glass down with a grimace. "Georgiana and Mary might hear something useful from the seemingly senseless talk of the *haute ton*. Those two have, after all, proved themselves time and again to be young ladies of resilience and fortitude." He grinned. "Just ask Ashton."

"I will not allow Georgiana to take part in any of this investigation—or Mary, for she would no doubt find a way to involve my sister." Mr. Darcy looked sternly at his cousin. "It is time for Georgiana to marry and start a family of her own. No more of this—" he searched for the word "—nonsense—" and set his glass down with a clatter.

Mr. Bingley looked pointedly at the delicate crystal. "The

question remains: should we warn Mary about Jameson's presence in London?"

Mr. Darcy answered, "She and Georgiana will not go to London for several weeks yet, at which point Lord Jameson may have already returned to Scotland." He paused. "It is also possible their paths would never cross while in town."

Colonel Fitzwilliam nodded. "It might be best to remain silent about the matter as far as Miss Bennet is concerned."

Mr. Bingley was thoughtful. "And Georgiana?"

Darcy's lips thinned. "If we tell *her*, she will tell Mary."

The colonel stood and yawned, stretching out his arms. "It is settled then. We will say nothing about it to either one of them." He went to the door. "I do not know about you two, but I took far too many generous portions at Mrs. Bennet's excellent table this evening. Such rich food, along with the thought of my impending journey to Rosings has made me tired. I am going to bed."

CHAPTER FIFTEEN

*(A Letter from Mrs. Edward Darnell
to Mr. and Mrs. Bennet)*

York, 10 March 1814

Dearest Mamma and Papa,

I write to you from the morning room of our townhouse, a nice room where I can sit and watch the river (one of two in town). If I lean forward far enough out the window, I can see the top of the Minster. It is an old cathedral, and only one of many historical buildings, York being one of the most ancient towns in the kingdom, founded by the Romans long ago (Edward has been teaching me). It is much colder here than in Hertfordshire, but we have fires in every room. Everything about the house is to my liking (except the housekeeper seems overly stern—I must find the courage to be firm with her).

Edward walks to his business each day (barring Sunday), and has promised to take me on a walk along the old city walls as soon as it is warm enough (he worries about my cough). We have been once to the assembly rooms for a concert, and will go to the Theatre Royal next week where we might see a famous actress—a Mrs. Jordan—who has reportedly returned to the stage after a long absence.

Several wives of businessmen in town have called, and I have returned each of their visits. They are all much older than me, and I find it difficult to remember their names.

I do not know how Lydia bears being so far away from her family. At least I have the hope of visiting Longbourn one day. Please give my best to everyone at Netherfield, and in Meryton.

I am sending the half-stockings I made for the baby, although they did not turn out as I had hoped.

Your loving daughter,
Catherine Darnell, née Bennet

CHAPTER SIXTEEN

(An Entry in Mary Bennet's Diary)

Rosings, 12 March 1814
We were only at Rosings two hours before Lady C ordered me to remove the scene in which Miss White and Miss Benjamin are subjected to opium, which has made me more determined than ever to keep it. And as Georgiana predicted, Lady C also insists upon an ending with at least two weddings. I have yet to convince her there might be some benefit in allowing one of the young ladies to remain independent, but her eyes did light up when I hinted at yet another continuation of The Turret Room *when this is complete. Mr. Egerton has added "by the authoress of* The Turret Room*" on the cover of* The Count of Camalore, *which he claims will generate interest in the first novel and any following.*

Georgiana and I have yet to visit Mr. and Mrs. Collins at Hunsford Parsonage, as Lady C does not like her carriages to get muddy, though we will undoubtedly be going by carriage to services tomorrow. I plan to pay close attention to Mr. Collins' sermon, so I might more accurately portray the parson I recently added to The Wine Cellar *(though I have no doubt Lady C will not approve). Georgiana has begun to teach Lucy, and we conclude each evening with a short reading by both of our maids—it is the part of the day I look most forward to here. (G warns against letting Lady C learn of our activities, fearing she might see it as radical and forbid us to continue. We are especially careful around the servants here, for they are completely under the dominion of their mistress.)*

The Colonel has helped pass many dull evenings, telling tales of his adventures, including some from his recent visit to town. (It seems the major regularly escorts Miss B to balls, the theatre, etc. I wonder if he has mentioned that he has in fact made an offer to another....)

CHAPTER SEVENTEEN

(A Letter from Elizabeth Darcy to Jane Bingley)

Pemberley, 12 March 1814

Dearest Jane,

We are now once again settled at Pemberley, and I daily look forward to the time when my own dear Jane is but a few miles away.

Mr. Greene tells us the modifications at Beechwood continue, despite the cold weather; based on his glowing reports, your home will be a veritable showplace by the time you arrive (the conservatory sounds lovely). Fitzwilliam tells me we must wait to see it until the weather permits, for the rain has made the roads nearly impassable.

Mr. Darcy approves the changes I plan for the nursery, and the re-painting of the walls is to begin next week. In the meantime I must choose fabrics and do a little sewing, though our nursemaid (a pleasant woman from Lambton) has asked if she might make some things for the baby, for she likes to keep busy. You know I have never been terribly fond of needlework.

Our midwife will soon come—she is Mrs. Halifax, and sister to Georgiana's former companion, Mrs. Annesley. At the same time, Mrs. Annesley is to be in London, where she will act as chaperone to Mary and Georgiana.

I have received no letters from Kitty, Mary, Georgiana, or even Lydia, and Mamma has written only once since we returned to Pemberley (I hope she is driven to distraction with *preparations for the journey to Derbyshire). Do write, and with many details—and please kiss little Eliza for me.*

Your affectionate sister,
Elizabeth Darcy

CHAPTER EIGHTEEN

At Hunsford Parsonage, Charlotte Collins drew her needle through the torn seam of a drab cotton dress. "Miss Darcy, when you are in London, will you be presented at court?" She had invited Georgiana and Mary into her own private sitting room, a place Mr. Collins rarely frequented for the window did not face the road—though at the time of their visit he was in fact out to see one of his parishioners, who, according to Charlotte, had erred by falling asleep during the previous Sunday's sermon.

"I think not," responded Georgiana, accepting a thin slice of buttered bread from the proffered tray. "It is not required as part of the season, you know, and the queen has been holding her drawing rooms less and less frequently these past years due to the king's poor health." She sipped her tea. "I would much rather attend lectures, concerts, or the opera than spend each day learning proper deportment."

Charlotte Collins looked up at her guest, surprised.

Mary added, "Based on Miss Bingley's information, the expense of a costume one wears only once is formidable, especially given the questionable outcome of any season." She took a delicate bite of toast.

"I have always thought being presented at court was crucial, especially if one wished to attend an assembly at Almack's Rooms." Charlotte frowned as she worked out a knot in the thread.

"It is a common enough assumption, but my Aunt Fitzwilliam assures me there is no immediate need. A presentation may be necessary at some point, especially if one of us should marry a peer—" she glanced mischievously at Mary

"—but until then, I will not be scouring the shops for the whitest of white ostrich feathers."

After a brief, presumably disapproving silence, Charlotte spoke again. "And who will be your chaperones while you are in London?" Her questions sounded very much as if Mr. Collins had something to do with them.

"Colonel Fitzwilliam is to be our escort, and my aunt, Lady Matlock, will act as our chaperone along with Mrs. Annesley, my former companion." Georgiana carefully set her teacup down, standing. "Thank you for the tea, Mrs. Collins. We must now return to Rosings—my aunt wished us to stay only long enough to issue her invitation for cards tomorrow evening." She glanced at Mary, who instantly rose to her feet, Georgiana barely allowing time enough for the nervous young maid to open the door before she stepped through.

Once inside the carriage, the bricks at their feet still warm, Mary commented, "I did not know Lady Catherine wished this to be so short a visit."

Georgiana shot her a fiery glance. "I could not help myself! Mr. Collins is having an unfortunate effect on his wife." She pulled the curtain closed. "I suppose it cannot be helped, being in his presence day after day, but the man is an inveterate busybody!"

Mary wondered at her friend's show of temper, but made no comment.

Eventually, Georgiana sighed. "I am sorry, Mary. I do not know what is wrong with me—I grow impatient so easily these past weeks."

"Never mind. Soon we will be in London, where there will be much to divert us." Mary leaned back against the cushions, though she kept a firm grip on the edge of the seat, for the winter ice had carved great ruts in the road, and even Lady Catherine's fine carriage was not designed to withstand such abuse.

～ула

"Cousin, will you not sit still?" Georgiana pointed her sketching pencil at Colonel Fitzwilliam. "Your fidgets make it impossible for me to catch any sort of likeness!"

Colonel Fitzwilliam sighed as he returned to his pose in one of Lady Catherine's least comfortable chairs. "You will have to stop soon at any rate, Georgiana, for our aunt demands punctuality above all things."

"Yes, she does, but it will take little time to complete the outline; please also refrain from speaking, as I am trying to capture your facial features."

The colonel rolled his eyes but maintained the posture. Mary sat nearby, reading through the final chapter of *The Wine Cellar,* which she was to give over to Lady Catherine for approval.

"How goes the latest novel, Miss Bennet?" the colonel asked, his lips barely moving. "Is it true my aunt has helped you create a masterpiece?"

Mary was more frustrated with the ever-changing story than she cared to admit, sorely tempted to abandon the project altogether. "I do not think anything I write will ever be considered a masterpiece, Colonel Fitzwilliam. If this book should ever be published you will certainly not be interested in reading it, for it will assuredly fall under the category of silly novels."

"No smiling!" commanded Georgiana. There was a slight pause. "Or facial contortions of any sort!"

"You may be surprised," said the colonel through his immobile lips, stubborn to the last, "but Major Ashton has convinced me to read *The Turret Room*, and even went so far as to purchase a copy for me when we were in London. Perhaps you will do me the honor of inscribing it?"

Mary viewed the colonel through her lashes, certain he was teasing her. "I would be happy to sign the book, if you wish it." She had in fact been hoping he would speak about Major Ashton, for she could not bring herself to broach the topic.

"Here you all are!" Lady Catherine entered the room with a swish of heavy silk skirts. "I see you are working on your drawing, Georgiana—one can never get enough practice in the arts, though it is now time to stop." She waved her hands dismissively before turning her narrowed gaze on Mary, who was quietly aligning the loose pages of the novel she was writing in collaboration with Lady Catherine in the hopes it would mend relations with the Darcys.

Lady Catherine rang a large bell, one of many always within her reach. "I see you have finished the final chapter, Miss Bennet, so I can now undertake the last reading of our novel." She cast narrowed eyes upon the colonel. "It was of course my wish to work directly with Miss Bennet on these final changes, but it appears there is no time and the responsibility falls to me alone." Her quick intake of breath did not allow for interruption. "When I am quite satisfied, I will see it is safely delivered to Mr. Egerton in London."

Mary did not like the only copy of her book being in the hands of anyone except Mr. Egerton (especially those of her hostess, who would now presumably change entire chapters at will). She stared at her clenched hands, wondering if (and how) she could prevent Lady Catherine's unsanctioned changes to the manuscript from ever reaching her publisher.

Mary was playing with the idea of refusing to give up the manuscript when Dawkins, Lady Catherine's faithful maid of many years, took it from her, her mistress taking on the appearance of a predatory bird as she looked on.

The maid walked out with the book in her hands, one wild idea after another coming to Mary's mind. But after a few silent moments, she had to admit defeat. She had after all agreed to the collaboration, and though she might have won a few battles, she had sadly underestimated the resolve of her hostess and had indeed lost the war.

Colonel Fitzwilliam broke the silence. "I am getting a cramp, Georgiana," he complained before addressing his aunt. "I would of course prefer the warmth and comfort of Rosings to the inhospitable air of London, but my time is not my own. It is Darcy's express wish for Georgiana to begin her season."

Lady Catherine struck the floor with the tip of her cane. "If it were not for certain developments—" her eyes rested on her daughter "—Anne and I could accompany Georgiana and Miss Bennet to London in the barouche box ourselves. I do not understand why you allow yourself to be at the beck and call of anyone, nephew—you are perfectly capable of choosing another lifestyle altogether."

The colonel's jaw tightened, but he was prevented from

commenting by the arrival of Mr. and Mrs. Collins.

As they proceeded to the drawing room, Lady Catherine took firm hold of her nephew's arm, turning to the others behind them. "Lord Wickford will be our guest tomorrow evening for dinner, Mrs. Collins." Her voice echoed in the cavernous hall. "You and Mr. Collins will join us, of course."

Charlotte dipped her head in lieu of an impractical curtsey. "We would be honored, Lady Catherine."

"Lord Wickford is so attentive to my Anne." Lady Catherine took her seat at the table closest to the fire. "I will not say for certain, but can *hint* there may soon be cause for celebration at Rosings." She turned to her nephew, seated at the neighboring table. "You would do well to remain with me, Richard, as I could easily find someone suitable for you as well. It is time you settled down and had a family of your own." She picked up the fresh deck of cards and smiled benignly upon her daughter, whose cheeks were distinctly pink. "The game is whist—the winning and losing pairs will play each other at the end of the first set."

The colonel dealt the cards with rather more force than was his habit, more surprised than anyone when he and Charlotte Collins defeated Mary and Mrs. Jenkinson five-to-one in the first game. While Mrs. Jenkinson dealt the next game, Mary heard Mr. Collins exclaim, "The boy should be sent to the workhouse!" Curiosity piqued, she continued to listen, disgusted when she learned he was speaking about a seven-year-old who had been caught chasing sheep in a local farmer's field.

"Mr. Collins, I do not believe the punishment you recommend for the poor child matches his alleged crime—if such a thing can be called a crime." Mary's hand stopped midway to the ace of diamonds—it was Georgiana who had spoken, and there was not a sound in the room, save from the crackling fire.

"I agree. The workhouse is certainly not an appropriate place for a boy who has only acted as any child his age might."

Upon hearing these words, Mary nearly dropped all of her cards, for it was Miss Anne de Bourgh speaking, the same young lady who had barely uttered more than 'yes, Mamma' in all the time Mary had been a guest at Rosings. Miss de Bourgh further shocked everyone in the room by adding, "His parents should be the ones to choose the punishment—I would think to bed without supper would do well enough."

The guests were silent until Colonel Fitzwilliam whispered, "Brava, cousin!"

Mary glanced over the top of her cards in time to see Georgiana's considering glance at her allegedly shy, retiring, and sickly cousin.

"You have laid the wrong card, Mr. Collins!" Lady Catherine snapped, her finger pointing at the stack in the middle of the table. "A heart was led!"

Mr. Collins quickly removed the offending card—a trump—and replaced it with a low spade. "I must apologize, Lady Catherine! I do not know how I—"

"Never mind, Mr. Collins!" Lady Catherine impatiently placed her own card down and took the trick.

Miss de Bourgh's delicate yawn marked the premature end of the evening, just as Mary and Mrs. Jenkinson were about to win their first game against the colonel and Charlotte Collins.

"Anne is tired." Lady Catherine rose regally from her chair. "She needs to rest, for tomorrow is an important day." With a flick of her wrist, the mistress of Rosings ordered Mrs. Jenkinson to follow her and her daughter after only the briefest of goodnights to her guests.

Like two little mice, Mr. and Mrs. Collins scurried out, quickly descending the stairs to wait in the immense, drafty hall while a carriage was made ready for them.

Georgiana endeavored to convince them to return to the drawing room where they could stay warm by the fire while they waited, but Mr. Collins refused. As a result, Charlotte, Georgiana, and Mary were thoroughly chilled by the time the carriage arrived.

After seeing Lady Catherine's guests out, Georgiana and Mary rushed up the grand staircase to their chambers, where Molly and Lucy had already warmed their beds and their nightdresses.

"Molly, you and Lucy may well have saved our lives this evening," Mary said, shivering despite the warmed clothing.

Molly tucked the down-filled cover up to Mary's chin. "You were standing in the hall ever-so-long, miss."

"Well, thank you for your thoughtfulness, but please now get yourself to your own bed—we would not wish to delay our journey to London by either of us catching a chill, would we?"

"No, miss." Molly placed another log on the fire and retired.

Mary watched the flames for a long while as she waited for the warmth to spread through her body, her treacherous mind dwelling on images of Miss Bingley taking Major Ashton's arm at a soirée, again at the theatre, again at a ball, until finally she turned on her side, punched her pillow, and closed her eyes with determination.

CHAPTER NINETEEN

"Miss Bennet!" Lady Catherine's piercing voice caused Georgiana to jump nervously, and Mary to lose her place, the symmetry of the fugue destroyed. "I will speak with you at once!"

Mary's heart sank. The next day they were to leave for London, and she had begun to hope her 'collaborator' would not have read the whole of *The Wine Cellar* by then, thereby forestalling this very interview.

Her hostess was clearly vexed, and Mary rose from the bench with a sense of doom before following the clicking heels down the hall (Georgiana tried to look encouraging).

"Sit there, Miss Bennet." Lady Catherine pointed to a plain wooden chair in her morning room (the one reserved for servants who were in trouble), and Mary obeyed. "I have finished the novel, and am quite displeased. You failed to remove reference to the drug, opium, and you made unsanctioned changes to much of my dialogue, *and* you wrote an ending completely different from the one I dictated!" Her voice rose with each infraction as she looked down her long nose at Mary. "I have re-written all of what you changed—thank heaven I have a capacious memory—and have corrected several errors in your depiction of rooms and finery. The novel now ends as I originally stated it should—with the two heroines marrying, each according to her station." Her narrowed eyes focused on the object of her discontent. "I have only to review the changes before the novel can be prepared for the post."

Apparently, Lady Catherine had said all she planned to say, and Mary managed to murmur something acceptable before slinking back to the music room, where Georgiana was still at the gilded harpsichord, practicing a well-known work by Handel Lady Catherine wished her to play for Lord Wickford's pleasure that evening.

"Georgiana!" Mary closed the door firmly before approaching the instrument. "We have a problem!"

Georgiana set her hands in her lap as she listened to the tale, frowning when Mary insisted they must get hold of the novel before it could be sent to the publisher. "The servants will know if it goes missing, and betray us in an instant." She stood and began to pace energetically. "However, we *could* make a fake package and exchange it for the real one."

"Such a plan might work—but how are we to know what the 'real' package looks like?" Mary drummed her fingers on the harpsichord casing. After a few moments, she turned to Georgiana with a devious look. "We could enlist Molly and Lucy's aid—not to steal the package of course, but only to discover what it looks like."

Georgiana looked dubious. "On second thought, it is not a good idea. We would have to copy the handwriting for the direction perfectly." She shook her head firmly. "And what will you do about the changes my aunt has made? She will eventually find out if you modified them—she has a prodigious memory."

Mary bit her lip, torn between the desire to appease Lady Catherine for Elizabeth's sake and the wish to maintain what she considered to be the integrity of her work. "I do not necessarily plan to change what she has written, but I feel most strongly about seeing those changes before Mr. Egerton does!"

"I cannot blame you." Georgiana went to the door, her hand halting just above the handle. "My cousin might be willing to help...." She gestured for Mary to come, just as she would Samson. "There is little time to find him before we must dress for dinner!"

⌒◡◡⌒

Lord Wickford arrived promptly that evening, his portly frame sporting an ornately-tied neckcloth, daring waistcoat, satin breeches, and tailcoat. His hair was carefully combed to cover any bare spots, and he looked every inch the prospective bridegroom. He gallantly bowed over Anne's hand to proclaim, "Miss de Bourgh, it seems like months instead of days since we last met."

Mary, who thought such words were only penned by novelists, was further amazed when Miss de Bourgh simpered in response. The not-so-young lady (being the same age as Mr. Darcy, who would soon turn thirty) actually smiled, and in a clear voice inquired as to Lord Wickford's health. She then asked after each of his four children by name, causing Colonel Fitzwilliam to stare openly until Georgiana caught his eye.

Mary, who had of late been thinking a great deal about the good and evil of matrimony, did not necessarily believe Anne and Lord Wickford suited one another in character, temper, or understanding, but Miss de Bourgh (who did not actually *need* a suitor) clearly welcomed the older gentleman's wooing. The normally sickly and pale young lady was looking almost pretty in a high-collared gown made from layers of diaphanous silk, her cheeks delicately pink. For Lord Wickford's part, the fortune his prospective bride would inherit was so considerable that any gentleman—even the worst of rogues—could manage an air of loving fascination (at least until after the wedding).

Throughout the pre-dinner hour, during which Lady Catherine never allowed drinks to be served, Georgiana and Mary sat with their hands in their laps, not asked to contribute to the conversation between Lady Catherine and her other guests, who in their turn were required to say little.

When the dinner bell finally rang, the colonel expelled a great sigh, holding out his arms for Georgiana and Mary. Lady Catherine and Anne were escorted to the dining room by Lord Wickford, leaving Mr. Collins with Charlotte and Mrs. Jenkinson.

At the table Mary was seated between Mr. and Mrs. Collins, the former taking full advantage of the opportunity to instruct and sermonize, pointing out all the evils of town, volubly abhorring the ease with which certain headstrong young people believed themselves above common societal habits and expectations. "You must control your two young charges while they are in town, Colonel Fitzwilliam," Mr. Collins said finally, moving his head to see him through the grand epergne.

The colonel set his silver down with a clatter before taking up his wine glass. "Mr. Collins, your concern is just and warranted, I am sure, but you need not remind me of my duty." He emptied his glass and motioned for a footman to refill it.

The number of courses increased exponentially at Lady Catherine's table whenever an eligible gentleman visited, therefore the party was at the dinner table for much longer than usual, requiring Mary to take part in more conversation with Mr. Collins than she was prepared to tolerate. Her strategy became to have just taken a spoonful of soup, a bite of fish or mutton, or to be in the midst of sipping wine whenever Mr. Collins addressed her, requiring only a slight nod of the head in response.

The conversation between Lord Wickford and Lady Catherine was far more interesting to her—at one point, he clearly requested a formal audience with her ladyship, and the other guests at the table sat with baited breath while the meeting was set for the following day.

Mary caught Georgiana's eye—if Lady Catherine's attention was so diverted, the colonel might more easily gain access to the manuscript.

Finally, the last table cloth was removed, the trifle and other desserts brought in, and the champagne wines served. Lady Catherine was all the while advising Charlotte on the proper way to maintain order in her kitchen. This allowed Lord Wickford the opportunity to tell Miss de Bourgh about his recently acquired phaeton, going so far as to invite her out in it on the next fine day.

Lady Catherine's expression showed her pleasure, though she pretended not to hear as she finished her lecture to Charlotte. She then stood, instructing the gentlemen to enjoy their port and cigars, adding with a sly smile, "But do not be at it too long."

When the gentlemen joined the ladies in the music room, Georgiana was already at work, playing Handel suites on the harpsichord, while Lady Catherine began her own recital of Miss de Bourgh's many accomplishments. Mary wondered if Lady Catherine's enthusiasm for her subject might have the unfortunate result of extinguishing any affection Lord Wickford held for her daughter, but he appeared to be as enamoured as ever, sandwiched between Miss de Bourgh and Mrs. Jenkinson on a smallish settee, and by the time Georgiana had performed nearly the entirety of Handel's keyboard oeuvre, it was clear that Miss de Bourgh was to have her proposal.

This time, Lady Catherine remained with her guests in the drawing room until the carriages were announced, and graciously attended them down the stairs and through the long hall. "Until our meeting tomorrow, Lord Wickford." (Mary thought a complete stranger might assume the lady expected a proposal herself.)

Mr. Collins could not leave without giving final directives to Mary, and made her promise she would act in a modest manner according to her station in life, and do nothing to blacken the name of de Bourgh or Darcy while she was in London. By the time he and his wife departed, Mary felt positively low.

"Never mind what Mr. Collins says," said Georgiana as they climbed the marble staircase, "we shall do exactly as we like. We will attend lectures and art exhibits, and visit the lending library every other day!"

Mary stopped at the landing and impulsively hugged her friend. "You are so good to me, Georgiana."

Georgiana dismissed Mary's words with a wave of her hand. Upon reaching the door to her own chamber, she whispered, her eyes bright, "Tomorrow we go to London. We will be free!"

Mary smiled in return and proceeded thoughtfully to her own room, her mind busy with possible strategies to prevent Lady Catherine's package from reaching Mr. Egerton, should Colonel Fitzwilliam's plan go awry.

After an abbreviated morning repast taken in their rooms, Colonel Fitzwilliam sent word to Georgiana and Mary via his batman (who relayed the message to Molly) that the carriages were ready for them and it was time to go.

"Have you become well-acquainted with the colonel's batman?" Mary asked curiously as Molly helped her into her heaviest traveling cloak.

Molly shrugged. "He doesn't speak much, but from what I've

seen of him, he's very loyal and would do anything for the colonel."

"Well, since you and Lucy will be riding with him in the other carriage, you might get to know him even better," Mary teased as she pulled on her gloves. "By the bye, have you seen a package on the table in the hall?"

Molly smiled. "I have seen it, miss, and so has the colonel. You shouldn't worry. Lawrence—that's the batman—says the colonel is one of the smartest men he's ever met."

"All he needs to do is outsmart Lady Catherine," Mary muttered as she left the room.

Georgiana and Mary were already wrapped in fur throws, their feet upon warmed bricks, when the colonel came outdoors to check the saddle on his horse before approaching their carriage.

"Would you not prefer to be inside with us, cousin?" asked Georgiana with a concerned frown. "I did not think you would be riding—it is so cold today and it looks likely to rain."

"I promised Darcy I would ride alongside until we reach the outskirts of London—I will keep his poor footmen company until then." He closed the carriage door firmly just as Lady Catherine appeared.

"I have ordered Anne to remain in her bed this morning," she said.

Colonel Fitzwilliam cleared his throat. "Cousin Anne appears to...appreciate the company of Lord Wickford."

Lady Catherine dipped her head in acknowledgment. "It will be a fine match." She stepped up to the first carriage with her niece and Mary inside, and tapped on the window. "Remember to keep your hood up for the entirety of the journey, Georgiana, or you will catch a chill." She then turned to Mary. "Miss Bennet, I will expect to hear news of the novel's publication soon after the publisher receives it. I will send suggestions for the title forthwith."

It took all of Mary's self-control to sound appreciative as she responded, "Thank you, Lady Catherine," trying not to stare at the parcel she held, wrapped in brown paper and clearly addressed to Mr. Egerton at his London office.

"Thank you for your kindness, Aunt Catherine," Georgiana

said prettily, while covering her head obediently with the hood of her cape. "Please offer my best wishes to Anne upon her engagement."

"She will certainly be happy—" Lady Catherine looked at her nephew with narrowed eyes "—likely more so than if she had married one of her cousins. I do not like to see her fortune go outside of the family, but Lord Wickford is understandably besotted, and *such* a gentleman." She looked up at the coachman. "Now, go, or I will catch my death!"

"Yes, m'lady," the coachman responded, and the horses slowly pulled the carriage around the circular drive and onto the straight path leading to the gates.

Mary looked at Georgiana, her eyes wide. "We did not get it!" She sank back into the cushions, biting her lower lip.

Georgiana pulled the hood of her cape off her head, straightening her lace-lined bonnet. "Never mind—we will come up with another plan." She thought for a moment, and her eyes grew brighter. "You can simply go to Mr. Egerton's office upon our arrival in London and ask for the parcel back, claiming you wish to make more changes. Given my aunt's singular style of writing, he would no doubt have asked you to make them anyway." She looked hopefully at her friend.

Suddenly, the carriage came to a halt, nearly tossing them to the floor. Mary was first to regain her seat, and she looked silently across at Georgiana, her brows raised. The last time their carriage had stopped so suddenly, it had been due to highwaymen.

Suddenly, there was a knock at the window and Georgiana pulled the curtain aside with some trepidation, laughing with relief. "It is only my cousin." She opened the window and the colonel handed the brown-paper parcel through it.

"However did you manage it?" Georgiana asked the colonel with a smile.

"As it turned out, I did not need to resort to subterfuge. I simply offered to see to its safe delivery myself—thereby saving Aunt Catherine the expense of the postage." He grinned and strode off, back upon his horse in an instant, and the coachman was soon directing the horses through the imposing gates.

Georgiana handed over the package and Mary placed it on

the bench beside her, effectively hiding it beneath the folds of her cloak lest Lady Catherine have a change of heart and send one of her footmen chasing after them. She then sank back into the cushions, pulling the fur rug up to her chin. "I had my doubts, Georgiana, but you and Molly were right to advise complete faith in the colonel."

CHAPTER TWENTY

(A Letter from Georgiana Darcy to Elizabeth Darcy)

Darcy House, 4 April 1814

Dearest Elizabeth,

Since arriving in London, we have had endless rounds of fittings, and never seem to finish the shopping. Miss Bingley calls each day (usually on the arm of Major A, which seems to cause Mary some degree of angst) and has not once mentioned Mr. P, or the termination of her wedding plans. (Is it possible she has forgotten?) Major A plays the part of courtier well, though Mary seems to doubt his attentions will garner the desired result.

We have had many visitors from amongst our acquaintances, including Mr. Clay (Cousin Richard and the major have asked us to tolerate his company for the time being, and we do, though the overpowering scent of the musk he favors remains behind for hours). Mr. Clay speaks with great freedom about his 'good friend Wickham' and is apparently a frequent visitor of Miss Bingley's (which must be the reason we are to be 'in' when he calls). Miss Burnaby and her mother are also in town—Miss Burnaby is to be presented, and nearly all her time is taken up with lessons for deportment and elocution, though I doubt she will utter a single syllable in the queen's presence. I must close, for we go to the theatre this evening. Please write soon with news of Pemberley, and give Samson a treat for me.

Yours sincerely,
Georgiana Darcy

CHAPTER TWENTY-ONE

The sight of her home growing smaller and smaller as the horse-cart carried the four of them down the tree-lined drive further hardened Miss Treadon's heart against their distant cousin and his odious wife.

Across the cart sat her silent mother, with eyes no longer capable of shedding tears. Her eldest sister sat stiffly upright, head high, features controlled, looking ahead, never back, while the youngest clutched a doll tightly, humming a tune sung by their mother during happier times.

"Mary! You must cease your work; we will have callers soon."

Having dared to slightly adapt only a few of Lady Catherine's changes to *The Wine Cellar*, Mary had completed the work during their first two days at Darcy House and had personally delivered the manuscript to the publisher's office. She then began immediately on her next, more serious, project: a story in which a mother and her daughters lose their home to a heartless, distant cousin, due to an entail. Her models for the main characters were of course Mrs. Leigh and her daughters. She had already outlined each of the characters for the book, including the ruthless adventurer who was to take advantage of one of the young ladies, and had only just begun to write the first chapter of the novel when Georgiana interrupted.

"Oh, Mary." Georgiana, perfectly coiffed and looking every inch the lady of the house, groaned. "You have ink on your face again! No—" she peered at the offending spots "—do not touch anything; you will only make it worse." She went to the bell-pull and rang for Molly. "You must promise to come as soon as she has finished."

Mary was frowning into the mirror, wondering how she could have transferred so much ink to her cheek and chin.

"It came from the edge of your palm—there." Georgiana pointed. "Perhaps we should order all of your gowns in ink-colored fabric. It would save Molly ever so much trouble." She shook her head in mock despair, wagged her finger at the clock, and left Mary in the care of Molly, who had responded to the summons without delay.

"A parcel has arrived for you, miss," Molly said as she rubbed an aromatic mixture she concocted herself onto the offending ink spots. "You'll be proud to know I could read the sender's name—it is from Mr. Egerton."

Mary watched the ink spots disappear. "It must be my copies of *The Count*." She held up her stained hand, and Molly clicked disapprovingly before working quickly to clean it as well. "Would you like a copy of your own?"

The young maid's face went pink with pleasure as she set down her cloth and went to the wardrobe. "I would like one very much, miss, if you can spare it." She chose a gown and turned towards Mary, who looked about to object. "You must change, miss—there's another ink stain on your cuff."

Mary looked down with surprise, for she had been wearing cuff protectors. "I apologize, Molly—what a frightful bother I must be to you."

"Never mind, miss, I have learned how to remove those as well." Molly paused in the middle of unbuttoning Mary's gown to say, "Miss Bingley has come with Major Ashton—would you not like me to do a bit more with your hair?"

Standing in front of the long mirror, Mary looked critically at her reflection, but shook her head. "Major Ashton has been much engaged with Miss Bingley of late—I do not think he will even notice me."

She did not see the speculative look on her maid's face.

When Mary entered the cheerful yellow-and-white morning room, recently redecorated under Elizabeth's guidance, Major Ashton was presumably with Colonel Fitzwilliam, who habitually refused to join them when they had visitors. Mrs. Annesley sat quietly in a corner with her sewing, while Miss Bingley expressed admiration for Georgiana's latest piece of fancywork.

"Dear Georgiana, how do you keep your stitches so even? I envy your patience!" Miss Bingley moved gracefully to the window to look out upon the street before turning to face Mary. "I understand Captain Jameson...oh, I am sorry—Lord Jameson—will be at the fête this evening with his wife. Have you met her? She is so well-bred, and so lovely!"

Georgiana responded quickly on Mary's behalf. "What good news—we did not think to have the honor of meeting her so soon."

Miss Bingley's eyes slid to Mary. "You must be looking forward to seeing your friend, the former captain, Miss Bennet— and his wife, of course."

Mary busied herself with stirring her tea, though had Miss Bingley seen her eyes she might have refrained from any references to the captain.

"How wonderful to be a countess," Miss Bingley continued, unaware that her barbs were falling a bit wide of their mark since Mary had long ago come to terms not only with Captain Jameson's marriage to a Scottish heiress, but also with her own feelings for him. She had since then even promised to consider Major Ashton's proposal of a marriage (based on friendship), which she never could have had her heart been still engaged. However, she had not spoken with the major about the matter since before Kitty's wedding day, and she was beginning to wonder if she had understood him correctly, and also if her first impression of the man as an irredeemable, inconstant, flirtatious, licentious libertine....

Georgiana broke into Mary's thoughts. "It would be nice to be a countess, of course, but I would not desire it unless I felt true affection for my husband, and my affection was reciprocated. Will you have a piece of cake, Caroline?" She indicated the assortment on the tiered tray. "Or perhaps a scone with some of Mrs. Babcock's lemon curd?"

Miss Bingley declined, but did accept a second cup of tea. "A bit more sugar, if you please," she instructed Mary, who was pouring. "When does Lady Matlock arrive, my dear?" She was facing Georgiana, but turned briefly to Mary when asking her next question. "Will you be removing to Grace-church Street when the countess takes up residence at Darcy House to watch over her niece, Miss Bennet?"

Again, Georgiana spoke before Mary could think of a response. "Mary and I will attend all the social commitments of the season together; my Aunt Matlock and Colonel Fitzwilliam will act as our chaperones, along with Mrs. Annesley." She smiled in that lady's direction. "We will of course frequently visit the Gardiners and their delightful children—perhaps you might care to join us one day?"

Miss Bingley's audience was in some doubt as to her true thoughts, but she said only, "Perhaps I will."

Mary then felt an irrepressible desire to broach the topic of Mr. Petersham, a subject absolutely forbidden by Colonel Fitzwilliam and Mr. Darcy ("we want her to believe that other than Colonel Fitzwilliam, only Major Ashton and Mr. Bingley know about the elopement"), but the arrival of Miss Deidre Burnaby and her mother prevented such an error in judgment.

The Burnabys had just come from the modiste for the final fitting of Deidre's court dress. Thus, during the next quarter of an hour, talk centered on the forthcoming Queen's Drawing Room. Miss Burnaby entertained them with predictions: her elaborate headdress would topple down when she knelt before Her Majesty; she would bump into a wall as she backed away, or worse, trip on her dress. "Or perhaps I will mistake the Prince Regent for Beau Brummell!" She laughed hysterically.

"Such a thing would hardly be possible, Miss Burnaby," Caroline Bingley asserted, "given the Beau's fine figure and the Regent's extreme corpulence."

Mrs. Burnaby, who had been the first of the Darcys' neighbors to welcome Elizabeth to Derbyshire, and whom Mary had always liked for it, focused her innocent-looking eyes on Miss Bingley. "I understand the Regent and Princess Caroline are sadly incompatible." She set her cup down and leaned forward to whisper, "They have not lived under the same roof since the birth of Princess Charlotte, and I hear the prince tried to prevent his wife from ever seeing the child."

Mrs. Burnaby took a bite of scone, and the next instant spoke of another subject altogether. "The poor Miss Leighs are now stuck so deep in the country in Buckinghamshire; they will have little chance of meeting anyone of quality." She leaned forward once more. "I have asked Mrs. Leigh if the two eldest might come to us—I have promised to show them the delights of the season. Poor Deidre misses her good friends so."

While Mrs. Burnaby took a breath, Mary was able to observe aloud, "I was not aware you were well-acquainted with the Leighs."

"Derbyshire is not so large as it seems, Miss Bennet. We have known them for years, although Mrs. Leigh has not been out in society for some time now—her husband, you know," she whispered. "But Deidre and Diana—the eldest daughter—are especially good friends." She gazed with pride upon her daughter, who was taking a brief respite from talk, about to consume the three fairy cakes on her plate. "They no longer have the advantages they once had, and are frightfully in need of new gowns—I have already notified my modiste, against their mother's express wishes, of course, but should I be expected to sponsor young ladies dressed in rags, I ask you? Surely they will not object to a few new, pretty things!" She finished the scone before adding, "Mr. Burnaby has had to return to the country, so I am left on my own to supervise, but I feel up to the task." She glanced at Caroline Bingley, whose smile looked a bit frozen. "I am determined to give those poor dears a season...and to extricate Catherine, the middle daughter, from a bad situation. It is said she has been seen far too often in the company of an infamous rogue...Deidre!"

Miss Burnaby started, caught her small plate before it fell to the floor, and blinked repeatedly, for she had fallen asleep.

"The season takes so much energy—so many late nights," complained Mrs. Burnaby. "We never seem to return from an evening's entertainment earlier than three in the morning, I swear, and I am forced to rest at least three hours before venturing out once more in search of—"

Mrs. Burnaby's soliloquy ended abruptly upon the butler's announcement of yet another visitor—someone both Georgiana and Mary had hoped not to see so soon again at Darcy House—

Mr. Clay.

The heavily-musked gentleman bowed and smirked over Miss Darcy's hand in a fine imitation of Mr. Collins, and when he approached Miss Bingley, greeted her with the familiarity allowed only the closest of friends, exclaiming, "Miss Bingley, what a beautiful ring! I swear it has the scent of spring flowers!"

"It is a perfumed ring, Mr. Clay—they are all the rage." Miss Bingley curtseyed prettily, holding out her hand so the others could view the ornament on her finger.

Deidre Burnaby wiped at the crumbs on her dress, stood, and stepped nearer Miss Bingley to view the ring more closely. "Mamma—I would like one of these," she said, sniffing. "The aroma is not unlike that of violets! Are there many scents to choose from, Miss Bingley?"

"There are innumerable scents available," Miss Bingley obliged, pulling her hand back.

Mr. Clay took the seat nearest Miss Bingley, and while half-listening as Deidre Burnaby described her ostrich feathers, Mary watched the two of them whispering together, their heads almost touching. She grew determined to speak with Colonel Fitzwilliam, perhaps even Major Ashton if she could pull him away from Miss Bingley, for she had long suspected—or perhaps hoped—Mr. Clay was in some way connected to Mr. Petersham, and now felt certain of it. He had been at Devonham at the crucial time and apparently enjoyed the confidence of Miss Bingley—who better to arrange the elopement?

Before Mary could study them further, however, Major Ashton entered, and on his face was the sardonic expression of old, though Mary thought he looked tired. He first bent over Georgiana's hand, then turned his attention to the Burnabys and then to Miss Bingley. When he came to Mary, his seeming indifference caused an onrush of an unfamiliar, distinctly unpleasant emotion. She greeted the major with the coldness adopted early in their acquaintanceship whenever she had the misfortune to be in his company, and observed the slight tightening of his jaw with satisfaction.

This cold greeting comprised the major's only address to Mary during the entirety of his short visit, and she thought his behavior typical of the popinjay she had always thought him to be. For rather than pay attention to the young lady he had almost asked to marry him on a family walk near Longbourn in the crisp, winter air, he paid court to Miss Bingley, who had fully intended to elope with one of the most infamous men any of them had ever had the misfortune to know. The same Miss Bingley whose invectives were often repeated in the presence of the major regarding a certain person's unsuitable upbringing and lack of fortune—even borrowing lines from Mr. Collins, referring to 'defects of temper' and going so far as to make pointed reference to 'headstrong and foolish young persons who were sadly unable to imitate the practices of 'elegant females'.

Mary was taken out of her reverie by Mrs. Burnaby, who insisted she and Deidre must be going. "We are to hear a musical concert tonight, and if I do not rest beforehand, I shall certainly fall asleep before the second note is played!"

Major Ashton then turned his attention to Mr. Clay, asking which of the coming balls and soirées he would be attending. Mary felt certain that the major too suspected Mr. Clay of nefarious dealings, but the time had passed when she felt comfortable approaching him to voice her own thoughts.

Soon afterwards, Miss Bingley took hold of each of the gentlemen's arms, insisting they accompany her home. "I will send away the carriage and you will walk with me—it is a fine day for exercise."

It was all Mary could do to look up when the major took his leave. She was able to catch his eye for a second and thought she saw a hint of affection there, but it was no matter. Miss Bingley did not allow for a single moment of conversation and the three of them departed, Miss Bingley's tinkling laughter echoing through the hall as the front door closed behind them.

When they were gone, Mrs. Annesley said something about needing a particular shade of purple thread. After she went in search of it, Georgiana asked, "Mary? Have you done something to cause a rift between you and the major?"

Mary managed to shake her pounding head before excusing herself, her surprised friend looking at her with concern.

To Mary's extreme mortification, the angry tears which she had so far controlled began to fall before she reached the privacy of her chamber.

CHAPTER TWENTY-TWO

It was at Almack's Assembly Rooms, nearly a sennight later (Lady Matlock having successfully procured the necessary vouchers) that Mary next saw Major Ashton. She watched from behind a large potted plant as he entered the ballroom with Miss Bingley's proprietorial hand on his arm—to Mary it looked as if they might soon announce an engagement.

Georgiana, ever vigilant, asked quietly, "Mary, are you unwell? You look entirely too pale."

Mary moved away from the plant when she noticed Lord Harold, whom Georgiana had known since childhood. He bowed and greeted Mary, asking if he might bring something for her comfort. "A glass of lemonade, perhaps? It is far too crowded and over-heated in here."

Mary looked up at Georgiana's dashing friend, whom Lady Matlock had taken under her wing after the death-bed request of one of her closest friends. If the prevailing rumors could be believed, Lord Harold was something of a rogue, and had been disinherited from his uncle for some unknown, but much-conjectured offense.

"I am perfectly fine, thank you. Something I saw took me by surprise." Mary did not elaborate.

They were standing near a group of matrons with large feathers in their hair, their bodices exhibiting an unnecessary amount of décolletage, each of them clearly listening to the exchange for some tidbit to whisper to one another behind their fans.

Georgiana spoke in a stage whisper. "Mary and I are indeed thirsty, Lord Harold. You are most kind—your offer of refreshment could not have come at a better time."

Georgiana took Lord Harold's proffered arm, Mary following suit, and the three of them made their way through the throng of people towards the drinks table. Unfortunately, there was a sudden opening of the crowd and Mary was treated to yet another clear view of Miss Bingley, smiling, and laughing, her hand still firmly upon Major Ashton's arm. When Miss Bingley's eyes caught her own, Mary was instantly metamorphosed into her former inelegant, graceless self. In that moment, she hated London—it was a horrible place—and decided to return to Hertfordshire as soon as arrangements could be made, where the relative tranquility of Longbourn would allow her to focus on writing, and where bothersome gentlemen were few and far between.

The next dance was announced directly after they had taken their refreshment, and Mr. Chandler, another childhood friend of Georgiana's, stood ready to take Mary to the floor.

The rest of the evening passed in a blur for Mary, who felt dull and uninteresting. She could not remember any of her partners except the colonel and Mr. Chandler, and when they were finally in the carriage, she breathed an audible sigh of relief.

Lady Matlock was instantly concerned. "You looked far too pale this evening, Mary, and seemed listless. Perhaps we should call for the physician."

Mary, angry at herself for worrying her friends, claimed to have taken too much pudding at dinner, and the countess said no more about physicians. Upon entering Darcy House, however, she ordered Mary immediately to bed.

Unfortunately, once there, Mary twisted and turned under the covers, going over each incident in which she had seen Major Ashton since his alleged proposal to her in December. After hours of analyzing what she decided was a chimerical character, she decided to think of the major as one who could not be trusted with a young lady's heart. As such, Mary was determined to harden her own against him. She finally fell into a troubled sleep, during which Miss Bingley haunted her dreams.

Despite her restless night, Mary rose comparatively early the next morning, determined to be her normal self and give no cause for further concern. When she entered the breakfast room, dressed in a becoming gown and displaying the latest of Molly's hair designs, Georgiana was clearly relieved.

"Oh, Mary, I thought you would have to remain in your bed today! Whatever upset you so last evening? I have never seen your face so pale."

Mary reached for the marmalade. "Unlike my heroines, I have not the temperament to pine, or to waste away due to *any* gentleman's behavior."

Georgiana tapped her egg, her expression knowing. "You are referring to the major—but surely you do not think his attentions to Miss Bingley are based on genuine affection?"

"I do not care about either Major Ashton or Miss Bingley," Mary declared stoutly, biting into her crumpet.

Georgiana did not look happy. "I found his coolness towards you a bit overdone, to be honest, but are not his attentions to Caroline part of his assigned duty? He escorts her in the hopes of extracting important information regarding Mr. Petersham."

Mary set down her cup with a clatter. "That may be so, but I do not understand why, considering his—" she hesitated "—*proposal*, he could not tell me so himself, or at least behave in a friendly manner towards me."

Georgiana considered the point while absently dipping her toast point. "We have not yet seen him without Miss Bingley in tow, and therefore he has not yet had the opportunity to speak with you in private."

Mary set her napkin on the table. "It is no matter, Georgiana. I was unable to sleep much of the night, and therefore had plenty of time to think." She paused dramatically. "I have come to a decision."

Georgiana, who knew Mary very well, did not smile as she waited silently.

"I will tell the major—should I ever have the fortune to see him without his paramour—that I release him from his proposal, or whatever it was, of December nineteenth, and that I wish never to see him again. As a matter of fact, I am wholly determined once again to steer clear of all gentlemen—they are a nuisance." She took a breath, but was not interrupted. "I decided long ago to remain a spinster, preferring to live life on my own terms, not subject to the whims of any man. I shall once more focus my attention on attaining my goal of having my own little cottage one day, sharing it with a companion for propriety's sake—" she did not see Georgiana's smile "—and will henceforth focus all my mental energies on writing so that one day my plans might come to fruition."

"If you think it best." Georgiana looked doubtful as she took a bite of toast.

"I do," Mary said firmly, reaching for a piece of fruit.

Later that day, Lady Matlock asked Georgiana to her private sitting room, where she was reclining on a settee with a book in her hands. "Well, my dear—I understand Mary is feeling better now, but do you think it might be a wise precaution to send for a physician? This is the second time she has complained to me of a troublesome digestion."

"I do not think a doctor will be necessary." Georgiana glanced at her aunt's book before sitting in the upholstered chair opposite. "You are reading *The Count of Camalore*."

The countess marked her page with braided silk threads and placed the book carefully on a side table. "Mary was kind enough to present me with an inscribed copy, and since then I have been disinclined to put it down."

"I wonder what her publisher's reaction will be to *The Wine Cellar*, given Aunt Catherine's input."

Lady Matlock looked apologetic. "Catherine is far too autocratic. She always had to have her way in everything when we were children—no matter what the circumstances. Perhaps it came from being the eldest of three fairly headstrong daughters, but I think our parents, and later her husband, enabled that particular quality in her, allowing it to grow out of proportion." She shook her head sadly. "Her poor husband never could control her."

Georgiana's curiosity was piqued. "I never knew this about my uncle."

"Well, you were far too young to observe their particular...dynamic whenever they had the misfortune to be together. I wonder sometimes if Catherine chose him because she knew she could wield complete control. To be honest, I was never certain if she or Sir Lewis first proposed the marriage."

Georgiana could not help laughing. "And what about my mother—how did she come to choose my father?"

Lady Matlock's eyes grew sad. "I wish she were here to tell you about her courtship with Mr. Darcy." She settled her feet more comfortably on the edge of the settee, covering them with her skirts. "But what a romance! Your mother was easily the most beautiful of all the young ladies in Derbyshire, and the most sought after. However, she noticed no one after she was introduced to your father, who was as handsome as your brother. It was always 'Mr. Darcy this, Mr. Darcy that,' and I felt sure it was only a matter of time before he would ask her to marry him." She paused, her eyes unfocused, and after a few moments, Georgiana cleared her throat delicately.

Lady Matlock stretched her arms above her head, smiling. "While your mother was falling deeply in love with Mr. Darcy, I was doing my best to *avoid* suitors—I was once a bit like Mary, you know, in my desire to remain single, at least until I was sure of the gentleman I would marry. I had several acquaintances who had rushed headlong into marriage, only to end up extremely unhappy. One of my closest friends was committed to the Bethlehem Hospital by her own husband—the one they call Bedlam. Horrible place." She noted the shock on her niece's face. "But let me save such sad tales for a later time."

"You need not fear on my behalf, Aunt, for I am no longer an innocent, naïve girl. I think Mary would like to hear the story— an evil husband committing his innocent wife to an asylum would make excellent fodder for another gothic novel."

The countess was thoughtful. "It is in fact an incredibly sad reality; perhaps she *could* write something to help enlighten people about the suffering there...but for now I will focus on your mother and father's courtship." She closed her eyes for a second. "At the time, I was certain Lord Matlock would propose to me—I knew him as The Honorable Mr. Fitzwilliam at the time. As the eldest son, he was sure to inherit his father's estate and title, and therefore my parents had no objection. At the same time, Catherine had set her sights on Sir Lewis de Bourgh.

"Now, Anne was besotted with her Mr. Darcy, but he sadly did not seek an interview with my father to ask for her hand—

and it was not until much later we learned why he did not."

Georgiana leaned forward, mesmerized by a tale she had never heard about a mother she never knew.

"Mr. Darcy was a man of property, but he did not have a title and therefore did not think himself worthy of your mother. It was as simple as that."

Georgiana waited for her aunt to continue, but the countess looked far away, a slight smile upon her lips. "Aunt Fitzwilliam?"

"Forgive me, Georgiana. One is lucky to have pleasant memories to look back on, but let me see—oh yes, your mother had come to a decision regarding Mr. Darcy." She paused, remembering. "She was determined to discover if he reciprocated her feelings, and by whatever means necessary. If he did not, she said she would forever denounce all gentlemen, vowing to take care of our parents in their dotage."

Georgiana again looked shocked.

"I am in earnest, my dear. Your mother was absolutely determined. Catherine of course tried to dissuade her from any rash action, suggesting she would soon find a more suitable, appropriately-titled gentleman. But your mamma would listen to no protestations against a man she was by then determined to have, and at the next opportunity—an evening at Almack's, and during a cotillion, if memory serves—she asked Mr. Darcy outright if he had intentions towards her."

Georgiana inhaled sharply. "She did not!"

"Yes, she did." Lady Matlock laughed at the memory. "And had she not done so, I do not think you and I would be having this conversation."

Georgiana sat back in the chair, her thoughts filled with the little she had gleaned over time about her mother, who by reputation had been a generous benefactress, a kind mistress, and a woman who enjoyed a truly loving relationship with her husband.

"My father did not often speak about my mother, and Fitzwilliam still finds it too painful, I believe."

"Yes, well—" Lady Matlock swung her feet to the floor, her expression determined "—now you must tell me what you think is ailing our poor Mary, for she is not usually one to be so glum."

Georgiana hesitated briefly before confiding in her aunt. She told her about Major Ashton's unusual proposal of marriage, Mary's initial reaction to it, and her reaction to his escorting Miss Bingley everywhere.

Lady Matlock listened patiently to the end of Georgiana's tale. "I am afraid we must wait to see what happens, just as Mary has forced us to do with her charming heroines—at least until such time as we deem it imperative to interfere."

Georgiana showed her agreement with a silent nod before going off to practice her most recently-acquired works for the pianoforte.

A few minutes after Georgiana left, Colonel Fitzwilliam responded to his mother's summons, and the two of them were in conference for nearly an hour.

Afterwards, Lady Matlock was busy writing invitations to a dinner to be held in two days' time.

~~~

Two days later, Molly insisted upon taking extra care with Mary's hair and choosing the prettiest of her new gowns.

Mary was thoughtful as she descended the stairs alongside Georgiana, whose maid had also taken special pains. "What has your aunt planned for this evening, I wonder? She has been uncharacteristically secretive."

Georgiana took Mary's arm. "All she would tell me is she has arranged an intimate dinner with friends."

When Georgiana and Mary entered the softly-lit anteroom adjacent to the dining room, Mary's eyes settled first upon Major Ashton, deep in discussion with Colonel Fitzwilliam, while Miss Bingley stood near the window, the flowing lines of her fine muslin gown emphasizing her delicate figure. Next to her was an elegant lady with shining chestnut curls whom Mary had not yet met (she was later introduced as Miss Grantly, a great friend of Miss Bingley's). Four gentlemen Mary knew from her time at Devonham were also there: Mr. Chandler, Lord Exeter, Lord Harold, and surprisingly, Mr. Clay.

Mr. Chandler approached them with a smile. "Miss Darcy! I was so pleased to get your aunt's kind invitation. And Miss

Bennet—how nice to see you again." He bowed smartly.

Georgiana greeted him politely, though she did not seem particularly excited to see him again. Mary was disappointed, for he was the very gentleman she thought would make her friend a fine companion, as well as a good father to her children.

Mr. Chandler turned to Mary. "Miss Bennet, I was at Hatchard's earlier, and picked up your latest novel—might I impose upon you at some point to sign the volume on my behalf?"

Mary, wondering exactly how the secret of her identity was becoming known outside her family and close friends, felt telltale color rising in her face. "Of course, Mr. Chandler. I would be honored."

Lady Matlock floated by and said, "My dears, it is so good to see you getting re-acquainted." She smiled upon Georgiana and Mr. Chandler, leaving Mary with the distinct impression that the assembled guests had been invited with definite purpose. She happened to see a knowing glance pass between Georgiana's aunt and Colonel Fitzwilliam at the same moment dinner was announced. Not sure what Lady Matlock and her son were about, but fairly certain the evening would be an interesting one, Mary accepted Mr. Chandler's arm for the procession into the dining room.

At the table, Mary was seated between Mr. Chandler and Lord Exeter (an inveterate gossip). Major Ashton was seated directly across from her, between Miss Grantly and Miss Bingley. He spoke with ease to each of them, appearing to enjoy himself immensely, while Mary made a special effort to be equally charming to her own dinner partners. When she glanced across to see if the major had noticed, she saw Mr. Clay deep in conversation with Miss Grantly, making her wonder if theirs was an acquaintanceship of long standing. As one course led to another, Mary tried to overhear what Miss Grantly was saying while at the same time respond with some sense to Mr. Chandler, who wished to discuss a play they had all seen the previous evening.

When Mary turned back to Lord Exeter, he began to make pointed references to certain books, seeming annoyed to have found they had been written, incredibly, by a woman. "Do you know of any such authoresses, Miss Bennet? Any perhaps who go by the overused pseudonym of 'a lady'?" At his question, she nearly stabbed his hand with her fork.

By the time their hostess rose and the ladies proceeded to the sitting room to while away the time until the gentlemen joined them, Mary was exhausted and wished only for the comfort and relief of her bed.

Lady Matlock suggested music, and Georgiana politely asked Miss Bingley if she would care to play. Remarkably, Miss Bingley demurred, suggesting Miss Grantly perform first— "for she has great facility at the keyboard and a highly-trained voice."

The ladies listened politely, and with pleasure, as Miss Grantly performed various arias with great artistry until the gentlemen joined them nearly a half-hour later. At that point Miss Bingley rose, and Miss Grantly cleverly brought the song to an end. Claiming the need for a rest, she exchanged places with Miss Bingley, who played with great skill and impressive speed.

Mary thought Miss Bingley's demeanor was more like a young lady newly out than that of a woman who had recently attempted to elope with an infamous traitor. She watched Major Ashton from behind her fan as he listened to Miss Bingley's performance with what appeared to be rapt attention.

When Miss Bingley relinquished the instrument to Georgiana, who chose to play country dances, Major Ashton passed by Mary, happening to speak just loudly enough for her to hear him say that he would be calling at Darcy House fairly early the following morning to meet with Colonel Fitzwilliam. She could not stop herself from looking up at him, and for the briefest of seconds caught sight of a familiar, welcome expression in his eyes. But Miss Bingley's sudden appearance at his side brought the return of his sardonic attitude, giving Mary good reason to wonder if her imagination had gotten the better of her.

Later, when the guests had all gone, Georgiana took Mary by the arm as they ascended the staircase. "Do you not think tonight's dinner was meant to disclose the person who orchestrated Miss

Bingley's elopement? Why else would my aunt and cousin gather these particular acquaintances together? Perhaps my cousin suspects the elopement was facilitated by the same person who helped Mr. Petersham escape from New Prison...." She peered at Mary, daring to add, "The major is to call early tomorrow—he will be here before Caroline arises from her own bed, and I think it is all in the hopes of seeing *you!*"

Mary did not relent. "The major can do what he likes; his actions do not affect me in any way. However, if there should arise an opportunity for private conversation between us, it will allow me to inform him of my decision to release him from any promise he feels he might have made to me."

Georgiana hugged her friend impulsively. "Oh, Mary!"

CHAPTER TWENTY-THREE

Mary woke early the next morning, her goal being to write an entire chapter of her new book before breakfast. Unfortunately, Major Ashton's proposed visit dominated her thoughts, and she found herself staring out the window more often than not. Before she managed to complete even a single paragraph, it was time to dress.

"Major Ashton came really early this morning," Molly said conversationally as she wound Mary's hair and pinned it into a flattering, modified chignon. She then went to the wardrobe and chose a morning gown, but Mary shook her head, claiming it was too fine. Molly did not argue as she normally would, but simply chose another. "He's meeting with the colonel right now." She leaned forward eagerly. "All the servants are talking about Miss Bingley. They say—" she looked around as if someone might overhear "—and you know I wouldn't repeat this to anyone but you and Lucy, miss, but they say she almost ran off with him!"

"With whom, do they say?"

Molly looked at Mary as if she had two heads. "Mr. Petersham, of course!"

"But she clearly did not run off with him," Mary said reasonably as she put on an ear-ring. "You should know better than to listen to gossip."

"Yes, miss." Molly looked deflated as she handed over the next piece of jewelry. "Do you think you'll be seeing Major Ashton today?"

Mary struggled with the second ear-ring. "I do not care one whit whether Major Ashton stays or goes, Molly. It is my first—

perhaps best—inclination to refuse to see him ever again."

"But he is so handsome and tall, miss, and you seemed to like him when we he visited at Longbourn—"

"—Major Ashton has done nothing but cater to the whims of Miss Caroline Bingley since leaving Hertfordshire, and as he appears to enjoy doing so, there is no reason for me to see him."

"Yes, miss," Molly replied, though she looked doubtful.

"But...given his propensity towards not hearing anything but what he chooses to, I *will* see him this morning, if only to tell him he need not concern himself with me any longer." Mary returned to her desk, sat, and dipped her pen in the ink bottle. "And Molly, should I spill ink on this dress, I will *not* change for him."

"Yes, miss." Molly hid her smile. "I will come back soon." She saw the look on Mary's face and hurried to add, "With a breakfast tray, and to remove the ink spot on your cheek."

Mary completed a sentence with a flourish before looking up, ready to assure her maid there was no need to remove ink from her face as it was only Major Ashton calling, but Molly had already gone.

An hour later, Molly came to remove the breakfast tray. "The countess has made me promise to put you in your finest morning gown, miss. She is expecting a special caller soon."

"Do you know the identity of this special caller?" Mary set her pen aside and blew on the manuscript page while Molly opened the wardrobe and took out the gown she had chosen earlier.

"I think it's Lady Castlereagh," she said, helping Mary into the dress.

"So early in the day?" Mary held her arm up while Molly fastened the line of tiny covered buttons at the bottom of the sleeve. "I would have thought she never rose from her bed until mid-afternoon, given her duties at Almack's."

"They say she's coming with Lord Castlereagh, who wants to talk to Lord Matlock—one of the footmen said that messages were going back and forth all night," Molly said as she began working on the other sleeve.

"I did not know Lord Matlock would be joining us so soon,"

Mary mused with a frown. "Why is he arriving so early in the day, I wonder?"

Molly shrugged—the doings of the aristocracy a complete mystery to her. "Maybe he missed his wife," she suggested.

Mary smiled at that. "In the case of most people in society, I would not hesitate to scoff at such a suggestion, but with Lord and Lady Matlock, it is possible."

"There, miss—" Molly repinned a strand of Mary's hair, patting it down "—you look like a princess."

Mary stood in front of the long mirror, tipping her head back and forth before turning around to view the back of the gown that had only just come from the modiste the day before. "Well, if I must see Major Ashton, perhaps it is just as well for me to be looking my best."

Molly hid her expression while busily straightening things on the dressing table.

Since coming to Darcy House, Lady Matlock met callers she considered friends in Elizabeth's morning room. When Mary entered, she was surprised to find only the countess and the major, who bowed and greeted her formally, his eyes searching hers until she was forced to look away.

"Major Ashton." Mary responded in kind with a tilt of her head, determined to maintain the upper hand in the forthcoming conversation. She then turned to the countess, about to ask after Georgiana, whom she had not yet seen that morning.

There was a light knock at the door and Lady Matlock's maid appeared, passing her a note on a silver tray. "Oh dear," the countess said, folding and pocketing the paper. "I must see Mrs. Babcock regarding dinner this evening, as she is unaware of the earl's intense dislike of mutton." With barely a glance in their direction, she left Mary and the major alone in the room (leaving the door slightly ajar).

Despite her assertions the previous evening, Mary was not mentally prepared for a private interview with the major. Momentarily disconcerted, she moved to the window to look at the gates to Hyde Park.

"Miss Bennet." The major had moved close, startling her, but she refused to show any sign of discomfiture and remained stationary, her eyes glued to a pretty, well-dressed nursemaid holding the hands of two little children as they passed through the gates of the park. "Miss Bennet—" Major Ashton's voice held a trace of amusement "—are you determined never to speak to me?"

Mary finally turned to face him, her hand accidentally brushing his, and blushed furiously, turning away again. "Major Ashton, before Lady Matlock returns, there is something I would like to say to you."

"You want to release me from my proposal of marriage given to you on the nineteenth of December, do you not?" The major's voice held a hint of humor, and something else Mary could not define.

She looked up at him warily, assuming he was mocking her. "Yes, major, that is exactly what I wish to do."

"May I ask why?" He was now uncomfortably close to her and she backed away, her hands gripping a chair.

"You may ask, Major Ashton, but I may not answer." She unconsciously imitated Elizabeth.

The major laughed. "I can only guess it is due to my inexplicable attentions to someone with whom you are well acquainted, a lady determined to run off with one of the world's greatest scoundrels without a thought about the consequences to her family and friends."

Mary looked at the floor, the ceiling, and the paintings on the wall opposite, her lips stubbornly closed.

"You do not have to answer, Miss Bennet, for I have long observed your different moods and if I were a betting man— which I am not," he hastened to assure her, "I would say you find my attentions to a certain 'Miss B' vexing."

She turned her head slightly. "Vexing?"

He shrugged. "For lack of better word, yes. Vexing."

Mary turned her back to him. "One never knows when you are being serious, Major Ashton."

"I am being serious right now, Miss Bennet." He took hold of her hand to turn her around, his grip growing tighter as she tried to pull it away. "If your feelings are of disappointment or anger, I cannot blame you, for I have only just learned that you have not been made aware of the details of Lord Castlereagh's plan to get much-needed information from the lady in question." He gazed into her eyes, and she forgot to try to pull her hand away. "If there is no other reason for your feelings of dissatisfaction regarding my proposal—and I did say I was a patient man—then I can assure you that my wishes are *exactly* the same as they were in December." He leaned down, his lips shockingly close to her own, at which point Mary successfully retrieved her hand and managed to back away without tripping over a side table.

"Major Ashton—" Mary began her prepared speech "—you have not addressed me in a civil manner since I came to London; you looked directly at me with no sign of recognition the first time I ever attended a function at Almack's; you simper and cater to *Miss B* in front of everyone—what was I supposed to think?" Mary realized her voice was rising, and she took a breath, adding in controlled tones, "I claim no hold on you; you may see *whom*ever and do *what*ever you like. But as we had not spoken since you left Hertfordshire to 'rescue' Miss B from her own folly, I do not know why you would assume, given your...proposal...that I would not be in some way affected by your actions." She turned to face him, a challenge in her eyes.

"You are absolutely right, and I apologize for assuming you had been told. Had I but known otherwise, I would have demanded to speak with you sooner. Thankfully, the countess confided in me, having only just learned about my proposal to you—which you are free to announce to anyone you wish. Since you apparently confided only in Miss Darcy, no one else was aware that my attentions to another might cause you pain, or give you reason to question my sense of honour."

"I would hardly say it caused me pain." Mary immediately regretted her petulance and asked, unable to prevent an element of wistfulness, "Must you continue this charade?"

"I have spoken with Colonel Fitzwilliam about being released from this assignment."

"And what did he say?" Mary did not like to admit even to herself that she was holding her breath.

The major did not answer immediately, for he was observing a carriage as it came to a standstill in front of the house, Mary wishing she could remove the furrow from his brow. "The earl has arrived," he said quietly, turning back to face her. "We have no more time, Miss Bennet. I only ask you to have patience—the colonel believes we are close to the conclusion of this unpleasant business. If you will but consider the reasons for my seeming indifference—" he stopped as they heard the countess greet the earl in the foyer. Without another word, he bowed and left the room, Mary standing stock still with a singular feeling of disappointment.

The countess entered before Mary could make her own exit, holding tight to the earl's arm, her smile brilliant. "Miss Bennet! Lord Matlock has finally joined us." She looked about the room with wide eyes. "I thought Georgiana would have been here by now."

In the days following, Mary was relieved to have little time to ponder the wishes and actions of Major Ashton, or her own feelings about him, for she and Georgiana were thrown into a veritable whirlpool of activity. Along with the earl and countess, and often in the company of the Gardiners, they visited Vauxhall Gardens, went to balls, routs, the opera, the theatre, and Venetian breakfasts. They attended a presentation at the Royal Academy of Arts, and the performance of an entire oratorio by Handel. They took walks and rode in an open carriage through Hyde Park, returned calls, made new acquaintances, visited dressmakers as well as purveyors of hats, gloves, stockings, and dancing slippers. During the course of events, they met many gentlemen who came to call the following day as society dictated, but none could catch the particular attention of either young lady.

"We have been out every day and every evening for nearly a sennight." Mary pulled off her gloves late one evening after they had returned from the opera. "I have not written a single word in all that time."

"But you have enjoyed yourself, have you not?" Georgiana looked anxious.

"Every moment," Mary hastened to assure her. "Especially the performance tonight—we can now add *The Magic Flute* to the list of operas we have seen this season, and what a treat it was!"

"Major Ashton appeared to enjoy it."

Mary removed her cloak and handed it to the waiting maid. "It is a wonder he could hear anything over Miss Bingley's chatter—I happened to see her through my glasses. The only time she was silent was during the Queen of the Night's second aria."

Georgiana smiled. "I noticed the major focusing his glasses on you once or twice. It was indeed a pleasant evening, but I am so tired I can hardly keep my eyes open."

The next day Miss Bingley and Miss Grantly called just as Georgiana and Mary were about to leave to visit the Gardiners at their home in Cheapside. Georgiana politely invited them to come along, though both she and Mary were a little disconcerted when their callers accepted.

At the Gardiners home they were treated to a short recitation by each of the four children, Miss Bingley proclaiming them to be angels (albeit through slightly clenched teeth).

Miss Grantly was extremely well-versed in many topics and entertained Mr. Gardiner with tales of the salons she frequented, often hosted by literary women. Mary listened to their exchange, wondering what such a maverick among her sex could possibly see in Miss Bingley. During the course of the conversation, Miss Grantly admitted her friendship with Miss Bingley was in actuality not of long duration, the two of them having become acquainted around the time of Miss Bingley's engagement to Mr. Petersham.

Mary later told this to Georgiana, who did not hesitate to share the information with Colonel Fitzwilliam.

After sternly warning his younger cousin not to get involved in any way, he admitted the information might be useful to the current investigation. "Good work, Georgiana," he added, pleasing her no end.

The next afternoon, Georgiana convinced Mary to venture inside Hyde Park despite the unpredictable April weather; it began to rain soon after they passed through the gates.

Georgiana, bent upon a private interview with Mary, did not seem to notice the inclement weather, but continued along the stone path far into the park. She need not have worried about privacy, for they appeared to be the sole visitors.

Still, Georgiana looked around to make sure she would not be overheard before announcing in careful tones, "Mary, I spoke briefly with Lord Jameson last evening at the assembly."

Mary was holding her umbrella so low to her head that she had to lift it to see Georgiana's eyes. "You did? Why did you not tell me sooner? Did he seem happy?" She was surprised to feel only curiosity.

Georgiana looked at her intently. "I did not think you would take the news so calmly, to be honest. Last night I did not wish to affect your evening—it was a pleasant ball, was it not, and you seemed content while dancing." She thought for a moment. "The atmosphere at Almack's often lends itself to artificial, calculated behavior, but if I read Lord Jameson's eyes and expression correctly, then no, I do not believe he is a happy man."

Suddenly, in a fierce gust of wind, Mary's umbrella turned inside out. Molly rushed forward and held it against the wind to right it (although both she and her mistress knew it would no longer be the pretty, functional thing it once was), before running back to stand with Lucy, sheltering under a large tree.

Georgiana added, her eyes on the maids, "He asked after you."

Mary's brows shot up as she tried to adjust one of the stretchers while still holding the umbrella above her head. "Surely, after all that happened, and with his new responsibilities, he does not still think of me?"

Georgiana shrugged. "It appears he does, but bears it like a gentleman, I am sure. But after what happened...I was concerned for you."

Mary rested her hand briefly on Georgiana's arm. "Thank you, but over time it seems reason has won over emotion. I never did feel like beating my hands against his chest as Miss White did in one of Lady Catherine's scenes, but I will admit to a few tears." She shook her head. "I could not have cared so very much for Captain Jameson if only months later I agreed to consider another's proposal. Even if *that* gentleman proved in the end to be a...I cannot think of an appropriate term."

Georgiana could not hold back her laughter. "I would not have chosen those exact words, Mary, but I believe I comprehend your meaning."

Another gust of wind brought the complete ruination of Mary's umbrella, and the rain dripped freely on her person. "Georgiana, I appreciate your wanting complete privacy for this conversation, but truly, I no longer harbor romantic feelings for Lord Jameson." She gestured towards their miserable maids and the footmen behind them. "Might we go in now?"

Georgiana nodded briskly, turning neatly on her heels—much to the relief of all the others.

~∪∿∪⌒

While Mary and Georgiana were outside in the rain, Colonel Fitzwilliam and Major Ashton were warm and dry, tucked inside a coffee house on King Street, near the offices of Lord Castlereagh.

Major Ashton sipped his coffee with care and set the cup down with a bang. "Why do they have to make it so hot?"

Colonel Fitzwilliam looked up from his fish pie, observing flatly, "You are unhappy with Castlereagh's decision about your continued close surveillance of a certain lady."

Major Ashton frowned across the small, round table. "You can complain all you want about following that reprobate Mr. Clay about, but you are not the one who has to escort said *lady* everywhere and anywhere—to the theatre, to the garden, to the opera, to the shops—it is exhausting, absolutely exhausting." He leaned back, tipping his chair against the brick wall. "It is time you took a turn."

Colonel Fitzwilliam shook his head. "I am sorry, Ashton, but what can I do? She prefers you. Besides, she has known me far too long and would no doubt suspect my motives."

The major set his chair back down and tried his coffee once more, this time without complaint. "I get the feeling the lady in question is not at all pleased with me of late. This cannot go on much longer."

"Five days is what he asked—only five days more. Then you

can attend to the other Miss B." Colonel Fitzwilliam grinned across the table. "I'm not blind, you know."

The major leaned forward to ask quietly, "Do you think Charles' sister suspects my feelings for the other Miss B?"

The colonel took the last bite of pie, shaking his head. "You fooled our little authoress, so I think you are safe there." He wiped his mouth, setting the napkin on the table as he looked around the crowded room. "Do you sometimes wonder if Miss B knows anything at all of use?"

"She is a female viper. Who can tell what she is about?"

The colonel reached inside his pocket and laid several coins on the table. "Well, what is on the program this evening?"

The major rolled his eyes, standing. "Almack's."

"Five more days, my friend!" Colonel Fitzwilliam laughed as he led the way through the throng and out into the rain.

In the meantime, a sodden Georgiana and Mary entered Darcy House, where the countess ordered hot baths for them and their maids, shaking her head in pure frustration as they went up the stairs.

Later, a thoroughly-warmed Molly took extra care with Mary's coiffure and dress, for the young ladies were to attend yet another assembly at Almack's. "You know—I think the major is only pretending to like Miss Bingley." Molly stuck a few pins in her mouth and held the first of Mary's curls up. "Sheeze nugh thu kie—"

"Molly—" Mary interrupted the young maid "—it is impossible to understand you with pins in your mouth."

Molly removed the pins, set them within reach on the dressing table, and repeated, "She's not the kind who'd attract him. I'm sure of it." She stuck the pin in and lightly patted the curl to see if it was secure. "It's you he likes, mark my words." Mary said nothing about her recent conversation with the major, content to listen to her maid talk about the poor servants under Caroline Bingley's thumb.

Molly put her hands on her hips. "If he doesn't prefer you to that persnickety Miss Bingley, there must be something wrong with him!"

CHAPTER TWENTY-FOUR

(An Entry in Mary Bennet's Diary)

Darcy House, 23 April 1814

Molly told me only today that her mother was at one time a seamstress for society ladies, and now she wishes to use the skills her mother taught her by trying her hand at a frock for me. I begin to think her talents are wasted in service. She is a fast learner, and in only a few lessons progressed far beyond primers. She is now reading my book aloud to Lucy. Thankfully, the income from my novels is sufficient for a rise in her wages.

Lady Matlock is inviting a number of Miss Bingley's friends to a card party (those in town at the time of the elopement) in the hopes that Mr. P's confederate might sooner be discovered. Surprisingly, Colonel Fitzwilliam has agreed to her plan, but has warned us all not to say a word, appear too curious, or act in any way unusual. With so many instructions as to what not to do, I am certain to err in one way or another.

Elizabeth wrote to ask if Georgiana is enjoying her season, and if she has met any gentlemen worthy of her. G has been introduced to several who stood up well to initial scrutiny, a few even passing muster after Colonel Fitzwilliam had them investigated. But all the while she is dancing with earls, lords, viscounts, and one foreign prince, her eyes are seeking Lord Harold, even though he treats her as he would an affectionate puppy. I do not think this season will end in marriage for her. She has gone so far as to say she would prefer to be married to a simple country squire than have to continue to laugh at poorly-executed jokes, tolerate her toes being trodden upon, and staying up until the wee hours each night—only to repeat the process the following evening.

For my part, I am learning much about societal rules (Lady Catherine was actually correct in changing a few of my descriptions). One small misstep could mean being turned away from Almack's, or lead to a cut direct by acquaintances, or never again being invited to salons and various entertainments. One certainly cannot wear the same gown twice, though it is a shameful waste. Molly tells me there are small children living in the streets of London who have neither sufficient clothing nor food. I have spoken to Georgiana about this, and we are determined to find a way to help them.

I have not heard from Mr. Egerton about The Wine Cellar, *and begin to have little hope of its publication. Lady Catherine will not be pleased.*

CHAPTER TWENTY-FIVE

*(A Letter from Lady Catherine de Bourgh
to Fitzwilliam Darcy)*

Rosings, 23 April 1814

Dear Nephew,

I write with good news. Your cousin Anne has won the affections of a noble, amiable gentleman, and has consented to be his wife (I believe you have met Lord Wickford on previous visits to Rosings). Our solicitors are drawing up the settlement, and the marriage will take place at Rosings, though I have not yet decided upon the date. The weather must be perfect for Anne's delicate health.

Anne and I must soon go to London to arrange for her wedding clothes, and since your house is open we will stay there (it would be a waste to open my own for so short a time). While at Darcy House I will undertake the chaperonage of Georgiana, despite my responsibilities to Anne, and will see to it my niece dances only with those gentlemen worthy of our family.

Mr. Collins tells me Miss Mary Bennet continues at Darcy House, and apparently goes everywhere with Georgiana. I need not remind you that she has not the education or experience of Anne, and therefore cannot be considered as suitable a companion as is her cousin, who will of course attend the events of the season as long as they are not too taxing on her health. This will allow Miss Bennet more time for her writing, which I intend to oversee while I am in town. I will *also supervise the running of the house, for my sister is far too lax with servants in general.*

Your aunt,
Lady Catherine de Bourgh

CHAPTER TWENTY-SIX

"Lizzy?" Mr. Darcy opened the door to his wife's morning room and found her seated at her desk, pen in hand. However, she was not writing a letter but staring out the window, lost in thought.

He cleared his throat and Elizabeth blinked, turning towards him with a welcoming smile as he approached. "I am trying to think what to write Mamma—she has once more put off the journey to Derbyshire."

Mr. Darcy stopped behind her chair to kiss her uplifted cheek. "Does she still think Mr. Collins and his wife will take up residence at Longbourn while she and your father are away? I recently asked the solicitor to write to her and allay her fears."

Elizabeth rested the pen in the silver stand Mr. Darcy had given to her for their seven-month anniversary. "If this continues, she will never see Pemberley or Beechwood Manor."

"I will write to your father after your required luncheon, my dear. In the meantime, we can devise something which will entice your mother to come."

Elizabeth accepted her husband's hand to help her from the chair, for the baby seemed to grow exponentially each day and her balance was not what it once was. "We must not say anything to alarm her."

A slight smile played about Mr. Darcy's lips. "We could tell her the nursery at Pemberley is in a shambles and we are in desperate need of her help."

Elizabeth tipped her head, considering. "She does enjoy giving advice, but I have just had the room repainted for the second time, and chose new fabric for the curtains only yesterday."

Mr. Darcy looked up at the vaulted ceiling of the long hall and sighed. "Sometimes we are called upon to make sacrifices, my dear." They entered the dining room and took their seats at the table for the mid-day meal they had been taking since returning to Pemberley per the midwife's orders.

When alone, Elizabeth and Mr. Darcy preferred their meals to be informal, with covered dishes set on the table so they could serve themselves. "I do hope Mamma is correct about this baby being a boy, for my appetite is a bit alarming." Elizabeth spooned fricassee onto their two plates. If I am carrying a girl, I fear she will not be the delicate flower of my dreams." Her words caused Mr. Darcy to cough and set his glass down abruptly.

Shortly after the luncheon dishes were removed and the dessert served, a footman brought a letter.

"Thank you, Thomas." Mr. Darcy set the envelope on the table.

Elizabeth took a spoonful of custard. "Do you not wish to open your letter, Fitzwilliam?"

"It is from Aunt Catherine. I thought—if only for the sake of our respective digestions—I should wait until we have finished."

Elizabeth continued to look at the neatly-folded paper with the embossed seal, the spoon forgotten in her hand. "Perhaps she has news? Georgiana and Mary were certain Anne was going to receive an offer of marriage soon after they left Rosings."

"My Cousin Anne becoming engaged would be news indeed, but there is always something about my aunt's letters which makes them better read away from the table."

Elizabeth took another bite. "I have never been overly fond of custard, Mr. Darcy, but Chef Renault makes it differently than what we had at Longbourn." She looked at the shiny, lightly-browned surface. "I think we should serve this when Mamma is here." She then set her spoon down, eyeing her husband's dish. "We appear to be finished, my dear—why not read your letter now?"

Mr. Darcy sighed, broke the embossed seal, and read the letter aloud.

Elizabeth listened to the end (it was a very long letter) without interrupting, and after delicately touching her napkin to the corners of her mouth. "Darcy House will no longer be a pleasant place of refuge for its inhabitants." Her eyes sparkled with mischief. "Perhaps we should ask Georgiana to cut her season short and return to Pemberley—bringing Mary with her. With three of her four daughters in Derbyshire, as well as her only grandchild and another on the way, how could Mamma possibly put off the dread journey any longer? "

Mr. Darcy slowly re-folded his aunt's letter. "Georgiana has been in London only a few weeks, Elizabeth. If we ask her to leave now, it will effectively end all chances of her marrying this year."

Elizabeth looked across the table with loving eyes at her husband. "Had you taken full advantage of any season, my dear, it is sadly possible we would never have met." She raised a single brow and waited.

Mr. Darcy's expression softened. "I did not like to force her to go to London, you know."

"We need not decide anything right now, but I am certain our sisters would like to be back in Derbyshire as soon as Jane and Charles are settled at Beechwood Manor. I must confess to missing dear little Eliza nearly as much as I do Jane."

Mr. Darcy looked through the window at the tower of water rising from the fountain. "Perhaps it would not be so bad if this first season came to an end. Richard tells me Georgiana is forever surrounded by coxcombs and rattlepates at the assemblies—thank heaven he and Lord Harold are there to prevent them from bothering her unduly." He thought for a moment. "I will wait until Aunt Catherine and Anne are in London before writing to Georgiana." Moving to Elizabeth's side of the table, he held out his hand. "You do realize, as Aunt Catherine and Cousin Anne will be guests at Darcy House, we should include them in the invitation to come here."

Elizabeth's eyes danced merrily. "Pemberley is quite large."

"Yes...but is it large enough?"

CHAPTER TWENTY-SEVEN

Darcy House, 25 April 1814

The cards of acceptance or regret for Lady Matlock's party had all arrived, and the countess, Georgiana, and Mary were standing over a large table in the library, laying the cards in sets of four to determine the most effective seating arrangement.

"Where shall we put Lord Exeter?" Georgiana picked up his card. "You seemed to be a favorite of his when we were at Devonham, Mary. Perhaps we should put him at your table."

Mary harrumphed. "His interest in gossip is second only to that of Mr. Collins. No—I fear Lord Exeter will find my company unsatisfactory, for I never have anything of interest to say about anybody." She thought for a moment. "He may enjoy Miss Bingley, however."

"They would make a fine couple." Georgiana set his card down next to Miss Bingley's, circling the large table to scan the cards once more. "I do not see Lord Harold here."

Lady Matlock was holding a lorgnette in one hand and Mrs. Babcock's final bill of fare for the party in the other. "He has not sent his regrets, my dear, but I expect he will simply appear, as is his habit." She pointed the ivory handle at the list. "Do you think we need two soups?"

"It would be unwise to argue with Mrs. Babcock about the supper. Elizabeth lives in fear that we will do something to cause her to give notice," warned Georgiana.

"Very well—two soups." Lady Matlock sighed and set the sheet down, picking up the guest list to re-tally the number. "When your Aunt Catherine comes, we must make sure she does not interfere with the kitchen." She looked up. "We will have enough young couples to merit a dance."

"Cards will allow for more conversation generally—between games, of course," Georgiana said, moving Miss Grantly's card to Colonel Fitzwilliam's table and Mr. Chandler's card to the earl's. "Not that Mary and I intend to do anything other than quietly observe, but should we overhear Mr. Clay refer to Miss Bingley's thwarted elopement, for example—"

"Georgiana!" The countess frowned at her niece. "Richard only agreed to this plan as long as we promised to do nothing whatsoever to interfere, or bring attention upon ourselves." She took Mr. Clay's card and put it at her own table. "You two have found yourselves in enough precarious situations."

Georgiana looked abashed. "If I should happen to overhear something interesting, I promise to do nothing other than report it immediately to my cousin." She looked across the table at Mary.

Never absolutely sure what her friend was planning, Mary said what she thought Georgiana wished her to say. "We have learned our lesson, Lady Matlock, and will leave the espionage to those in the service of His Majesty."

Lady Matlock did not seem convinced, but said no more on the subject as she circled the table once again.

～ᴗᴗ～

On the evening of the card party, Lady Matlock, dressed in a stunning gown of deep green with perfectly-matched emeralds, checked to see that the felt-covered tables were well situated in the drawing room. Satisfied, she then entered the dining room, which was set for the supper with sparkling crystal, the finest silver and china, and several ornate candelabras. Music from the small orchestra in the anteroom wafted through the hall as she went to meet the earl before their guests arrived.

"Ready, my dear?" the earl asked.

The countess smiled, clearly pleased with the preparations. "All is laid ready."

"This plan of yours and Richard's had better bear fruit—I am tired of this business with Petersham. As soon as it is settled, we will return to Devonham."

Lady Matlock patted her husband's arm. "It will all end soon, I am sure. But we cannot leave too soon, for it would shorten Georgiana's season unnecessarily."

"Has she met anyone other than puppies and hobbledehoys in all this time?" the earl demanded.

"She is not at all interested in those few who have passed muster with your son," the countess began thoughtfully, "but I have a feeling—" She could not finish, however, for just then the Burnabys were announced.

As soon as she had greeted her hosts, Deidre Burnaby rushed across the room to tell Georgiana and Mary about her recent presentation at court, giggling all the while, admitting she had nearly tripped on the unwieldy skirt of her gown as she backed away from the queen. "We waited in the carriage for hours, until I thought I should faint from hunger! And once inside, my headdress kept slipping—I was sure the feathers would fall over my eyes, and I felt about to sneeze the entire time!"

While she continued the tale, Mr. Chandler was announced. When at Devonham, Mary was convinced he and Georgiana would make a perfect couple, if only Georgiana could see it. But now, as Mary observed their greeting, she saw nothing to indicate they were anything other than friendly.

On the other hand, when Lord Harold arrived (without having sent his acceptance), Georgiana's smile brightened, and her responses to his teasing remarks were playful. Lord Harold was admittedly handsome—dangerously so—and because he was working closely with Colonel Fitzwilliam and Major Ashton to uncover a spy network (possibly acting as a spy himself, adding even more to his attractions), Mary thought it no wonder Georgiana seemed smitten. There was the slight problem of his being disinherited by an uncle who thought him a debauched wastrel. But even if it were true, his faults were as nothing when compared to those of Mr. Petersham, with whom Georgiana once believed herself in love.

Mary moved away, planning to walk about idly so she could overlisten the conversation of others. Most of the guests had been at Devonham during the time of trouble with Mr. Petersham, and unexpectedly, the sight of them all together again brought a rush of nerves. For an instant Mary was back in the wine cellar; she could feel the cold of the stone floor, and could almost taste the odious, perfumed cravat used to bind her mouth.

Mrs. Pierce was nearest to her. "Are you feeling unwell, Miss Bennet?"

Mary shook her head, primarily to clear her thoughts, and turned to the Pierces, smiling. "I was just thinking of Devonham, to be honest, for the party seems to be reunited this evening." Mary searched her memory for something to say. "Remember the ungainly footmen? Did not one spill soup on Miss Pierce's gown?"

"Thank goodness it was cold soup, Miss Bennet, or my daughter could have been burned." Mrs. Pierce leaned forward to add in a soft voice, "I noticed many of the servants were accident-prone during that house party; I sincerely hope they have since been dismissed."

Mary did not respond, knowing full well those particularly clumsy "servants" were no longer at Devonham. She turned to Miss Pierce. "I hope your gown did not suffer too much damage?"

Miss Pierce, giggly and over-loud when in the company of the Miss Webbs (favorites of Lady Catherine, not yet in town), seemed almost shy without them. "My mother's maid was able to remove the stain, Miss Bennet. Thank you for your concern."

"My daughter's maid does not have the same talent with removing stains as my own," Mrs. Pierce hastened to assure Mary, who wondered why she felt the need to say so.

Just then Miss Bingley entered, her face upturned to better display the graceful line of her neck as she laughed lightly at something the major had said.

"I wonder if we will soon hear of an engagement," Mrs. Pierce half-whispered, her eyes on the newly-arrived couple.

Mary chose not to respond, fully aware that the most innocent looking members of society were often the most vicious gossips.

Mr. Chandler, ever the gentleman, joined them to ask Mr. and Mrs. Pierce's opinion about a play they had all recently seen. Mrs. Pierce changed positions with her daughter, and the poor young girl was forced to stammer out a response to Mr.

Chandler's inquiry while her eager mother looked on.

In the meantime, Mary looked over Miss Pierce's head to observe Colonel Fitzwilliam in conversation with Mr. Clay, but she could not tell if it was his gesticulations or his fondness for musk scent that caused the colonel to lean away from him.

Miss Bingley approached, her hand on the major's arm. "Ah, you are still here, Miss Bennet."

Mary looked up and caught Major Ashton's eyes briefly, thinking (or perhaps only hoping) she saw something like anger there, but in the next instant his face was like stone as the Pierces were introduced.

Mary excused herself on some conjured errand, but could not leave before witnessing Miss Bingley tap the major flirtatiously with the tip of her fan as she said, "There are others with whom I am not acquainted, Major Ashton. Perhaps you can introduce them to me before the games commence, so we need not incommode Miss Darcy?"

From her place by Mrs. Annesley, who insisted on keeping to the fringes at any social gathering, Mary watched the major introduce Miss Bingley to Lord Exeter, who had been conversing with the Burnabys, and for a moment the sound of Deidre Burnaby's excited laughter eclipsed the strains of music as she showed Miss Bingley her own scented ring.

As if there had been an announcement, attention was suddenly focused on the most recent addition to their party, Miss Grantly, whose superior beauty and grace were undeniable as she appeared to almost float into the room. Her silver muslin overlay enhanced her perfect figure, though Mary could have sworn the underdress had been dampened. Miss Grantly greeted the earl and countess in her usual charming manner before coming to Miss Bingley's side, whose greeting of her 'great friend' seemed less effusive than normal.

It was as if the whole room breathed a sigh of relief when Lady Matlock finally suggested they adjourn to the drawing room for cards. Lord Harold said he had another engagement and excused himself. Georgiana hid her disappointment before anyone (except Mary) saw it, and she joined good-naturedly in the search for the assigned seats.

When looking for her own card, the countess seemed at a loss and turned narrowed eyes on her son. The colonel's expression was one of innocence as he took a seat at the table his mother had meant to sit at herself.

Having witnessed this, Mary was not surprised to find herself seated at a table with Mrs. Burnaby, Mrs. Annesley, and Mr. Pierce, instead of the one with Mr. Clary and Miss Bingley as they had planned. None at Georgiana's table could be suspected of being Mr. Petersham's confederate either.

The countess quickly resumed her normal placid air, announced Long Whist as the game, and the guests dutifully began the play.

Mrs. Burnaby and Mr. Pierce won every hand but one over Mary and Mrs. Annesley, who took their defeat in stride as it was a fairly common occurrence. Mary was frustrated, overhearing nothing of seeming value throughout the evening, and breathed a silent sigh of relief when the players at each of the tables had finally reached nine points and supper was announced.

Before the party could proceed to the dining room, however, the butler appeared with a note for the colonel. Shortly afterwards, both he and Major Ashton excused themselves with the briefest possible explanation.

Lord Exeter gallantly offered his arm to escort Miss Bingley, who accepted with a brilliant smile.

At supper, after the salmon à la sage had been served, Lord Exeter leaned slightly to the side to whisper to Mary, "I know your secret, Miss Bennet."

Mary carefully lifted her fork and took a bite of the fish, fully aware of the amount of drink some of the gentlemen had consumed during the course of the evening. After a moment she responded coolly, "It is no secret if you have learned of it, Lord Exeter. To what do you refer?"

He lifted his eyebrows in a 'don't-you-wish' attitude, forcing Mary to choose between quizzing him further or changing the subject. Assuming the secret was about her being the anonymous authoress of The Turret Room, she chose the latter, and asked how he was enjoying the season. While half-listening to his response, Mary caught a glimpse of Miss Bingley's face, and felt certain she was looking at the source of Lord Exeter's information.

The colonel had not tampered with Lady Matlock's supper arrangements, and Mary found Mr. Clay seated to her left. During the next course (as part of her determination to learn more about his acquaintanceship with Miss Bingley), she feigned great interest in his tale about an incident he claimed to have witnessed.

"The Regent cut Brummell direct, Miss Bennet! But in the next moment, Brummell retaliated by asking the man next to him—" and thankfully, he lowered his voice at this point "—'who is your fat friend?'"

"You've got it all wrong, Clay!" Lord Exeter was eyeing Mr. Clay over the top of Mary's head. "It was not on the street the cut-direct occurred, but at a ball hosted by Brummell and his friends. Excuse me, Miss Bennet, but I could not bear to have such misinformation go uncontested. My sources are far more reliable, I assure you." His glance rested momentarily on Miss Bingley, whose attention he had successfully caught.

Mr. Clay snorted and took a great gulp of wine before turning to a confused-looking Miss Pierce on his other side. Mary could have kicked Lord Exeter, for it had been her last opportunity to speak with Mr. Clay, her chief suspect.

It was towards the end of the evening, when they were all taking tea in the drawing room (now free of card tables), that Mary spied Lord Exeter leading Miss Bingley towards a secluded corner of the room, steering her behind a large painted screen.

It was not acceptable behavior for an unmarried lady, but Miss Bingley had after all been twice engaged and twice disappointed. As far as Lord Exeter was concerned, Mary thought him a gossip monger, but had never seriously considered him to be Mr. Petersham's confederate, and had no reason to suspect he was party to the elopement. However, she had been wrong before, and vainly tried to catch Georgiana's attention. She had to be satisfied with covertly watching the others, noting how closely Mr. Clay and Miss Grantly sat together.

A short time later, just after Mrs. Burnaby set her cup down and declared it was time to take Deidre home, Miss Bingley reappeared, her eyes sparkling, clearly pleased as she departed with her hand on the arm of Lord Exeter.

Mary remained in a dark corner to watch the other guests depart, making special note when Miss Grantly left on the arm of Mr. Clay.

CHAPTER TWENTY-EIGHT

(A Letter from Charles Bingley to Fitzwilliam Darcy)

Netherfield, 26 April 1814

Dear Darcy,

The physician has approved travel for both Jane and little Eliza (who looks more and more like her beautiful mother each day), as long as we inch our way to Derbyshire. The journey will therefore take four days rather than two. I will send you a note when we depart, for the exact day seems to change each time we decide upon one. Perhaps having difficulty committing to travel is a Bennet trait, for our parents-in-law are still unsure when they will join us (Mr. Bennet now doubts they will leave Longbourn before the end of May).

My man of business recently told me of an exciting new invention in Northumberland, near Newcastle. It is called a 'steam locomotive'—a carriage that uses steam to move, not horses! The incredible machine hauls coal directly from the mine to the shipping port. I should like to see this myself, but for now must be satisfied with sending a representative. It may make for an excellent investment, especially if it can be used for transporting goods to my ships at the London Docks.

I look forward with great pleasure to our first game of billiards at Beechwood Manor. How grand it will be to finally have an estate of my own—do you remember when I first mentioned the idea to you, and we began the search? What a fortunate day it was for us all.

Yours sincerely,
Charles Bingley

CHAPTER TWENTY-NINE

Pemberley, 26 April 1814

"Fitzwilliam?" Elizabeth moved the newspaper away from her husband's face. "Will you come with me to look at the nursery? There is something wrong with the color—the walls seem to be a light yellow in the morning light, but turn an unpleasant shade of green in the afternoon!"

Mr. Darcy set his paper aside and stood up without complaint, although it was the third interruption that morning. "Now, my dear, tell me exactly what color you wish the walls to be." He took firm hold of Elizabeth's arm. "Allow me to assist you up the stairs, for you are not as...well-centered as on the day we first met," and was gratified to see the dimples appear in her cheeks.

"Before little Eliza was born, Jane was exceedingly grateful for her husband's arm, I assure you, just as I am for yours." At the top of the stairs Elizabeth leaned against him for a moment. "Though I do not remember her being so short of breath after only a bit of exercise."

In the nursery they found three workmen, each painting a separate wall in a different color. Mr. Darcy looked confused. "I thought you wished me to see a yellow wall?"

"It is the new color I wish you to approve. I could not bear the green in the afternoon—it reminded me too much of the walls of Charlotte and Mr. Collins' dining room."

"Of course." Mr. Darcy smiled and moved closer to one of the walls, pointing. "This is a pleasing color, is it not?"

Elizabeth stood back with a hand on her hip, nodding her head as she considered the paint. "There is something about it—

but do you not find it too bright?"

Mr. Darcy considered each of the walls before turning to his bride and future mother of his child. "I have an idea, Lizzy. Would you not like a miniature model of Pemberley just as Jane has for Beechwood Manor? You could change the walls in any number of rooms on a whim, rearrange miniature replicas of the furniture...."

"It would prevent me from taking the workmen away from the stable renovation." Though she feigned calm, Elizabeth's eyes were shining in anticipation of the gift.

Mr. Darcy offered his hand. "I believe we will find Mr. Greene in his office at this hour. You can tell him yourself exactly what you desire in the model—he knows a fine draftsman."

———

Longbourn, 26 April 1814

"Mr. Bennet! Mr. Bennet!" Mrs. Bennet's voice carried down the hall of Longbourn and through the heavy door of Mr. Bennet's study, where he was attempting to read his daughter's most recent book, The Count of Camalore, in private. With a rueful shake of his head, he carefully placed the book inside a drawer.

Mrs. Bennet entered the room without ceremony, waving a letter, the criss-crossed lines creating dark blotches on the paper. "Kitty has asked us to visit her in York, Mr. Bennet! What are we to do?"

Mr. Bennet removed his pince-nez and frowned. "I do not see a problem, my dear. Derbyshire is nearly halfway to York—an historic city with many interesting sites and buildings, according to your daughter. We could easily make the journey from Jane or Elizabeth's home, and I believe there would be some merit in seeing Kitty settled."

Mrs. Bennet sat down, her lips in a thin line. "Mr. Bennet, we will be away far too long as it is. Mrs. Long informed me only yesterday that Charlotte and Mr. Collins will be at Lucas Lodge on the very day we leave—does not their sudden appearance seem a bit coincidental to you?" She looked impatiently at her uncomprehending husband. "If we are not here to prevent it, they will take up residence at Longbourn!" She pulled out a handkerchief and covered her eyes. "Oh, what are we to do?"

Mr. Bennet spoke firmly. "Mrs. Bennet, I promise you: Mr. and Mrs. Collins will under no circumstances enter our home while we are absent from it."

"But how can we prevent them?" cried Mrs. Bennet.

"I will instruct Mr. Hill to refuse them entry, should the attempt be made—and I must say I think it highly unlikely. Mr. Collins may be my heir, but I am still very much alive, and I plan to remain so until I have seen each of my daughters bear many healthy babies. Now—do you feel better?" He took a sturdy handkerchief from his pocket and dabbed at his wife's eyes.

Mrs. Bennet sniffed. "You will have to stay alive for many, many more years if you choose to wait for Mary to have children." She pouted prettily. "Very well, we will go to York as well, but you must make Mr. Hill promise not to allow Charlotte or Mr. Collins inside this house!"

Mr. Bennet went to open the door. "I will make sure he fully comprehends your orders, my dear, and carries them out to the letter."

Mrs. Bennet's steps quickened. "See that you do, Mr. Bennet, for I have not the time. I must discuss tomorrow's dinner with Cook. It will be the last time we have Jane and Mr. Bingley at our table for some time."

Once she had gone, Mr. Bennet returned to his chair, replaced the pince-nez, and retrieved Mary's novel from the drawer, leaning back in his chair with a contented sigh.

~~~~~

Netherfield Hall, 26 April 1814
"Well, my dear, what have you been doing? You have been closeted with Mrs. Nicholls nearly all afternoon."

Jane lifted her cheek to receive Mr. Bingley's kiss and motioned for him to take a seat next to her. "We have been discussing what should be done at Netherfield before the next tenants arrive." She handed him several sheets of paper, which he viewed with wide eyes.

"Surely you do not think it necessary to have all of this

completed before we leave for Derbyshire?"

Jane smiled fondly at her husband. "Certainly not. Mrs. Nicholls and I agreed there will be plenty of time for everything to be completed after our departure, but before the new tenants arrive." She closed the lid on the ink jar. "Mamma and Papa will be ever so pleased to have a retired naval officer living nearby. His wife and family sound charming, and I want Netherfield to be in perfect condition for their arrival."

Mr. Bingley set the long list on the table, a look of pride on his face. "Only you would think of someone else's comfort at a time like this. The admiral and his wife will make a fine addition to local society. I only hope they decide to stay, for I have heard they are both fond of the sea."

"The sea is a magical place—one cannot blame them," Jane said with a smile.

Mr. Bingley's eyes lit up. "Would you care to go again?"

Jane placed a hand over her husband's. "When our six children are old enough to accompany us, yes, I would."

"Six, eh? I had thought you would follow your mother's example and stop at five."

"With the reported size of Beechwood Manor, we could have twenty children and there would still be room for our extended family—each with their own rooms."

"We have yet to decide upon a new name for the estate."

"Charles, I have been thinking. Why not keep the name as it is—in part out of respect for the Leigh family—but the tenants and the villagers have always known it as Beechwood Manor, just as this house will always be known as Netherfield Hall."

Mr. Bingley was thoughtful for a few moments, looking at nothing in particular. "I have never considered it in such a way before, but I think you are absolutely right. We would not want the tenants to think we do not honor the history of the place." He slapped his hand on the table. "Beechwood Manor it will remain!"

Darcy House, 26 April 1814

Major Ashton turned on his heel to face Colonel Fitzwilliam.

"Miss Caroline Bingley is one of the most astute liars I have ever come across—the most scheming, vicious—"

Colonel Fitzwilliam watched lazily from the comfort of his chair in Mr. Darcy's library as his friend and colleague marched back and forth across the room. "I believe it is time for you to bring your close acquaintanceship with the lady in question to an end—" he examined his fingernails "—my good aunt has pointed out that your continued attentions might put you in danger."

Major Ashton stopped pacing. "Danger?" He scoffed. "In what way?"

"In the marriage way, if you must know." Colonel Fitzwilliam stood and went to pour a drink for each of them. He handed one to the colonel before returning to his chair, pointing to the one opposite. "Sit down, Ashton; your pacing makes me nervous."

Major Ashton, with a slightly hunted look in his eyes, sat. "You cannot be serious."

The colonel shrugged. "The alliance would have certain benefits, for she has £20,000, in addition to a handsome annuity."

"You know I care nothing for money." The major ran a hand through his hair. "We must put an end to this fiasco—immediately." He took a long drink and set the glass down, shaking his head. "Marriage to Miss Bingley would be an exercise in disaster for any man, especially for one foolish enough to fall in love with her."

"Lord Harold is ready to take over where you have left off if necessary, though I believe she finds Exeter's attention—who, by-the-bye, will one day be a baron—more than gratifying. For all we know, she has already made plans to replace you."

Major Ashton almost smiled. "I think she and Exeter would make an excellent couple."

"As do I." Colonel Fitzwilliam studied the play of light in his glass. "It matters not, for she is no longer of use to us. It had to be Clay and Miss Grantly who acted as informants to Petersham and his valet, and it is only a matter of time before we have the rascal they used as a messenger. Once we have him in custody, and convince him to give evidence against them, I am sure Clay and Miss Grantly will be happy to confess all in exchange for clemency, or perhaps their very lives."

"Lord Harold has become an excellent scout; I was surprised to learn of Miss Grantly's long association with Petersham—she has hidden her alliance to France well.

The colonel nodded. "What Georgiana learned about the timing of her friendship with Miss Bingley adds sense to the matter."

"As long as Miss Bingley is finally taken off my hands, you know I will help in any way I can to catch the messenger."

Colonel Fitzwilliam nodded, satisfied. "Exactly what I thought, my friend—exactly what I thought." He leaned forward. "This is Castlereagh's plan...."

"Mary? Whatever are you doing?" Georgiana entered Mary's chamber late that night, clad in a favorite night-rail, her golden hair in a long braid down her back.

Mary looked up from the page on her writing desk. "I am trying to outline the plot for my next book before Lady Catherine arrives." She glanced up, the light from her candle revealing either a dark shadow or an ink stain on her cheek. "If she discovers I am writing another book, she will insist upon working with me, and change the complexion of it altogether. I only want to get the plot and characters written down so I do not forget—if only I can stay awake long enough."

"If you feel you must work at this late hour because of my aunt, then the least I can do is help you to stay awake." She put her hands around the teapot. "The tea is not hot, but still warm—may I pour you a cup?"

Mary nodded. "And one for yourself, if you are intent upon remaining." She took up a few pieces of the carefully trimmed foolscap. "If you would be so kind as to read what I have written so far—"

Georgiana took the pages, catching sight of a thick volume on Mary's desk entitled The Art of Cookery. "Are you reading a cookery book as part of your research?"

Mary smiled. "It is for my own interest, although what I have learned might be useful in some book or other. If ever I should be allowed in a kitchen, I would like to learn first-hand how to boil the water for tea, or how to prepare a breakfast egg properly."

"You plan to cook for yourself in your little cottage?" Georgiana teased.

Mary smiled, shrugging. "It may seem silly, but I should like to be able to fend for myself if need be."

Georgiana set the book down as if it were forbidden reading. "You will not get the opportunity to experiment in Mrs. Babcock's kitchen."

Mary grinned and re-sharpened the tip of her quill pen before dipping it in the ink. "Not her kitchen, but there will be others."

Georgiana plunked down in a nearby chair and began to read.

CHAPTER THIRTY

(A Letter from Catherine Darnell to Mary Bennet)

Garden Place, York, 27 April 1814

Dear Mary,

Thank you so much for sending your new novel! I have already read it twice, and now Edward has asked me to read it to him in the evenings.

It is so long since I said good-bye to my family and friends in Hertfordshire, and since then I have met many ladies whose husbands are in business like Edward. However, in their presence I feel silly and young, foolish and useless, and can never think of anything to say. Edward says I am being a mouse—perhaps I should endeavor to become more like your brave Miss White? There is a younger lady who calls frequently; she has been friends with Edward since they were children, and tells me many stories of their adventures.

We have been to one ball, two performances at the theatre, and yesterday we went to see the Minster, an enormous church. Edward is so good to me, but he is away during the day and I am often alone. I have begun to read books to pass the time (I thought you would be happy to hear), and am committed to writing frequent letters to all my sisters (including Lydia, though heaven knows when I will get a response) in the hope of receiving them in return.

Our housekeeper, Mrs. Kepplar, is in complete control of all the servants here, and I have to admit she frightens me. Edward says I must be firm with her, and I do try. My own maid is younger than I am and barely speaks a word to me—

nor I to her for that matter, for I fear she will report everything I say to Mrs. Kepplar. I wish I could have someone like your Molly, but Edward insists I have not tried hard enough with this one.

I have written to Mamma to ask her to come to us, but as yet have received no reply (I remember Papa telling Mamma that Elizabeth received letters because she wrote letters, though I do not think she completely understood his meaning). Jane has sent me a drawing she made of little Eliza, which sits on my bedside table. How unfair it was to have had to leave before seeing my niece! But, if I am lucky, I too will one day have a little baby of my own to take care of and to keep me company. Perhaps if Miss Darcy can spare you, you could come to us in York? We have splendid, bright rooms for our guests—you could write in complete privacy each morning. You would be ever so welcome, I am certain of it.

Edward's parents are to visit soon. I do like them, even though his father can be intimidating (at Longbourn he asked me what types of books I read, and I nearly forgot my own name). But Mrs. Darnell was excessively kind to me, and later told me not to concern myself about books and such things because her son chose me for who I am. Perhaps you would not mind sending me a list of things to read before they come so I might better impress them. I have never been fond of fancy work, as you know, and do not have the patience for drawing. Edward wants me to sew for the children of the poor, as the ladies here do, and I have begun the slow, tedious work.

I must close as it is time for the postman—I like to hand him my letters personally, for then I know for certain they have been sent.

Please give Miss Darcy my best, and tell her I would be so happy if she would ever be so gracious as to visit us in York. It would be delightful if you could come together. We could have so much fun.

Your affectionate sister,
Catherine Darnell, née Bennet

n.b. Perhaps Lizzy and Jane will invite us to visit them in Derbyshire, so we might all be together again.

CHAPTER THIRTY-ONE

"Are you young ladies ready? You know how the earl does not like to be kept waiting." The countess peeked her diamond-bedecked head around the doorway of Georgiana's dressing room, the two young maids adding final touches to the gowns of their mistresses. As they were clearly not ready, the countess entered, circling first around Mary, who stood on a stool while Molly fussed with the hem of her dress. "You know, Mary, when you made it clear you would only join us this evening if you were responsible for your own gown—a ridiculous notion—I imagined all sorts of atrocities, but this one is perfectly lovely."

"It is Molly's creation, Lady Matlock," Mary said, raising her arm to better exhibit the lines. "She asked if she might try her hand at a frock and here you see the result."

The countess eyed Molly consideringly. "You are a talented young woman."

Molly blushed to the roots of her hair, dimples showing in her childishly round cheeks. "Thank you, your ladyship." She curtsied before fussing with more, seemingly unnecessary adjustments to Mary's gown.

Georgiana turned upon her own stool per Lucy's request. "Molly could well become a great seamstress, but she claims she does not wish to leave her post." She twisted about in front of the mirror, comparing the lines of her gown to Mary's. "I hope one day she will design a gown for me."

The countess looked at Mary, her brows raised.

"Molly's future is in her own hands," Mary replied as her maid pulled a thread through the Van Dyke points along the hem.

The line of carriages along Hanover Street gave testament to the number of patrons of the musical arts among the *haute ton*. The program for the evening was to include a short symphonic work by Beethoven (dedicated to the Prince Regent), along with works by Handel, "John" Bach, and new piano works called nocturnes, written by a relatively unknown Irish composer.

When they entered the principal room, Mary was astounded by its size, holding what appeared to be hundreds of people.

"Do you like it?" whispered Georgiana behind her fan.

Mary nodded, her wide eyes trying to take in everything at once.

As the earl and countess led them to their seats, Georgiana whispered, "Do you think the queen will attend this evening?"

Taking the seat next to Mary, the colonel whispered, "She does make the odd appearance—but should the prince deign to come, *he* will no doubt be late."

"But the work dedicated to him is the first on the program," murmured Mary, reading the description in the booklet.

They were prevented from further comment by the appearance of the Philharmonic Society on a raised stage on the opposite end of the hall from the royal boxes. The orchestral piece, written to celebrate the Duke of Wellington's victory at the Battle of Vitoria, was not at all what Mary expected. When the strains of *Rule, Britannia* were heard, the audience cried out, clapping loudly; when the national anthem was played, they stood, many with tears in their eyes. It was the most emotional and definitely the loudest orchestral work Mary could ever have imagined.

At the break, the audience members sought refreshment and conversation. Not wishing to disturb any of her party, Mary slipped away to the dressing room to adjust (or perhaps remove) the elaborate headdress Molly had insisted she wear. Once inside the mirrored space, she chose a seat next to a young lady with red hair who was unfamiliar to her, but one to whom she felt obliged to speak—she had obviously been crying and was attempting to wipe away the evidence with an already-saturated handkerchief.

"Please excuse me," Mary said softly, leaning towards her, "but is there any way I might be of assistance?" Without waiting for a response, she reached inside her reticule and pulled out a clean handkerchief, embroidered by Kitty, who had made one for each of her sisters and her mother, anticipating tears at her wedding.

The young lady attempted a brave smile as she accepted the daintily-trimmed muslin. "You are too kind," she said, and dabbed at her eyes. She sat up straight and looked into the mirror. "But it is hopeless," she whispered to the reflection, seeming to forget Mary was sitting next to her.

Mary did not wish to inquire further into a stranger's private affairs, and so began the business of fixing the headdress, trying to re-center it but succeeding only in making a mess of her hair.

"Please, allow me, for the attendant is busy at the moment," said the red-haired lady softly, looking across the room where the attendant was indeed busy repairing the ripped hem of a corpulent woman's dress. "My name is Morna," she said, her accent sounding Scottish to Mary's ears.

"Mine is Mary—Mary Bennet." She turned obediently at Morna's direction, whose fingers were deft and competent, and in a few short minutes Mary's hair was put to rights.

"Your headdress is most unusual," Morna said, and almost immediately her eyes widened, a look of horror on her face. "I am so sorry—I meant that as a compliment. I am forever making mistakes in this country. My husband has told me several times never to make personal comments, especially to someone I have only just met. Please accept my sincerest apology."

The poor young woman looked about to cry again, and Mary reached out to her with a smile. "Please do not worry on my account. I find many of society's rules ridiculous."

Morna studied Mary's face for a moment, as if to determine the truth of her words. "You make me feel so much better; I cannot thank you enough."

"I thank *you* for helping me this evening, for how could I have returned to the concert, given the mess I made of this?" Mary pointed to the headdress. "You managed to put it exactly as it should be." She picked up her reticule. "But now I must return to my party, for they will soon miss me."

"Wait a moment, if you please," begged Morna. "How am I to return your handkerchief?" She studied the fine embroidery.

"It must be precious."

Mary quickly gave the address of Darcy House and dipped a curtsey. "I look forward to seeing you again, Morna."

"And I to see you," Morna replied, her eyes catching Mary's in the mirror as she leaned forward, rubbing ineffectually at her cheeks. "I must remain a bit longer to allow the blotches to fade, I am afraid."

Mary had no time to tell the curious members of her party what had kept her, for the bell announcing the recommencement of the concert rang, and the audience returned to their seats with surprising alacrity.

Each of the works by Herr Handel performed in the second half of the programme were clearly old favorites to many in the audience, but the best of the evening's concert for both Mary and Georgiana were the piano pieces performed at the end. The melodies were plaintive and the accompaniments simple, but somehow the music was dissimilar from anything they had heard before. The sweetly haunting phrases brought tears to Georgiana's eyes, and Mary knew without a doubt they would soon be scouring the shops in search of any sheet music by Mr. Field—or if necessary, borrowing the music and copying it out themselves by hand.

～⌣⌣⌐

"The work by Herr Beethoven was nothing like I expected," Georgiana said, sitting near the window in the morning room the next day, a neglected piece of sewing in her hand. The countess was reclining on the most comfortable of the settees, while Mary was ostensibly reading her cookery book. The three were taking advantage of the little time remaining before Lady Catherine's arrival at Darcy House.

"There is to be another performance by the Philharmonic Society of his works this week. Shall we attend?" The countess reached for a small scone on a nearby tray. "The earl is fond of music—much more so than of dancing."

At that moment, Steinman, the butler at Darcy House, solemnly announced the arrival of a visitor—Lady Jameson. "Shall I say you are at home, my lady?"

Upon hearing the name, the three ladies nearly jumped from their seats, hurriedly plumping pillows and placing sewing and books out of sight, the countess signaling the butler to remove the tea things. "We will be home to her in but a few moments," she replied, her eyes on the other two as she handed him a napkin before he left to slightly delay their guest's entry.

Georgiana looked about the room for any signs of recent activity. "Whyever would Lady Jameson call at Darcy House? I thought after she visited you at Longbourn it would be the last time any of us would set eyes on her."

Mary shook her head dumbly, more confused than Georgiana. Had the countess not been with them, she knew she would have been somewhat afraid, for Captain Jameson's mother was as much a tyrant as Lady Catherine.

"Girls!" The countess hissed, her hands motioning for them to attend, and the two moved near her with placid smiles, ready to receive their guest.

When Lady Jameson entered the room, Mary had to work hard to hide her surprise, for it was not the captain's mother who had come to call.

"Lady Jameson," announced the austere butler before departing.

For a brief moment, Mary was too stunned to speak. For before them stood the miserable young woman with beautiful hair Mary had met in the dressing room the previous evening, who she knew only as Morna. The poor young girl Mary had assisted was the same "horse-faced" heiress about whom Captain Jameson had spoken so disparagingly, and whom he had married.

Morna was tall, certainly, and her complexion spoke of her fondness for the outdoors, but the captain's description was wholly unfair. Mary could not quite come to terms with the fact that the sad but kind young lady who had straightened her hair and headdress was none other than Miss Drummond of Dunwar Castle, the rich heiress who was to save Lady Jameson and her daughters from penury by her marriage to Captain Jameson. The very same young lady Mary had instinctively liked upon their first meeting.

Lady Jameson did not wait upon ceremony, but approached

Mary with a smile. "Miss Mary Bennet—how good it is to see you again." She held out a small, wrapped package. "I have come to return your precious handkerchief, and to thank you once more in person for coming to my aid during the concert."

Georgiana and Lady Matlock looked on with undisguised curiosity, and Mary recalled herself. "Lady Jameson—please allow me to introduce you to The Countess of Devonham, Lady Matlock, and her niece, Miss Georgiana Darcy."

Georgiana looked puzzled. "Please pardon my curiosity, Lady Jameson, but we are acquainted with another lady by your name; she is from Scotland and is the mother of an acquaintance—Lord Jameson. Are you in any way related?"

Morna's expression was difficult to read. "I believe you are referring to my mother-in-law, the Countess of Sinclair—my husband's mother." She looked down at her gloved hands. "She did not accompany us to London; I am here in the company of my husband, who I believe you know well." She looked directly at Mary. "When I said where I was going today, he told me you are the authoress of *The Turret Room,* a book I thoroughly enjoyed reading."

Mary's state of mind allowed her to respond with only a slight inclination of her head, and Morna continued, "He speaks highly of you—of all of you. Mary...forgive me, Miss Bennet found me in a state of discomposure in the dressing room last evening and kindly lent me her handkerchief; I have come to return it."

"It seems an unnecessary formality to call me Miss Bennet." Mary finally found her voice. She instinctively liked *this* Lady Jameson. "Please do continue to call me Mary."

"I will," promised their guest, "but you must all promise to call me Morna."

"Can you stay for tea?" The countess looked as though she was still trying to reconcile what she had just heard with her memory of past events.

"I would dearly like to," Morna said eagerly. "I have not been in London long and feel like a fish out of water."

"How are you liking London?" asked Lady Matlock.

Morna's expression was rueful. "I have to admit that I do not care for it. I am not comfortable in society; I never have been.

My mother gave up trying to teach me social graces long ago and I fear my husband is embarrassed by the lack."

Mary reached forward and covered the young Lady Jameson's hand with her own. "You need not worry about such things with us, I assure you."

Lady Matlock smiled and gestured towards a chair. "It would be but a simple thing to help you feel more comfortable in London, Lady Jameson. We would be more than pleased to introduce you to some of the more accommodating members of the *ton*."

Morna's reply was forestalled by Steinman, who announced more late-afternoon callers—Miss Bingley and Miss Grantly.

Lady Matlock was a wise woman, and when the two newcomers entered with their usual pomp, she introduced Lady Jameson as formally as she would a queen.

———

"You had no idea Morna was in actual fact Lady Jameson?" Georgiana asked Mary after all their guests had gone.

Mary shook her head. "I only knew her as Morna, and would never have guessed she was the young lady Captain Jameson described both unkindly and unfairly."

Georgiana half smiled. "But we should forgive him, as he was then in love with another young lady, was he not?"

Mary turned towards the window. "He might have been—but I no longer believe I know what true love is."

"Nor I," said Georgiana ruefully. "Before we left Hertfordshire, I asked Elizabeth if she thought I had a propensity for being attracted to men with less-than-desirable characters."

"And what did she say?"

Georgiana shrugged. "She said I have probably learned my lesson and will no longer be so easily taken in by reprobates."

Mary grinned. "Let us hope she is right."

CHAPTER THIRTY-TWO

Molly had just completed running a brush through Mary's hair a full one hundred times (something she claimed was absolutely necessary) when Mary asked, "Now you have finished reading my book to Lucy, what will you choose next?"

Molly pulled a slim volume from her apron pocket, clearly excited to show it to her mistress.

"*The Mirror of the Graces*?" Surprised, Mary opened the book.

"The countess said I could borrow it from Mr. Darcy's library. It's by a lady of dis...disting—"

"Distinction," Mary said absently as she turned a page. "It is a word not commonly found in primers." She frowned. "In the first paragraph alone I find six words which merit keeping a copy of Dr. Johnson's dictionary handy. How are you getting along?"

"I've written down the words I don't know." Molly pulled a much-worn, folded scrap of paper from her pocket.

Mary scanned the long list. "Molly, this is the action of a true scholar. After we return from the shops tomorrow, I would be happy to go over each of these with you, if you wish." She pointed at the list. "This first word—'discoursing'—means 'to talk about,' for example."

Molly took the sheet of paper eagerly, choosing a pencil from the many items she kept in her pocket before slowly, painstakingly writing the definition alongside the word.

Mary was grateful for the distraction. The dinner Lady Matlock had planned in honor of Lord and Lady Jameson was only an hour away, and would be Mary's first meeting with the former Captain Jameson since she had refused his offer of marriage and told him in no uncertain terms that she would *never* marry. She had been fretting ever since the invitations had been sent, and now, shaking her head to dispel the memory of the elder Lady Jameson's visit to Longbourn, she closed the book and returned it to Molly. "Why have you chosen to read this? It has no plot—no distressed young ladies in need of rescue by handsome gentlemen."

"I can't say I've read much of it, miss, because it's pretty hard going. But you've been saying for a long time now that you don't think I'll be staying in service forever. So, if I was ever to change positions—I'm not saying I would, but if I should ever decide to try my hand at seamstressing, I'd want to make dresses for ladies in society, you know. And I'd like to talk more like they do."

Mary smiled at the unintentional slight. "It is an excellent scheme. But when it comes to pass, I will miss you terribly."

"Don't you worry, miss—I promise to make all of your gowns, and at a discounted price!"

Later, as Georgiana and Mary waited in the drawing room for the guests to arrive, Georgiana leaned over to whisper, "You must try to relax—your face looks like a porcelain mask!" She hesitated briefly before adding, "You need only think of Major Ashton's proposal—" she correctly interpreted the look on Mary's face "—or...perhaps you might prefer to think about how you already have two books published, with a third in the making!"

The earl, standing near the window, grumbled, "I wonder why you insisted upon hosting this evening, my dear. If Jameson's wife does not care for society, poor thing, why force it upon her?"

"Because, my dear, I think she really *does* wish it—you should have seen her face when I proposed introducing her to our friends." The countess pouted slightly and adjusted the lace overlay of her gown. "Miss Bingley and Miss Grantly will not be here, for they had a previous engagement—they are to attend the theatre in the company of Lord Exeter and Mr. Clay this evening...." The countess looked pointedly at her husband.

"If Castlereagh is right about the situation, Clay will soon be in prison—in the meantime, we may as well keep a close eye on him while he remains at liberty," said the earl, returning her glance. "Richard, Major Ashton, and Lord Harold will also be at the theatre."

"Lord Harold will not be coming this evening?" Georgiana tried too late to hide her disappointment.

"He has other duties," stated the earl firmly.

"We will be a small party, with no one to disturb poor Morna," the countess said, just before Steinman announced the arrival of the first guests.

Later, when Lord and Lady Jameson were announced, Lady Matlock whispered, "Chin up, Mary," for she knew the whole of the story behind Mary's refusal.

Mary's heart performed nervous acrobatics upon Lord Jameson's entrance, the memory of the last meeting with the former captain fresh in her mind.

"Miss Bennet." He bowed and moved quickly away, not allowing her the opportunity to congratulate him on his marriage. However, Morna greeted Mary as she would a long-time friend.

The other guests were Lord and Lady Castlereagh, Mrs. Burnaby and her daughter, Mr. and Mrs. Gardiner, and Mr. Chandler, with Mrs. Annesley completing their number. The countess had wisely seated Mary and Lord Jameson on the same side of the table, with several people between them.

After an excellent meal, Mrs. Babcock having prepared many of Lord Jameson's favorite foods from earlier times, the ladies retired to the music room.

Georgiana sat with the young Lady Jameson, while Mrs. Annesley sat down at the harp and began to play. "I hope you are enjoying the evening," Georgiana ventured.

"I am, thank you—your aunt is most kind." Morna took a handkerchief from her pearl-covered reticule. "You all have such easy manners, and make me feel so welcome. I do not recall stuttering even once at dinner!" She directed a glance towards Mary, who was obligingly admiring Deidre Burnaby's ring. "Miss Bennet is so different from what I expected."

"Oh?"

Morna twisted the handkerchief in her hands, keeping her eyes down. "I have known James—Lord Jameson—ever since I was a child. His family's estate borders mine, and we were often thrown together, though I know he thought me a terrible bore. When he proposed to me, it seemed nothing short of a miracle."

"Did you play together as children?" Georgiana was truly curious. "Lord Harold and I—he was unable to come this evening, I am sorry to say—we were playmates. He used to tease me mercilessly." Her tone was wistful as she added with a smile, "He still does."

"I am sorry to say I was most frequently in the company of James' sisters, whose interests were dissimilar to mine." Morna grinned. "All the while I was playing with dolls, I wished only to be outside playing with the dogs or riding my horse." Her head was down as she said quietly, "I am not ashamed to say I have always loved him, and when he finally asked me to become his wife I thought my happiness could not be more complete." Her eyes were on Mary. "But he does not love me."

Georgiana did not respond, for she did not know what to say.

"Having met Miss Bennet, I cannot blame him." Morna sighed. "I understand she wishes to remain anonymous, but I had to tell her how much I enjoyed reading *The Turret Room*—I did not like to put it down. Will she write a sequel, do you know?"

Georgiana thought for a moment. "I would not like to speak for Mary—perhaps it would be better to ask her."

Morna peered intently at Georgiana. "Please excuse my impertinence, but can you tell me if there was at one time something between them? Female writers and actresses are of a different breed than we are, I believe, and—" she stopped upon seeing Georgiana's shocked expression. "Oh no, I have done it again!" She went back to twisting the handkerchief. "Forgive me, Miss Darcy. You see how unsuitable I am for society?"

"You do not need to worry when in my company, Morna, but I must tell you that nothing even remotely improper occurred between Mary and Lord Jameson." Her cheeks grew pink. "And should anyone say otherwise, I am prepared to defend Miss Bennet's reputation with everything in my power, if need be."

~~~

"It was not too disturbing to see him again, was it?" Georgiana and Mary, already dressed for bed, were lounging near the low-burning fire in Georgiana's sitting room.

"No—it was not at all bad if you discount the fact that Captain—er, *Lord* Jameson said not a single word to me after his cold greeting. After tonight, I think I understand a little of what it would be like to be a ghost."

"Something you might find useful for your next gothic novel," Georgiana teased. "Poor Morna. His actions only strengthen her notion that he continues to have feelings for you."

"His feelings are primarily of anger," Mary replied stoutly. "I have never felt so uncomfortable—well, at least not recently."

Georgiana studied her fingernails for a moment before asking, "How exactly did you feel, apart from uncomfortable?"

Mary took a long breath. "It is hard to explain, but after the initial shock I felt only a little sad, as at the loss of a friend. But friend or foe, I cannot like his cold behavior towards his wife, who clearly adores him."

Georgiana tipped her head to the side, but said nothing, and Mary held up her hands in a defensive posture. "I already told you my feelings regarding the captain changed substantially over time, especially once I knew he had married Miss Drummond of Dunwar Castle—do you know, I think it was Lord Exeter who told me first." Her smile was slight. "Having met Morna before realizing exactly who she was—well, I felt sympathy for her from the first moment I met her, and will do all I can to make her husband see what a treasure she is."

"It might be difficult, seeing as he will not even look in your direction, let alone speak to you. Between the two of us—and my clever aunt—we might just be able to achieve your noble goal!" Georgiana hid a yawn behind her shawl.

Mary stood, also feeling the lateness of the hour. "You were disappointed when Lord Harold did not come to dinner this evening."

Georgiana looked a little embarrassed. "I know you would

have me choose Mr. Chandler, Mary, but I cannot." She followed Mary to the door, twisting her long braided hair. "Lord Harold has certainly redeemed himself, working for Lord Castlereagh."

"He has indeed." Mary did not like to think of the day when Georgiana admitted to Mr. Darcy that she had given her heart to yet another man with questionable merit, at least in her brother's eyes. Could he possibly sanction a match with Lord Harold, or would he assume it was yet another whimsy on Georgiana's part (so blind to the significantly-flawed characters of the two men she had once thought herself in love). By comparison, Mary saw Lord Harold as a paragon of virtue—if only Mr. Darcy could see it.

Mary asked gently, "Does he reciprocate your feelings?"

Georgiana lifted her shoulders. "He is unfailingly polite at all times, even when he is teasing. Perhaps I only imagine his eyes reserve a certain sparkle only for me and I am doomed to experience yet another broken heart."

"We must do something to prevent it, and before you are fully committed to loving him."

"But what is there to do?"

Mary opened the door with a determined smile. "As my good Aunt Philips is wont to say, 'If I have a problem to mull over, I like to sleep on it.'"

The following day, Georgiana slipped down to the breakfast room at the very time her cousin habitually took his morning meal. She was pleased to find him alone and after pouring a cup of tea for herself, came to sit across from him at the long table.

"Yes, Georgiana?" Colonel Fitzwilliam looked up from the letter he was reading.

"Cousin Richard, I have come to speak with you about Lord Jameson and Mary."

The colonel picked up his silver. "The two of them should not be mentioned in the same sentence."

"I know," Georgiana replied a trifle impatiently. "It is about Lord Jameson's coldness to her that I have come to speak."

He took a bite of eggs, eyebrows raised.

"Lady Jameson—Morna—is intimidated by Mary, though she is unaware of both her husband's proposal and Mary's rejection of it." She ignored her cousin's impatient expression. "It is my belief that if he were told the truth, he could finally forgive Mary and learn to love his wife."

"I find meddling in other people's affairs abhorrent, Georgiana." The colonel pushed his empty plate away. "But in this case I must agree with your assessment. Jameson has been acting like a wounded lion ever since coming to London. He does not want to hear Miss Bennet's name one second, and the next is anxious to hear all about her."

The colonel took a warm roll from the basket on the table, breaking it in half and chewing thoughtfully. "In what manner do you propose he learns the truth? After all, Mary did promise the Dowager Lady Jameson never to tell anyone—let alone Jameson." He pointed the other half of the roll at Georgiana, shaking his head. "Should he learn the truth, he may actually admire her all the more; her refusal was truly honorable."

Georgiana bit her lip, sipped her tea, frowned, and thought, while the colonel wiped his fingers and went back to reading his letter. Finally she said, "It is the only way—he must know the truth."

Colonel Fitzwilliam folded the letter and pocketed it with a great sigh. "I will be seeing him today at any rate. I will find a way to tell him the story, and make him swear never to repeat it, under threat of death."

Georgiana smiled before moving to the sideboard. "Thank you." She paused after taking up a plate. "There is one more thing...Mary must not hear a word about this."

Colonel Fitzwilliam held his cup out for Georgiana to refill, muttering, "Women!"

⌒⌒⌒

Lady Catherine had not indicated an exact time or date of her arrival, and Lady Matlock claimed all the waiting around made her nervous. She therefore took Georgiana and Mary out in her carriage for an afternoon of shopping—first to Hatchards (where they went to view the volumes of *The Count of Camalore* on display, the 'new novel written by the authoress of *The Turret Room*'), followed by the Clementi store for Georgiana (who purchased a copious amount of sheet music, including the latest new sonata by Beethoven and a prized nocturne by John Field), then to the milliner for the countess, and finally to a warehouse where Molly chose fabric for the frocks she was to design for Georgiana and Lady Matlock as part of what she liked to call her apprenticeship, having only just learned the word.

After leaving the warehouse, Lady Matlock declared she could not go one step farther without sustenance, insisting they stop for a decent tea.

It was therefore late in the afternoon when the ladies arrived to find an elegant, closed barouche stopped outside Darcy House, and poor Mrs. Jenkinson struggling with a large birdcage as she approached the entrance.

"Would this not be an opportune time to visit your Aunt and Uncle Gardiner?" Georgiana asked Mary as they stepped from the carriage.

Mary dared not respond as they passed through the open door where Steinman stood at attention, his gloved hands formed into tight fists at his side.

Upon entering the house, they found anxious servants scurrying about.

Lady Catherine had arrived.

CHAPTER THIRTY-THREE

(A Letter from Georgiana Darcy to Elizabeth Darcy)

Darcy House, 2 May 1814

Dearest Elizabeth,

Aunt Catherine and Cousin Anne are with us now, and it appears they will be for some time to come. Our aunt has so far not allowed Anne to accompany us to dances, but she may be able to go to the theatre tomorrow (Mary said she was happy to stay at home and write instead of going out in the evenings, as Aunt Catherine said she must, but Uncle Matlock would not hear of it).

Cousin Anne appears to be happy about her forthcoming marriage to Lord Wickford, though Mary says it is having a home she can call her own that Anne anticipates with the most joy (I argued against the point, for there are those four children). At any rate, there is a bloom in Anne's cheeks, and at times a sparkle in her eyes I have never before seen. Last evening, she laughed out loud on two separate occasions, almost making one wonder if Aunt Catherine has not been exaggerating the state of my cousin's health all these years.

You ask if I have been enjoying my first season. As you know, I am by nature more retiring than most young ladies, and find making conversation with people I have only just met a severe trial. Consequently, each time I am taken to the floor by a newly-introduced gentleman I am ill at ease and wish only for the dance to end (save when I dance with Lord Harold).

In regard to other activities, however, Mary and I are enjoying ourselves tremendously. Remember the presentation we all attended on static electricity? We recently went to the Royal Institute to see a scholarly presentation about the fossils found in Lyme Regis—a place I dearly want to visit one day. There were ever so many curios of bone and shell, and the remains of an extremely large bird the likes of which defy description. The presentation was given by a Mr. Anning, though his entire family helps him in his work. He claims the collection of fossils has become a popular past-time, though warning it can be dangerous as it is often done on cliff-sides.

We regularly walk in the park, visit the circulating library and bookshops, and go to concerts. We have so far heard several symphonies by Herr Beethoven, Mozart, and Haydn, and only last evening we were fortunate to see Mr. John Bach perform his own works in the Hanover-square rooms. As it turns out, Mrs. Annesley is a particular friend of his eldest sister, and she introduced us to the composer after the concert (I feared both Mary and I would require sal-volatile).

We have met Captain J's charming wife, Morna (of course he is Lord J now). They came to dinner at Aunt Matlock's invitation, but he would not speak to Mary.

Neither Major Ashton nor Lord Harold have called in the past few days; my uncle assures us they are about to bring the whole business regarding Mr. P to a close.

I began the season with little hope of finding someone suitable, and have not—but I will continue to attend all of what society deems necessary for a marriageable young lady of my station.

I count the days until we are all together again at Pemberley, eagerly awaiting the arrival of my own nephew or niece.

Affectionately,
Georgiana Darcy

CHAPTER THIRTY-FOUR

(A Letter from Jane Bingley to Elizabeth Darcy)

Netherfield, 2 May 1814

Dearest Elizabeth,

This will be the last letter I write from Netherfield, a place very dear to me as you know, for it is where Charles took such gentle care with me after I fell ill from riding a horse in the rain, and where I fell in love with him. It is the thought of living so close to my most beloved sister which makes me look forward with great anticipation to the future, and to feel less heartache at leaving our dear home in Hertfordshire. Charles can hardly remain in one place above five minutes, he is so excited. As you know, neither he nor I have seen Beechwood Manor, yet I feel as if we have been there many times.

Charles has asked that the model of our new home be placed in a position of prominence so we can see it first thing and judge how closely it resembles the actual house. How does your own model of Pemberley progress? I am almost as anxious to see it as I am to see the real house and my sister.

Little Eliza turns three months old tomorrow—you will wonder at how much she has grown. There is much to tell, but I will wait until I see you in person. However, I will relay one piece of information which will surprise you. There was recently a wedding in Meryton: Miss King to young Mr. Webb.

Mamma is beside herself—which is also all I will say for now.

Your loving sister,
Jane Bingley

CHAPTER THIRTY-FIVE

"What are you writing, Miss Bennet? Let me see!" Lady Catherine had entered Mary's private sitting room without knocking, causing Mary to start, her pen flying across the page, the ink blotting several carefully composed lines. The mistress of Rosings leaned down to examine the paper, lifting a lorgnette to her eyes. "What is this? I do hope you have not begun to write another sequel without my guidance!"

"How nice to see you, Lady Catherine." Mary stood, attempting to block access to the manuscript pages. "It is not another sequel, but a completely new story. Please—do sit down." She indicated the chair farthest from the desk, but was ignored.

Lady Catherine pushed Mary aside and picked up the pages, flipping from one to the next impatiently, a great frown creasing her forehead. "Who is this Mrs. Winters? Who are her daughters? What is the plot of your story? Are they people of society?" She turned to face Mary, her lips pursed. "I do hope you have benefited from my tutelage, and have remembered how to properly describe their homes, clothing, and behavior, for otherwise there will be much to change."

Mary dared not take the manuscript from the clutches of Georgiana's aunt, though it was with great effort she restrained herself. "It is but the first draft of a novel about three young ladies who have lost their home to an entail, Lady Catherine."

"A worthy subject," Lady Catherine observed, temporarily diverted. "I never have understood the reason to take property out of the hands of daughters. Miss de Bourgh, as you know, will inherit Rosings one day, according to the wishes of her dear departed father, Sir Louis de Bourgh. He would have it no other way."

Mary tried to look as if it were the first time she had heard the circumstances of Miss de Bourgh's inheritance. "I am happy to hear you have sympathy for my characters, Lady Catherine, as I was afraid the subject matter might be objectionable to society."

Lady Catherine laid the pages down to pick up the one with the ink blotches. She read a few lines and set it aside carelessly. "I do not pretend to have sympathy for anything I have not read, Miss Bennet, and when the shopping is complete for Miss de Bourgh's wedding clothes, I will read all of what you have written of this new book." She moved to a chair and sat down. "Now, tell me what have you heard from the publisher about our book? When is it to be published?"

Mary took a deep breath. "Mr. Egerton has not yet informed me of his decision regarding *The Wine Cellar*, Lady Catherine." She spoke honestly, for Mr. Egerton had not yet contacted her about the book Lady Catherine had insisted on writing with her, but she did not say what she had begun to think (he did not care for it).

Lady Catherine sniffed. "He should be contacting me, not you, Miss Bennet, for I am the one who sent the package. It is only because of me that you managed to finish the book at all, and it will become popular in society only through my influence."

Mary was saved from replying by Georgiana's entrance.

"Georgiana! I understand you plan to attend a musical concert this evening." Lady Catherine turned her imperious gaze upon her niece.

"Yes, Aunt Catherine. The Philharmonic Society is to feature a work by a student of Signor Clementi, who is also to perform."

Lady Catherine signaled for them to sit across from her. "Anne and I will accompany you this evening. A night listening to music will not tire her as a dance or cards would." She focused narrowed eyes on Georgiana. "It is time you and I discussed the gentlemen you have met since the commencement of your season. Has my nephew had each of them thoroughly investigated?"

"Colonel Fitzwilliam has been doing so assiduously, Aunt Catherine." Georgiana glanced briefly at Mary. "And to date neither he nor my Aunt Matlock has found a single gentleman worthy of my attention."

"Now I am here, I will discuss the qualifications of these young men with Richard. My sister's judgment cannot always be trusted; she has always been far too lenient with you."

Mary saw the playful look in Georgiana's eyes disappear in an instant, and wondered what Lady Catherine would make of Lord Harold, as well as how many unsavory details of his allegedly colorful past she might uncover.

It was at that moment Mary decided to do whatever she could to bring her friend's dream closer to fruition—before Lady Catherine could destroy Georgiana's hopes for happiness in the marriage state.

***

The opportunity for Mary to assist Georgiana came sooner than expected, as Lord Harold was invited to sit with the Darcy party at that evening's concert. In league with Lady Matlock (who was fond of Lord Harold despite his transgressions), Mary managed to have him seated right next to Georgiana, with Lady Catherine at the opposite end of the row where she could not see them without considerable effort.

Mary quickly took the seat on the other side of Lord Harold, effectively blocking Miss Burnaby by pretending not to see her. Mary could certainly not fault the poor girl for her taste, but she was determined to intercede between two people who might never admit their feelings to one another.

Lady Matlock, taking the seat on the other side of Mary, opened her fan to hide a complacent smile. While they waited for the concert to begin, Mary turned to speak to the countess, giving Lord Harold no choice but to wait for Miss Darcy to turn to him.

Georgiana was no fool, but she did not appear at all discomposed by Mary and her aunt's orchestrations, and began an animated conversation with Lord Harold about the nocturnes they had recently heard. In fact, it was only the start of the programme that caused them to cease speaking to one another—Mary noting with pleasure the frequency of Georgiana's laughter.

During the first intermission, Mary was sipping a glass of claret when she caught sight of Miss Diana Leigh leaving the room with determined steps. A worried frown marred her normally placid countenance, and Mary set her glass down to follow and see if she could be of assistance.

When Mary caught up with her, Diana Leigh had stopped at the wide entrance to the Principal Room to look upon a scene that was clearly distressing to her. Mary's eyes followed Miss Leigh's sight line, and for a moment could not tell what had her so transfixed. Then it became clear: Miss Catherine Leigh was approaching a group of young, fashionable people, her face pale, eyes red-rimmed. Her eyes were focused on a young man dressed at the height of fashion, his dark curled hair just touching the edge of his high collar.

Mary watched as the gentleman purposely turned away and escorted the dark-haired young lady from the room, leaving poor Miss Leigh standing there alone, exposed, her hand outstretched.

As if a spell had been broken, Diana rushed forward, and to Mary's surprise nearly collided with Lord Harold, who had already taken firm hold of Catherine Leigh's arm and begun to lead her from the room, making it seem as if she had suddenly taken ill. However, his efforts were too late, for as they passed through the archway, fans went up and the whispers began.

Undaunted, Lord Harold's eyes searched the room, catching those of Major Ashton, who managed to reach him without bringing attention to himself. After a few whispered words, Diana Leigh and Lord Harold conveyed her nearly-overcome sister to the main door, while Major Ashton called for his carriage.

Upon its arrival, Lord Harold lifted the overcome Catherine Leigh inside, Diana asking him to inform Mrs. Burnaby of their whereabouts before stepping in herself.

Meanwhile, Major Ashton had climbed up alongside his

coachman, and as there was little traffic they were soon out of sight.

Mary, who did not wish to bring further attention to the incident, returned to Georgiana's side to describe in a soft voice what had happened. Colonel Fitzwilliam listened, asserting the gentleman in question was an unredeemable rake, and one who would likely be called out before the year was over. He watched with cold eyes as the man in question strutted down the length of the Principal Room with the dark-haired, well-dressed lady on his arm.

While Mary watched, she noticed Miss Deidre Burnaby in close conversation with another young lady, the two of them insensible to what had just happened to her mother's guests. Mary turned to Georgiana and whispered, "Do you think we ought to call on the Burnabys tomorrow?"

After the concert, Lady Catherine insisted upon their immediate return to Darcy House, where she and Anne retired to their rooms. Georgiana therefore had a few moments to speak with her Aunt Matlock.

"If we visit Mrs. Burnaby and her guests tomorrow, it might help alleviate some of the gossip, for Miss Leigh is in great danger of being cut-direct from all quarters, given her actions this evening."

The countess laid a consoling hand upon her niece's arm. "We will call tomorrow, Georgiana, with all the pomp and circumstance devisable. I will ask Catherine to come as well, although I will refrain from telling her the reason."

Lady Matlock became serious. "It is kind of you to want to help Miss Leigh, but you must know there is bound to be gossip, and we may not be able to save her." She turned to her son who was pulling on his gloves, preparing to return to his own house. "Richard, before you leave, I would consider it a great favor if you would tell me all about this unredeemable rake who has caused so much distress to poor Miss Leigh."

Colonel Fitzwilliam sighed, glancing at his pocket watch. "Yes, Mother, but I think Lord Harold knows the story much better than I."

As soon as Lady Catherine entered the carriage waiting to take them to the Burnabys, she demanded, "What was all the fuss about last evening? Mrs. Jenkinson said a young person made a complete fool of herself, became nearly prostrate, and had to be practically carried from the hall." She clucked her tongue. "I am shocked she was allowed entrance to the Principal Room in the first place."

"The young lady you speak of is the daughter of a gentleman, and an acquaintance of Miss Darcy and Miss Bennet, Catherine," said Lady Matlock in a stern tone. "She was overcome by the heat—it is as simple as that. We are calling on her this afternoon in the hopes of finding her fully recovered."

Lady Catherine's eyes narrowed but she said nothing more on the subject, busying herself instead by nearly swaddling her daughter in a wool shawl.

Diana Leigh was seated in the drawing room with Mrs. Burnaby and Deidre when Lady Matlock's party arrived, but Catherine Leigh remained in her room, reportedly too ill to receive anyone.

Lady Matlock spoke first. "We do hope Miss Leigh has recovered from the heat in the hall last evening—it was stifling."

Diana Leigh responded astutely, "It was only through the kind attentions of a gentleman we have only recently met—Lord Harold—that we were able to leave the concert hall and return here so quickly." Her eyes were shaded as she added, "My sister has not been well of late; the closeness of the hall was too much for her to bear."

"I am so sorry to hear it," murmured Lady Matlock with genuine sympathy before drawing Mrs. Burnaby and Lady Catherine into a conversation, which left Georgiana and Mary free to speak with Diana Leigh.

"I do thank you for coming today," Diana Leigh said softly. "Major Ashton has already called to see if Catherine is recovered." She glanced at Mrs. Burnaby, who was happily talking with her auspicious guests, Miss Anne and Lady Catherine de Bourgh, about the much-anticipated birth of the

Darcys' child. "Mrs. Burnaby has been so kind, but my greatest wish is to see my sister safely back home with my mother." She lowered her voice even more. "The journey is long, though, and Catherine may not be strong enough to endure it just yet."

Georgiana leaned forward to ask, "Has she seen a physician?"

Diana Leigh smiled ruefully. "She absolutely refuses to see one." She looked down at her fingers, entwined so tightly they had gone white, then looked at Mary. "You were one of few people, I hope, to witness what really happened last evening, Miss Bennet." She did not wait for Mary's response. "My sister believed—we all believed—she would soon be engaged to the gentleman you saw treat her with such disdain." She took a deep breath, closing her eyes. "It is only since we came to London that we became aware of his attentions to another—a young lady with a great fortune, if the gossips can be believed." Her expression turned hard. "I know what they will say of Catherine; it is of no account to us except I would not wish to have the Burnabys' reputation tarnished because of their association with us. My sister and I hate London and count the moments until we are able to return home." She looked up. "Forgive me. We will never forget Mrs. Burnaby's kindness to us—nor yours. My sister has had so many disappointments this past year. And this latest, complete disillusionment about one she truly believed loved her...well, never mind." She smiled determinedly. "She will soon be better, and we will return to our mother and sister, where we belong." She lifted the teapot, her expression polite. "More tea?"

CHAPTER THIRTY-SIX

Mary took advantage of Lady Catherine's absence the following day (she had taken Miss de Bourgh to the milliner to purchase the required head coverings) to capture on paper the scene in which poor Catherine Leigh had played such an unfortunate role, one which Mary considered a vital illustration of how entails could adversely affect young ladies' fortunes, hopes, and dreams.

A knock at the door interrupted her musings, and Molly appeared with the long-awaited letter from her publisher. While Mary read the few lines from Mr. Egerton, her maid hovered, redundantly straightening and dusting.

Finally, Molly could no longer contain herself. "Well, miss? Does he like the book?"

Mary set the letter aside and began to pace. "He wishes to discuss changes to the manuscript." Her mind was awhirl—how to meet the publisher without Lady Catherine in attendance. "Molly, we need a plan...."

It was due to Georgiana's complete understanding of her Aunt Catherine's nature, as well as the unparalleled snobbery of her lady's maid, that Mary's plan to leave her writing partner behind when she met with Mr. Egerton in New Burlington Street came to fruition.

The prospect of drinking tea with one of the influential, exclusive ladies who determined the fate of so many at the proverbial gates to Almack's Assembly Rooms would be irresistible to Lady Catherine, so Georgiana proposed Lady Matlock invite Lady Castlereagh to tea on the very day of the appointment with the publisher.

Lady Matlock obliged her niece by issuing the invitation, and only after it was accepted did Mary tell Lady Catherine of the scheduled meeting with Mr. Egerton.

The second part of Georgiana's plan took place on the actual morning of the appointment. Below-stairs, in front of Lady Catherine's maid, Dawson, Lucy "accidentally" let slip the fact that Lady Castlereagh was coming to tea. The outcome was as predicted: Dawson flew up the narrow stairs to report to her mistress.

Once Lady Catherine was made aware of the auspicious lady's visit, bells began to ring insistently and incessantly. She and Miss de Bourgh must have hot water; they must have their finest gowns freshly pressed, their shoes brushed, and their hair arranged (by Molly). Dawson and Mrs. Jenkinson between them simply could not complete the necessary toilette for the de Bourghs, and therefore the services of all the ladies' maids would be required.

While having her hair coiffed, Lady Catherine had lectured both Mary and Mrs. Annesley (who was to accompany Mary in lieu of Lady Catherine) on the "proper handling of publishers."

Two hours later, Mary skipped down the steps to the waiting carriage.

When Mary and Mrs. Annesley entered Mr. Egerton's book-lined office, he gestured towards the chairs facing his desk. "Would you ladies care for tea?"

Mary, a lump in her throat from a hurried breakfast due to the last-minute summons by Lady Catherine, shook her head, while Mrs. Annesley accepted the offer with a look of relief. She too had been nearly run off her feet with the demands of Georgiana's aunt.

When Mr. Egerton pulled the manuscript in question from a drawer and pushed it across the shining desktop, Mary felt a sudden ringing in her ears. There were an astonishing number of comments written on the cover page alone. "You do not care for the title?"

Mr. Egerton smiled indulgently. "I have only suggested a few, Miss Bennet, for you did not give it a title."

Mrs. Annesley set her teacup down and leaned forward to view the top page, which was indeed without a title. With her eyes filled with humor, she prompted, "You had difficulty deciding upon one, Miss Bennet?"

Mary, her nerves in a state, nodded. "I had thought to name the book *The Wine Cellar*, but Lady Catherine de Bourgh of Rosings, who saw it as her duty to make sure my portrayal of all things involving society were absolutely correct, did not care for it."

Mr. Egerton leaned forward and began to rifle through a number of pages, each with an alarming number of editing marks. "Lady Catherine de Bourgh, you say?" He frowned as he flipped, Mary's heart sinking with each page. "I had a feeling there was more than one author to this book!" He slapped his hand on the desk and laughed.

Before she lost her nerve, Mary asked, "Do you think the book can be made acceptable for publication, or should I consider this a failed project?" She dreaded his response, but held her chin high.

"Of course it can be published!" Mr. Egerton stopped at a page on which many notations had been made. "However, I would like you to consider various suggestions given by my assistant, Miss Paige."

"Assistant?" Mary was confused.

"Yes, Miss Bennet. At least one of my assistants reads each book before I publish it, checking for spelling errors, inconsistencies—that sort of thing. These are Miss Paige's markings, not mine, though I have discussed the book with her at length. You need not make all the changes she suggests, but as you read them, please do consider why she wrote each particular comment." He looked at Mrs. Annesley. "The first two of Miss Bennet's books were something of an aberration." He rang for an assistant, asking the eager young man to wrap Miss Bennet's manuscript for her.

Mary stood and held out her gloved hand to the publisher. "I will try to justify your faith in me, Mr. Egerton."

"I am sure you will, Miss Bennet," he said, his grip firm. To her surprise he winked. "But you will need to do so without the help of Lady Catherine de Bourgh of Rosings, eh?"

Mrs. Annesley took the brown-paper parcel from the assistant, and with firm steps led the way through the glass door and down the block to a teashop.

Once the tea was ordered, Mary said, "I am so grateful to you for coming today, Mrs. Annesley. I felt so—"

Mrs. Annesley patted Mary's hand comfortingly. "I did nothing at all. You did just fine." She removed her gloves and placed them carefully in her reticule. "The difficult part is how you are going to manage those changes without the knowledge—or interference—of Lady Catherine!" She poured their tea before reaching for a tiny frosted cake.

～⌣⌣⌐

"Shall I arrange your hair now, miss?" Molly wielded her brush.

Mary sighed. "After reading through Miss Paige's suggested changes for only the first chapter, I would like only to slip between the covers, close my eyes, and not wake until sometime tomorrow afternoon."

"If you wish me to tell Her Ladyship's maid you are ill, I will do so."

"No—hiding away will do me no good. Besides, it would be insulting to the Miss Leighs."

Molly nodded sagely. "There was a girl once in my village who fell in love with a man and thought he would marry her." She began to braid a section of Mary's hair. "He abused her affection for him—if you know what I mean."

Mary twisted around on the dressing stool, shocked. "Molly! Such a tale of woe is not for tender ears!"

Molly, unfazed, continued her work. "My mother says it's far better to learn by others' misdeeds than your own."

Mary sat up straighter and turned back to the mirror. "Your mother is a wise woman. Do you think she would mind if I used her philosophy in my book?"

"No, miss. She'd be happy to hear of it. She's always saying things like that." Molly began another braid.

Mary thought it time to change the subject. "Have you learned anything useful from *The Mirror of the Graces*?" she asked, though she had her doubts.

Molly set the brush down on the dressing table and pulled the book from her apron pocket. She turned the first few pages, frowning. "There is one thing, miss, that has me confused. Here it is, on page nine." She held the book out to Mary, pointing. "Can you read this for me?"

Mary took up the book and read: "*In order to give a regular and perspicuous elucidation of the several branches of my subject....*" She paused. "Do you understand a word of this?"

"I did what you told me, and found every word I don't understand in the dictionary, but it still doesn't make much sense to me." Molly used the brush as a pointer. "Together, what do these two long words mean?"

"Perspicuous elucidation?"

Molly nodded.

Mary read the sentence three times over, frowning. "I guess what she means to say is she wants to give a clearly understandable explanation of the subject matter." Mary returned the book to her maid.

"Then why doesn't she just say so?"

Mary laughed. "I cannot say for certain, Molly, but I guess it is fashionable for writers to make their meaning obscure."

"Obscure—" Molly tried the word experimentally. "Then this writer must be a very fashionable lady," she said, making Mary laugh even harder.

That evening, before the dinner guests arrived, the earl and countess passed the time by including Georgiana and Mary in their discussion about a particular concert of the Philharmonic Society, the earl being the only one in the room to prefer the bombastic Beethoven work over the pianoforte pieces. "Too sleepy for me," he stated firmly. "I like a bit of excitement in my music."

Their conversation came to an end when Lady Catherine's clicking mules foretold her imminent appearance. Upon entering the oval anteroom, she immediately turned to a footman and barked, "Close those doors! The frigid air will make Miss de Bourgh ill!"

Lady Matlock, accustomed to her sister's behavior, did not belay the order to close the French doors, but instead nodded her acquiescence with a look of apology to the footman before asking, "Catherine, what is that in your hand?"

Lady Catherine's lips formed a thin, disapproving line. "I have just caught one of the maids—the one tending to Miss Bennet—" her narrowed gaze found Mary "—with this book!" She held up the evidence so everyone could see. It was *The Mirror of the Graces*. "She claims she had permission to read it! I of course seized it immediately, told her to pack her bags, and have only now come from seeing Steinman about the matter of her dismissal."

Georgiana's eyes grew wide with dismay while Mary took a step forward, but further movement was stayed by Lady Matlock's hand. She whispered through barely moving lips, "I will see to this, Mary," before turning to her husband. "My dear, would you please inform Catherine about Lady Castlereagh's card party next week? I will return in a moment." The earl turned immediately to his sister-in-law to do his wife's bidding, forcing Lady Catherine to remain, though her gaze followed the countess out of the room.

Mary felt a strong urge to leave also, to right the wrongs of the lady standing so officiously before them, but Georgiana's whispered words prevented any rash action.

"My aunt will take care of this. Molly will be all right—never fear."

When Lady Matlock returned, she gave Mary an encouraging nod, the color still high in her cheeks. Mary was of course more than anxious to learn what had transpired, but the first guests were announced.

Colonel Fitzwilliam, Major Ashton, and Lord Harold arrived together, Mrs. Burnaby, Deidre, and the two Miss Leighs close on their heels. The last to arrive were Lord and Lady Jameson, and Mary was grateful when Georgiana immediately introduced them to the Leighs, Catherine Leigh standing by silently, her face pale, expression vacant.

Mary, standing next to Miss de Bourgh, only half-listened as Deidre Burnaby described her recent presentation at court. Miss de Bourgh looked worried when Miss Burnaby claimed she nearly tripped on her gown when bowing out of the room. "I practiced walking backwards for days, but still I was in danger!"

Dinner was soon announced, and Mary was surprised to find Major Ashton standing next to her. "Miss Bennet?" He inclined his head, the usual sardonic smile on his lips. Mary hesitated only briefly before taking his arm, and felt an unexpected sensation, causing her to wonder why physical contact with *all* gentlemen did not have such a deleterious effect on her nerves. With such thoughts flying about, and another gentleman in the room who had once offered his arm to her with frequency, she kept her eyes down as they proceeded to the dining room, unaware of the thoughtful look on Lord Jameson's face.

The evening passed pleasantly enough, Major Ashton doing his best to draw Mary out, the attention pleasing, but she was preoccupied by worry for Molly and the presence of the frowning Lord Jameson.

Mary was gratified, however, to see Colonel Fitzwilliam and Lord Jameson speaking freely and at great length with one another. Happily, their relationship seemed to be much as it had been despite the captain's sudden elevation to a title.

Lady Catherine, meanwhile, took particular pleasure in quizzing Lady Jameson about living conditions at the castle in Scotland, recommending various remedies for small closets, ant infiltrations, and for servants who took too much lamb at dinner.

The dinner party was meant to help bring an end to the gossip about Catherine Leigh, as well as to make Morna feel more comfortable in London society, but none of the guests were at their best. It was therefore with a collective sigh of relief they all said goodnight, Lady Catherine the only one who seemed disappointed when the evening finally came to a close.

Immediately after the guests had gone, Mary sought an audience with Lady Matlock, but was perforce to wait until Lady Catherine climbed the stairs, volubly comparing them disfavourably to all at Rosings, even those used by the servants. Once she was far out of earshot (Lady Catherine had excellent hearing), Mary left her quiet corner of the room and approached the countess, who was speaking with Steinman.

"I am sorry to hear that Molly was brought to tears and will speak with her myself in the morning. There is to be no change in her status—none whatsoever, and I would appreciate it if you would convey this to the rest of the servants. Molly is highly valued by all of us, and she is to suffer no repercussions whatsoever from this unfortunate incident."

"Yes, My Lady," responded Steinman with a stiff bow and the closest thing to a smile Mary had ever seen on his face.

Once he had gone, the countess rubbed her forehead wearily. "Oh, Mary, be grateful you enjoy such communion with your sisters." She started for the stairs. "I have retrieved the book, and my maid has returned it to Molly. I am sorry to say, however, that my sister has upset her terribly. I will speak to Molly tomorrow—to both of them, actually."

"Thank you, Lady Matlock—Molly is sure to understand." Mary spoke with confidence. "She has spent a good deal of time at Rosings, you know."

Minutes later, when Molly came in response to the bell, Georgiana was with Mary, fully prepared to apologize on behalf of her Aunt Catherine.

However, Molly responded with admirable equanimity when asked about the incident. "I was worried at first, miss, but I've seen enough of Lady Catherine to know to ignore—" Molly's eyes grew wide "—I'm so sorry! What I mean to say is—"

Georgiana set her cup of cocoa down and impulsively hugged the young maid. "I understand your meaning, Molly. But was the book recovered?"

Molly nodded vehemently. "Lucy overheard Mr. Steinman say that Lady Matlock demanded the book back from Lady Catherine, and told her not to interfere with the servants at Darcy House again."

After Molly left, Georgiana said stoutly, "Aunt Catherine should never have taken the book from Molly; this is my brother's house, not hers."

"It is a good thing Lady Catherine has not discovered we are teaching our maids to read," Mary said thoughtfully. "Has she indicated how much longer she and Miss de Bourgh will remain in London?"

Georgiana shook her head. "She has made no mention of her plans. But my Aunt Matlock's reaction to this incident might accelerate things a bit."

CHAPTER THIRTY-SEVEN

(A Letter from Lord Matlock to Fitzwilliam Darcy)

Darcy House, 4 May 1814

Dear Fitzwilliam,

Our agents in America have sent word of Petersham's arrival in Boston, where he and his valet were apparently welcomed as heroes (we can only presume he was working for them all along). The two scoundrels managed to gain passage aboard a mail packet with an American captain, a faster boat than any of ours. Petersham's confederates in London will not fare so well, I assure you; it is but a matter of little time before arrests are made and this episode will be behind us. It is my greatest desire to return within the month to Devonham, where we can comfortably await the news of the safe delivery of our grand-nephew at Pemberley. If it were up to me we would leave for home tomorrow, but your good aunt tells me these things take time, and believes a little more of the season will do Georgiana good. Richard and I will remain vigilant, of course; there seem to be far more dandies and popinjays about than when I was a young man. To date my niece does not seem inclined towards any of them in particular, which is all for the best, for I have met none worthy of her.

Your Aunt Catherine is with us, and we are of course happy for Anne (although I believe Lord Wickford is closer in age to me than to her). I am more than ever grateful for the refuge of my club.

Yours affectionately,
Lord Matlock

CHAPTER THIRTY-EIGHT

(A Letter from Elizabeth Darcy to G Darcy & M Bennet)

Pemberley, 4 May 1814

To my dearest sisters,

I write one letter to you both, as I know you will share its contents regardless. You will be happy to learn that the Bingleys are safely arrived at Beechwood Manor, and could not be more pleased with the house and the estate. Mamma and Papa have finally decided to leave for Derbyshire in a fortnight, unless Mamma concocts yet another reason for delay.

Mrs. Annesley's sister is with us now, though the baby is not due until the third week of June, and it is my dearest hope you will both be back in Derbyshire long before then. Kitty has written several times, and sounds terribly home-sick and lonely. I have invited her to visit us, but Mr. Darnell cannot think of leaving his business right now and she will not come without him.

I want to hear more about your experiences in London, and would especially like to know how poor Miss Leigh fares. Given her current state of health, it would seem best for her to return to her mother. Should the two of them decide to leave, do you think they might care to stop at Pemberley for a few days to break the journey?

We all miss you—poor Samson looks in your rooms each day, and is sure to splatter your dresses with mud the minute you step from the carriage.

Until I see you again, take care and enjoy yourselves. My

best to Lady Matlock, Mrs. Burnaby, the Miss Leighs, and of course Lady Catherine and Cousin Anne.

Your loving sister,
Elizabeth Darcy

CHAPTER THIRTY-NINE

Mary had read through nearly half of Miss Paige's suggested changes to *The Wine Cellar,* all the while shaking her head and talking aloud as if Mr. Egerton's assistant were there with her.

"Mary, who on earth are you speaking to?" Georgiana looked about the otherwise empty room.

"This manuscript! Miss *Paige* completely misunderstood my meaning here—" Mary rifled back through several sheets "—and here—" she rifled through some more "—and here!"

Georgiana looked on, shaking her head sympathetically. "She does seem to have written an inordinate amount. Perhaps you are in need of a respite?"

Mary stood, stretching her arms to the ceiling. "I am *very* hungry."

"Mrs. Babcock must be clairvoyant, then, because she has prepared a luncheon for us, fearing we will not have the opportunity to take anything before the ball tonight."

"Then let us partake of the viands, by all means." Mary made a sweeping motion. "After you, my good friend!"

⌒⌣⌣⌒

When the Matlock party entered Almack's that evening, already brimming with London's most fashionable people, Mary was much surprised by Lady Castlereagh's singular attention. "Miss Bennet, I have only just learned you are the authoress of *The Turret Room*! I cannot tell you how much I look forward to reading more adventures of Miss White and Miss Benjamin!"

Mary was grateful Lady Catherine had already greeted the grand mistresses of the place, and was at the moment leading

Anne to a seat amongst the older, married ladies. "You are most kind," she replied to the grand lady, who, along with a select few, could refuse a duke entry to Almack's with the merest flick of her finger, and had actually done so.

"It is something of a feat to gain Lady Castlereagh's notice," whispered Georgiana behind her fan as they followed her aunt and uncle Matlock into the ballroom.

Mary could not help but be excited at the thought of Lady Castlereagh's influence on her book sales, and for a moment her little cottage grew a bit larger. But her ascension to greatness was short-lived as she looked upon the grand scene. All of a sudden she felt as if she were the Miss Mary Bennet of earlier days, a bane to her sisters and something of an embarrassment to her own mother—to the time when she decided to forgo her disguise as the proud, pedantic, proselytizing...she started at the sound of Colonel Fitzwilliam's voice.

"Miss Bennet, might I have the honor of the next set?" Mary looked about her, but Georgiana was already being escorted to the floor by Lord Harold. She was thankfully mistress of herself enough to respond graciously. "Thank you, Colonel, it would be a pleasure."

While waiting for the music to begin, Mary was pleased to see Lord Jameson escort Lady Jameson to the floor. At the next turn in the dance she watched Mrs. Burnaby enter, with Deidre and the Leigh sisters in tow. The younger Miss Leigh's dress looked far too large for her thin frame, and her face was like chalk—not unlike the fashion of the previous century, but her complexion was not by dint of a powder puff. The efforts of the countess to vanquish the gossips were successful in a small way, for only about half of the matrons' fans went up to hide their whispering when the Leighs passed by.

As Mary and the colonel passed down the line in the simple dance, she continued to watch, impatient with herself for feeling something she did not like to admit when Major Ashton offered his arm to the elder Miss Leigh. She was particularly interested to see Mr. Chandler leading Anne de Bourgh to the line of dancers.

"You appear to be most interested in who is dancing with whom," remarked the colonel drily.

Mary turned back to him, refusing to be embarrassed. "I cannot help but wonder why certain people are still free to come and go, rather than being in prison." Her glance rested briefly on Mr. Clay, in animated conversation with someone she did not know.

The colonel performed a sharp figure and returned to her. "You need not apologize, Miss Bennet, for I too am most anxious to see the end of all this play-acting and posturing. I wish to heaven I had never heard of Mr. P., and that the man had never been allowed to set foot in England."

Mary did not have a chance to reply for, the dance required they each move down the line to another partner. From her place Mary could see Mr. Clay scanning the room. She followed his gaze and thought she saw a moment of silent communication between him and the divinely-gowned Miss Grantly, who passed by in the crisscross pattern of the dance.

At the end of the set, Colonel Fitzwilliam uncharacteristically claimed the need for fresh air and he led Mary to the terrace, at the moment empty of people. "If you will pardon me a moment, Miss Bennet, I will soon return with refreshment." Mary obeyed what was clearly an order, but did wonder why he escorted her outdoors only to leave her alone.

Moments later, she heard someone approach from behind and turned around, the breath catching in her throat when she saw it was not the colonel, but Lord Jameson.

"Miss Bennet—" Lord Jameson was apologetic, and seemed nervous "—we have only a few seconds, but I wish to speak with you most urgently."

Mary was dismayed at what could only be construed as a tête-à-tête, worried Morna might come looking for her husband, but Lord Jameson held up his hand to prevent her from protesting. "I have recently learned the true reason for your refusal last autumn."

Mary could not stop herself. "What do you mean by 'true reason,' Lord Jameson?"

"Colonel Fitzwilliam has told me why you felt it imperative to turn me away—to treat me so coldly. My mother..." he looked deeply into her eyes, a habit of old. "But there is no time to say everything I wish; for propriety's sake I can remain but a few seconds. I wish only to say how much I admire you for what you have done—how I will never forget how you sacrificed your own wishes, possibly your future welfare as well, for the sake of my sisters and my mother. They will forever be in your debt, as will I." He seemed about to reach for her hands, but dropped his own to his side.

Mary looked up at the man who was first to admire her as the new Miss Mary Bennet, who had listened to her, who joined in conversation with her, who seemed to enjoy her company, and who had ultimately saved her life. As she stood on the terrace in the soft night air, a romantic moon shining overhead, she knew without a doubt she was no longer in love with him—perhaps never had been—but because he had applauded her when she spoke her mind, encouraged her to think independently and to believe in herself, he had played the part of a hero so well she had *thought* herself in love with him.

This epiphany gave her courage. "Lord Jameson, since you say I made the ultimate sacrifice to ensure the happiness of your mother and sisters, I would like to ask something of you in return."

"Anything, Miss Bennet." His looks and tone were sincere, and in her novelist's eye Mary saw him leaving her forever, his figure disappearing into a thick Scottish fog.

"I would ask you to see your wife, Morna, for the treasure she truly is, to treat her well, and to love her." She was not happy with her words, and had they been in a novel she would have rewritten them, but did not wish to delay the end of their meeting.

Lord Jameson had the grace to look ashamed. "Your noble actions are humbling, Miss Bennet—I will do better by Morna, please believe me." He stepped back and bowed, adding softly, "Please allow me to wish you the best of all fortunes, and to again offer my sincerest gratitude for what you have done."

Mary's heart was beating rapidly as she looked upon him for what she knew would be the last time, all the while fearing that the greatest gossips in all of London (namely Miss Bingley and Lord Exeter) would appear at any moment. "You must go, Lord Jameson. I wish both you and Lady Jameson joy, with all my heart."

He nodded and was gone.

Seconds later, Colonel Fitzwilliam appeared as if in a play, carrying two glasses and looking as innocent as could be.

～～～

Late that evening, after everyone in Darcy House was tucked in their beds, two men dressed in soiled, faded traveling clothes entered a dingy tap room on Drury Lane. The regular clientele looked up briefly before returning to their drinks.

"Two of your best ales," one of the men ordered as he placed the proper coins on the sticky surface of the bar.

The newcomers claimed the last vacant seats and appeared intent only upon drinking, soon banging their empty pints on the bar to catch the proprietor's attention.

The second man paid for the next round. After taking a deep draught of the bitter ale, he turned on his stool to view the others in the dark, crowded room. His friend remained facing the bar, observing the patrons through a mirror on the wall opposite.

After the fourth pint was poured and served, one of the patrons they were surreptitiously watching donned his cap and walked unsteadily to the exit, almost tripping as he stepped outside.

Immediately, the two newcomers followed the man out, shadowing him down the street and into a narrow alleyway. The first man grabbed the dunk man's arms and twisted them round his back.

"What do you want? I haven't got any money!" The intoxicated man struggled in vain against the stronger, sober one.

"We want information," growled the first man, who was in actual fact Colonel Fitzwilliam, his appearance so altered his own mother would not have known him. He dragged the weakly-protesting man back into the street, pushing him into a waiting carriage.

Major Ashton, similarly disguised, scanned the area with shaded eyes before following. Once inside the carriage, he tapped the roof and they were away in seconds.

The next afternoon, Lord Matlock called a conference at Darcy House. When all but Lady Catherine and Anne had convened in the study (Miss de Bourgh was being fitted for new riding boots), the earl cleared his throat and said, "Since you all know what occurred at Devonham in regard to Mr. Petersham and his valet, I thought you might like to hear about recent events.

"Last night, Colonel Fitzwilliam and Major Ashton apprehended the scoundrel who has been assisting Mr. Clay. After only a little encouragement, their captive admitted that Clay and one other person were involved in Miss Bingley's planned elopement, and that Clay has long been helping Petersham in whatever dastardly scheme he had up his sleeve." The earl paused briefly, allowing his words to sink in. "We now know for certain it was Mr. Clay who helped the valet escape Devonham, who arranged the elopement, and who assisted in Petersham's ultimate escape from England."

The earl was sitting on the edge of Mr. Darcy's desk and leaned forward to impart the last of his news, enjoying every moment. "I think this last bit of information will surprise you—" he looked at the ladies "—it was Miss Grantly who convinced Miss Bingley to elope and to sign her fortune over to Mr. Petersham. Miss Grantly has been in league with Petersham all along, and is in fact his legal wife!" Lord Matlock leaned back, triumphant.

Georgiana looked incredulous. "Wife!"

"Yes," said Colonel Fitzwilliam with a quick, apologetic glance at his cousin. "They have been married for many years, and somehow managed to keep their relationship completely secret. I am sorry to say she is as much a spy as Petersham ever was."

"I have long wondered how anyone could convince Miss Bingley to elope," Mary said before anyone—especially her good friend—could think longer about Mr. Petersham having been married while paying court to Georgiana.

Major Ashton most definitely winked at Mary. "We believe Petersham's vast wealth played a large role in her decision. Miss Grantly...er, Mrs. Petersham, is now in custody. She admitted to telling Miss Bingley if she did not elope with Petersham the marriage might never take place."

"And Miss Bingley believed her?" Mary was incredulous.

Georgiana, on the other hand, was thoughtful. "Caroline was angry about the postponement of the wedding. It is possible she was also worried about becoming an item for the gossips and thought an elopement would be better than no marriage at all." She paused, stressing her next point. "She would, after all, have become one of the wealthiest women in England."

The earl looked fondly upon his niece. "It is as plausible as any explanation we have at this point, but Mrs. Petersham will be undergoing further questioning."

"What will happen to her?" It surprised no one that Georgiana's first concern was the welfare of another, even if that person had committed treason.

Colonel Fitzwilliam unfolded his arms and pushed away from the wall. "The most lenient sentence she can be given is transportation."

"And Mr. Clay?" The countess looked worried.

"He has disappeared—but will soon be caught," said the colonel through clenched teeth.

Mary's mind went back to an incident never fully explained and directed her question to Lord Harold, who had been very quiet. "Was it you who met Mr. Petersham in the maze at Devonham on the day we went to Lady Matlock's cottage?"

Lord Harold's smile was apologetic. "I was under orders to play the part of Petersham's confederate for a time." He glanced at the major and the colonel. "Unfortunately, he never confided in me."

Lady Matlock looked hurt. "You never told me as much."

Lord Harold had the grace to look abashed. "My apologies, Lady Matlock—my orders for secrecy were given by Lord Castlereagh."

"Never mind all that," said the earl. "The reason I have called you together is to tell you it is all over. As soon as this Mr. Clay is in custody, we will have no need for further concern." He looked pointedly at Georgiana. "It is time for you and Miss Bennet to get down to the business of the season so we can all return to Derbyshire before Darcy's baby is born!"

CHAPTER FORTY

(A Letter from Mrs. George Wickham to Mary Bennet)

Kingston, Jamaica, 20 February 1814

Dear Mary,

Mrs. Lottington, a dear friend to George and me, said something very interesting at tea the other day—she said you had written a novel! And called yourself "A Lady" of all things! George and I were quite diverted, I tell you, and laughed and laughed—people can be so stupid! One wonders how such stories get started. You must write immediately to deny this, for despite all my arguments, Mrs. Lottington stands firm (she likes to be right in all things, so it would be great fun to prove her wrong). It was difficult enough to believe Kitty when she wrote and said your looks had improved—but to be an authoress? Ridiculous! I understand you continue to stay with the Darcys. I suppose it is better than becoming a governess.

Mamma wrote to say Mr. Webb is to marry Miss King (I never could see anything in her), when we all thought you were destined for him. Perhaps you are disappointed and I should be very sorry for you, but I will feel sorry for Miss King instead—to be tied to the vicar's son! If you want to catch a husband, follow my advice: smile and laugh at everything gentlemen say, for they surely do prefer it to all things. Also, pinch your cheeks for color and press your lips together frequently. Do not talk about books or music, and for heaven's sake, never perform on the pianoforte!

I must close, for we are to attend a masquerade tonight, and my costume will take some time to prepare. When you next see or write to Elizabeth and Jane, please remind them of my letters, for they are very slow in responding.

Your sister,
Lydia Wickham

CHAPTER FORTY-ONE

The day after Mary's clandestine meeting with Lord Jameson, Morna came to call at Darcy House. "James has tired of London and wishes to return to Scotland," she announced almost immediately upon entering the morning room, her face beaming. "I will soon be back at home with my horses and my dogs!"

Lady Matlock gestured to a chair. "This is a sudden plan, is it not?"

Morna nodded, her eyes bright as she sat down. "He told me he has finished his business in town and wishes to return to Scotland." She smiled shyly. "I hope you are not disappointed in me, after introducing me to your friends. How can I ever thank you?"

Georgiana looked towards her aunt. "We did nothing at all out of the ordinary, Lady Jameson—"

"Oh! You must always call me Morna. And I will always call you Georgiana." She turned to Mary with a shy smile. "Will you both write to me?"

Georgiana, who knew of Mary's private interview with Lord Jameson, prevented her friend from having to think of an appropriate response. "Of course, Morna; we will be eager to hear your news." She grinned. "I too am fond of horses and dogs—there is a spaniel at Pemberley—"

"Steinman!" Lady Catherine's raised voice coming from the hall brought all pleasantries to an end. "Where is Lady Matlock?"

When Lady Catherine entered the morning room seconds later, Morna stood. "You must all excuse me," she said breathlessly, "but I cannot stay——there is much to see to before our departure." She curtsied and made as if to go.

"I will see you out," Georgiana offered, and they left the room together, unaware of either the displeased look on Lady Catherine's face, or her exclamation, "Well, I never!"

‧‧‧

At Pemberley, Mr. Darcy did not find his wife in the nursery, where she was in the habit of going each afternoon. While passing through the portrait hall, he came across their housekeeper and asked, "Mrs. Reynolds, have you seen Mrs. Darcy recently?"

Mrs. Reynolds, ever ready to assist, tapped a finger to her lip, thinking. "I believe she is in her morning room, sir."

Mr. Darcy thanked her and proceeded to the empty morning room, where Elizabeth's desk was littered with plans for her miniature model of Pemberley. As he left the room, he encountered one of the housemaids, who was in such awe of her master she could barely form the words "no, sir" when asked if she knew Mrs. Darcy's whereabouts. Mr. Darcy thanked her and passed through the portrait hall on the way to his study.

Elizabeth was there, sitting in the chair behind his desk, pouring over an architectural drawing. When Darcy moved closer, a smile forming on his lips, he saw it was the original plan for Pemberley.

"Fitzwilliam! How good of you to join me." Elizabeth pointed at a particular section of the large sheet. "While studying the plans for the model, I found a curious discrepancy in the guest wing." She made room for him to examine the page more closely, pulling a large sheet from under the drawing of Pemberley. "If you look on the plan for the little house—" she refused to call it a doll house "—there is a significant difference in the size of one of the rooms." She laid the miniature-version drawing of Pemberley alongside the original. "Do you see what I mean?"

Darcy leaned forward and compared the two. "Lizzy, I believe you might have discovered something."

Elizabeth's eyes grew round. "How exciting! Do you think it

might be a hidden room?" She looked back at the drawing. "Where exactly is this?"

Mr. Darcy drew a chair closer to the desk, and together they compared the drawings.

"This is just the type of thing to interest Georgiana and Mary." Elizabeth tapped her finger against her cheek. "Do you have any reason to hope Georgiana has yet found a gentleman worthy of her?"

Darcy grimaced, leaning back in his chair. "No, I do not. Richard has sent reports on every caper-witted mushroom competing for her attention; I have begun to think this venture is a complete waste of time and am days away from ordering her back to Pemberley."

Elizabeth's dimples appeared. "Ordering, my dear?"

Darcy bowed his head. "Forgive me. I will write to ask if she would care to return home sooner than planned. Will that do?"

"It would indeed, Mr. Darcy." Elizabeth's shining eyes returned to the drawings. "In the meantime, we can discover the meaning of this."

Suddenly, she gasped and Mr. Darcy looked up, concerned. "Lizzy?"

She took a deep breath, forcing a smile to allay his fears, and placed a hand on her midsection. "It is only this baby of yours— it has been kicking all morning." She took hold of Mr. Darcy's hand and held it next to her own. "Mamma believes a boy will kick more often than a girl."

They waited in silence for the baby to kick again, but were not rewarded. "Our son seems to like it when you sing—" Mr. Darcy spoke in earnest "—perhaps we could both hear you this evening? You know how much it pleases me."

Elizabeth said cheekily, "As I told Charlotte eons ago, I do not care to sing in front of everybody and anybody. However, I will grant your request, Mr. Darcy, if you will grant mine and help me discover if there is anything to this—" she pointed to the plans.

"Done," he promised.

Once inside Darcy House, Colonel Fitzwilliam stamped his feet. "I do not mind going out in the rain, but to have to endure the rattle-pated nonsense of jingle-brained idiots—pardon me, mother—who are clearly out to make a match with any female as long as she is attached to a fortune! The entire evening was intolerable! Father was far better off meeting with Lord Castlereagh."

Georgiana removed her gloves, sighing. "I agree wholeheartedly, and do not know how many more of these fêtes I can attend—the constant talk of nothing is so exhausting! My uncle was wise to remain at home tonight."

Lady Matlock, after removing her cape, gave whispered instructions to her maid before directing her son, niece, and Mary to the sitting room. When they were inside with the door closed, she stood at the mantle and faced her audience, her manner stern. "Georgiana, I do not believe you will ever agree to marry even the most kind, handsome, and eligible man in the kingdom." She turned her eyes towards Mary. "And you, Miss Bennet, would task the most dedicated match-maker beyond endurance." There was a light knock on the door and the butler entered carrying a tray.

"Thank you, Steinman," said Lady Matlock, waiting until he departed and the door was closed once more. "Lord Matlock and I are of the opinion that it is no use trying to force you to choose a marriage partner, Georgiana, and although we are both willing to continue here and accompany you wherever you wish to go, we think we might just as well bring this season to an end so we can return to Derbyshire where we will all be more comfortable." She watched as Georgiana attempted to hide a yawn behind her hand. "And far less tired," she said pointedly.

The atmosphere in the room fairly crackled, and even Colonel Fitzwilliam dared not speak while his mother indicated with only the slightest nod for him to pour. "We will make a pact to keep this amongst ourselves—my sister Catherine would not for an instant sanction forfeiting the season." Lady Matlock lifted her glass and waited while the others solemnly chose one from the tray. "Agreed?"

Her audience touched their glasses together.

Later that night, when Mary and Georgiana were fast asleep, Colonel Fitzwilliam and Major Ashton were once more dressed in their disguises, crouched on the servants' stairs across the street from a particular house on Bridgewater Square.

"He should have come out by now," the colonel said quietly.

"I agree." Major Ashton tried without success to stretch his left leg, which had begun to cramp. "Is it possible he slipped out the back unseen?"

"I do not see how he could evade so many of our men." The colonel was clearly frustrated. "We have seen no one in the street since the groom left with the carriage."

"The groom did seem similar in height and build to Mr. Clay."

"We could not have been fooled by such a simple ploy," insisted the colonel, though there was some doubt in his voice. "But if Clay left, disguised as the groom—"

"We may never find him," growled the major.

The colonel stood. "Get two of the men to relieve us—we must get to the mews!"

CHAPTER FORTY-TWO

Mary set her pen down with finality and a great sigh.

"How do you think Mr. Egerton will react?" Georgiana sat across the room, sketching Mary 'for prosperity.'

Mary twisted round and shrugged. "He will no doubt refuse to publish the book. But as it is primarily *my* work, other than a fair number of Lady Catherine and Miss Paige's suggestions to appease each of them, I believe I must have the final say." She straightened the pages and pulled out a large sheet of brown wrapping.

"I thought the publisher's office would make for a pleasurable excursion, as Lady Catherine has taken Miss de Bourgh for the final fitting of her wedding dress."

Georgiana laid her sketch-book aside, grinning. "Then there is no time to lose!"

Lady Matlock could not accompany Mary and Georgiana to the publisher as she was expecting callers, but insisted they take Molly and Lucy, and assigned two footmen to ride outside the carriage. "For Mr. Clay is not yet found."

When they arrived at the publisher's office, Mary was secretly relieved to learn Mr. Egerton was with another client, and left the manuscript for *The Wine Cellar* with one of his assistants (Miss Paige was happily out), who said shyly, "My mother, wife, and two daughters will be pleased to know there is to be a sequel to *The Turret Room*, Miss Bennet."

The two young ladies left the publisher's office in high spirits. Upon reaching the Darcy carriage, Georgiana stoutly instructed the coachman to take them to Ludgate Hill, where they could purchase gifts for Elizabeth and the baby.

When they returned to Darcy House, Steinman immediately led Georgiana and Mary to the library, where Colonel Fitzwilliam and Major Ashton were waiting impatiently.

"Where have you been, Georgiana? It is nearly half-past four!" Her cousin looked more displeased than worried.

"We had a number of errands to see to, and were well protected," responded Georgiana a trifle defensively. "Whatever has happened?"

The colonel handed a sealed letter to Mary. "While you were out, this urgent message was delivered—it is from a Mrs. D'Arblay, whose husband is a French émigré."

Mary took up the letter, curious. "I know of no one by that name." She looked at the two men with no idea why they should be interested in her correspondence.

"Given the current state of our investigation and the unfortunate disappearance of Clay, we were hoping you might read it in our presence, Miss Bennet. The messenger said it was urgent." The colonel's brows rose.

Mary broke the wax seal without hesitation.

> *11 Boulton Street, Mayfair*
> *10 May 1814*
>
> *Dear Miss Bennet,*
> *We have not yet been introduced, but I send this note to you by request of Her Majesty, Queen Charlotte. May I beg the favour of your call tomorrow afternoon at three o'clock?*
> *Yours sincerely,*
> *Mrs. Alexandre D'Arblay*
> *(aka Fanny Burney)*

Mary handed the note first to Georgiana, who after reading it, protested, "You act as though you think Mary is a spy!" She huffed. "I think you owe Miss Bennet an apology, gentlemen." She held the letter out.

Colonel Fitzwilliam and Major Ashton read it simultaneously, and the major was the first to speak. "I am sorry we were officious, Miss Bennet—had the lady used the name by which she is better known—"

"Well, she can hardly go about calling herself by her maiden name, can she?" demanded Georgiana, who went to the bell-pull. "Would anyone else care for tea?"

Mary looked from one to the other of them. "Can you please tell me what you all appear to know, which I do not?"

"Fanny Burney is the daughter of a renowned music scholar, and at one time was in the service of the Queen. I am sorry to say neither the colonel nor I knew she was also called Mrs. D'Arblay." The major looked very apologetic.

Georgiana waited for Mary's reaction before prodding, "She is also an extremely popular authoress, best known by her maiden name."

Mary looked again at the signature on the letter, embarrassed. "Miss Fanny Burney? Did she not write the book you are reading now...*Evelina*?" Mary re-read the note. "Whyever would she beg a favor of me?"

Georgiana responded with a grin, "You shall have to visit her tomorrow and see!"

At precisely three o'clock the following afternoon, Mary, full of nerves and curiosity, was shown into an ornate drawing room crowded with heavy furniture. A woman who by Mary's calculations had to be well over fifty years old, but looked much younger, rose to greet her.

"Miss Bennet! How good of you to come! Please sit down."

Mary did as her hostess requested, not daring to speak for fear she would breech some societal rule, remembering that the lady before her was on intimate terms with the queen.

"I am Mrs. D'Arblay—perhaps you might know me better by my maiden name—Fanny Burney."

Mary's eyes lit up. "Yes, indeed, Mrs. D'Arblay. I cannot express how honored I am to meet you."

"Please call me Fanny, Miss Bennet. I was raised in a household where formality was not highly regarded." Mrs. D'Arblay waited while a housemaid set a tray on the table between them. "Thank you, Jenny."

"I am not currently residing in London, Miss Bennet—"

At her hesitation Mary begged, "Please, do call me Mary."

"I will be happy to." Mrs. D'Arblay said cheerily as she prepared the tea. "Do you take cream, Mary?"

"A little, if you please...Fanny." Mary marveled at the woman's ability to put a complete stranger at ease so quickly.

"My husband and I have made our home in Bath, and my time in London is short, for we leave tomorrow. As such, I will dispense first with my commission, and then I want to hear all about you." Mrs. D'Arblay smiled kindly. "I have enjoyed your books immensely—your use of irony is unique and entertaining."

Now Mary blushed, for she had not yet read Miss Burney's works (the circulating librarian in Meryton had taken a dislike to Miss Burney's father—no one had been clear on the particulars—and the end result was the librarian had refused to stock books written by anyone connected to him). "Thank you, although you are much too kind. *Your* books have paved the way for female authors; it may otherwise have never occurred to me to try to publish myself."

"As you have been published anonymously, you must wonder how I learned your identity." She handed Mary her cup. "Sadly, few secrets survive in society, and your identity has become generally known." She smiled at Mary's dismay. "I would not let it concern you. I know of another authoress who has published books anonymously and calls herself 'A Lady' as you have done—her books are rather a favorite of mine. She is from the country and is somewhat retiring, her father having been a vicar of no great wealth. She is not without connections, however, for one of her brothers inherited a vast estate, and another is married to a former comtesse. Perhaps when we are next in town I might introduce you to her—the writer, I mean. I think you would get on quite well." Mrs. D'Arblay was apparently satisfied with Mary's slight nod, for she continued. "But I must get to the reason for my request.

"When I was thirty-four years of age and unmarried, a good friend of mine introduced me to Queen Charlotte, who offered me a post as Second Keeper of the Robes. At the time it seemed foolish to refuse, although I did not wish to be separated from my family and feared I would not have enough time to write. I remained in the post for four years, despite being under the thumb of the domineering, pestering woman who was my direct superior.

"In those years I grew close to the queen and the young princesses." She lifted a tray of sweet biscuits and Mary took one. "The queen is a great reader, especially since the onset of poor King George's trouble. She has read each of your books, and wishes me to convey her wishes for you to write a sequel to *The Turret Room*. Should you write one, it would please Her Majesty if you would dedicate the book to her." Mrs. D'Arblay had clearly dispensed with her duty, and watched Mary's expression closely.

Mary felt as if her face had changed color several times, and wondered if it were natural to feel parched just after taking a sip of tea. Queens simply didn't ask favors of the Bennet family. She cleared her throat and swallowed nervously, thinking of the sequel resting upon Mr. Egerton's desk, with her corrections and comments written next to those of Miss Paige.

"I *have* written a sequel," she admitted reflectively, "but Mr. Egerton, my publisher, asked for some changes to be made...."

Mrs. D'Arblay laughed. "And you felt your offspring had been criticized without just cause, did you not?" She looked at Mary, her expression rueful. "It has happened to me as well, more often than I care to admit. I have had to train myself to see beyond the emotional response to what feels like a personal attack and try to decide without prejudice whether what is being suggested might actually be an improvement. On the other hand, there are times when you must simply trust yourself."

Mary thought back to her reaction about one rather large section Miss Paige had wanted removed completely. "You describe it as if you had been there."

"The first time is the worst. It will get easier, I promise."

"If Mr. Egerton will publish the book, I will be pleased to dedicate it to Her Highness," Mary said before finally taking a bite of the biscuit. Her words were unnecessary, as any 'request' by the queen would never be denied by anyone with sense.

"The queen will be most pleased to know the book is so close to publication." Mrs. D'Arblay adjusted her skirts. "You are not married, Mary?"

Mary shook her head.

"Nor engaged?"

Mary paused briefly before shaking her head once more, which did not go unnoticed.

"When I was nearer your age, I turned down more than one offer of marriage, believing it best to remain unmarried so I might write freely. I enjoyed the company of my father, you see, and as my books had begun to make a profit I did not feel the need to marry. It was not until I was...let me see, I must have been thirty-eight at the time—" she grinned "—I was quite the spinster! I fell in love with a gentleman who sadly married another, wealthier woman." She turned a shrewd eye on her audience. "You need not look so concerned, Mary; it was all for the best, as some novelists tell us. Three years later I married Monsieur D'Arblay, and have been content ever since. But I will tell you this—" she pointed her index finger "—those years before I married my husband were long and lonely, and there was plenty of time for regret. Being a writer was *not* enough, and I have a feeling it may not be so for you, either."

Throughout the carriage ride back to Darcy House, Mary could not attend to Molly's complaints about the laxity she witnessed amongst the servants at the Boulton Street house, for her head was swimming.

Once at Darcy House, it took a full thirty minutes to describe to the others all that was said and to answer their questions, and it was not until she was in the privacy of her own room that Mary allowed herself to ponder Mrs. D'Arblay's words.

When Georgiana married, it would no longer suit Mary to be the perpetual guest of her friend, and as she sat in front of the mirror reflecting a young lady with fear in her eyes, she wondered if Captain Jameson's attentions had been welcome because she secretly feared loneliness? And what about Major Ashton's offer—she had actually considered accepting him, but for what reason? Mary sat for a long time at her dressing table, staring into the mirror. What was to become of her?

Early the next morning, Georgiana rushed into Mary's room. "Mary! Lucy has just told me news of a most disturbing nature!"

Mary punched her pillows and sat up higher, her eyes still blurry with sleep. "What has happened?"

Georgiana took up Mary's dressing gown. "It is Catherine Leigh—her sister writes to say they must leave London as soon as possible, for she has become seriously ill. My cousin and the major are devising a plan to take her home!"

Mary threw aside the covers and put on the dressing gown, impatiently pulling her long hair from underneath the collar. "What is their plan?"

"They are to personally escort the Miss Leighs to Pemberley, where they will stop to allow Dr. Braxton to assess the state of Catherine's health." She leaned forward to whisper, "Miss Bingley says it is all due to the man Catherine Leigh saw at the concert in the company of another young lady. Apparently Miss Leigh believed she was about to become his wife."

Mary's eyes opened wide. "Breach of promise?" And in the next second asked, "Miss Bingley said this?"

Georgiana went to the door. "There was evidently no promise made—the strength of his affections was assumed by those who witnessed his behavior with Catherine."

"What can we do to help?" Mary asked.

"Get dressed quickly, and fix your hair simply, for we have not a moment to lose. I believe I have a plan which will suit us all."

Mary recognized the gleam of determination in Georgiana's eyes.

CHAPTER FORTY-THREE

The earl and countess thought Georgiana's plan to be a fine one, and Colonel Fitzwilliam and Major Ashton were soon recruited to approach Mrs. Burnaby. Just after noon on that very day, they were shown into her drawing room in Mayfair.

Mrs. Burnaby was filled with the beneficence of one who was not to be put out. "Miss Darcy is too, too kind to offer her carriage! And you gentlemen—to offer to take the poor dears to Derbyshire and then on to their mother! Deidre and I would have done so ourselves, if only we had Mr. Burnaby to protect us on the journey." She wrung her hands and turned in half-circles as she spoke. "I will have the Miss Leighs ready as soon as may be, but there is much to be done!"

Major Ashton suggested, "If we might speak with the elder Miss Leigh, Mrs. Burnaby, it might help put her mind at ease."

Mrs. Burnaby stared blankly at him for a moment before bobbing a slight curtsey. "Yes, yes, of course, Major Ashton. I will have her brought to you immediately. If you will forgive me, I must go to instruct the servants." With a last, grateful glance, she rushed from the room, calling out to a passing servant to gather the trunks.

As they waited for Diana Leigh to appear, Major Ashton walked about the room, picking up a china figure here, an ornate vase there.

"What are you doing, Ashton?" the colonel grumbled.

The major set a carved wooden animal down, presumably an elephant. "Such an inordinate number of trinkets makes me nervous."

The colonel's response was a great sigh, but before the major could do anything more to irritate him, Diana Leigh appeared, her hair pulled back with a plain ribbon, her dress not at all fashionable, her face pale. She was clearly distracted and wore an air of exhaustion, but thoughtfully asked the two men to be seated.

"I understand Miss Darcy is offering us a place in her carriage to Derbyshire, for which we are extremely grateful." Diana Leigh's voice shook slightly. "I have not informed my mother about the seriousness of Catherine's condition, for I did not wish to worry her unduly and did not know when we might be so fortunate as to return home." She looked down at her clasped hands. "My father is away on business—" her face colored "—and we cannot rely upon his assistance." She looked up and said, "To put it plainly, I would like to accept her offer, but do not know how we will get from Derbyshire to our mother in Buckinghamshire."

Colonel Fitzwilliam spoke firmly, brooking no argument. "Miss Leigh, the major and I will accompany the four of you to Derbyshire; once we reach Pemberley, he and I will personally escort you and your sister to Buckinghamshire—it will be our pleasure."

"I regret having to beg such a favor, but I do not believe my sister's health will recover as long as we remain in town. It is her wish—and mine—to leave London as soon as possible. Your offer is as a miracle to us." Diana Leigh stood, her eyes showing signs of threatening tears. "I must see to the arrangements. We will be ready for the journey at whatever time you specify."

"Will tomorrow morning suit?" Major Ashton asked, watching her face carefully.

Miss Leigh nodded, her relief clear. "It would, Major Ashton. We will be ready."

Just as the colonel and the major stepped into the bright sunshine, Lord Exeter exited a carriage and turned to assist someone, whose soft kid slipper, delicate ankle, and lace-covered hem forewarned them of Miss Bingley's presence.

"Ah, Colonel Fitzwilliam—Major Ashton." Lord Exeter smiled as Miss Bingley took his arm possessively while pointedly not looking at the major. "Are you leaving? We have only just arrived to call on the poor Miss Leighs." He shook his head in fine imitation of pity. "Miss Caroline has not been looking at all well of late, and we have come to cheer her."

After a brief exchange, the colonel and major made their apologies and departed. As they strode down the street, Colonel Fitzwilliam mumbled, "Cheer her, indeed. If only Exeter could have been the one to arrest instead of Clay!"

~~~~

At dinner that evening, Lady Catherine was not pleased. "Why not simply send a servant with those two Leigh girls? Surely my niece and Miss Bennet need not return to Derbyshire so soon, and on such an errand!" She set her narrowed eyes on Georgiana. "If you leave now, you will have accomplished nothing this season."

"It is Darcy's desire that Georgiana return to Pemberley, Catherine," said the countess gently. "And Mrs. Darcy would like her sister with her, for the time of the birth is fast approaching."

"What of Mrs. Annesley?" Lady Catherine was not one to give up easily. "Surely it would be no hardship for her to accompany them?"

"It is Mrs. Annesley's desire to return to Bath to care for her nieces—her sister has gone to Pemberley to act as Mrs. Darcy's midwife," responded the countess patiently.

Lady Catherine lifted her napkin, dabbing somewhat violently at the corners of her mouth. "And what of our novel, Miss Bennet? Of course I must now act as its representative. It will take time away from Anne and the wedding preparations—" she glanced down the table at her daughter, who was having difficulty with the capon on her plate "—but I will manage."

Mary had not yet heard back from Mr. Egerton regarding *The Wine Cellar*, but had no intention of allowing Lady Catherine to take charge of the book. She took a deep, calming breath. "There is no need for further action on the novel, Lady Catherine, but I thank you for your kindness at a time when Miss de Bourgh's wedding must necessarily demand all your attention."

Lady Catherine looked upon Mary with narrowed eyes for a moment before turning towards Colonel Fitzwilliam. "And who will accompany Anne to the fête tomorrow?"

"Mr. Chandler has kindly offered to escort Anne, my dear." Lady Matlock was firm. "He is a charming gentleman of long acquaintance and has been kind to her, as you have seen for yourself—" she looked down the table, and Miss de Bourgh blushed, causing Mary to wonder if perhaps the young and handsome Mr. Chandler might be a challenge to the much older Lord Wickford. In the next second she dismissed the idea, for Miss de Bourgh could never do anything so rash, no matter how great the temptation. No, her fate was sealed.

"It is all very well for you to say so, dear sister, but Richard is far more familiar with Anne's needs." Lady Catherine looked accusingly at her nephew, who took a bite of fowl.

⁓

At ten o'clock the following morning, Georgiana and Mary were comfortably situated in Mr. Darcy's landau, spacious enough to seat six people. Seeing they were ready, Colonel Fitzwilliam issued orders to the footmen, and he and Major Ashton mounted their horses, both striking in their regimental uniforms.

As the carriage began to move, Mary sat back, her mind awhirl. She had hoped for the opportunity to thank Major Ashton for what he was doing on behalf of the Miss Leighs, but had only managed to say "you are most kind" when he had helped her inside the vehicle. Upon his response, "It is my pleasure to see all of you safely home, Miss Bennet," she had replied without thought, "Derbyshire is not my home." His response had then been, "Who knows where your home will be in the end, Miss Bennet?"

Mary was kicking herself for having no reply at the ready.

The Miss Leighs were waiting in the Burnabys' morning room when the Darcy carriage arrived, and the colonel insisted they leave immediately. Mrs. Burnaby kissed her two young charges and wished them well, alternately waving her handkerchief and holding it to her mouth as they drove off.

Catherine Leigh did not look well, the dark shadows under her eyes deeper than ever. Neither Georgiana nor Mary wished to disturb her, and after only the minimum of conversation were quiet.

So great was Catherine Leigh's exhaustion she was asleep on her sister's shoulder before they reached the outskirts of London. The gentle movement of the carriage lulled the others to sleep as well, Mary's eyes closing after reading only the first chapter of Fanny Burney's epistolary novel, *Evelina*.

They all came awake, however, at a sudden explosive noise. The carriage shifted violently and the young ladies were thrown against the wall, their cries lost amongst the neighing horses and shouting men. The four inside held on to each other for dear life as the carriage swung violently back and forth.

"What is happening?" cried Diana Leigh.

Outside, Colonel Fitzwilliam and Major Ashton tried to draw their horses close to the swinging carriage so they might jump aboard, but they soon found it was impossible. The colonel pushed his horse harder to get alongside the front of the carriage, where he used hand signals to convey orders to the coachman and groom, while ahead of them the four horses galloped out of control.

Quickly comprehending what the colonel wished him to do, the groom released his grip on the bench and threw himself to the floor where he waited, crouching. In the next instant he jumped onto the back of one of the horses, fighting for a grip on the harness.

For a few moments it appeared the groom would fail, but suddenly he righted himself, his arms wound around the horse's neck as he struggled to stay on the frightened animal.

The colonel continued riding alongside the carriage at a dangerous pace, miming to the coachman to try to separate the horses from the carriage. The frightened man gripped the reins as he too crouched low in front of the seat, ready to leap from the wildly swinging vehicle in the hopes of landing safely on the back of another horse. Suddenly he jumped, the reins he had wrapped around his forearm saving him from falling under the horses' beating hooves.

Inside, the others were sobbing and Mary knew they expected to die. She realized then how very much she wanted to live. She wanted to see a healthy Elizabeth holding her newborn baby; she wanted to see the proud look on her Mamma and Papa's face as they looked upon their two grandchildren; she wanted to play duets with Georgiana; she wanted to finish reading Miss Burney's novel; she wanted to see Molly's dream of becoming a seamstress come true...she realized all these things at once. She also realized she wanted to tell Major Ashton she would *seriously* consider his offer of marriage—whether it be one based on friendship or on love.

Meanwhile, the coachman and groom were preparing to cut the strapping that would separate the carriage from the panicked horses. They had their folding-knives ready, and on a silent count of three cut through the leather. In the next instant, the horses and their riders were away, the carriage careening violently along the rough, gravel-covered road.

All the wheels had broken and the frame of the carriage scraped along the road, a rising wall of dust and debris behind it. Suddenly, it struck against a boulder and skidded to the grassy edge. Inside, the four helpless ladies were tossed about like ragdolls, unable to brace themselves for the inevitable crash.

The men watched in horror as the now horseless carriage flipped over, landing on its side only a few feet from the edge of a precipice. They feared the worst, when suddenly the carriage came to a dead stop, the only thing preventing it from tumbling down the hillside being the trunk of a single tree.

In the same instant, Major Ashton and Colonel Fitzwilliam pulled hard on the reins and jumped from their horses. They ran as fast as they could, reaching the ruin of Mr. Darcy's carriage just after it came to a halt.

The colonel rushed to the side of the carriage that was leaning against the tree, he and one of the footmen using their backs to brace against the vehicle.

The major scrambled up the side of the carriage, ripping the door from its frame and throwing it to the ground. He looked inside where the four young ladies had landed in a heap, one upon the other.

In the sudden, eerie stillness, Major Ashton called through the opening, "Miss Bennet—Miss Darcy—Miss Leigh! Can anyone hear me?"

"Major Ashton?" The thin, shaking voice was Georgiana's. "I think I am all right—Mary?" she cried out fearfully. "Diana? Catherine?"

Diana Leigh's voice was muffled. "Catherine and I are bruised, but I think unhurt." There was a pause. "Miss Bennet is underneath us and has not made a sound; I cannot move to help her."

"We will get you out." The major spoke with the determined calm of a soldier. "Miss Darcy—" he carefully lowered himself inside, placing one foot on the battered window frame for support "—can you take hold of my hand?"

Georgiana had to lean into the side of one of the Miss Leighs in order to raise her arm, causing Diana Leigh to gasp. "I am so sorry," Georgiana whispered just as the major managed to take hold of her gloved hand. He pulled, lifting her off the others until he could grasp her upper arm, her feet dangling free for a moment while he lifted her through the opening. One of the footmen was there, waiting to help her to the ground and safety.

The men worked quickly and efficiently, Colonel Fitzwilliam and now two of the footmen using all their strength to hold the carriage in place, the small tree creaking ominously with each movement inside the carriage.

Inside, Mary was aware of a great weight being lifted from her chest and she struggled to take a breath. The simple action brought searing pain. She tried to speak, but only managed to whimper pathetically before she lost consciousness.

Major Ashton heard the sound and looked with great concern upon the still form below him. "Miss Bennet? Are you in pain?" When she did not respond, he used the bench as a brace and lowered himself even more, until he could place his feet on either side of her. He put his hand to her cheek. Finding it warm, he held his hand close to her nose and mouth, the relief upon feeling her breath evident in his features. He called out, "Miss Bennet is unconscious! I need help!"

CHAPTER FORTY-FOUR

Mary was confused and in pain. A man was calling out to a Miss Bennet, but Mary did not know such a person. She only knew she was in great pain and discomfort, and tried to turn her head to see the person, causing her head to pound. She cried out in a small voice, "Please—I am hurt!"

When he saw Mary was once more conscious, Major Ashton's relief was palpable. He leaned closer to her still form. "I will help you, Miss Bennet, do not be afraid." He began to look for signs of serious injury. "But I must lift you up and get you out of here—the coach is not safe."

Mary opened her eyes to see a handsome gentleman with kind eyes and a worried expression. "Please."

"You must let me know if I hurt you." He began to lift her, the confined space giving him no small amount of trouble. Mary stifled a cry as he gathered her in his arms. "You may have some broken ribs—we will try not to cause additional pain." He looked up through the opening at the waiting footman, who had heard and was nodding his understanding. The two of them worked in concert to lift Mary from the carriage, and she ground her teeth together to stifle any cries until she was laid down on the soft grass alongside the three ladies, who were bruised and shaken, but otherwise unhurt.

After Major Ashton handed out whatever he could of the belongings inside, he quickly climbed out of the carriage. Colonel Fitzwilliam then signaled to the footmen to go away from the carriage before he himself left his post, its fate up to one small tree.

After seeing for himself that Georgiana and the Miss Leighs

were relatively unhurt, Colonel Fitzwilliam turned to Mary, lying on the ground with Georgiana's traveling cloak for a blanket. "Miss Bennet, are you in pain?"

Mary looked up at the second man to call her 'Miss Bennet.' "My head hurts, sir." She did not wish to exaggerate the pain, though it was difficult to bear, and was embarrassed to admit to the men that she felt a great deal of discomfort in the area of her chest as well.

Georgiana, kneeling closer to her friend asked in a small voice, "Mary? Why do you call Colonel Fitzwilliam 'sir'? Do you not know him? Do you not know me?" She looked up with fear in her eyes.

Mary did in fact not recognize the beautiful young lady with golden hair and dirt-smudged face, or any of the faces looking down upon her with such worried expressions. She shook her head and immediately closed her eyes again. "I am sorry—" she whispered "—my head—"

The colonel rose to his feet, his eyes squinted from the bright sun. "She needs a physician, and soon. There is a coaching inn fewer than two miles down the road—" he pointed "—but we cannot risk taking her on horseback, and must go for some type of transport." His gestured for the major to follow him, and the two spoke quietly with the footmen. Soon, two of them were galloping off in the direction of the inn, the other two going in search of the coachman and groom, who had last been seen on the bare backs of the carriage horses.

The major then returned to Mary's side. "You will be fine, Miss Bennet—we are getting help." Mary opened her eyes to look upon his kind face, wishing she could comfort him in some way. He turned to Georgiana. "We need to keep her awake."

Georgiana responded immediately to his words, turning to Mary to ask softly, "Do you remember what happened? There was an accident."

Mary tried to remember, but she could not. She looked at the others, and though they seemed kind, they were complete strangers to her. Finally she whispered, "I do not remember...I cannot remember anything."

Georgiana gasped and looked away, while Diana Leigh leaned forward, her tone soothing. "Did you hit your head when the carriage flipped over, Miss Bennet?"

Mary thought again, wondering why her head hurt so much, but with no memory of the incident. "No. But I must have, for there is such pain—" she closed her eyes again.

The major stood and addressed Diana Leigh. "Miss Leigh, will you please remain with Miss Bennet for a moment? I would like to speak with Miss Darcy." He held a hand out to Georgiana, who accepted his help in standing.

"Of course, major," Diana Leigh was a practical young woman, and spoke with confidence. "Catherine and I are unhurt, and are well able to look after her."

Georgiana and the major then went to speak with Colonel Fitzwilliam who was frowning over part of a broken wheel.

Georgiana spoke first, though she was clearly fighting tears. "Mary does not know who she is; she does not even remember the accident!"

"The major and I have seen cases of memory loss before, Georgiana. Sometimes it lasts but a short time—it is possible she will soon remember everything." His eyes were upon Diana Leigh. "Keep Mary still, and be sure she is warm. We should have some sort of conveyance soon." As he spoke, the coachman and groom returned. The carriage horses appeared to be unhurt and were much calmer, but the groom, when he dismounted, walked with a pronounced limp.

Before the two could reach the colonel and major however, the small tree gave way with a loud crack and Mr. Darcy's landau crashed into the ravine, flipping over twice more before landing at the bottom with an unimpressive thud.

An hour passed before one of the footmen returned with a conveyance from the coaching inn. It was only a simple cart, but a welcome sight.

The major and the colonel had fashioned a narrow cot-like conveyance to lift Mary into the cart, and soon the party was away, the driver adhering to the colonel's orders avoid ruts and other obstructions in the road. Their progress was slow, and another hour passed before the cart pulled into the yard of the coaching inn.

There was much rushing about, the publican and his wife

clearly ill-prepared for so many guests, especially one who had to be carried up the narrow stairs on a cot.

Once Mary was situated as comfortably as possible, Georgiana absolutely refusing to leave her bedside, the colonel wrote a brief message and sent one of the men with it to Pemberley.

In the meantime, the publican's wife had laid out a pot of stew and a basket of bread in the common room, where the Miss Leighs waited with the colonel and the major, who paced relentlessly.

The colonel watched for the physician through a grimy window. "If the doctor does not come soon, Miss Bennet may have to stay the night in this odious place—we all might."

"In which case, should we not bring some food to Miss Bennet and Miss Darcy?" asked Diana Leigh.

Major Ashton looked blankly at the table before shaking his head firmly. "With an injury such as hers it is best to wait. The physician should arrive soon." He then recommenced his pacing.

Diana Leigh went to the sideboard and took up a pitcher, looking inside with an expression of distaste before filling a glass. "There is no tea, Major Ashton," she said quietly as she handed him the ale.

The major took the glass from her, but did not drink. "Why does he not come?" he asked no one in particular.

Later, after Colonel Fitzwilliam had finally managed to convince the others to partake of the humble offerings of the proprietress, and Georgiana had unwillingly gone downstairs to join them, Diana Leigh sat at Mary's bedside with a piece of sewing. Her tone was soft, but determinedly cheerful as she described their new home in Buckinghamshire. "The house is much smaller than Beechwood Manor, of course, and is something of an adjustment for my mother and sisters. But happily, just before we left for London, my uncle had a pianoforte brought to the house for Catherine—it is a great comfort to her." She stopped for a moment, deep in thought. "I am certain she will be her cheerful self again once we reach home." Even Mary, in her current state, could discern an element of doubt. Diana Leigh moved to another topic.

Mary tried to maintain the appearance of interest, but the great number of unfamiliar names and places was confusing, and made her head hurt even more. It seemed however, that Miss Diana Leigh's commission was to keep the patient awake, and she was determined to do so.

"I do hope Mr. and Mrs. Bingley are happy at the manor—Mrs. Bingley is your sister, I understand. We were always happy at Beechwood, you know, until—" she hesitated, frowning "—you may not have heard, and probably cannot remember, even if you had, but my father has long had a propensity for high-stakes gambling; we were ultimately forced to leave our home because of it. I am certain our situation provides entertainment for the gossips—there are no secrets in society, are there?" She looked kindly down upon Mary.

Mary, who was forced to lie on her back for fear of further endangerment, blinked, and made an encouraging sound.

"Perhaps we might meet Mrs. Bingley in time. I have heard her described as a great beauty. Your sister Elizabeth certainly is."

"I seem to have a great many sisters," Mary observed quietly just as Catherine Leigh entered the room.

"I will sit with Miss Bennet, Diana. You must be hungry."

"I am *very* hungry," complained Mary.

Diana Leigh looked down with regret at her patient. "When the physician declares it safe for you to eat, Miss Bennet, I will see you get something to appease your appetite. Though I am afraid the choices at this inn may not completely satisfy your taste." She shuddered as she looked around the small, dingy room.

"I promise not to be particular," promised Mary as Catherine Leigh took the chair near the bed.

"Are you fond of novels, Miss Bennet?" she asked after her sister had gone, looking at Mary with wonder. "I have only just learned that you are a writer, and have two books published." Mary's brows shot up, and Catherine held up a book for her to see. "I would be happy to read to you. This book is by Miss Edgeworth, my favorite authoress. Perhaps you have already read it—it is called *Belinda*."

Mary did actually feel in great need of distraction. "You are so thoughtful—" she could not recall the name of the pretty, far too thin young lady "—and I am certain to enjoy it, for I will not know if I have read the book before or not."

Catherine Leigh's rare smile appeared. "Of course not," she responded, a thoughtful look on her face as she opened the book and began to read aloud:

Mrs. Stanhope, a well-bred woman, accomplished in that branch of knowledge which is called the art of rising in the world, had, with but a small fortune—

"Miss Bennet, I must apologize for disturbing you, but the colonel and the major were firm about the need for you to remain awake until the physician comes." Catherine Leigh was leaning over Mary.

"I am so sorry." Mary's voice sounded weak. "Please continue—I promise to keep my eyes open, though I feel so sleepy."

"Then I will read louder," Catherine said cheerfully, and continued:

...with but a small fortune, contrived to live in the highest company....

Catherine Leigh set the open book on her lap. "You know, Miss Bennet, this is a remarkably accurate description of what my sister and I so often observed while we were in London. We no longer have any pretensions to wealth, you understand, which perhaps made us able to see it so clearly in others...."

Mary was the one to interrupt this time. "Do you know, Miss—" she searched her memory for the correct name.

"I am Miss Leigh—but I hope you will call me Catherine."

"Very well," replied Mary. "I think it might be easier to stay awake if you continue in this manner—reading a little, and then talking about what you have just read. I believe it will be a pleasant diversion...Catherine."

Catherine Leigh sat back with a smile. "As you wish, Miss Bennet." However, before she could continue with the book, Dr.

Braxton arrived, entering the room with all the pomposity and officiousness requisite to his position.

Georgiana and the Miss Leighs stood by silently while Mary suffered through the brief examination, the doctor not saying a word to her, but addressing the others as if she were not there. He sighed impatiently if Mary was slow to respond to his orders to move this way or that, his expression unreadable when he asked her to stick out her tongue, his muttering indecipherable when he struck her knees with a stick.

As a final insult, instead of making his report to Miss Darcy, whom he had attended at Pemberley, he left the room to report to Colonel Fitzwilliam and Major Ashton.

"Well, Doctor Braxton?" Colonel Fitzwilliam was impatient. "What is the status of your patient?"

"She has suffered a head injury which has resulted in apparent loss of memory."

"And?" The colonel looked ready to shake the man.

Dr. Braxton shrugged his shoulders. "If, as you say, Miss Bennet was the first to fall to the ground and the other young ladies fell on top of her, and if her head struck something hard— say the bench—the damage could be severe and irreversible. There might be swelling or bruising, resulting in a brain attack. Whatever the cause, Miss Bennet has certainly suffered some form of trauma." He pulled out a handkerchief to wipe his hands. "I have heard of cases in which patients recover from this state after a brief period of rest, and of others who never do."

Major Ashton, a great frown on his brow, stopped pacing to inquire, "What can be done for her?"

The doctor shook his head solemnly. "There is nothing to be done for her at this point, I am afraid to say, except to bleed her, and not to allow her any food. I am sorry, but her fate is not up to mere mortals."

"Bleed her?" the Colonel barked, raising his eyes to the ceiling before demanding, "How soon can she be moved?"

The doctor was unfazed. "Even if it were to be done with the greatest care, I cannot recommend it."

The colonel and major exchanged glances, but before they could ask anything else, the bewildered proprietor appeared.

From behind him came a most impatient Mr. and Mrs. Darcy.

Elizabeth almost pushed the publican aside and rushed up to the colonel. "How is Mary?" Her voice was shaking.

"Mrs. Darcy! You should never have made such a journey!" Dr. Braxton looked accusingly at Mr. Darcy before appearing to recall their last discussion, when he had diagnosed Georgiana's condition as 'hysteria,' and softened his officious tone. He wiped his brow. "Please, Mrs. Darcy—you must take extreme care with yourself and the baby until the birth. If you would but take a seat now and rest."

Elizabeth ignored his request. Instead she came to stand directly in front of him to ask again, "How is my sister Mary, Dr. Braxton?"

The colonel responded for the physician. "The doctor has just told us she has lost her memory due to a head injury, and cannot yet be moved." He shot a warning glance towards Dr. Braxton. "But he believes there is hope for improvement."

Elizabeth frowned. "What can be done for her? Is she in pain?"

The physician held up his hand to stem the flow of questions, and addressed Mr. Darcy, his tone at this point deferential. "Miss Bennet should remain where she is, undisturbed, until such time as it is safe for her to travel." He frowned. "Where exactly *is* her home?"

"She is to be taken to Pemberley," replied Mr. Darcy without hesitation.

The doctor pulled a watch from his waistcoat pocket, squinted at it for a moment, and clicked it shut. "I will return tomorrow to see Miss Bennet, but I must go now, for another of my patients has taken a turn for the worse." The doctor bowed stiffly and departed, his nose going up a notch when he noticed the woman standing behind Mr. Darcy.

Elizabeth did not miss his reaction and said clearly, "This is Mrs. Halifax, our midwife." She turned to that lady. "Will you come with me to see my sister?"

Mrs. Halifax followed Elizabeth up the narrow stairs, both their faces registering extreme distaste as they noticed the general lack of cleanliness. "We must remove her as soon as may be," Elizabeth whispered to Mrs. Halifax behind her, who agreed with vigor.

Upon entering the room, Elizabeth cried out and ran to Mary's side, tears streaming down her cheeks. "Oh, Mary!"

Meanwhile, Mrs. Halifax approached the opposite side of the bed, and spoke in a quiet, unaffected tone. "Good day, Miss Bennet. I am Mrs. Halifax." She indicated Elizabeth with a glance. "Do you remember your sister, Miss Bennet? This is Mrs. Darcy."

Mary dutifully studied Elizabeth's features, hoping to spark a memory, but none came. "I am sorry, but I do not." Her expression clearly showed her regret. "But I am pleased to meet you."

Elizabeth gasped, her eyes wide, a hand moving involuntarily to her throat.

Mrs. Halifax's eyes were kind and understanding, showing none of the fear so easily discernible in Elizabeth's. "Mrs. Darcy, I would like to complete a brief examination, if you do not mind." She waited until her meaning became clear, and Elizabeth, after taking hold of Mary's hand for a moment, left the room, Catherine Leigh following closely behind.

Mrs. Halifax immediately began her examination, making soothing noises when Mary groaned at the touch of her rib cage. She moved on to Mary's neck and head, massaging the tender areas ever-so-gently with careful fingers, humming softly as she did so, lessening the severity of Mary's headache.

"Miss Bennet—" Mrs. Halifax's gentle voice woke Mary "—I would like to examine your ribs once more. "If you will let me know exactly where it hurts," instructed the midwife.

Mrs. Halifax met with the others a quarter of an hour later. "If Miss Bennet is to have any hope of recovery, she must have nourishment."

"Doctor Braxton said she was not to be given any food, and suggested bleeding her," said Colonel Fitzwilliam, his expression dubious.

Elizabeth looked horrified. "Mamma thinks the practice of bleeding only makes people weaker, and she certainly has never been in favor of starving someone in the interest of their health!" She turned to her husband. "Fitzwilliam, I would prefer to take the advice of Mrs. Halifax in this matter."

Mr. Darcy nodded briefly before ringing for a servant. When the harried maid appeared, he suggested Mrs. Halifax request whatever she felt appropriate from the kitchen in aid of Mary's recovery.

After trying to glean from the maid what the kitchen actually had by way of ingredients, Mrs. Halifax threw her hands up in frustration, declaring she would prepare a nourishing broth herself.

The poor confused girl looked frightened as she followed the officious midwife from the room.

CHAPTER FORTY-FIVE

After Mary had consumed the last spoonful of Mrs. Halifax's gruel, a tearful Elizabeth came again to see her. "It is the baby, or so Mamma claims," she explained her tears away, dabbing at her eyes with Mr. Darcy's handkerchief. "She said she used to cry at the sight of overcooked potatoes." Elizabeth smiled and proceeded to tell of Jane and Mr. Bingley's recent arrival in Derbyshire, all about Beechwood Manor. "You have been there numerous times; it is the former home of the Miss Leighs, who have been so good to you...although we might wish to refrain from talking about their former home while in their company." Elizabeth also described Mary's other sisters—leaving some particulars regarding Lydia for later—until Georgiana came to relieve her.

Elizabeth stood as quickly as a woman in her condition could, resting her cool palm briefly on Mary's forehead. "It will not be long before we take you home to Pemberley, my dear." She looked about the room, dimples showing in her cheeks. "And since you cannot remember what it is like there, I believe you will be pleasantly surprised!"

After Elizabeth left, promising to request something sweet from the kitchen, Georgiana sat down next to the bed. "Do you remember anything at all about the past, Mary? Anything about our time in London, at Rosings, or our recent, unfortunate, carriage ride?"

Mary looked regretful. "I do not, but Mrs. Halifax claims it is a good sign I can remember what has occurred *since* the accident."

Georgiana fished for something in her small traveling bag.

"Major Ashton managed to retrieve this from our carriage before it crashed to the bottom of a ravine." She held it high so Mary could see. "You have been reading it of late."

"*The Art of Cookery*?" Mary was extremely puzzled. "I thought I was a writer of sorts. Am I also a cook?"

Georgiana laughed, a pleasing sound to Mary's ears. "No Mary, you are not a cook. You have long desired to be an independent woman, and were reading this to learn how to make tea and a few simple things. Would you like me to read it to you?"

Mary thought for a moment. Sadly, the gruel Mrs. Halifax prepared had not been filling. "It might prove taxing, for I am still hungry."

"You sound like your old self, at any rate...but you must remember to call me Georgiana." She grinned. "To save you from fear of starvation, I shall read instead from *A Romance of the Forest*—thank heaven Major Ashton was able to retrieve it as well." She examined the book, sighing over the damage. "Even though you have read this many times, today it will be as the first!"

⁓⌣⌣⌐

Mr. Darcy, Colonel Fitzwilliam, and Major Ashton strode across the yard to the stable, all three eager to examine what little the footmen had been able to retrieve of Darcy's landau.

"Do you see, Darcy?" Colonel Fitzwilliam picked up the same part of the broken wheel he had examined directly after the accident. "It is hewn nearly halfway through."

Mr. Darcy studied the wheel before running his fingers along the edge, a great frown gathering on his brow. "It is a clean cut; one made with a single purpose." He looked again. "But who would have had the opportunity? And when?"

The major's expression was grim. "The groom admitted that a man stopped near the carriage before the colonel and I arrived at Darcy House this morning."

Mr. Darcy's eyes narrowed. "And this man fell suddenly ill and asked the groom to fetch him some water?"

"Something like that," replied the colonel. He looked up from his own study of the broken bits and pieces. "Miss Bingley and Lord Exeter called at the Burnabys' house the day before our departure, and while there would have learned our plans."

Major Ashton explained to a confused-looking Mr. Darcy, "Lord Exeter and Miss Bingley are frequently in each other's company and are friendly with Clay. We all know Exeter to be a consummate spreader of tales." He shook his head in disgust. "I did not agree with Lord Castlereagh's decision to allow Clay to remain at large, claiming he was harmless."

"You think Clay was responsible for the accident?" Mr. Darcy asked the two men, who nodded, their expressions fierce.

"He must be apprehended without further delay!" The colonel strode angrily back to the inn.

Major Ashton ran his hand through his hair, clearly frustrated. "Unfortunately, I did not think to warn the servants not to trust Clay—he had a full day to devise a plan, and could easily have hired someone to sabotage the wheel." He faced Mr. Darcy. "I take full responsibility."

"No one could have foreseen this action." Mr. Darcy shook his head impatiently. "But my cousin is right; the man must be caught and questioned thoroughly. My sister—any one of you—could have been killed!" He looked up into the dark shadows of the rafters. "When will we be free of this evil?"

All but Mrs. Halifax and Mary convened late that afternoon in the public lounge for stale bread, questionable cheese, and lukewarm, weak tea.

Georgiana leaned towards Elizabeth. "Perhaps Dr. Braxton was right, and you should not have risked coming. This place is horrid," she whispered. "Do you think they have re-used the tea leaves from earlier today?" She gazed with horror into her teacup.

"Elizabeth would not be put off," Mr. Darcy said as he too gazed suspiciously into his cup.

When everyone had finished pretending they were drinking tea or eating bread, Diana Leigh cleared her throat. "My sister and I are extremely grateful for your help in getting us this far." She faced Colonel Fitzwilliam and Major Ashton. "But you have far more pressing matters to attend to. We must not burden you any longer, and will find another way home."

Colonel Fitzwilliam pushed his chair away from the rough-hewn table and stood to face Diana Leigh. "Major Ashton can remain with the Darcy party, Miss Leigh, while I continue on with you and your sister to Buckinghamshire, as promised." He glanced at Mr. Darcy. "If you can spare a couple footmen?"

Mr. Darcy nodded. "I will have one of the servants ride to Pemberley for another carriage."

Colonel Fitzwilliam acknowledged his cousin's offer with a grateful nod before asking the Miss Leighs, "Will tomorrow morning suit you?"

Diana Leigh's eyes were filled with gratitude. "We will be ready at whatever hour you wish, Colonel Fitzwilliam—thank you."

Shortly afterwards, the three gentlemen stood near the stable, watching as two Pemberley servants rode off with orders to return as soon as humanly possible with a carriage for the Miss Leighs. Preferring the outside air to that inside, they remained where they were.

Mr. Darcy looked up at the front-facing windows. "Elizabeth is to ask Mrs. Halifax how soon we can safely take Mary away from this place. Neither she nor Georgiana will leave without her." His eyes were on the peeling paint of a window sill.

"It is hideous, Darcy," said the colonel. "You might find the stables more...habitable."

Mrs. Halifax examined Mary once again with great care, focusing on her head, neck, and ribs. After nearly half an hour, she met the others in the public room. "In my opinion, Miss Bennet's injury will be temporary—she speaks clearly, and I see no indications the brain fever mentioned by Dr. Braxton." Her expression left little doubt of her opinion regarding that doctor's diagnosis. "Your sister is young and strong—" she addressed Elizabeth "—and though I believe her ribs are fractured, which is quite painful and will take some time to heal naturally, there is no reason to think she will not experience a complete recovery."

"Can she be moved?" whispered Georgiana.

"If Miss Bennet were in cleaner, more comfortable

surroundings, it would greatly increase the speed of her recovery, in my opinion." Mrs. Halifax looked encouraging, adding two lumps of sugar to her cup. "She is sleeping peacefully now, and should take more nourishment upon awaking. I believe she will be strong enough for the journey to Pemberley tomorrow. But you may not get the same opinion from Dr. Braxton."

Mrs. Halifax allowed Georgiana to take the second watch over Mary that night, but not until after she had tucked the covers up to her patient's chin and opened the sole window, its creaking a testimony to how infrequently any guest had attempted it. "The fresh air will help you sleep, which is what you need most to recover now," Mrs. Halifax said softly, her eyes on Georgiana as she whispered, "Be sure she remains covered."

Mary watched the midwife go before turning her head towards Georgiana. "I am sorry to cause so much trouble."

"You would do the same for me." Georgiana's tone was determinedly cheerful "It is but another experience you and I have shared—who knows, in time you may find this temporary memory loss useful in a novel."

Mary considered the possibility before voicing a pressing fear. "What if I cannot remember how to write novels?"

Georgiana laughed. "You are sounding so much like your normal self that it is hard to remember you have no memory of past events." She took up Mary's copy of *Evelina*. "You had tea recently with the lady who wrote this book—she is now Mrs. D'Arblay, but her books are published under her maiden name, Miss Fanny Burney." She peered at Mary but saw only curiosity. "She invited you to dedicate the sequel of your first novel to the queen, with whom Miss Burney is intimate. You agreed to do so, writing the dedication and sending it to your publisher only shortly before we left London."

"How gratifying. Then the book itself is finished?" Mary felt inexplicably nervous.

"Your publisher may or may not ask you to make revisions, but you need not concern yourself with it now since he was instructed to send all correspondence to you at Pemberley. I can help you." Georgiana smiled and patted Mary's hand. "I did not speak of it to make you feel anxious, but happy." She glanced at the book. "You only just started reading this; it is written as a series of letters, similar to Mr. Richardson's *Pamela*—a favorite novel of mine, and yours." She looked up apologetically. "I hope references to things you cannot remember do not disturb you."

Mary smiled. "Perhaps one of those references will spark a memory and I will be cured—" she snapped her fingers "—like that."

Georgiana laughed. "You remember some things quite well!" She attempted to snap her own fingers without success before opening to the first chapter. She read aloud:

Letter One: Lady Howard to the Reverend Mr. Villars, Howard Grove, Kent. Can any thing, my good Sir, be more painful to a friendly mind than a necessity of communicating disagreeable intelligence?

Georgiana looked up to remark upon the question, only to find Mary's eyes closed, her breathing even.

CHAPTER FORTY-SIX

Beechwood Manor, 6 May 1814
Eight days before Georgiana, Mary, Diana, and Catherine Leigh left on their ill-fated journey, the Bingley carriage came round the curve in the long drive, allowing Jane the first sight of her new home. "Charles! The house is beautiful!" She turned to face him for a second before turning back. "It must be twice the size of Netherfield at least!"

The mansion house was three full stories, composed of four sections, the two on either end topped with a square belvedere tower, and was (just as Elizabeth had described) the equal to Pemberley in both elegance and scale.

Mr. Bingley handed his wife from the carriage, the footmen dressed in new livery, the maids wearing starched white aprons over their new dresses. Walker, and one of the footmen (eager for the adventure of moving to Derbyshire), had left Netherfield in advance of the Bingleys, and it was those two who first welcomed the happy couple to their new home.

The housekeeper, a friendly, efficient woman chosen by Elizabeth, introduced Mr. and Mrs. Bingley to each of the servants in turn, the last being the three young scullery maids, who smiled shyly at their young, beautiful mistress as they curtseyed.

When Jane and Mr. Bingley entered the grand foyer of their house, they were clearly pleased with everything they saw. The housekeeper took them first to the largest drawing room, the one to which the Darcy party had been taken when first visiting the house on behalf of the Bingleys. In the middle of the room was Jane's model of Beechwood Manor, handsomely displayed on a marble-topped table.

"Oh, Charles—the little house!" Jane walked around the model with a critical eye. "It will take days to compare this with the original—where on earth shall we begin?"

Mr. Bingley took gentle hold of his wife's hand and led her to a large bank of windows. Together they looked out upon the immediate grounds, the sunken garden alive with color, and the folly clearly visible in the distance. Neither spoke as she leaned her head against his shoulder.

⌒⌣⌣⌒

Despite receiving word that Mr. and Mrs. Bennet had indeed left Longbourn for Derbyshire, Jane and Charles Bingley were still somewhat amazed when the Bennet carriage was spotted passing by the gatehouse exactly four days later.

When Mrs. Bennet entered the grand home of her eldest daughter, no amount of praise for the house and surrounding property would suffice. She examined each room over the course of the next several days, taking Jane with her, declaring it to be "the most beautiful house in the world!"

In the days following, when Mr. and Mrs. Darcy came to call and Mrs. Bennet was more than content to spend the time with her daughters and baby granddaughter. Otherwise, when the child was sleeping, she spent much of her days passing from room to room, shaking her head in wonder.

Mr. Bennet was in his element, assisting Mr. Bingley in planning the organization of the Beechwood Manor library, opening box after box of the precious books, oftentimes taking one to a wingback chair near a window, a glass of port somehow appearing at his elbow.

Time passed peacefully by until one of the housemaids brought a note directly to Jane's dressing room, where her lady's maid had just begun her coiffure. Upon reading the note, Jane's face grew pale, and she did not allow her maid to finish pinning her hair before she hurried from the room to seek her husband's counsel.

Mr. Bingley, fully dressed, excused his valet and quickly read

Elizabeth's hastily-scrawled note from the coaching inn. He frowned. "Your parents must be told, of course—but this news will alarm them."

He held his hand out to his wife and together they descended the stairs and entered the sitting room adjacent to the largest dining room, Mr. Bingley preferring the room due to its incomparable view of the folly.

Mrs. Bennet was quick to perceive her daughter's troubled state. "What is it, Jane? What has happened? Is it Longbourn?" She turned to her husband. "I knew we should not leave it all to the Hills, Mr. Bennet—see what has happened!" She chewed her lip, her eyes moving back and forth. "I knew it! Mr. Collins and Charlotte have invaded our home!"

"Mamma, it is a note from Lizzy. You may rest easy; Longbourn is safe." Jane attempted to sooth her mother as she gave Elizabeth's note to her father. Mr. Bennet remained calm as he read the brief report of the accident, and of Mary's current condition. He calmly set aside the letter and took hold of his wife's hands. "My dear, Elizabeth writes to tell us there has been a slight accident." Before Mrs. Bennet could cry out, he added, "No one is seriously injured, but it would seem that our Mary is experiencing a temporary loss of memory." He let go of her hands to show Mrs. Bennet the letter. "Look, my dear—Lizzy writes that Mary is in good spirits and perfect health."

Sal volatile and two small glasses of sherry were required to revive and calm Mrs. Bennet, who demanded they leave immediately for the inn.

Jane, ever-practical, insisted, "Lizzy will be sure Mary is well cared for, Mamma. It would be unwise for us to travel this late in the day; it could be dangerous."

The reference to dangerous travel removed all thought of leaving immediately from Mrs. Bennet's mind, and eventually she recovered enough to make a good dinner, though she insisted they all retire early to prepare for the next day's short journey to Pemberley, where they would await the arrival of the Darcy party.

~~~

The next day at the coaching inn, Dr. Braxton briefly examined Mary, and recommended she remain where she was until her memory returned. His words were not well received.

"The dirt, grime, and chill of this decrepit building is more a detriment to Miss Bennet's health than moving her ever could be, Doctor Braxton!"

"Mr. Darcy, I do not think it wise to listen to—" Dr. Braxton appealed, pointing a long finger at Mrs. Halifax "—amateurs and meddlers who fancy themselves midwives. It is my official, medical opinion that Miss Bennet's recovery will be slowed considerably by moving her—perhaps even irrevocably."

So great was Mr. Darcy's distaste for their current accommodations, as well as his respect for Mrs. Annesley's sister, he said firmly, "Mrs. Darcy and I take note of your concern, Doctor Braxton, but I am inclined to agree with Mrs. Halifax's assessment."

His words had the effect of turning Dr. Braxton's face an unpleasant shade of red. "Then I will wish you good day, Mr. Darcy, and offer my best wishes for Miss Bennet's health." The physician lifted his chest. "Should you wish me to attend her at Pemberley—"

"We will contact you, Doctor Braxton. Thank you." Mr. Darcy's words were a clear dismissal, though Elizabeth softened them by offering her hand and thanking the doctor for his care of her sister.

While Mary was being examined at the inn, the Bingley party arrived at Pemberley. It was Mr. and Mrs. Bennet's first visit to the great house, and to prevent Mrs. Bennet from fretting while they waited for the Darcy carriage to arrive, Mrs. Reynolds kindly accepted the commission to take Mrs. Darcy's parents on a tour of the primary rooms, just as she had done with Mr. and Mrs. Gardiner on that fateful visit when Elizabeth saw Mr. Darcy at his own home for the first time.

Rather than join them, Jane went to the nursery where Elizabeth had spent hours planning the separate alcoves, each with a crib and soft draperies to protect her own children and her nephews and nieces from unwelcome breezes or too much sunlight. The space was large enough to accommodate comfortable furniture, including two rocking chairs set side-by-side, facing out upon the large lake.

Jane sang a lullaby to Little Eliza, restless after the journey, and left in search of her family only after the child was sound asleep. When Jane eventually caught up with her parents, she found them in the portrait hall, Mrs. Bennet staring up at the recent painting of Elizabeth which Mr. Darcy had commissioned shortly after they were married.

"After seeing Beechwood Manor," Mrs. Bennet said, her eyes enormous, "I thought I would be prepared for the grandeur of Pemberley, but I am absolutely speechless—to have two of my own daughters situated so! The park must be a hundred times larger than ours at Longbourn—" at her near-accusatory look, Mr. Bennet pulled out the spare handkerchief he was in the habit of carrying for his wife and wiped his forehead. Mrs. Bennet lowered her voice, much to her oldest daughter's relief. "And to think I was so rude to Mr. Darcy when he first came to Hertfordshire. Granted, he did refuse to dance with Lizzy, but after seeing his house, I begin to wonder he ever deigned speak to any one of us!"

Jane's soft smile appeared. "He could not help himself, Mamma—he fell in love with Lizzy." Her eyes held a faraway look. "Sometimes I wonder what would have become of us had Mr. Bingley never returned to Hertfordshire, as his sister Caroline once predicted."

"Perish the thought, my dear!" Mrs. Bennet waved her hands about as if to cleanse the air. "Now, Mr. Bennet tells me he wishes to go off on his own to find Mr. Darcy's grand library, where he will disappear and we will never see him again, and little Eliza is down for her nap—what shall we do, for if we do not keep ourselves busy...."

Jane, recognizing the signs which would have normally sent Mrs. Bennet to her bed at Longbourn, quickly suggested they first visit their own rooms in the family wing before going outdoors to stroll along the cascade.

After allowing Mrs. Bennet time enough to exclaim over their spacious rooms and fine furnishings, the mother and daughter descended the grand stairs, proceeded through the long gallery, and left through the front door held open for them by a footman. All the while, Mrs. Bennet's eyes were wide with wonder, and she was uncharacteristically silent.

Just as the two ladies reached the end of the reflecting pond, the Darcy carriage arrived. Molly and Lucy had been anxiously awaiting the arrival of their young mistresses, and ran down the stairs to stand with the other servants to greet the party and wish Miss Bennet well.

When Mary stepped from the carriage, she was astounded at the number of people standing outside the grand house, and was even more astonished when they each wished her well, addressing her as "Miss Bennet" as she passed. But it was with greater surprise—and wide eyes—she perceived a dog running full tilt towards her, as if determined to knock her down.

Georgiana leaned down in front of Mary to catch hold of the black and white spaniel. "Oh, Samson! I have missed you," she said, wrapping her arms about the wriggling puppy and looking up at her friend. "Mary, this is Samson—he is my brother's dog, and a great friend to both of us. You have known him almost since the moment he was born."

Mary considered the animal for a moment, any fear vanishing as she looked into its brown eyes. Instinctively, she knelt down and opened her arms, just as Georgiana had done, and after looking at both Mr. Darcy and Georgiana as if for permission, the puppy ran to her, nearly toppling her over.

Mary laughed. "How could anyone forget you, Samson?" Suddenly, she became aware of many eyes upon her and stood, worried she had just breached a rule of etiquette.

Mr. Darcy smiled and lifted his hand, Samson leaving Mary's side to stand obediently by his master. Georgiana then pulled Mary along the rest of the line of servants, introducing each one by name, until they reached the entrance.

Mary looked up at the high ceiling as they stepped inside the foyer, the beauty of the painted ceiling taking her breath away.

Molly and Lucy had followed them inside, but before a teary-eyed Molly could assist in the removal of Mary's bonnet and pelisse, Mrs. Bennet rushed in, her breath coming in short gasps. "Mary! Oh, my dear, dear Mary!"

A small, elegantly-dressed woman rushed towards her, arms open wide. Mindful of her painful ribs, Mary instinctively took a step back.

The movement caused Mrs. Bennet to stop in her tracks. "Mr. Bennet! Mr. Bennet! Where are you?" she cried. "Mary does not know me! She does not know her own mother!"

Elizabeth and Jane did their best to comfort their mother while Georgiana attempted the same with Mary, who was mortified at having caused such a disturbance. She apologized, but her formality only made matters worse, Mrs. Bennet burying her face even deeper in a handkerchief. Thankfully, Mr. Bennet appeared to take charge of his wife.

Elizabeth sighed as her maid helped her out of her traveling cloak, spying Jane and quickly assuring her that Mary was well enough. "The inn was so very dirty, Jane. Mr. Darcy and I looked upon the peeling paper in our chamber and decided to think of it as rustic—at least until we had vacated the premises." She shuddered as she ordered hot baths for herself, Mary, and Georgiana, leaving Mr. Darcy and Major Ashton to the care of their valets.

Georgiana escorted Mary to the suite of rooms she had occupied in the past, hoping to spur a memory, but Mary's exclamations upon seeing the luxurious accommodations were as one who was looking at them for the first time.

"My sister Elizabeth was right—after the inn, this house is definitely a surprise."

Disappointed, but happy to see signs of good humor, Georgiana spoke briefly to Molly. "While you prepare her bath, you might recount some of your shared memories; it is difficult to know what might help her remember." She then went to her own apartment to bathe and rest, for Miss Darcy had slept little since the accident.

Major Ashton, who had graciously accepted Mr. Darcy's invitation to stay on at Pemberley, descended the grand stairs much refreshed by a bath and change of clothes. After asking the direction from a passing housemaid, the major found Mr. Darcy in his study.

"Ah, Ashton—good of you to come down so soon." Mr. Darcy clasped him by the shoulder. "Elizabeth and I hope you will remain at Pemberley as long as Lord Castlereagh can spare you—we think your presence will be of great benefit to Miss Bennet, as you are one with whom she is well acquainted."

"I will do whatever I can to help." Major Ashton paused, assessing his host. "However, I should tell you what has passed between Miss Bennet and myself."

Mr. Darcy looked very curious, but did not interrupt.

"This past December, I proposed marriage to your sister-in-law." The major allowed some time for his words to soak in. "She said she would consider my offer."

Mr. Darcy hid his smile. "Consider, eh?" He sat down at his desk and the major chose a chair opposite. "You need not have scrupled to tell me, but may I ask if you have received any encouragement since then?"

The major looked rueful. "My wishes have not changed, but I have not had many opportunities to press my suit, you understand. Prior to our departure from London, I had no reason to believe Miss Bennet had changed in her desire to remain a spinster."

"I can tell you, based on personal experience, that the Bennet daughters are not short on determination." Mr. Darcy leaned back in his chair. "Given what you have just told me, escorting Miss Bingley to society events must have been somewhat...difficult."

Major Ashton smiled in response. "It was not the easiest of assignments. Unfortunately, Miss Bennet was not made aware of Lord Castlereagh's plan, and consequently thought I was harboring feelings for Miss Bingley."

"Did she indeed?" Mr. Darcy went to the sideboard. "She obviously has no memory of it now—shall we drink to the success of your campaign?"

After Mrs. Halifax helped Mary into the bath filled with the salts Molly mixed with lavender and chamomile, Mary took some time to explore her rooms. She was drawn first to the bookshelves, where she opened each book, flipping open to random pages in the hopes of remembering something—

anything. No sudden return of memory occurred, however, and she moved restlessly from the bookshelves to the window, where she looked out upon the walled herb garden, the wide green field beyond it currently void of animal life. She chose a comfortable chair nearest the window and looked out, thinking about each of the people she had met since the accident.

Miss Darcy was the first to come to mind—her angelic features and golden hair making her seem almost unworldly at times, but it had not taken long for Mary to recognize a superior strength of character and resolve not to be underestimated. The Miss Leighs had been kind and attentive (the younger looked as if she had been through a prolonged illness), but Mary had not had sufficient time to draw any particular conclusions about them other than what she had learned from Georgiana. Her sisters Jane and Elizabeth appeared to be kind ladies, but were very fine, their husbands handsome and extremely civil. The grandness of the Darcy carriage, the fine livery of the servants, and the sheer size of the Darcy estate were overwhelming. Mrs. Bennet was an affectionate woman, though she seemed inclined to hysterics, while Mr. Bennet appeared to be a kindly, well-read man who took time to think before speaking. He was apparently fond of chess.

Of Colonel Fitzwilliam Mary had seen little, and now he had gone to take the Miss Leighs to their mother. Major Ashton had been particularly kind to her when they left the coaching inn, solicitous of her comfort. He was a handsome man, both in features and figure, with an easy wit and seeming lightness of heart that was attractive. Since Mary had taken his hand to step inside the Darcy carriage (and he had winked at her), she had begun to wonder if there was some sort of relationship between them, and if so, why no one had told her.

Growing impatient with her thoughts, Mary began to study the personal belongings Molly insisted were hers. Amongst the books—the titles brought no recollection—she found a journal, apparently given to her by one of her sisters.

Taking it with her, she resumed her seat by the window and began to read.

Mary was startled awake by Mrs. Halifax, who gently chastised her for falling asleep in a chair. "Has your headache lessened any, Miss Bennet?"

Mary's hand went without volition to her temples. "The headache is better, thank you, Mrs. Halifax. I find the most pain to be in my ribs." She touched the area with care, feeling the tightly-wound bandage beneath her frock.

Mrs. Halifax did not seem surprised. "It will take time, my dear, for either the bruises to stop hurting, or the bones to heal."

When Mary asked if she might join the others at dinner, Mrs. Halifax agreed, so long as her patient did not overly exert herself and was asleep at an early hour. The midwife moved to the bell-pull and rang for Mary's maid. "Until then, however, you will rest—this time in your bed."

Molly, who had at first been shocked at the formal manner in which her young mistress had greeted her, had risen to the occasion. While arranging Mary's hair, she chatted in a friendly manner, not requiring any response, before changing the subject to that of books. She relayed the story of the kidnapping which had been loosely retold in Mary's first novel, describing in vivid detail the wicked people at the derelict castle who had locked Mary and Miss Darcy inside the windowless turret room.

"However did we manage to escape such a horrid place?" Mary asked, holding her arms up as high as she could without causing pain.

Molly was gentle as she buttoned the back of the gown. "Well, miss, I do not want to give away too much if you decide to read the book—Mrs. Darcy thought it might be a good way for you to remember." She leaned forward to whisper, "But it was Mr. Arbuthnot who rescued you."

"Mr. Arbuthnot." Mary tried the name. "He must be an exceedingly brave man."

Molly shook her head vehemently, her eyes wide. "No, he isn't, miss! He is a horrible man!" She circled Mary to view her work, apparently satisfied. "When you come back after dinner, I can tell you how the story ended, if you wish it."

"I would enjoy that, Molly, as long as Mrs. Halifax approves."

Molly nodded. "Of course, miss. Lucy—she's Miss Darcy's

maid in case you've forgotten again—told me Major Ashton is staying on for a time. Do you remember him at all, miss? He's ever so handsome and tall—a fine gentleman, just like in your books."

"He has been especially kind to me since the accident." Mary looked towards the door, Georgiana having just entered the room. "But I do not remember him," she said firmly, unaware of her maid's worried expression.

In the sitting room, after greeting those gathered there, Mary approached Mr. and Mrs. Bennet in the manner of one who wished to be introduced.

Mr. Bennet looked kindly upon his daughter, his eyes searching hers for signs of recognition. "I am your papa, my dear—do you not know me?"

Mary did not like the sad look in his eyes, and leaned up to kiss him dutifully on the cheek. "Good evening, father," she said, the formality causing Mrs. Bennet to bury her face in her handkerchief.

When Mary dipped a curtsey upon greeting the Bingleys, Jane could not hide her dismay. Mr. Bingley, however, was cheerful as he took hold of Mary's hand, shaking it energetically. "It is so good to see you looking so well, Mary. We were all very worried about you."

Major Ashton bowed formally, with no hint of a wink when he asked after Mary's health.

"It is good to see you again, Major Ashton. I understand you are fond of opera." She had learned the fact from Georgiana.

He bowed. "The pleasure is mine, I assure you, Miss Bennet. And you are correct—I am indeed fond of opera. May I say how pleased I am to see you looking so much recovered. I do hope you are not in any pain."

Mary thought when he smiled it actually made the room seem brighter, and a second later wondered why her cheeks felt hot. She turned to the others to hide her momentary discomfiture and addressed them all. "Thank you all for your kindness. I am certain my memory will soon return, and may I apologize now for anything inappropriate I might say or do before then."

Mary wondered if she had committed another faux pas, for her words seemed to have made everyone in the room laugh.

Mary's first dinner at Pemberley was a wonderful revelation, her memory of food being limited to that served at the coaching inn.

"Chef Renault planned the meal himself, Mary—choosing dishes he knows you favor," Elizabeth said as she took her place at the end of the table, opposite Mr. Darcy.

Mary was seated between Major Ashton and her father, and at one point during the first course, the two gentlemen began discussing books over the top of her head. "I find Chetwood's description of the stage insightful," commented Mr. Bennet. "What is your opinion, Major Ashton?"

The major leaned back in his chair to better see Mr. Bennet. "You are referring to his General History of the Stage, are you not? It is a book I have enjoyed reading many times, having taken it with me on more than one campaign."

Thus began a lively discussion, the others at the table joining in at will about the theatre.

At the commencement of the second course a new plate was set before her, and Mary looked across the table at Georgiana, who silently indicated the proper fork and knife to use for fish.

"It is such a pleasure to share a meal in a casual, friendly manner." Major Ashton spoke to the table in general.

Mr. Bingley nodded enthusiastically. "My sister Caroline never allows us to enjoy family meals in this way, but it is a pleasant change from the formality of turning first to speak to the person on my left, and after the soup turn to the one on the right, saying exactly what I did half an hour before."

"Some rules were meant to be broken," Mr. Bennet said with a smile.

"Here, here!" cried Mr. Bingley.

The second course passed pleasantly, although the discussion led to the unfortunate loss of memory Mary had suffered.

"Mr. Bennet tells me you have seen this sort of thing before," Mrs. Bennet addressed Major Ashton from down the table.

"I have seen a few cases, as has Colonel Fitzwilliam, Mrs. Bennet," the major replied politely. "And though each circumstance was unique, the majority regained their memory within the span of a fortnight."

It was at this moment Mary took a bite of the aligot, unaware of the close attention the Darcys were paying to her reaction, being well aware of her fondness for the dish.

Finally, Elizabeth could bear the suspense no longer. "Mary, how do you like the potatoes? They are one of Chef Renault's specialties."

Mary dabbed the corners of her mouth with the soft napkin. "Since the only memory of food I have since the accident was of Mrs. Halifax's gruel—which tasted well enough, please do not misunderstand me—I never imagined food could be so delicious."

Her reaction seemed to please everyone at the table, and the subject soon changed to opera, Mary noting how gracious Major Ashton was when asked his opinion, and how clearly he expressed his thoughts. She thought at that moment she might use him as a model for a hero in one of her books—should she ever write again.

After dinner, they assembled in the music room, where Georgiana chose to play music on the pianoforte with which Mary had at one time been familiar.

Mrs. Bennet sat next to Mary on the settee, her handkerchief in hand. "You used to play concertos beautifully, Mary. If only Kitty and Lydia were here with us, they would laugh and dance, and make you remember." She sniffled, her eyes brightening as she turned to Jane, who was holding her baby, Mr. Bingley cooing over her shoulder. "Perhaps now you and Mr. Bingley are established at Beechwood Manor, and with Mary suffering such a horrible fate—" she patted Mary's hand absently "—Mr. Darnell might agree to bring Kitty to Derbyshire." She shook her head sadly. "But poor, poor Lydia—in her last letter, she said she has no idea when she and Mr. Wickham will return home to England."

"I will write to Kitty in the morning," Elizabeth promised before holding her hands out to Jane, who graciously relinquished the baby to her sister.

Mary noted that when Lydia's name was mentioned someone nearly always changed the subject.

CHAPTER FORTY-SEVEN

The next morning Mrs. Halifax insisted Mary remain in her room until the afternoon. Georgiana therefore went to the music room, Mr. Bennet went to the library, Mr. Darcy, Mr. Bingley, and Major Ashton went riding, and Jane and Elizabeth went to the morning room, where they turned their good mother's attention to one of her new favorite topics: Beechwood Manor.

"Everything about the house is pleasing—though Mr. Bennet and I have not seen even a quarter of the rooms," said Mrs. Bennet. "Jane and Mr. Bingley are lucky the old housekeeper stayed on, for she knows the ways of the shopkeepers in the village, and is efficient as any I have ever seen." Her eyes lit up as she leaned forward. "And the ballroom! Jane, you and Mr. Bingley must have a ball soon!"

Jane and Elizabeth shared an amused glance as their mother described the refurbished room down to the new cornices on the ceiling. "And the model of Beechwood...such a delight! You described the ballroom perfectly, Lizzy. And the immense doors leading to the large dining room...."

"This may take a while," whispered Elizabeth as Jane smiled down at the baby resting in her arms.

"As long as Eliza continues to sleep, I will ask Mamma to describe every flower in the sunken garden," Jane threatened. "Wait until you have your own, Lizzy—you will understand."

Just then, Jane's tiny daughter stretched, and her little arm escaped the swaddling. Elizabeth held out her finger, her eyes alight with wonder when the baby took tight hold of it. She whispered, "If we are not careful, Mrs. Bingley, we will become terribly unfashionable, and spend far too much time with our babies. Our poor husbands will either have to tolerate us or lock us in the attic."

Mrs. Bennet stopped in the middle of describing the new glass panels for the orangery at Beechwood. "Who is locked in the attic?" she demanded.

Jane and Elizabeth held their breath as they looked down at the baby, breathing a collective sigh of relief when she slept peacefully on.

Prior to dinner that evening, Georgiana and Mary were summoned to Mr. Darcy's study, each of them surprised to find Mr. Darcy and Major Ashton in conference with Dr. Braxton.

Mr. Darcy looked up when they entered. "Miss Bennet, Dr. Braxton has expressed his desire to see how you are progressing." His face was turned away from the doctor as he spoke, only Mary and Georgiana able to see his look of apology. "I had hoped Mrs. Darcy would have joined us by now," he added.

"You are a fortunate young woman, Miss Bennet." The officious physician rose from his chair, reaching out to touch her, and Mary instinctively stepped back. Undeterred, the doctor took hold of her chin, turning her face this way and that, using the fingers on his other hand to open her eyes wide.

Tut-tutting, Dr. Braxton finally let go of her chin and Mary stepped well out of his reach behind Georgiana.

"It is rare for a person suffering from a head injury such as this to show no outward signs of trauma," the doctor stated.

"Have you treated many cases of head injury and memory loss?" Major Ashton looked deferential.

The doctor hesitated briefly. "I have read about such cases."

"Read about them?" Major Ashton now looked menacing.

Mary, worried she was the cause of bad feelings and argument, came out from behind Georgiana. "My good health must be a credit to your care, doctor. I will be forever grateful."

Mr. Darcy added, "We all appreciate your expertise, I am sure." He opened the door to his study and gestured for the doctor to precede him, smiling when he caught sight of Elizabeth coming down the hall. "It is time we joined the others, for dinner will soon be announced."

A good many steps behind them, Georgiana whispered, "The doctor was apparently bent on examining you, Mary."

The major nodded, his eyes on Mary. "He was. Mr. Darcy felt it was the only way to appease the man, for he was most insistent, though your sister was meant to be there to help protect you," he said with an apologetic glance at Mary.

Georgiana mused, "If Elizabeth and Fitzwilliam invited that man to dinner, it must mean they wish to keep him on as the official physician at Pemberley."

Mary frowned "I do hope I have not been the cause of any discord."

"Not at all," Georgiana hastened to assure her.

As they passed through the hall of statues, the major said a litter of puppies was expected soon in the Pemberley stables.

"You adore puppies, Mary," Georgiana declared with a glance at the major.

"I do?" Mary asked, wondering what she could have said that was so funny.

Georgiana was in the midst of describing each of the puppies born in the same litter as Samson when they came to the drawing room, stopping when she saw Colonel Fitzwilliam, and pulled Mary over with her.

"It is good to see you, cousin—are you not surprised to see Miss Bennet looking so well? She is close to a complete recovery, is she not, Doctor Braxton?" Georgiana turned to face the doctor, who had been discussing Mary's condition with Mr. and Mrs. Bennet nearby.

"She *might* recover, Miss Darcy," the doctor answered as he frowned at Mary.

Georgiana would not countenance doubt, however, and turned back to the colonel. "She improves daily."

Colonel Fitzwilliam bowed. "It is good to find you looking yourself again, Miss Bennet."

Mary had taken to mimicking nearly all of Miss Darcy's mannerisms, and dipped her head slightly in response.

"I do hope the Miss Leighs were in good health when you delivered them into the care of their mother." Georgiana was clearly asking.

The colonel smiled easily. "They were indeed, Georgiana—as a matter of fact, I believe Miss Catherine was in far better health than when she left London." He glanced at Mary. "Miss Diana actually credits Miss Bennet's accident, for it gave her sister something else on which to focus her attention."

"They were so kind to me—as was everyone," said Mary. "I must think of a way to thank you all properly."

"Have you received any word about your latest novel?" Major Ashton came to stand near them, his query surprising not only Mary but all those within hearing.

Georgiana answered, "We expect a packet any day from the publisher, at which time Miss Bennet may need some assistance should he require changes to the manuscript." She looked directly at the major.

Mary was uncomfortable with so many eyes upon her and spoke haltingly. "I fear I will not remember *how* to write novels."

Mrs. Bennet, having only just entered the room with her husband, let out a small cry.

Doctor Braxton looked nonplussed. "Miss Bennet has written a novel?"

"She has written *three*," Georgiana said proudly. "Two have already been published, and have caught the attention of society."

"Did Aunt Catherine's...assistance create problems with the publication?" Colonel Fitzwilliam addressed his question to Georgiana.

"We shall see when the manuscript arrives—if Mr. Egerton does not send the original copy, I am afraid Mary is the only one who would have known exactly what changes Aunt Catherine suggested." Georgiana looked at Mary, who tried to disguise her increasing discomfort by copying her sister Jane's placid smile.

Mr. Bennet joined them. "Mr. Darcy tells me Her Majesty has asked you to dedicate your next novel to her, Mary." His eyes were filled with pride. "We could not be more proud of you, my dear."

Mary nodded slowly. "I have heard of the queen's request—it is a tremendous honor."

Mrs. Bennet's eyes went from Mary to her husband and back

again. "The queen? Our Mary? Why does no one tell me these things?"

The dinner bell rang, and Mr. Bennet tried to satisfy his wife's curiosity as he led her to the dinner table.

Once they were all seated, as if sensing Mary's increasing discomfiture, Elizabeth deliberately asked Mr. Bennet how he liked Beechwood Manor, whereupon Mrs. Bennet exclaimed, "It is charming! Absolutely charming!" She faced Major Ashton. "Mr. Darcy and Elizabeth were the first to view the place, you know, and it was on Mr. Darcy's advice Mr. Bingley made the purchase. You must see the manor to appreciate all that has been done."

The major smiled politely. "It would be an enormous pleasure."

Mr. Bingley had been listening to the exchange, and addressed the room in general. "Perhaps we might all go to Beechwood Manor for an afternoon excursion—I would like to visit it myself."

"Mrs. Darcy cannot be allowed to travel until well after the baby is born!" Dr. Braxton's expression was fierce.

Mrs. Darcy herself looked about to argue the point, but lowered her eyes and sipped her glass of diluted wine (prescribed by Mrs. Halifax). "I am sure Mary would appreciate an outing." She spoke directly to the major. "The Bingley's home is so close—there is no reason why you should not go. If only Jane and little Eliza will stay behind it will appease me, just so long as you all promise to return to Pemberley prepared to describe everything you have seen in great detail."

"My horses can get us there in under an hour." Mr. Bingley sat back, crossing his legs, his challenging eyes on Mr. Darcy, who refused to rise to the bait.

A plan was formed to travel the few miles to Beechwood Manor in two days' time, and the conversation became formal, the presence of the physician preventing the Bingleys, Darcys, and Bennets from speaking freely to one another as they enjoyed doing at family dinner. After dessert was brought in, many had to hide their relief when the doctor said he must leave, as he had another patient to tend to.

Before the doctor departed, however, he took Mrs. Bennet

aside to warn her of what he saw as her daughter Elizabeth's 'willful propensity' to disobey his orders.

"You must take her in hand, Mrs. Bennet. She is headstrong and prefers to listen to the advice of the *midwife*." His lips curled slightly at the mention of Mrs. Halifax. "Mrs. Darcy would do well to heed my advice. As regards your daughter Mary, if she does not remain in her bed I cannot say with any certainty that she will *ever* regain her memory." He shook his head, looking deeply concerned. "Mrs. Darcy refuses to have her bled, which leaves only the strictest of diets as a remedy, though I see my advice was not followed this evening. Miss Bennet must be allowed only the thinnest gruel until she shows definite signs of improvement."

Mrs. Bennet looked on with a worried expression as the physician gave his bows to the Darcys. She turned to Mr. Bennet, who had overheard the doctor's words, and had tucked his wife's hand under his arm.

"I do not think we need to worry about Lizzy, nor starve or bleed Mary to death, my dear," Mr. Bennet said. "You too were a headstrong patient, and preferred to follow the advice of the midwife over either the apothecary or the physician. If you will but recall, you did manage to give birth to five healthy daughters."

Mrs. Bennet looked up at her husband. "I am surprised you remember those days."

He smiled down at her in response.

CHAPTER FORTY-EIGHT

(An Entry in Mary Bennet's Diary)

Pemberley, 17 May 1814

I have read every page before this in the hopes of bringing memories to the fore. Unfortunately, though it makes for interesting reading, I am still completely disassociated from this Mary Bennet, and feel pity for one whose sole confidante was this diary. When I look in the mirror I am not familiar with the reflection, and wonder if I will ever again be the person who wrote these entries.

I begin to wonder if some information is being kept from me, for it is incredible that I could forget all the experiences this Mary Bennet claims to have had. The kidnapping, the derelict castle, the near-drowning, the kindness of the former Captain Jameson, his awful mother, the experience I shared with Miss Darcy in the wine cellar at Devonham, the wickedness of Mr. Petersham and of Mr. Wickham, and the bravery of Colonel Fitzwilliam and Major Ashton. All of it reads as if from a novel.

Memory loss appears to be fickle, for I was able to read and understand French today, but cannot remember having learned it. Nor English, for that matter. If my memory should fail to return, how will I ever know all I have forgotten?

It is odd (and diverting) to read about the various people whose names are sprinkled through the pages of this diary. For some reason I was attempting to thwart Miss Darcy's aunt, Lady Catherine de Bourgh—a great lady by all accounts—in her attempts to help me to write my latest novel. (I now feel in great need of help, although when I brought up the possibility of Lady Catherine coming to Pemberley to assist me, Elizabeth could hardly reply for laughing.)

It was in the pages of this diary that I learned of Major Ashton's proposal (thus solving the mystery of our relationship—or lack thereof). Imagine my surprise! Apparently, his attention turned to this Miss Caroline Bingley, whose name is so frequently mentioned, and because of it I told him I released him from any duty in regards to me or his proposal.

I must ask Miss Darcy to explain the situation to me, for the major is so kind to me, and I do enjoy his company. Why did I not accept him when he offered? Am I so stubborn and shortsighted? Perhaps there is a defect, something abhorrent about his character, which I cannot recall. From all appearances, he has excellent manners and a sharp wit, and reads prolifically (he and my father talk incessantly of books). I feel at ease in his company but wonder why it was not always so. According to the early entries of this diary, he used to tease me relentlessly.

Given the state of my memory, I wonder if Major Ashton would want me now. That is, if he does not prefer this Miss Bingley. Whatever the situation, I have done as Miss Darcy clearly wishes, accepting Major Ashton's kind offer to help with my novel.

My maid, Molly, is a wonder. This morning when I came back to my room for a shawl, I found her making a pattern from one of my gowns. She plans to make a new frock for me— apparently she is a talented dressmaker (she claims I taught her to read, and showed me the strangest book about manners). The gown she made for me prior to the accident (which she tells me I have worn on more than one occasion) is lovely. This afternoon I learned from Mr. Darcy that Molly is actually in my personal employ—her wages paid through the profits of my books.

I do hope she is happy in her work, for I have quickly grown extremely fond of her.

CHAPTER FORTY-NINE

The long-awaited package containing *The Wine Cellar* arrived at Pemberley, along with a sheaf of handwritten notes.

"It appears I have some work to do." Mary was at a complete loss as she rifled through the pages before facing the others in the sitting room.

"The major and I will be happy to help you." Georgiana spoke for him, his face being hidden behind a large newspaper.

"You are most kind," Mary replied.

"Not at all," said the major from behind his paper.

Georgiana turned to her brother. "May we make use of the larger library? It is where Mary was used to working."

"Of course." Mr. Darcy did not look up from his copy of *A General History of the Stage*.

"You will require a chaperone," Mrs. Bennet declared, her elbow making contact with her husband's ribs.

Mr. Bennet kindly offered his services.

After working on the changes to the first five chapters, Georgiana, upon seeing Mary rub her temples a second time, suggested they stop for the day. Mary was surprised at how easy the work had been—Major Ashton and Georgiana had taken turns reading the chapters aloud as they were originally written and then with the changes inserted as suggested by the publisher's assistant. Since Mary did not remember writing the book in the first place, she was unprejudicial and more than happy to make the changes. Mr. Bennet, sitting nearby with an open book in his hand, often stopped to make suggestions of his own.

After Mary put her pen away, Georgiana suggested they join the others, who had made a plan to go out walking. "Unless you would rather go to your room to rest."

Mary said she did not require rest, for she had enjoyed the time spent with her new friends (and father) immensely and much preferred to remain in their company.

Little Eliza was carefully swaddled and placed inside her basket, which was carried by Mr. Bingley who stopped frequently to re-tuck the blanket and to make funny sounds.

The fourth time he did this, Mr. Darcy stopped walking. "Charles, I thought we came outdoors to walk."

"Just you wait, Darcy," replied Mr. Bingley with good humor. "Look! Her eyes are open!"

Behind them, the colonel increased his stride. "Come along, Georgiana, Mary, Ashton; if we continue at this pace, we will reap no benefit."

As they followed behind the two gentlemen, Mary was silent, observing that the major was perhaps an inch over the colonel's height and how his dark hair curled about his high collar in a pleasing manner.

"Mary, what are you thinking?" inquired Georgiana, her head tipped to the side.

Mary, taken suddenly out of her reverie, was embarrassed to say exactly where her thoughts had gone. Instead she said, "I was thinking how beautiful the reflection of the sun is on the water, and wondering if Samson likes to swim."

"Does he ever!" Georgiana whistled for the puppy at Mr. Darcy's side while picking up a stick. "I had a feeling you were thinking of something else entirely."

"Mind your dresses!" called Mrs. Bennet from up ahead as Georgiana threw the stick and Samson jumped into the water.

~~~~~

"Do you not think Major Ashton is a patient, well-read gentleman?" Georgiana was perched upon the arm of a sofa, watching as Molly completed Mary's coiffure.

"He *is* patient." Mary frowned into the mirror. "And well-read. He is also intelligent, all of which makes him a skilled and interesting conversationalist—"

"And so handsome!" Molly interrupted, her cheeks pink.

Mary eyed her maid through the mirror. "He is at that, as are *all* of the gentlemen assembled here, so I have observed."

Georgiana examined her fingernails. "He was especially helpful with your novel."

"You all were—even my father, whose suggestion for the humorous treatment of the vicar vastly improved the scene." She thought for a moment. "It is as if everyone here is already familiar with the story."

"As it is based on something that actually happened, are you so surprised? I especially liked the major's suggestion for the scene in which the two young heroines are tied up and forced through the narrow, secret passage—his description brought me right back to Devonham."

Mary shook her head in disbelief. "How is it possible I could forget having experienced anything so chilling?"

Georgiana's response was simply to shrug, while Molly added the last pin to Mary's hair. "Since we are all family at dinner this evening, I think a discussion of your novel might make for interesting conversation. That is, if you are willing." Georgiana did not wait for Mary's response before jumping to her feet. "But we must not alarm your mamma, Mary, who does not know there is truth in some of your tales."

After dinner, the laughter increasing with each new ridiculous suggestion for plot twists, all adjourned to the music room. Elizabeth offered to play duets with Georgiana, who again chose pieces with which Mary had once been familiar.

"Will you not play for us sometime, Mary?" Mr. Bennet asked.

"I am sorry, father, but I do not even know if I can play." Mary blanched at the thought of performing in front of anyone.

Elizabeth lifted her hands from the keyboard in mid-phrase. "Perhaps you could try playing some pieces tomorrow—privately, with the help of Georgiana," she suggested gently. "Or Major Ashton might consent to play the violin to your accompaniment?"

Mary was saved from responding, for the nursemaid came to tell the Bingleys the baby was awake. Jane and Mr. Bingley excused themselves, Elizabeth and Mr. Darcy soon following behind them.

Mr. and Mrs. Bennet remained behind, though Mr. Bennet soon asked his wife to join him out on the balcony from where he thought they could see the moon.

Mrs. Bennet did not hesitate, but took her husband's arm, turning back to say, "Mary, why do you not try a duet with the major now?"

Colonel Fitzwilliam, who looked increasingly amused with each of the departures, bowed mockingly at his friend. Major Ashton returned his bow and crossed the room to open a violin case. He removed it and ran the bow experimentally across the strings before adjusting the tuning. He then looked at Mary, his comprehension of her mental state clear when he suggested, "Perhaps it might be better if you play the piece first, Miss Darcy. Miss Bennet can watch and try to play another time when she feels comfortable."

Mary looked up gratefully, and Georgiana went to the cupboard to choose a piece, inviting Mary to sit with her at the keyboard.

While Mary sat staring at the strange notes on the page, Georgiana suggested, "Try to think of it as another language. Hold your hands above the keys like I am doing, and see if you can follow along with the music." She looked over at Major Ashton. "Ready, Major?"

The major nodded, and the two of them began to play. To Mary it sounded as if they had been playing together always, and wished with all her heart she could play as well for him.

When the Bennets returned, Mrs. Bennet could not hide her disappointment when she saw it was Georgiana playing the pianoforte and not Mary.

At the end of the piece Georgiana turned to the Bennets. "I am certain Mary will remember how to play."

Mrs. Bennet raised her handkerchief, while Mr. Bennet walked over to place his hands upon Mary's shoulders. "You must not worry over such trifles, my dear."

Mary smiled, realizing she already felt a strong affection for the man who everyone claimed was her father.

～◡◡◠

Elizabeth had written Mr. and Mrs. Gardiner about the accident, asking if they might come to Pemberley, and it was on the day of the planned excursion to Beechwood Manor they arrived.

It was not the first time the Gardiners had visited Pemberley, having first toured the home at a time when they (and Elizabeth) had been assured the family was away. Mr. Darcy had appeared unexpectedly, much to Elizabeth's mortification.

Mary liked Mr. and Mrs. Gardiner on sight and was amused to see how their children behaved when in the company of Miss Darcy, who appeared to be several years younger when she joined in their games out on the lawn, rolling in the grass with them and several puppies.

The children seemed a little frightened at first by Mary, as they had been told of the accident and her loss of memory, but at Georgiana's urging, Mary began telling them a made-up story, adding new twists each day to what was becoming a ridiculously long plot, and they warmed to her—and she to them. Mary knew from her diary entries that she had not planned on becoming a mother, but the time she spent with her nephews and nieces was precious to her, and she began to wonder at another of her former self's resolutions.

A sennight had passed since Jane and Mr. Bingley had come to Pemberley, and Jane gently broached their proposed return to Beechwood Manor. She patted her sister on the hand. "The baby is not due until later in June," Jane reminded Elizabeth, who would of course prefer every one of her guests remain at Pemberley indefinitely. "We will of course be traveling back and forth frequently, as we are but a short carriage ride away."

"Mary has not yet recovered her memory, Jane. Would it not be best to stay? You would feel terrible if she remembered everything while you were gone, would you not?" Her look was both teasing and hopeful.

Mrs. Bennet, who was particularly fond of her new granddaughter, said she and Mr. Bennet must go with the Bingleys when they returned home, but supported Elizabeth's wishes. "It would be unthinkable for us to leave before Mary has her memories back, Jane; we are perfectly comfortable where we are, and all together." She leaned forward to whisper, "And if I am right, we will soon have another wedding to plan." She mouthed dramatically "The major has been to see your father!"

Elizabeth looked surprised for a moment, but then laughed. "Mamma, you are incorrigible! Our poor sister does not yet recall a single thing from her past—how can you expect her to be in love with someone she cannot remember?"

Mrs. Bennet did not reply, but took a delicate bite of a tiny savory egg pie.

In the meantime, Mary read through her diary a second time, and though she had not regained her memory, had by then some familiarity with her past. She thought a great deal about her declared preference to remain a spinster-authoress, deeply contemplated her former propensity for reading Fordyce's sermons, and questioned the reasons behind her earlier determination to be as physically and socially unappealing as possible (all the while thinking she must have been a ridiculous creature). She thought about one entry in particular—her meeting with Fanny Burney and Miss Burney's assurances that being a successful writer could never make up for the loneliness Mary would surely experience.

Watching Elizabeth one day, who was clearly comfortable in her grand surroundings, and extremely happy, Mary wondered how the gauche girl from the diary entries could have ever felt comfortable either at Pemberley or in Miss Darcy's company. Jane and Elizabeth, on the other hand, seemed completely at ease in their fine homes and incomparably happy with their husbands (who in turn clearly held their wives in great esteem). Was it possible for sisters to be so different from one another?

Focusing her attention on another object, Mary covertly watched as her mother chatted happily with the major and blushed to think what she might be saying. The major looked up and before either of them broke eye contact Mary felt sure she had been given a message, and one not unpleasant to her.

Meanwhile, Mr. Bennet was in deep conversation with Mr. Darcy about a recent purchase for his library—Mr. Darcy frowning upon the mention of a man called Byron.

"Have you finished your novel?" Mrs. Gardiner's soft voice broke into Mary's thoughts. "I understand you have been getting some help." She glanced in the major's direction.

"Both Miss Darcy and Major Ashton have been a great help—as has my father," Mary answered with a smile. "I think I can safely say things will be resolved soon."

CHAPTER FIFTY

"Charles, do you think it is normal for Elizabeth to require so much rest?" Mr. Darcy was frowning as he offered his good friend a glass of claret. "She takes more naps than Sampson recently."

"Jane slept more as her time grew nearer." Mr. Bingley absently accepted the glass and took a deep draught. "Sometimes she would fall asleep at her desk in the morning room directly after breakfast," he added with a grin. "You need not worry, Darcy—Mrs. Halifax is taking good care of your wife."

"But Dr. Braxton thinks—"

"I thought the physician's opinions were to be superseded by those of Mrs. Halifax. It will not do for you to lose confidence in your wife's care." Mr. Bingley was uncharacteristically insightful.

"Elizabeth trusts Mrs. Halifax completely, and Mrs. Bennet herself had five children with only the assistance of the midwife." Mr. Darcy drank half the contents in one gulp. "But one hears so many stories...."

Mr. Bingley well knew the history of Darcy's mother, who had died tragically after giving birth to Georgiana. "Keep the physician on hand when the time comes," he advised, "but only as a measure should something go wrong or if Elizabeth wants him. And remember, Mrs. Bennet will be here; she will be a great comfort to Elizabeth just as she was to Jane."

"I do not know how you survived it, Charles." Mr. Darcy shook his head. "Your advice is sound, though, and I will do as you suggest." He hesitated. "There is another—perhaps more delicate matter...."

Mr. Bingley did not interrupt, but held out his glass.

After topping off each glass, Mr. Darcy sat down. "Last night, Elizabeth woke me to ask if I would ring for whatever food the kitchen could manage with the least delay, and insisted I join her in a repast of cold potatoes, piccalillo, and kippers!"

Mr. Bingley grinned. "Jane asked me to procure cake and boiled mutton in the middle of the night more often than I care to remember."

"It would not be so bad, but Lizzy does not seem at all...affected by it. Apparently it all goes to the baby, but—" Darcy patted his front "—I fear my waistcoats are less comfortable as a result of these midnight forays."

Mr. Bingley shook his head, smiling. "Welcome to fatherhood, Darcy."

Tea that afternoon was held in the music room, where the Gardiners' only daughter, Hannah, wished to perform a sonata by Signor Clementi.

"What a charming piece," Mary said, clapping along with the others, though it was one she had played herself many times.

"Georgy taught it to me," Hannah said shyly.

There was an uncomfortable, worried silence, which Mr. Gardiner broke by addressing Major Ashton. "You would do me a great honor, my boy, if you would consent to play a duet; the violin is my favorite instrument."

Mary watched the major's face for any adverse reaction to being called 'my boy,' but he seemed not to mind. "I would be happy to, Mr. Gardiner—perhaps Miss Darcy would agree to play this evening?"

"Of course—it would be my pleasure, Major Ashton," Georgiana replied.

Across the room, Mrs. Gardiner was telling Colonel Fitzwilliam about the near-accident Mr. Darnell's parents experienced in their own carriage prior to Kitty's wedding. "Travel abroad comes with its own dangers. Highwaymen, broken wheels, treacherous roads...."

Jane had been listening. "Netherfield has been taken by a sea captain and his wife. It is said she has accompanied him on every one of his voyages, and hopes to continue to do so again in the future."

"I find travel to be good for the soul," Major Ashton commented, catching Mary's attention. "I hope to take my own wife with me everywhere I go—once I am married, of course," he added with a slight smile, sharing a glance with Georgiana. (Mary thought the man inconstant in his attentions, it being the second time she had seen him share such a glance with Miss Darcy.)

"Jane and I were at sea for part of our wedding trip." Mr. Bingley spoke from his place near the window. "I hope to take my family back to Italy one day to see our vineyard."

Mr. Darcy looked about to comment but was prevented by the noisy entrance of the Gardiner boys, who had been asked to recite for the benefit of the assembled party. After taking extended bows and consuming all of the cakes on the tray, the eldest of the three dared to ask Mr. Darcy if he would give them a fencing lesson.

Mr. Darcy smiled tolerantly, for he too had come to know them well. "I think the tutelage of the colonel and the major would be more helpful to you, but I will enjoy watching the lesson."

Colonel Fitzwilliam looked towards the Gardiners for consent, Mrs. Gardiner agreeing to the scheme as long as the major and colonel promised to demonstrate only the rudiments of the sport.

The colonel solemnly agreed. "Back to work, Ashton!"

⁓⌣⌣⌐

Mr. Darcy leaned against the stone wall of Pemberley's gymnasium, arms crossed, watching the eager Gardiner boys who were dressed in the white jackets and protective face masks he and Mr. Wickham had worn as children. Sticks at the ready, the three boys looked on with awe as Colonel Fitzwilliam demonstrated the proper form.

"Passe arriere!" the colonel ordered, and the boys stepped backwards. During the next half-hour, the colonel and major alternately demonstrated the basic movements, having the boys replicate them until the two men agreed it was time the first lesson came to an end.

"You have brought us to the brink of exhaustion," the major complained, much to the delight of their pupils. After agreeing to one final foot drill, he and the colonel removed their masks, bowed to one another and to each of the boys, and declared the first lesson a success.

Mr. Darcy stepped farther into the large room in which he had practiced fencing not only with Wickham but with his father. He had not entered the gymnasium after his father's death until feeling an urgent need to exorcise the memory of a certain young lady's smiling eyes (the lady he had since married), and it was with a cheerful countenance he congratulated the boys on their posture and footwork. "You are model teachers." He watched the contented young Gardiners follow their tutor out as the colonel and major placed their practice sticks in the stand. "And you both will make good fathers, if this is any example."

"Never mind him, Ashton," the colonel said. "Darcy's mind is forever on his impending fatherhood these days."

Mr. Darcy pulled a letter from his waistcoat pocket and waved it at his cousin. "Not solely on fatherhood, Richard. You might enjoy reading this."

The colonel took the letter and as he read a broad smile appeared. "We have him! Lord Harold has done it—we finally have Clay in custody." He handed it to the major. "We were right about Clay and Miss Grantly being in league. It was Clay who assisted Petersham with his escape both from Devonham and New Prison, and Miss Grantly who convinced Caroline Bingley to elope—as well as to hand over her fortune." He released a great sigh. "It is over then."

Mr. Darcy nodded solemnly but with a look of satisfaction. "And in good time, for I am soon to become a father and wish to have no further distractions."

As they left the gymnasium, Colonel Fitzwilliam said in a casual way, "I would like to hear the full story from Lord Harold."

Mr. Darcy considered for a moment. "I had become used to

thinking he was a weak character, but he has begun to redeem himself." He was unaware of the scrutiny of the other gentlemen as he continued, "I will speak to Elizabeth. It *would* be good to hear the story directly from him."

"Georgiana will be pleased," said the colonel quietly to the major as they followed their host down the hall.

During the fencing lesson, Mary went alone to the large library to complete the final changes to *The Wine Cellar* (writing, as it turned out, being one of the things her memory loss had not greatly affected). After editing the final scene—a wedding—she set her pen down. With a sigh, she stood, stretched, and began a casual perusal of the countless books on the balcony level. The first one she took up was a volume called *Sermons to Young Women* by James Fordyce. She read part of one page and flipped impatiently to the next, and then the next, scanning paragraph after paragraph, her color rose and her lips formed a straight line.

She set the book down on a table and leaned her forehead against the cool glass of the window. Suddenly, and coincidentally, a ray of sunshine broke through the clouds. Mary looked up, her eyes exhibiting a certain brightness not apparent since the carriage accident. She looked all about her, at the hundreds of shelved books, at the table she had so often used for writing, at the despised book.

She opened the tome to read a particular passage in the middle. Disgusted, she slammed it shut and returned it to the shelf.

Laughing out loud, Mary almost skipped down the spiral staircase to the first level, her expression a mixture of resolution and excitement.

"You remember *everything*, Mary?" Georgia looked amazed, excited, and extremely happy as she placed her paint brush in water, removing her protective smock before giving Mary a crushing hug. "How did this happen? And when?"

Mary told her about the book of sermons and how angry she had become. "It was as if I had nothing in my brain one moment and it was full the next." She knew she could never do justice to the experience. "I *do* remember everything! I remember all about Lady Catherine's help with my book while we were at Rosings, about Anne's engagement to Lord Wickford. I remember earlier events such as Lydia's elopement, Lizzy and Jane's wedding, that awful turret room, Wickham pushing me into the Thames, Captain Jameson's rescue—" she frowned "—I remember the first time Mr. Bingley and your brother came to Hertfordshire, why I wore those spectacles, which hurt my eyes by the way, and why I pulled my hair back so tightly—" she looked up, smiling "—I remember when I first came to Pemberley, and how we became friends. I remember all our adventures." It was as if she were afraid she would forget again, her words were coming out so fast. "I remember Captain Jameson's mother, his sister Elspeth—it is all there. Everything!" She could not stand still, pacing back and forth with great energy.

"Come, we must tell everyone!" Georgiana pulled at Mary's hand, but experienced resistance.

"Georgiana—wait a moment, if you please." Mary was thoughtful. "I remember every single second, including Major Ashton's proposal on our walk near Longbourn in December." She took hold of both of her friend's hands, excited. "Since losing my memory, I have questioned why I did not accept him." She looked shyly up at her friend. "I actually began to suspect you and he..." she blushed "...well, just know that I was not completely sure about either of your hearts." She let go of Georgiana's hands and began to pace, hands on her hips. "Perhaps we could delay telling him about my memory returning so I might learn how he truly feels about me—*before* he learns that I remember his proposal. I need to know whether he loves me, or simply holds me in high esteem before I can give him my answer...."

"Mary?" Georgiana eyed her. "What exactly are you thinking?"

"Nothing scandalous, I assure you, but since reading Miss Burney's words in my diary, they have played over and over in my mind. I have had plenty of time to reflect and had come to think that being unmarried and alone may not suit me after all."

"Oh?" Georgiana could not prevent a teasing smile. "What do

you propose?"

Mary looked through the window, unseeing. "While reading those diary entries, which to me seemed to be written by someone other than myself, I frequently wondered why I did not accept the major's fair and decent proposal—one which could only benefit me, allowing far more freedom than I would have experienced as a spinster." She looked up, her eyes bright. "But now I begin to understand—despite all my protestations to the contrary, I wanted him to say he loved me." Mary paused but Georgiana did not interrupt. "With the return of my memory, it would seem I have the added benefit of clearer understanding regarding affairs of my own heart; I think I have been in love with him for some time without having any idea of it."

"And Captain—er, Lord Jameson?"

"He was the first gentleman to treat me like a lady, and one worthy of attention. I was flattered and I liked him, but the feelings I had for him are different than those I feel for the major." She faltered. "Before the accident, I had come to realize that my feelings for Captain Jameson were along the lines of hero worship, where in the case of the major—well...."

Georgiana's sweet smile appeared, the frown lines gone. "I have wondered about your first attachment for some time, Mary, and you know I have experience in this. Perhaps it is because of what one reads in novels, but I thought a truly broken heart could not be so practical as yours, though I do believe you did care for him." She took hold of Mary's hand to pull her from the room. "Never mind what has passed, when we go to the others I will propose a walk to the little cottage—Major Ashton will without a doubt offer to escort us. While walking, I will contrive a broken shoelace and ask you to go on ahead while I see to it." She smiled deviously. "I do not believe we will encounter resistance, for Elizabeth has also come to believe you were unable to admit to your true feelings."

"Has she indeed?" Mary asked, all the while wondering about Georgiana's own heart, for she also remembered her good friend's feelings for a certain gentleman, whom her brother considered the worst of rakes. "But what of you and Lord Harold?"

Georgiana stopped in her tracks, turning to her friend with a sigh. "He sees me only as his childhood playmate, and treats me as he would a sister. It would seem it is I who will remain the spinster."

Her tone was determinedly cheerful, but Mary felt sure that Miss Georgiana Darcy's heart would not so easily recover this time.

CHAPTER FIFTY-ONE

Inclement weather postponed Georgiana's proposed walk, and therefore the announcement about Mary's memory, causing that young lady no small amount of anxiety.

While waiting for the others to join them in the drawing room before dinner that evening, Elizabeth told Georgiana and Mary of Mr. Clay's capture. "Mr. Darcy has asked Lord Harold to come, and we must wait for him to give us the details." Her relief at the closure of the business was clear.

"It was Lord Harold who finally found him?" Georgiana's cheeks were pink.

Elizabeth looked with interest at her sister-in-law. "Yes," she replied, with no other reference to the gentleman, being well-acquainted with her husband's opinion of him.

Earlier, Mary had suggested they tell all but Major Ashton about the return of her memory, but Georgiana had demurred. "If you tell the others, some one of us will assuredly make a slip of the tongue. Your secret will be out and our experiment ruined."

Mary did not like keeping anything secret from her hostess, who happened also to be her sister, but with the return of her memory she also knew of Elizabeth's propensity towards matchmaking. Believing their plan to be of vital importance, she agreed to remain silent on the subject and as a result did not speak much during the evening so as not to compound her crime of omission with active dishonesty.

In the music room after dinner, Elizabeth approached Mary to ask quietly if she were feeling ill, nearly bringing about a full confession for her guilt-ridden sister, but Georgiana distracted her sister-in-law by asking about her miniature replica of Pemberley.

"My heavens!" Elizabeth looked at them with wide eyes. "We have totally forgotten about the hidden room!"

"Hidden room?" the two of them echoed.

"Yes—there was a discrepancy in the plans for my model of Pemberley and those for the house itself. Fitzwilliam and I found the room, with a little help from the carpenter, and we planned to surprise you when you arrived back home." She looked at Mary with a sad expression. "But you had your accident, and we did not think of it again."

Mrs. Gardiner, Mrs. Bingley, and Mrs. Bennet left off their discussion about French food, Mrs. Gardiner declaring that every house should have at least one secret room.

When the gentlemen entered the music room, they each took up candles and walked the entire length of Pemberley to view the recently-uncovered room.

Inside the small chamber was a plain wooden chair, a heavily-curtained bed, a desk with letters still tucked inside its cubbies, and a few spent candles. Everything was covered in dust and webs, the room clearly having been closed off for decades, perhaps longer, the Darcy ancestors possibly not passing down the secret of having been in service to the prince when it would have been considered treasonous. Mr. Darcy and Elizabeth had read the letters left in the desk when the carpenters had removed the walls concealing the room, Mr. Darcy deducing his family had hidden supporters of Charles II during the reign of Cromwell.

The late hour and the state of the room discouraged further investigation and they dispersed, but not before Georgiana proposed a walk for the next day.

After everyone had retired to their own rooms and Mr. Darcy was busy with his valet, Elizabeth creeped down the hall to Mary's room, the two young ladies she found there looking decidedly guilty.

"Mary?" Elizabeth came to Mary's side to check for fever. "I came to find out if you were feeling any better. You were so quiet this evening I feared your headaches had returned—" her eyes narrowed as she looked from one to the other.

"She is not ill, Elizabeth...Mary has remembered everything!"

"Everything?" Elizabeth's eyebrows went up.

"Everything," Mary admitted, hanging her head.

"But Mary, this is almost miraculous! Why are you so despondent?" Elizabeth cried, taking her sister's hands.

Again Georgiana answered for her. "Mary wished to keep her situation a secret until—" she looked at Mary helplessly.

Elizabeth Darcy put her hands on her hips and faced her two sisters, demanding they tell her everything, which they did, and with great relief.

"Some of us would not have betrayed your secret, you know, but I understand." Elizabeth sat down. "I suggest we do as you propose, Georgiana, and go for a walk along the lake tomorrow—but as early in the day as it can be arranged." She tapped her lip as Georgiana and Mary waited, barely breathing as she plotted and planned, mentally moving each of her relatives around Pemberley as she did the tiny furniture in her model of the house. "Fitzwilliam and the colonel must be separated from the major somehow, and of course we have to consider the possibility of our plan being thwarted by the arrival of Lord Harold."

"Yes—" Elizabeth nodded slowly "—I think we can manage something. You two can continue on to the cottage when suddenly Georgiana will need to stop and tie her shoe—"

Georgiana laughed. "Elizabeth, I believe you read too many novels."

Elizabeth assured them all would be well on the morrow before claiming Mr. Darcy would soon send the servants in search of her. She did not, however, tell them she fully intended to tell her husband what she had just learned.

The next afternoon, Elizabeth feigned tiredness when they had gone about half-way along the west side of the lake. The married ladies immediately insisted upon returning with her to the house, and Mr. Darcy asked Colonel Fitzwilliam and Major Ashton to see to Georgiana and Mary.

Shortly after resuming their walk, Georgiana claimed to have left her parasol behind a tree when they had stopped to throw sticks for Samson and the other dogs, who had taken to walking with them.

Strangely, the colonel suggested he go with her and told Major Ashton to walk on ahead with Mary. "Georgiana and I will catch up to you shortly."

Once alone with the major, Mary became nervous about her plan. But when she took his offered arm she felt something almost undefinable, the word 'rightness' coming to mind.

The major broke the silence as they approached the rustic cottage the elder Mr. Darcy had designed for his wife, Lady Anne. "Now you have completed the changes to *The Wine Cellar*, have you thought of what you would like to write next, Miss Bennet?"

Mary's mind went to the Miss Leighs and Beechwood Manor. "I have—it is to be a novel about a mother and her daughters who lose their home to an entail."

He looked thoughtful for a moment. "It is a sad fact of our society, but one you need not be concerned with, surely?"

Mary smiled wryly. "Mr. Darcy and Mr. Bingley saved us from that worry, for which my family will be forever grateful. I think it time I wrote about something other than kidnapping and castles—something important." In his expression she could discern only friendly interest. "Rather than spend the rest of my days writing what Colonel Fitzwilliam calls 'silly novels' I thought I would try writing something with—" she stopped, thinking she had given away the state of her memory, but the major seemed unaware.

"Social significance?" he asked with a smile.

Mary simply nodded in reply, for they had arrived at the little house. "Might we go inside?" she asked, and when the major tried the door it swung open easily.

"We may as well wait for Miss Darcy and the colonel in comfort." His expression was unreadable as he gestured for her to precede him.

Mary's heart was beating unreasonably fast as she realized her plan for a tête-à-tête had succeeded. "It is a lovely place," she murmured, looking through the tall windows out upon the lake.

"But small."

Mary laughed. "At one time I dreamt of such a place as this—of having my own little cottage."

In the next moment, he took hold of her arms and turned her to face him. "What did you just say, Miss Bennet?"

Mary's breath caught in her throat, and she looked at the wall opposite. "I meant to say Georgiana has told me about my wishes for it."

Suddenly, he released her and moved away. "I am sorry, Miss Bennet, but for a moment I thought—" he ran a hand through his hair, his eyes on the entrance to the cottage. "There is something I would like to say—about what has occurred between us."

"Between us?"

"Yes—on December the nineteenth—on a walk with your family in Hertfordshire, just before the colonel and I were called away to go in search of Miss Bingley—you know the story of her planned elopement, I presume?"

Mary nodded, not wishing to interrupt him knowing the others could appear at any moment.

"I spoke of my parents' marriage—how they were friends when they married, and how happy they have been." His eyes searched hers. "If only you could remember. It was difficult enough to put this into words the first time."

Mary felt a twinge of guilt, but still she would not interrupt.

"On that day in December I proposed a similar arrangement between us, Miss Bennet—a marriage between two people who esteem one another. I asked you to consider marriage with me, based on friendship."

"Indeed?" Mary's brows rose, and she experienced a definite warming in the region of her heart.

"I did—and at the time thought it a most prudent course of action, given my feelings."

"Your feelings?"

He began to pace. "I was not completely truthful, Miss Bennet, in my proposal, for I made it sound as if the only feelings I had for you were those of esteem. There are feelings of love, which I did not mention for fear it would result in your immediate refusal."

Mary could bear it no longer. "I remember my response well." She smiled. "I said I would consider your proposal."

"Exactly—" he stopped pacing and turned to her. "Did I hear you correctly?" His eyes narrowed.

She looked up at him. "Yes, Major Ashton. Since late yesterday afternoon I have experienced a total recollection of past events. It was when I—"

"—You did not think to tell anyone?"

Mary blushed, worried now that her actions would have the opposite effect of those she had hoped. "I told Georgiana...but decided to wait to tell everyone else until I had the opportunity to speak with you privately."

This time the major was silent.

Mary searched for the right words. "I did not wish you to feel obliged to keep a promise you made to me so many months ago, especially given my almost uncivil response, and thought to give you an opportunity to retract your...." She lowered her eyes.

"My proposal." He gently lifted her chin. "I will not retract my proposal, but repeat it." He stood straight before her, his expression serious. "Will you, Miss Mary Bennet, do me the honor of becoming my authoress-wife, my closest friend and confidante, and my helpmate?"

The novelist in Mary heard his words with pleasure. She raised her face to his. "I will be your wife, Major Ashton, and do my best to ensure you never regret this moment."

Outside, Colonel Fitzwilliam had been peering through the window. He held a finger to his lips and quietly led Georgiana back down the path. "A few seconds more," he said firmly.

CHAPTER FIFTY-TWO

Later in the day, Major Ashton received the requisite approval of Mr. Bennet, and the Darcys' guests convened for a surprising announcement—not only had Miss Mary Bennet's memory returned, but the confirmed spinster was engaged to be married.

"Oh, Major Ashton!" Mrs. Bennet linked arms with her future son-in-law. "I had a feeling!" Her eyes twinkled. "You never knew Mary in days past, but there was a time when she absolutely refused to marry!" She turned to address her husband, who looked bemused after his recent interview with yet another future son-in-law. "Do you remember, Mr. Bennet, the morning when Mary first appeared at breakfast without her spectacles?"

Mr. Bennet accepted a glass of prosecco from Mr. Bingley. "I do indeed, my dear. It is my understanding that it symbolized the shaking-off of a persona devised to turn away all suitors, and had she not succeeded so well at the time, we might not be having this conversation."

Lord Harold arrived soon afterwards, Mr. Darcy watching him closely as he joined Georgiana and the newly-engaged couple, all of them laughing.

Elizabeth's brow lifted as she too watched. "You know, my dear, it is now only Georgiana and Caroline Bingley who are in need of husbands—would you ever have believed our Mary and your cousin, Miss de Bourgh, would be first at the altar?"

Mr. Darcy looked down at his wife, his expression teasing. "Do you have someone in mind for Georgiana, my dear?"

Elizabeth smiled back at him, but did not voice her thoughts, nor did she look in the direction of Lord Harold.

Across the room, Georgiana became serious. "I do not like to think of Mary leaving us, Major Ashton, and would ask you not to take her too far from me."

"Where will you live, Ashton?"

Mary was grateful the colonel voiced the question she had not yet found the courage to ask.

The major turned to Mary. "Miss Bennet and I have not yet discussed the matter, but I expect we will never be far from Miss Darcy."

"I would not expect it either." Colonel Fitzwilliam grinned as he rested his hand upon Lord Harold's shoulder. "We are of course anxious to hear the details of Clay's capture, and especially about his involvement in the carriage accident."

The major nodded. "Your skills have proved to be exemplary, Lord Harold—I do hope your service to the Crown will be amply rewarded."

Despite the praise, Lord Harold did not look happy. "We would have found Clay much sooner had he not disappeared in the Dials—it is a maze of narrow streets and decrepit buildings."

"The entire area should be burned to the ground," the colonel agreed.

Any further comment on the matter was curtailed by the announcement of dinner, and it being the first time Mary had been taken into a dining room on the arm of the man to whom she was betrothed, she did not know if her feet ever touched the ground.

Dinner was served in the most intimate of Pemberley's dining rooms, and was a lively affair with much toasting and laughter. At one point Mrs. Bennet claimed, "I for one never doubted Mary would recover her memory, for the brain has marvelous healing powers." Her words initiated a spirited dialogue which lasted until after dessert.

At a silent signal from his wife, Mr. Darcy suggested they reconvene in the drawing room to hear Lord Harold's tale. The ladies rose, and during the short time the gentlemen took for their port Mr. Bennet asked Lord Harold to tell them how Mr. Clay had managed to sabotage the carriage, for he did not wish to unnecessarily alarm the ladies—especially Mrs. Bennet, for whom any type of travel was a trial.

Lord Harold told of discovering evidence in Miss Grantly's home, where Clay had at first been hiding. "The informant caught by the colonel and major—" Lord Harold gestured to the two men with his cigar "—was happy to enlighten us in the hopes of having his punishment lessened to deportation. We know without a doubt that Mr. Clay was involved in all the activities at Devonham, including Petersham and the valet's escape. Clay has not yet admitted to tampering with the wheel of Mr. Darcy's carriage—" Lord Harold looked briefly at his host, whose expression was murderous "—but the coachman has identified him as the man who, on the morning of the ladies' departure, appeared to have some sort of bilious attack and asked for something to drink.

"The servant was gone but a minute, but Clay probably hired someone to damage the wheel—it needed only a single man with strength and a sharp saw blade once the coachman and groom were distracted." Lord Harold held his glass by the stem, absently twisting it on the shining table. "Clay is charged with treason, but Lord Castlereagh may lighten the sentence if he admits to this additional crime."

Colonel Fitzwilliam was furious. "He should be facing a charge of attempted murder!"

The others clearly agreed with him.

Mr. Bennet rose from his chair. "Lord Harold, I would like to thank you personally for your work in getting that man captured."

The men solemnly joined in the toast before joining the ladies in the drawing room, where a much-edited version of events was told by Lord Harold, though it was horrific enough to cause Mrs. Bennet to gasp more than once.

All the while, Elizabeth and Mary watched Georgiana who was looking upon Lord Harold with an expression that might have had Mrs. Bennet choosing flowers for the wedding, had she but observed it.

After everyone else had gone to their beds, Mary and Georgiana stood on the balcony outside Georgiana's room, the temperature pleasant and the stars brilliant in the night sky.

"Though I am happy for you Mary, I am sad as well, for this means the end of our adventures together." Georgiana kept her gaze focused on the stars as she spoke.

"We still have one rather difficult task before us, Georgiana—we must convince your brother of a certain gentleman's viability as your suitor."

Georgiana wiped at her cheeks impatiently. "I have little hope of Lord Harold sharing my feelings, nor of Fitzwilliam ever accepting the connection." She turned to face Mary, a faint glimmer of hope in her eyes. "But I am willing to try—have you a plan?"

"Not yet, but I will have by morning."

The next morning, Major Ashton went to personally inform his parents of his engagement, intent upon returning to Pemberley within three days. Mary had risen early to see him off, and very soon afterwards was surprised to receive a summons from Elizabeth.

"What is it, Lizzy?" asked Mary upon entering the bright yellow morning room, filled with the scent of fresh air and spring flowers.

"I would like your opinion about this letter—" Elizabeth held up the single page filled with Kitty's scrawl "—as well as this one from Lady Catherine."

Mary perused Kitty's letter quickly, then traded it for Lady Catherine's.

"I am growing concerned about Kitty, for with each letter she sounds increasingly unhappy." Elizabeth rummaged through the cubbies of her desk and pulled out four letters, rising from her chair to place them in order by date on a table.

Before Mary began to read them, she asked, "What of Lady Catherine's invitation? Surely you cannot think of attending Anne's wedding?"

Elizabeth's expression was difficult to read. "I certainly cannot travel to Kent, and Fitzwilliam refuses to go without me. But as Anne has little family to witness the occasion, he and I think it best that *someone* from Pemberley attend. We hope Georgiana and Colonel Fitzwilliam will go—if he can delay returning to his duties in town."

Mary looked up, her attention caught. "Georgiana is to go to Rosings?" Her mind was racing with thoughts of her recent engagement, her promise to Georgiana about Lord Harold, and of Kitty, whose final letter sounded a little desperate if one read between the lines.

"Fitzwilliam could of course ask Lady Catherine to include Major Ashton in the invitation, for you are invited as well, Mary." Elizabeth smiled gently at her sister as she placed a metal tip at the end of her quill and pulled out a sheet of paper. "But I think Mrs. Halifax might have some objection to your traveling so far. It is actually Kitty who concerns me most. I am writing now to invite her to Pemberley, and will use your engagement to convince Mr. Darnell to bring her to us." She waylaid Mary's words with a wave of her hand. "I realize the date has not yet been set, but I would like to attend the ceremony..." she turned away suddenly.

Even before regaining her memories, Mary had realized how worried Elizabeth was about the birth. "Mrs. Halifax will not allow anything to happen to either you or the baby, Lizzy. And neither will Mamma or Jane."

Elizabeth blotted her eyes with a handkerchief. "I am so sorry. I seem to worry about everything and anything these last few weeks, and cry for no reason whatsoever. Jane tells me this is but another stage when one is expecting and should not last long."

The major had not spoken of a wedding date prior to his departure, but Mary felt secure in saying, "I do not believe Major Ashton will object to a brief engagement." She blushed furiously.

Elizabeth spoke to Mr. Darcy soon afterwards.

"I think your plan to invite Kitty is a good one, my dear. Mary's wedding makes a perfect excuse for the Darnells to come to us, if you think Ashton can convince her."

"I think Mary will comply." Elizabeth took his hand and rested it against her cheek. "Have I told you how much I love and esteem you today, Mr. Darcy?"

He pretended to think. "No, I do not recall you doing so."

Mrs. Darcy of Pemberley told him, in tender terms, how very

fond of him she was before broaching the subject of Miss de Bourgh's wedding.

Mr. Darcy paced the thickly carpeted floor of their private sitting room, his hands behind his back. "Georgiana must go, of course, but it would be unfair to expect your sister to oblige my aunt at such a time." His expression was quizzical. "What does Mary have to say?"

Elizabeth shrugged. "She will be happy to go with Georgiana anywhere, of course. I told her you might ask Lady Catherine to invite Major Ashton."

Mr. Darcy looked skeptical. "They would go to Rosings on their wedding trip?"

Elizabeth laughed. "Fitzwilliam, if it were to be a wedding trip, they would have to marry even sooner than I had thought." She paused, considering the idea.

"The major might be in favor of such a plan, for a speedy wedding would not allow time for Mary to change her mind. And Rosings, as you know, has the benefit of a large park."

Elizabeth patted her husband's hand. "Mary will not change her mind—I am certain of it." Her eyes shifted with her thoughts. "It is too bad the major left before the two of them decided upon a date. Otherwise, I might have written to Kitty today."

Mr. Darcy leaned closer to whisper, "You could invite them to come without giving a firm date, you know, Mrs. Darcy. If the major had his way, the wedding would be tomorrow."

"You will not mind so many guests at Pemberley? Four of five Bennet daughters, my mother and father...."

Mr. Darcy smiled. "Mrs. Darcy, must I remind you once again how large is Pemberley and how many servants there are to assist us?" He turned to her with a sudden thought. "We could always remove temporarily to the little house on the lake."

Elizabeth's eyes twinkled. "The little house on the lake would make for a perfect retreat for a recently-married young couple, would it not?" She thought for a moment. "You know, my dear—I know very little about Major Ashton's situation."

Mr. Darcy rose, stretching. "You need not worry about him, Elizabeth. He is situated well enough, I assure you. Ashton told me himself that he wanted Mary to accept him solely on his own merit—a noble thing, and as she has never questioned him he never saw a reason to broach the subject." He grinned. "Your father certainly has no objection to the match."

Elizabeth considered her husband for a moment, frowning. "Can you tell me *some* of the particulars of his situation, my dear?"

Mr. Darcy laughed, pulling her to her feet. "I wonder you did not ask sooner. Major Ashton's father is a viscount, and Mary's husband will one day inherit the title, though he wishes to continue in the service of the crown." He held up his hand to stop the inevitable flow of questions. "You need not worry— Ashton will tell Mary when the time is right."

"It would seem we are to keep a secret from her now." Elizabeth tipped her head to the side. "How extraordinary Mary turned out to be."

"I would never have thought it possible after first meeting her in Hertfordshire." Mr. Darcy looked apologetic. "Georgiana will be happy to hear that the major's family home is so close to Pemberley."

"You never consider anything under fifty miles as far away, Fitzwilliam." Elizabeth's dimples appeared. "We must now find Georgiana a husband whose estate is close by as well. Just think—our Mary, a viscountess." Her eyes shone. "Does Mamma have any idea?"

Later, all the ladies joined Elizabeth on her daily walk, Mrs. Halifax encouraging the exercise. As they entered the new maze, modeled after the one at Devonham, Georgiana asked Mary quietly, "Is something bothering you? You have a defined furrow on your brow."

Mary looked up, her eyes not immediately focusing. "I only just realized something rather important—I do not know Major Ashton's first name." She shook her head in disbelief. "I know very little about his parents, his situation in life, or what the future holds for us—and yet I have consented to be his wife." She looked with wide eyes at her friend. "Does this sound like me at all?"

Georgiana laughed, wiping her eyes. "It sounds neither like the Mary Bennet I first met nor the Mary Bennet of only two months ago!"

Elizabeth had heard the exchange. "But it does sound like a Miss Mary Bennet who has finally fallen in love, does it not?"

CHAPTER FIFTY-THREE

(A Letter from Caroline Bingley to Charles Bingley)

Belgrave, 24 May 1814

Dear Charles,

Louisa and I are feeling quite deserted in London, and I know not who else to turn to for this favor—it is in the nature of having a certain gentleman thoroughly investigated as to fortune, reputation, etc. The gentleman in question is Lord Exeter, who I first met at a party given by Lady Matlock at Darcy House (designed to bring eligible gentlemen to meet poor Miss Darcy). Since then, with Louisa and Mr. Hurst acting as chaperones, I have accompanied Lord Exeter to many events and find his company quite above any other. I can only hint that should your investigation prove him worthy, you might soon call him 'brother.'

I understand you have finally left Hertfordshire for good. I must admit, I never could feel comfortable with those country folk. Louisa and I have many obligations, of course, and the delights of town are particularly sweet now I am a young lady of means once more, but we would be happy to help Jane with the settling of her new household, and in the training of the servants as well, for she has not had the benefit of our upbringing (Mr. Hurst has some experience with landscape design, which you may find useful). I daresay if we do not hear from you soon, we may well surprise you.

I understand Major Ashton and Colonel Fitzwilliam escorted the Miss Leighs to Derbyshire, though perhaps those *two gentlemen would not have done so were they aware of the rumors flying about regarding the younger Miss Leigh.*

Your loving sister,
Caroline Bingley

CHAPTER FIFTY-FOUR

"Jane—" Mr. Bingley approached his wife in the Pemberley nursery, a letter in his hand "—Caroline has written to ask if I might have a certain gentleman investigated on her behalf, and is hinting she may be married soon."

Jane placed their sleeping baby in the crib and lifted a finger to her lips. Mr. Bingley understood and tiptoed the rest of the way. Together, the new parents watched their sleeping child until Mr. Bingley took Jane's hand to lead her from the room, Jane making silent gestures at the nursemaid, who nodded before going back to her book (she had only just begun to read *The Turret Room*).

When they reached their own sitting room, Jane read the letter from his sister with a slight frown. "Charles, now that Mary has regained her memory, do you not think it is time we return to Beechwood? The servants will think we do not mean to live there."

Mr. Bingley took hold of his wife and kissed her soundly. "We will go as soon as Eliza wakes from her nap—I must speak to Darcy immediately!"

Jane, a half-smile mixed with a look of determination on her face, went to find Elizabeth.

A short time later Mr. Bennet informed his wife of their imminent return to the Bingley's home, and Mrs. Bennet rushed off to instruct her maid about the packing, though there was comparatively little to do as most of her things were at Beechwood Manor.

Mr. Gardiner too said it was time he returned to his business in London and made arrangements to depart the following day.

Two hours later, Elizabeth smiled sadly and kissed her sister Jane good-bye. "We will be a much-diminished party tomorrow."

"We are but a short carriage ride away, Lizzy, and can come at a moment's notice, especially once the date is set for Mary's wedding."

Mrs. Bennet made Elizabeth promise to allow Mr. Darcy to help her up the stairs, to walk only a short distance each day, and to be watchful of changing weather when she went out. "The wind is not our friend, Lizzy," she warned before stepping into the waiting carriage. Once inside, her head appeared through the window. "And remember to carry your parasol, my dear!"

That afternoon, Major Ashton returned to Pemberley and was conducted to the back terrace, where he found Mr. Darcy, Mr. Gardiner, Lord Harold, and Colonel Fitzwilliam.

A drinks tray soon followed and after his guests had been served, Mr. Darcy cleared his throat. "Earlier today, Richard received an express from Lord Matlock: talks for peace between France and England have begun, and a treaty is soon to be signed. A toast, gentlemen—" he lifted his glass "—to the end of war with France, and to the end of Napoleon!"

"To the end of war!" the other men echoed.

Mr. Darcy then proposed a tour of the stables, the modifications finally complete.

After a thorough tour and a look at Darcy's prized horses, the colonel proposed a ride. "Your fine horses look in need of fresh air, Darcy," he said to his cousin with a grin. Mr. Gardiner declined to join them, leaving the younger men to celebrate in their own way while he returned to the house to share the good news with the ladies.

After exercising their horses on the wide expanse along the western edge of the estate, the four younger men rode into Lambton, intent upon taking pints of ale at Lambton's public house.

The news had traveled fast, and the public house was full to brimming when they arrived. Mr. Darcy ordered drinks for all the men there, and toast after toast was made as well as plans to burn Napoleon in effigy in the clearing just outside of Lambton.

When the crowd grew too boisterous Mr. Darcy suggested they return to Pemberley and the four gentlemen rode back the way they had come, albeit much more slowly.

After taking their horses to the stable Mr. Darcy caught Major Ashton by the arm to hold him back as the others went into the house. "I do not know the best manner in which to present this request, Major Ashton, for it is beyond our right to ask—" he looked apologetically at his future brother-in-law "—but Elizabeth and I were hoping you and Mary might consider having your wedding here, at Pemberley Chapel." He hesitated briefly. "Perhaps before the end of this month—so that Mrs. Darcy might attend?"

The major smiled, relieved, for Mr. Darcy had looked so serious. "I would be more than happy to wed Miss Bennet as soon as may be—tomorrow if she were willing. But it is she who must be asked. Have either you or Mrs. Darcy spoken to her?"

Mr. Darcy shook his head. "We thought it best to consult you first. Would you prefer to broach the topic yourself? I can arrange for the two of you to be left undisturbed...."

Major Ashton laughed outright. "Mr. Darcy, I do believe you have missed your calling."

Mr. Darcy acknowledged the words with a nod. "Now we are to be brothers-in-law, I hope you will call me Fitzwilliam—or Darcy if you prefer."

"And you must call me Christopher, er...Darcy." The major looked consideringly at the man he would soon be calling his brother. "There is something I would like to ask of *you*, Darcy."

"Anything."

"There is the matter of my father's title, and the probability of my inheriting it one day."

Mr. Darcy lifted a single brow, waiting, for the major was clearly having difficulty finding the right words.

"Miss Bennet believes my income comes solely from my post in His Majesty's Regiment."

Mr. Darcy inclined his head, waiting.

"I have not yet said anything to her about my family situation, for she has never asked me."

"Miss Mary Bennet is a remarkable young lady, Christopher."

"Indeed she is." He kicked at a stone in the path. "I wish to tell her myself—at the right time."

Mr. Darcy smiled. "You may rest assured—those few of us who are aware of your situation will say not a word about it." He thought for a moment. "But your parents?"

"I have asked that they call themselves Mr. and Mrs. Ashton in the meantime."

Mr. Darcy shook his head. "You are playing with fire, my friend, but Elizabeth and I will do as you ask."

Ultimately, Mr. Darcy's contrivance for a private conference between the major and his fiancée was not needed. After questioning many servants and searching the various places Miss Bennet was wont to go during the day, he found her more or less alone, kneeling in the large grassy area near the stable block. She was surrounded by the new litter of spaniel puppies (Georgiana had run inside to change her dress but had not yet returned).

"Miss Bennet—" Major Ashton looked as if he were deciding whether it would be better to join her on the ground or help her to her feet "—I have told you a little of my parents, but I would like to tell you more about my family's circumstances."

Mary picked up a puppy, unmindful of dirty paws, and made as if to stand, the major moving quickly to help her. "You need not tell me anything, Major Ashton, for Papa assures me you are a gentleman of some property who can comfortably support a wife." She could not bring herself to mention children. "I am certain either Mr. Darcy or Colonel Fitzwilliam would have said something if they thought you were a less-than-desirable marriage partner, or if you had an unfortunate propensity for betting on the horses." She smiled up at him, the puppy wriggling in her arms. "There is the matter of my own small income, which I hope will contribute to our household expenses."

The major looked away to hide his smile, turning back to her to say with great seriousness, "The income from your novels will indeed be useful to us, Miss Bennet, and I am pleased to know you are willing to share it."

Mary continued, undeterred. "I would also like to continue

to be responsible for Molly's wages—though I do not know how much longer she will remain with me."

"No other young lady of my acquaintance would be so generous, Miss Bennet, nor so sanguine regarding her fiancé's circumstances."

Mary patted the female puppy's head gently before setting her on the ground. "I cannot explain it, other than to say I trust you implicitly. However, I would like to know one thing before we are married."

"And what would that be, Miss Bennet?"

"I would like to know by what name I should call you."

The major laughed. "My full name is Christopher Stanhope Benning Ashton, Miss Bennet. But when we are married, you may call me by whatever name you choose." He picked up one of the puppies, busily attacking his boot.

"There is one other thing...Christopher."

The major stood to face her, his brows raised.

"Do you think we might manage a little cottage of our own at one point or another?"

The major laughed, causing Mary to wonder why she had never before acknowledged how pleasurable it was to hear.

"Yes, Miss Bennet. I think we can have a little cottage. We only need to find it."

"You need not call me Miss Bennet any longer."

The major took up one of Mary's hands to study her fingers. "I wish to call you Miss Bennet until we are married, if you do not mind."

"Of course not—I will in turn call you Major Ashton, though I will think of you as Christopher, for I like the name." Mary looked up at him, the depth of her feelings for a man who used to vex her with his teasing clear in her expression. "And your parents? Do they approve the marriage?"

The major pretended to think for a moment, setting down the puppy and picking up a stick. He threw it, Samson running off with three short-legged balls of fur tumbling after him. "After I told my father I wished to marry the lady who wrote *The Turret Room* and *The Count of Camalore*, and promised an inscribed copy of *The Wine Cellar* as soon as it becomes available—" he raised an eyebrow at Mary, who inclined her head ever so slightly "—he thought it an excellent idea."

"And your mother? Perhaps she had hoped you would marry an heiress at least, if not a titled lady." Mary frowned at the thought.

"Thankfully, my mother is as fond of your books as is my father."

"And they will come for the wedding?"

"The questions you ask, Miss Bennet!" He threw the stick once more. "Yes, they will come. As a matter of fact, Mrs. Darcy is poised to invite them as soon as the date is set."

Georgiana finally joined them with two of the puppies in her arms, rubbing their soft coats against her cheeks. "What has you two smiling at each other so?"

It was then that the major broached the Darcys' request for a wedding date within the next fortnight, and not even Georgiana could predict her friend's reaction.

Mary bent down to brush at the grass stains on her dress, keeping her face averted until she regained her composure. "A wedding might very well finally convince Mr. Darnell to bring Kitty—"she smiled, mischief in her eyes "—and I know for certain it would please Mamma no end to tell her friends that the least likely of her daughters was married by special license." She tipped her head to the side. "Can we afford it, Major Ashton?"

⌒﹏⌒

By the time Kitty and Mr. Darnell arrived from York, only four days remained before the wedding of Miss Mary Bennet and Major Christopher Ashton.

Mary thought Kitty's traveling cloak far too heavy for the time of year, noting with concern how thin and pale her younger sister was as she clung to Mrs. Bennet before Mr. Darnell came to take her arm.

Mr. Darnell greeted everyone in his easy, pleasant manner, but seemed disappointed to hear that the Bingleys would not be at Pemberley until the day before the wedding. He then asked if they might be shown to their rooms, for he said Kitty needed rest after their journey.

It was not until just before dinner when Elizabeth managed to speak with Kitty in semi-private, Kitty making light of her condition, saying only that she had not been sleeping well. "It is much colder in York than in Hertfordshire," she said, pulling her shawl more tightly about her too-thin shoulders. "But I am growing accustomed to it."

After dinner, Elizabeth expressed her concerns to Mary.

"Perhaps the colder climate is truly affecting her," Mary suggested, though she did not believe it herself.

Elizabeth shook her head firmly. "When Kitty left Netherfield for York, she was as happy as any young bride could be—and healthy, mind you. But now look at her." She frowned as she looked across the room where Kitty was in conversation with Georgiana. "She will become ill if she grows any thinner." Elizabeth's considering eyes went to Mr. Darnell. "They were like two turtledoves when in Hertfordshire—is it possible after they were married Mr. Darnell turned into a monster?"

Mary looked across the room just as Kitty laughed, her face animated. "Perhaps we have read too many novels, Lizzy, and are imagining trouble." She watched Mr. Darnell come to sit with Kitty and Georgiana, and the laughter ceased. "Though I think it might be wise to ask Molly and Lucy to become friendly with Kitty's maid—perhaps they can learn something we could not."

The two sisters looked across the room at their subject, the candlelight casting shadows on their faces.

CHAPTER FIFTY-FIVE

Three days before Mary's wedding, a messenger arrived from Beechwood manor with news of the Bingleys' newly-arrived guests: Miss Caroline Bingley, Mr. and Mrs. Hurst, and Lord Exeter.

"Fitzwilliam!" Elizabeth rose from her dressing-table.

"Yes, my dear?" Mr. Darcy's head appeared in the doorway.

Elizabeth waved Jane's brief note and he closed the door, striding across the room to take it.

"What are we to do?" Elizabeth automatically reached up to adjust his cravat, even though it had been expertly tied by his valet.

Mr. Darcy looked again at the letter with a slight frown. "Mary would not be expected to invite Miss Bingley, the Hursts, and Lord Exeter to her wedding, though I am not certain Jane would relish the thought of Caroline remaining behind at Beechwood Manor while she and Charles are here."

Elizabeth walked to the door, speaking almost to herself. "They might think it odd not to be invited to the wedding breakfast, if not the wedding itself. I must find Mary."

Mr. Darcy looked fondly upon his wife, whom Mrs. Halifax had begun watching closely, certain her time was near.

～⌣～

On the day of the wedding, Miss Mary Bennet was still asleep when Molly opened the curtains, allowing the early-morning sun to shine upon the face of her mistress. For one brief moment Mary did not remember the significance of the day, but was soon reaching for her dressing gown.

Mary wondered at feeling no nerves as she sat obediently before the dressing table, taking small bites of a warm crumpet, changing positions per her maid's orders. Molly was far too excited to allow time to respond to the myriad questions she had about everything, and Mary was therefore able to eat an entire crumpet and drink two full cups of tea while her maid wound strands of pearls throughout the complex coiffure.

The gown Mary had chosen to wear had been specially made by Molly weeks prior to the accident, her design taken from one of the Greek statues at Pemberley. As the prospective bride stood before the mirror, fully dressed and ready to become Mrs. Ashton (Molly making last-minute adjustments to the headdress), a misty-eyed Georgiana appeared.

At exactly ten o'clock in the morning, the bride and groom, the Darcys, and their guests (Miss Bingley, the Hursts, and Lord Exeter had in fact been invited) walked the short distance to Pemberley Chapel.

Happily, the vicar proved to be a man of few, well-chosen words, and began the solemnization ceremony after only a brief sermon on maintaining affection in marriage. Mary was too excited to listen carefully to the entire ceremony, though she did hear certain things with which she did not agree, especially the part about the wife being the 'weaker vessel', and pondered briefly about the line, 'Husbands, love your wives, and be not bitter against them.'

Mary chose to ignore those sections of the service, having complete faith in her own ability, and that of her soon-to-be husband's, to maintain a healthy partnership in marriage. It was again with that feeling of rightness she finally placed her hand in his, as well as when she experienced an unusual, tingling feeling as he slipped the gold ring on her finger. She looked up at him, more attractive to her than she had ever cared to admit, and wondered if someday she might be able to accurately describe her feelings.

Later on, after the wedding breakfast and the dancing, and the toasting, and the laughter, which continued late into the evening, she and her husband walked along the lake path.

Mary knew she could describe exactly how she felt the moment the door of the little lake cottage closed, and she and her husband were finally alone.

She sighed with satisfaction when Christopher Stanhope Ashton wrapped his strong arms around her, looking deeply into her eyes, his lips close to hers as he whispered, "How do you do, Mrs. Ashton?"

"I do very well, Christopher, thank you." Mary closed her eyes as his lips finally touched her own.

She also knew what she felt at *that* moment would never pass from her pen to paper.

CHAPTER FIFTY-SIX

(A Letter from Mary Ashton to Georgiana Darcy)

Pemberley, 14 June 1814

Dear Georgiana,

I do hope the journey to Rosings was pleasant and that you and the colonel are enjoying your time there. You must remember everything when you return to Pemberley, which I hope will be soon after Miss de Bourgh is safely wed. Will Mr. Collins be reading the service?

Despite all my former misgivings about marriage in general, I can happily say the state is a most pleasant one. You will be surprised to hear I have now made breakfast twice, the lake cottage being a perfect place for me to practice such skills. The major prepared the fire each morning, thank heaven, for otherwise we would have had neither tea, eggs, nor slightly burnt toast. After the second breakfast he offered to procure a basket of provisions from the Pemberley kitchen, claiming I need not work so hard during these first few days of our marriage. I would like to surprise him with biscuits as described in my cookery book, if I can only contrive to get the proper ingredients.

Mrs. Halifax is now convinced Elizabeth will have her baby earlier than Dr. Braxton predicted. Your brother has already begun to pace and will not leave the house for anything—the major, Mr. Bingley, and my father play billiards with him each day in an effort to keep him calm, but I cannot say it is working. Elizabeth takes it all in stride—I believe having Mamma and Jane here gives her great comfort.

Kitty and Mr. Darnell left for York yesterday. It is a disappointment to us all, especially Kitty, who would have liked to be here for the birth of Lizzy's baby. I heard her say on more than one occasion how very much she hopes to have a child of her own, though one wonders if she is strong enough.

Molly and Lucy tried to become friendly with Kitty's maid, whom Molly does not trust and calls sullen and willful, but the only information they could glean from her was that Kitty was not at all the type of mistress the housekeeper expected Mr. Darnell to bring home.

Before leaving, Kitty did mention something of interest: they have a frequent caller at their house in York—Miss Bloomfield is her name—who is apparently a long-time friend of Mr. Darnell. I gather this Miss Bloomfield feels comfortable calling at any time of the day, and is a regular guest at their table. When I asked Kitty for particulars she would not say anything more, but the situation seemed to upset her. I have therefore asked the major if we might accept the invitation to visit the Darnells in York and he has agreed to the plan. We will of course not leave until a few weeks after the baby is born.

I see my husband walking down the path with one of the puppies at his heels (the one with the most white in her coat). Mr. Darcy noticed she likes to follow us about and asked if we might like to keep her. We answered at the same time—the major saying, "It is up to Mary," while I said, "It is up to Christopher," and of course we both said yes. We are calling her Georgy.

Please do write with many details. I miss my good friend more than I can express.

> *Yours sincerely,*
> *Mary Ashton*

n.b. I believe Miss Bingley will soon be engaged.

CHAPTER FIFTY-SEVEN

(A Letter from Georgiana Darcy to Mary Ashton)

Rosings, 16 June 1814

Dearest Mary,

I write to you with astonishing news, which I hope you will share with my brother and Elizabeth for I do not think I will be allowed to write again. There is an absolute uproar here at Rosings. As you know, today is the day of Anne's wedding, but when it came time for her to be dressed she could not be found. It took a long time to find the note she left behind (one assumes it was hidden with purpose) and by then she had been gone for hours. She wrote that she simply could not marry Lord Wickford as she was in love with someone else—will you be surprised to learn his name, I wonder—but here is the news: Anne has eloped with Mr. Chandler!

Aunt Catherine has sent all who could be spared to search for her, demanding Cousin Richard go as well. Of course she threatens to disinherit Anne irrevocably unless she returns to Rosings and agrees to marry Lord Wickford. For the past two hours she has been closeted with Mr. Collins, and her bell is constantly ringing. I do not know when I can return to Pemberley, for my aunt is so very angry and upset (she has begun to look quite ill). Of one thing in particular I must warn you—my aunt blames my brother for marrying Elizabeth, and also blames the entire Bennet family in general. The sad case of Lydia's elopement was of course mentioned several times.

Should anyone from Pemberley write to me here, I am certain my aunt will intercept and possibly burn the letters. I will write again as soon as I am able.

Yours sincerely,
Georgiana Darcy

EPILOGUE

(An Entry in Mary Ashton's Diary)

Pemberley, 20 June 1814

When Christopher learned that Mr. Darcy was making plans to travel to Rosings to bring Georgiana home, he proposed going himself. I am not surprised at this generous action on my husband's part, for I have come to realize he not only looks the part of a gallant. He vowed to be back again before midnight, though I hardly think it possible and begged him not to risk traveling in the dark.

I find myself quite equal to the solitude, and write this last entry by way of gathering my thoughts before returning to my sadly neglected novel. Progress is slow, for I often catch myself looking out the window, woolgathering.

I think Miss Anne de Bourgh must have long been living in fear of her mother, for why else would she not act in a manner more in keeping with her station? Why could she not simply break off her engagement with Lord Wickford before starting anew with Mr. Chandler? Lady Catherine blames us all, just as Georgiana warned in her letter, and has reminded Mr. Darcy several times that she told him long ago they would all rue the day he married my sister. Mr. Darcy was concerned his aunt's vituperative communications were upsetting Elizabeth, but she seems to appreciate the diversion.

Since Jane and Mr. Bingley are once again staying at Pemberley, Miss Bingley, the Hursts, and Lord Exeter remain as well. Only yesterday I overheard Jane asking Caroline if she were missing London. Miss Bingley claimed she was perfectly *happy in Derbyshire visiting her dear friends, but there was a certain look in her eyes that made many of us hopeful.*

Of Lord Harold and Georgiana, I know not what will happen. He has returned to London and Mr. Darcy never speaks of him. Lizzy has praised the poor man many times in Mr. Darcy's presence, but so far without any discernible effect.

Lord and Lady Matlock are back at Devonham, awaiting the news of Lizzy's safe delivery. The countess wrote that all of London is agog over the elopement of Anne de Bourgh and Mr. Chandler, and that the gossips have them living on one of his family's estates in Ireland. I have not yet asked Lord Exeter his opinion on the matter.

The Burnabys have returned home, ostensibly to be at the ready to greet the new heir to Pemberley. Miss Burnaby seemed decidedly put out by Mr. Chandler's actions.

Both Diana and Catherine Leigh have written to say how pleased they were to hear I had recovered my memory, and Lizzy has invited them to come to Pemberley after the baby is born. Catherine has reportedly regained her good health and they have promised to come.

Papa is happy wherever there is a good library and is helping Mr. Bingley fill the shelves at Beechwood Manor. There is to be an auction of books at a nearby estate in three days, and we are all to go as a party (excepting Elizabeth, Jane, and Mamma).

Molly has been busy designing gowns for Elizabeth, having told me in no uncertain terms that ladies who have only just had a baby need to feel pretty. She is also concerned about Kitty, and does not understand why Mr. Darnell insists on keeping certain of the servants on. The major does not believe there is any mystery—only poorly-behaved servants taking advantage of a young, inexperienced mistress whose husband is preoccupied with his business. I think differently, of course, but am holding my tongue.

Sadly, my efforts to heal the breach between Elizabeth, Mr. Darcy, and Lady C with the co-authorship of a novel seem to have been in vain. However, Mr. Egerton did agree with Lady Catherine that The Wine Cellar *must end with a wedding. I have written the scene and sent it on (it was a simple matter, for I have now experienced one myself), and the book is to be published at the end of the summer months. By then I expect the major and I will be situated in London.*

Lydia once claimed she would have no time to write letters as a 'married woman,' which at the time I found ridiculous—and still do. Of course a married woman has time to write letters—I even have time to write novels. Last evening, while Christopher and I sat together by the lake, I proposed writing the story of a young woman so determined to remain a spinster that she wears spectacles through which she cannot see, pulls her hair back so painfully tight it narrows her eyes, chooses unbecoming gowns, and plays long concertos badly—all the while preaching and lecturing incessantly—in order to prevent her mother from forcing her to marry. My husband thought it all sounded perfectly reasonable.

As it turns out, I think I showed great foresight in my actions of old, for otherwise I would never have met the major, who I now see approaching the cottage.

~ *The End* ~

...or is it?
The tale of
Mary, Mary, How Extraordinary
continues in
Mayhem at the Minster
An Above-Stairs/Below-Stairs Mystery
by S.M. Klassen
(preview on the following pages)

Readers' Reviews for *Spies, Lies, & Shoo-Fly Pie*
A Jamey Knight Mystery
by Shelly McDunn (AKA S.M. Klassen):

"This is a fun and engaging read with surprising plot twists. There are real people portrayed here that maneuver through dangerous circumstances acting honorably or despicably, but with actual behavioral expectations. No cartoonish excess here."

"The locations are beautifully depicted...the Mennonite community shines through with love and warmth."

"Ms. McDunn has created a wonderful first installment on hopefully a series that will develop the stories of these very interesting characters. We will want to know where they are going."

"Just finished reading Spies, Lies & Shoo-fly Pie. What a wonderfully refreshing read. This book is fast paced and exciting. Very difficult to put down. Interesting tie in from Philadelphia to The Florida Keys to PA Dutch Amish Country. I am so looking forward to the next Jamey Knight Mystery. Congratulations to Shelly McDunn on her very successful Jamey mystery. Simply, a most enjoyable read."

"I want to know lots more about these characters. For a job well done, congrats Ms. McDunn. (We could set that to music.) I have lots of delicious questions about these book inhabitants. "

"Great read!! Kept my attention from the start until the end. Looking forward to this author's next book. Would definitely recommend this."

PREVIEW

Mayhem at the Minster
A Regency Era Above-Stairs/Below-Stairs Mystery

by S.M. Klassen

*Seldom, very seldom, does complete truth
belong to any human disclosure;
seldom can it happen that something is not
a little disguised or a little mistaken.*
~ Jane Austen, *Emma*

Chapter 1

Pemberley, Derbyshire
25 June 1814
ی

The chimes of the pendulum clock echoed against the marble
floors in the vestibule while the servants, roused early from their
beds, went about their tasks with a decided air of anticipation.

Molly Turner, lady's maid to Mary Ashton, entered the main
kitchen where one maid was pouring hot water over tea leaves in
an enormous pot, a second was cutting thick slices of bread, a
third was rolling pastry dough, another was removing piping hot

croissants from the oven, another was seeing to the eggs, while all the others followed the orders of Chef Renault, who spoke in a mixture of French and English, in the preparation of an unusually early breakfast.

"You're here for the hot water?" One of the cooks wiped her hands and led Molly to the pot, grabbing two kitchen towels. "You be careful, now—it's heavy." She considered Molly's slight frame. "You might want help." She looked about the room, searching for an available servant.

Just then, however, Lucy Pearl, lady's maid to Georgiana Darcy, entered and rushed to Molly's side. "Sorry, Moll, I was stopped by Miss Bingley."

"I never thought she could wake up this early, even if a cannon exploded." Molly handed Lucy a towel. "Ready?"

Together they hefted the pot from the stove, not spilling a single drop as they carried it all the way to Elizabeth Darcy's chamber, where Mrs. Bennet was dabbing at her second eldest daughter's damp brow with a handkerchief.

Jane Bingley was on the other side of the bed, doing her best to encourage her younger sister. "It will all be over soon, Lizzy, I promise. Just take deep breaths." She puffed in and out to demonstrate.

Elizabeth puffed obediently five times before inhaling sharply. "Where is Fitzwilliam?"

"We sent Mr. Darcy to the billiard room with your father and Mr. Bingley, for he was wearing out the hall carpet," answered Mrs. Bennet as she dabbed.

Suddenly, Elizabeth cried out, and Mrs. Halifax, the midwife, silently shooed Molly and Lucy out the door. Mrs. Bennet had given birth to five daughters and began to puff furiously along with Elizabeth and Jane.

Out in the hall, Molly spied her mistress, who, given the state of her hair and clothes, had dressed hurriedly and run all the way from the cottage by the lake where she and Major Ashton had been staying since their wedding nearly a sennight earlier.

"How is Mrs. Darcy?" Mary rested her hand against the wall as she caught her breath.

"She is doing very well, madam," Molly replied. "Mrs. Bennet and Mrs. Bingley are with her now." A sudden sharp cry came from within the chamber and she hastened to add, "My mum says it's best to leave this part of things to people who know what they're doing, if you don't mind my saying so, madam."

Mary sighed. "Mrs. Halifax was quite firm yesterday when she said Georgiana and I were not to be allowed in the birthing room."

"My mum also says it can take days for a baby to come." Upon seeing Mary's face, Molly quickly added, "But since Lucy and I just brought up the hot water, it should be soon."

Mary straightened her shoulders and turned to Lucy, whose eyes grew even wider as they heard another cry. "Do you know where Miss Darcy has gone?"

"To the music room, madam."

"Then I will go to her there...and Miss Bingley?"

"I think she has gone back to sleep," Lucy answered.

Molly couldn't help but look disapproving at the mention of Miss Bingley. "If you don't mind, madam, I'd like to finish the last of the dresses for Mrs. Darcy." She had taken to designing various items of clothing for Mrs. Darcy since Mary's marriage, which had resulted in—at least temporarily—much lighter duties.

Mary nodded. "Of course, if you wish to. But take care to have adequate light—the sun will not be up for some time yet." She hesitated a moment. "Molly, you wouldn't by any chance consider calling me Miss Mary, as you did before I married Major Ashton, would you? This new manner of address seems unnecessarily formal."

Molly shook her head firmly. "My mum says I am always to call you madam now."

Mary sighed. "Very well." She then began the long walk to the music room, the two young maids skipping off in the opposite direction.

Long before Mary reached the east entrance to the room, she could hear strains of a melancholy work, and she frowned with concern. Ever since Miss Darcy had returned from her abbreviated visit to Rosings, where she had gone to witness the wedding of her cousin Anne de Bourgh to Lord Wickford, she had been prone to periods of deep contemplation. Mary suspected the cause to be Lord Harold, who was as charming as he was handsome. Unfortunately, his unverified actions had the consequence of his being disinherited by his uncle and being labeled a rake by society.

Poor Georgiana had lost her heart once—no twice, Mary corrected her thoughts—to the most undesirable of men. Firstly to Mr. Wickham when she was but sixteen; secondly to Mr. Petersham, more recently, who eventually became engaged to Caroline Bingley. About Mr. Wickham, the less said the better, and about Mr. Petersham very little could be said except he had good teeth and an enormous fortune.

Now, poor Miss Darcy believed herself in love with Lord Harold, of whom Mr. Darcy would never approve, and though Mary thought her good friend's affection was returned, apparently Lord Harold's high standards would not allow him to approach her while his reputation was sullied.

Mary realized she'd been standing outside the music room for some time. She gently pushed aside one of the pocket doors and entered quietly.

The pianoforte was a recent gift from Mr. Darcy—the latest model on offer from Broadwood and Sons. It was a gorgeous instrument with a rich, vibrant sound, giving full voice to Georgiana's facility at the keyboard. It was not until the final notes had died away and Georgiana had removed her hands from the keyboard that Mary approached.

"What a lovely piece, Georgiana. But it is so very sad." Mary wrung her hands as she paced. "I'm afraid I don't know what to do with myself while Lizzy is...she is....."

"Giving birth?" Georgiana's gentle smile appeared as she turned on the bench. "Elizabeth is strong, Mary, and Mrs. Halifax is a fine midwife, which must give us comfort. But since you and I are not allowed to witness the event—an old-fashioned notion, in my opinion—why do we not play duets to keep ourselves from worrying? I have missed our time together since you became Mrs. Ashton."

Mary ran her hands along the smooth wood surface. "Perhaps we might at first choose pieces with slow tempos, for since becoming a married woman I have had no time to practice." She smiled at her own words, her youngest sister, Lydia, coming to mind.

In the billiard room, Major Ashton's shot went awry.

"Unfortunate." Mr. Darcy moved to the table and leaned over, his cue suspended for a moment. No footsteps could be heard however, and he made the shot, his ball striking Mr. Bingley's.

"Have you told my daughter that your father is a viscount, my boy?" Mr. Bennet's question to Major Ashton was deceptively casual.

"Not yet, Mr. Bennet—the time has not yet seemed right." The major moved aside while Mr. Bingley took his turn.

"Such happy news might change her determination to learn cookery." Mr. Darcy kept a straight face as Major Ashton prepared his own shot.

Mr. Bingley frowned. "I don't know of many women who would enter into marriage without some knowledge of their husband's prospects—oh, good shot, Ashton." He smirked at Mr. Darcy, who sighed.

Major Ashton shrugged. "It pleases me to know she has little interest in such things."

Just then there was a light knock on the door and Mr. Simms, Darcy's butler, appeared. There was the hint of emotion in his voice when he announced, "Mrs. Darcy is safely delivered of a child, sir, and requests your presence." He made a formal bow. "May I be the first to offer my congratulations?"

Mr. Darcy, in an uncharacteristic display, hugged Simms (who had in fact been at Darcy House since before Mr. Darcy was born and therefore had an unwavering, avuncular affection for his master). He then hugged Mr. Bennet, Mr. Bingley, and Major Ashton before rushing out, calling behind him, "All the servants are to have a glass of punch!"

By the time Mary and Georgiana had graduated to transcriptions of opera arias, Jane appeared at the music room door to announce the happy news: the baby was, as Mrs. Bennet had long predicted, a boy, quite healthy, and gifted with a strong set of lungs.

When the three ladies entered the chamber a few minutes later, Mrs. Bennet was holding her second grandchild in her arms, while a tired but contented Elizabeth looked on with a smile.

Mr. Darcy, his suspiciously damp eyes upon his heir, was holding Elizabeth's hand as if he would never let go. Mrs. Bennet was uncharacteristically silent as she approached them, presenting the baby to his father.

Mr. Darcy was no novice, having held the Bingleys' daughter soon after she was born. But still, the others watched in wonder as he gently accepted the swaddled bundle and began to hum to his son, something none of them could have foreseen upon first meeting the proud master of Pemberley.

"He's beautiful," Georgiana whispered. "Have you decided upon a name?"

Elizabeth turned tired, but teasing eyes upon her husband. "Have we, Fitzwilliam?"

Mr. Darcy returned her look. "Which of the thirty or so names still under consideration should we choose, my dear?"

Elizabeth held her arms out for the baby. "We can now eliminate nearly half, but tomorrow will be soon enough. At this moment I wish only to admire our son."

Mrs. Halifax was unable to stave off a sniffle as she shooed everyone but the parents of the newborn child from the room.

ACKNOWLEDGMENTS

My thanks again to Sharon Marie Saunders, to Mary Paula Ball, Jim Ball, and Mary Kjos for their unending support, and to my husband, Kevin. Lastly, thanks to all the readers of the *Mary, Mary* series, and to the wonderful imagination and humor of Miss Jane Austen.